Other Books by Florence Love Karsner

The Highland Healer Series
Highland Healer (Book 1)
Highland Circle of Stones (Book 2)
Highland Bloodline (Book 3)
The Wolf, The Wizard, and The Woad (Book 4)

The Dr. Molly McCormick Series
We All Have Secrets

Tobacco Rose

Even Saints Have Secrets

Even Saints Have Secrets

A Novel

Florence Love Karsner

SeaDog Press

This book is a work of fiction. Any references to historical events, real people, or real places are used fictitiously. Other names, characters, places, and events are products of the author's imagination, and any resemblance to actual events or places or persons, living or dead, is entirely coincidental.

Cover Design: Dar Albert, Wicked Smart Designs
Ship Logo: © Dn Br | Shutterstock

The serpent is an ancient symbol of healing. Early drawings show two serpents wrapped around the caduceus of the Greek god, Hermes. Many ancient cultures regarded the serpent as sacred and used it in healing rituals.

A serpent devouring its tail is called an ouroboros. It is symbolic of immortality, the eternal unity of all things, and the cycle of birth and death. It unites opposites such as the conscious and unconscious mind. It has a meaning of infinity or wholeness, and is the Western world equivalent of Yin-Yang.

Chapter 1

Thanks to the loud, jarring clang of his alarm clock, Adam awakes with a jerk, sits up, and begins his morning routine of wrenching his threadbare emotions from the tortuous dream that now occurs as regularly as sunrise. It no longer surprises him with its sense of impending doom, but he so wishes it would allow a brief interlude in which he can sleep without it creeping into his room every night.

Sitting on the edge of his bed for a moment, he tells himself he will eventually be free of this middle-of-the-night, uninvited visitor. His attempts at analyzing this nocturnal play are fruitless. What does it mean? The smothering darkness? The gun? The woman?

The sharp crack of the gun is a sound he's most familiar with as he regularly runs marathons—the latest exercise craze—which always begin with a gunshot. And the woman is easy enough. The luscious, long dark curls can only belong to Colleen.

But presently he'll not entertain any more analysis of his visitor. He has more pressing issues to take care of now that morning has arrived.

Shake it off. Like you did yesterday. Like you will tomorrow.

With that final thought, he rushes to the shower, pulls on jeans and tee shirt, grabs a cup of strong coffee, and starts this day as he always does—saying goodbye to the love of his life.

His long legs take him down the hallway to an open door. He enters, bends down, and plants a kiss on his young daughter's cheek, then delivers his daily reminders of his written-in-stone rules she's to abide by.

"Hey, Sweet Pea, I've got an early charter this morning so I gotta go. Tony the Tiger is waitin' for you when you get up. So, after you drown him in milk and gobble him up, don't forget to brush your teeth."

"You're funny, Daddy," the child said sleepily. Eyes still closed. But she did give him half a smile.

"And Wesley, stay within your boundaries. You can ride your bike along the sidewalks downtown, go to the park with Mila and Ariane, and visit Sassy at her shop. But you're not to go close to the water without an adult with you. That's off-limits. I know you can swim, but sometimes those waves can pull you out before you know what happened. Got it?"

"Yes, Daddy. I know the rules. Don't go to the ocean without an adult. That's off limits," she repeated, as she did every morning. She turns over in bed and Adam tucks the light blanket around her before leaving her room.

Wesley's active, young mind churns as she lays there for a few more moments. Just long enough to formulate a plan for her day. Then, the minute she hears Adam's pickup truck pull away from their bungalow she hops up and steps into her favorite red shorts and a yellow tee shirt that advertises The Hook, Line, and Charter, the bait and charter shop her dad owns.

But looks like Tony the Tiger will escape his drowning this morning. Wesley flies out the door to the carport, straddles her pink bicycle— with its colored streamers hanging from the handlebars—and starts on the morning ritual she began a couple of weeks ago.

A few minutes later she's standing at the ocean's edge, her tiny body tucked behind a large Australian Pine that leans slightly toward the water, its dark green, feathery limbs providing a perfect place for a nine-year-old, very curious, rule-breaking munchkin to hide. And even at nine years old she knows she'll be in real trouble if anyone sees her here.

She kicks off her flip-flops and wades into the water as the first pink streaks of light appear on the horizon.

The sky looks like cotton candy, she thinks.

A few yards to her right are the remains of a dock that had originally been attached to a cottage up on the dune. Portions of the dock still stretch far out into the water, but in the aftermath of a storm a few years ago most of it collapsed, leaving only one small section still standing.

A spreading mangrove hugs the edges of the dock and is serving breakfast to several roseate spoonbills. Wesley watches them wade through the shallow water, sweeping their heads from side to side hoping to trap something within their flat bill. She walks a few steps closer to the dock, sending one of the smaller spoonbills scattering, seeking another avian diner for his morning feast.

Continuing on her path alongside the dilapidated dock, she walks

2

along and kicks at the loose sand, hoping to find pieces of sea glass to add to her collection.

Getting down on her knees, she combs through the sand with her fingers. The first item she comes across is pretty exciting. A large shark's tooth.

Maybe it's from a great white! She giggles.

She turns it over several times, decides it's worth keeping, and places it in the small net bag she carries when she searches for sea glass or shells.

After a short time combing the sand and finding nothing else interesting, she gets up, pushes her bike along, and walks up the dune toward the section of the dock that's still standing. This part leads up to the Sandpiper Hotel—just a short distance from the Gasparilla Inn—if you walk far enough. The boards of the dock are weathered, warped, and several have sharp, rusty nails sticking up through them. Wesley notes the nails and decides she'll not climb up on the dock, but rather, maybe dig around the pilings beneath it.

She's higher up on the dune now, so she lays her bike down and looks toward the beachfront. It is barely daylight, but she sees a man walking along the beach tossing a stick for his dog who appears to like this game. Just beyond him several people are bent over, looking for shells. Wesley calls them "stoopers." She stands for a moment longer, then goes on about her search.

I'll look farther up the dock. Closer to the part that's still standing. The tide sends the water up there at high tide. Maybe I'll find some glass beneath it.

She walks a bit farther, then gets to her knees to take a look beneath the dock. There, just under the edge of the dock near a piling, is a small pile of sand. She crawls under and gets herself settled. Swatting at a couple of large green flies that buzz about her face, she begins to dig at the base of the pilings. A few moments later she looks up from her pile of sand and sees a sight that has her widening her eyes, jerking her hands back, and dropping her mouth open.

"Oh!" she calls out in a loud voice.

Too loud, she thinks as she backs out from beneath the dock. She'd not expected to come across someone taking a nap under the dock. She's sure her outburst must have awakened them. A few seconds pass and still the person says nothing. Wesley isn't sure she should look again, but can't stop herself. Being inquisitive is bred into her bones.

"It's just how you're wired, dear girl," her Gran would have said. She sits still for a minute, twisting a strand of hair, wondering how to proceed.

Why didn't the person say something when I crawled under the dock?

She leans down once more, takes a quick peek, then hesitates. A foot is sticking out from beneath the sand. A foot with toes. Toes with bright red polish. She edges back under the dock a short way and, of their own accord, her eyes move farther upward. Now she can see her silent friend is a woman.

Oh, it's a lady. She hasn't moved, so looks like I didn't wake her up. That's good.

But something about the way the woman is positioned gets Wesley's attention. The lady is lying on her left side, her cheek resting on the sand and her left arm twisted behind her back. Wesley leans slightly forward for a better look.

No. She's not asleep. Her eyes are open. I guess I did wake her up. But why is she lying like that? She'll get sand in her eyes. Maybe if I call out she'll hear me.

But Wesley doesn't call out. This little mite is braver than that. She lightly touches the woman on the foot and even though the morning is already quite warm, the woman's foot is cold—too cold. Wesley blinks a couple of times when she notices the woman is staring straight ahead. And—unlike Wesley—the woman does not blink.

"What . . ."

Wesley's mouth opens to say something more, but no words come out. Her young mind is whirring like the tires on her bicycle when she pedals as fast as she can. But her brain simply can't make sense of the images her eyes are sending it. The message it wants to register is one Wesley doesn't want to accept. No, that message is simply too much for a nine-year-old to comprehend.

Now, scared but unable to refrain from doing so, Wesley looks again, more closely this time. And when a large fiddler crab skitters across the woman's face—and she still doesn't blink—Wesley's frightened little brain finally arranges all the visual clues her eyes have been sending. And she has no choice but to understand their messages.

She's dead. I think she's dead. But her eyes are open. Wouldn't her eyes be closed if she's dead?

She can hear her heart pounding in her ears. When a shiver passes through her body, she thinks she's going to be sick. Then, with no prompting from Wesley, her breath begins to come in gasps, faster and faster.

With great effort, she tells herself to keep calm, but that thought only lasts half a second before she starts screaming as she scoots out

4

from beneath the dock and stands.

"Daddy! Daddy! Where are you? Daddy! I need you!"

She swings her head about, looking in every direction. The "stoopers" are now far down the beach and no one hears her screams. She calls out again as loudly as her small voice will allow.

"Help me! Somebody! Please!"

She stumbles across the sand and falls to her knees next to her bike. She calls again and again, but the offshore ocean breeze swallows her voice, and her screams disappear as quickly as ocean foam when it reaches the shore.

The Hook, Line, and Charter is just a few blocks down the beach, so Wesley's first thought is to hop on her bike and go there.

I'll go to the shop—get Daddy.

But no sooner does that thought run through her mind than another follows on its heels.

But he's gone on his charter.

She knows the shop will be closed until Kokomo Joe opens it at 7:30 a.m. And that's at least another half hour from now. By this point she's crying so hard she has the hiccups and is afraid to look back under the dock again. Thoughts are clicking through her mind so fast she doesn't know which ones to believe or what to do next.

Is she dead? When Gran died, she was lying in a soft, satin-lined casket. But her eyes were closed and she looked like she was sleeping.

She takes one more glance from a safe distance as she can't fathom crawling back under and taking a closer look. Then she has a thought that has her grabbing her bike, still crying and hiccupping, tears streaming down her face.

I'll go tell Sassy. She'll come. I know she will.

She hops on her bike, leaving the dock behind. Her hands shake on the handlebars, and she pedals so hard and fast she begins to get cramps in her calf muscles. Still she sobs, hiccups, and pedals on.

Chapter 2

The ocean breeze that crept in through the open window brought its constant companion: a slightly salty, pungent scent that Molly found inviting. This early morning caller was a reminder she was lying in her soft, comfy bed in Keeper's Cottage on the island of Cayo Canna. Every day on the island began with this briny breeze, and Molly knew she would never tire of waking to its enticing scent. She even liked the dampness that accompanied it, causing her auburn curls to awaken and respond whether she wished them to or not.

Next came the sound of laughter. Not from a person, but from a pack of laughing gulls making their way to the Gulf. Seeking breakfast most likely. Molly turned her head, listening to them as they "laughed" across the beachfront and headed out to the open sea. She found it amusing when she learned these birds had a white head, gray wings, and blackish markings—except during the mating season when males of the species donned a black cap. She supposed that meant female gulls are mad about fellows wearing black hats. One of nature's many idiosyncrasies.

She stretched her arms over her head, threw back the top sheet, and inhaled another scent equally as enticing as the others: lavender. Compliments of Solana's attention to detail.

Scents of you, Mimi. I wish you were still here. I still feel your presence even though I know that isn't possible.

When Mimi, her grandmother, was alive she made a lavender paste out of potpourri and sprinkled it in her laundry. Mimi was gone now, but Solana continued to make the paste, and Molly was glad. Somehow, she would always associate the scent of lavender with Cayo Canna. And Mimi.

But these comforting sounds and scents disappeared in the wee hours of the morning when they made room for a different caller—

much like the one that haunted Adam—to enter her cocoon of safety and warmth that life in the lighthouse provided. She'd thought these night terrors would cease once the ordeal with Sam had passed. But not so. This frightening, nocturnal visitor was a constant reminder of events that changed her life. She lay there, listening, remembering.

The first attack happened in September. In Baltimore. She was returning from the ceremony that marked her graduation from the Internal Medicine Residency Program at Johns Hopkins Hospital. Upon entering her apartment that evening, she was brutally attacked by Sam, a deranged, psychiatric patient whom she had treated during her residency program clinical time.

This hideous fiend, Sam, broke into her apartment and waited for her. He then tortured her by placing a lighted cigarette to her breast, slashed her wrists with a scalpel, smashed her skull with the butt of a pistol, carved the letter "S" in her left temple, and placed her in a locked closet from which she could not escape. He planned to return and complete his work. "I'll be back, Dr. McCormick. We have unfinished business," he'd whispered as he locked the closet. Even though terribly wounded, she'd been able to call Papa Jack, her grandfather, on her ham radio that was housed in that same closet. He had come to her rescue and brought her to Cayo Canna to recover from this ordeal.

Cayo Canna was an ideal place to recover. Papa Jack and Solana, his housekeeper, took care of her every need. But even though her physical scars were healing well, her psychological ones ran deeper. One person on the island had a special gift. He connected with people. Father Patrick O'Brien, a friend of Papa Jack's, was taking a sabbatical from his church in Boston. This young priest was dealing with his own psychological scars and pain, so understood Molly's needs. Spending time with Patrick was like applying the finest healing medication to an open wound.

The second attack occurred on this island paradise. Molly was gaining her confidence daily, and looking forward to starting a family medicine practice in this special place. But just as she was about to take action to make this happen, Sam made good on his promise. He found her again and tried to complete his task. But this time around Molly was prepared. Father Patrick had taught her to keep a loaded pistol on her person at all times. So, when Sam sneaked into the lighthouse late one evening and attempted to finish his task, Molly stabbed him with a long-blade knife, and then shot him in the upper part of the thigh, where the femoral artery is located. Still, he wasn't dead. Father Patrick showed up at the last moment and ended this macabre play by placing his Walther PPK to Sam's head and sending him to his next life. So Father Patrick had a special place in Molly's heart and she thought of him often even though he had left the island shortly following this event.

She shook her head back and forth briefly. To clear her thoughts. *Papa would tell you to stop this rehashing of the past and 'engage Molly Mac. Life is waiting for you.'*

She got out of bed, brushed her teeth, slipped on a pair of white Bermuda shorts and a blue, sleeveless blouse, then slid her feet into leather sandals. Next, she ran a brush through her thick hair, which now shone with streaks of gold from living on the island for a few months.

As a matter of routine, she avoided looking too closely at her face. Her wound from Sam carving an "S" in her left temple had healed, but she now had a scar that was quite visible. Probably the first thing anyone saw when they met her. If nothing else, the scar was a constant reminder of the attack. Presently, her way of coping with the problem—the scar—was to ignore it. As much as possible. Some days her coping mechanism worked. Other days not so well.

She spread her bed quickly as she read somewhere that if you make your bed every day, first thing, it gets your day off to a better start. You've already accomplished something before you tackle more challenging situations that may present later during the day. Even so, she was sure Solana would chide her about doing that chore. This Cuban housekeeper had been "majordomo" of the lighthouse for eons, and the running of the place was her domain. Or so she thought. She didn't like anyone usurping any of her duties, and that included Molly.

Solana had cared for Mimi during her long, losing battle with cancer. Since then she'd taken care of Captain Jack, and Molly was relieved he wasn't pining away, wishing for times that were long gone. Although there were times she longed for that very thing. Times that were long gone. Today, however, she was thankful to be alive and determined to regain some semblance of normalcy in her life again. And that meant taking steps to establish herself as a physician on the island of Cayo Canna.

She took a deep breath and headed from Keeper's Cottage to the breezeway leading to the kitchen in the lighthouse. They had recently celebrated Thanksgiving, a small affair with the three, Papa Jack, Solana, and Molly. And Molly sensed things were getting back to normal.

She stared out the open kitchen window and watched a brown pelican making a head-first dive from the sky, plunging into the waves below. Molly smiled as he crashed into the waves and came up with a large fish in his mouth, then winged back upward, breakfast now in beak. Fresh fish. Which reminded her once again that she simply must have a meal at The Lazy Flamingo over on Sanibel Island, which was only about thirty minutes or so by water if she used Papa's 24-foot Chris-Craft, an old wooden boat Papa had taught her to operate when she was only twelve years old. And he refused to part with it for something newer.

Today she had something else in mind. She wondered if perhaps her moving into Keeper's Cottage may have caused a ripple in Papa's usual activities as well as Solana's. And maybe they would like to return to their previous morning routine? Without her presence? Perhaps it was time for her to find a bungalow of her own. And, of course, she needed to find a place to establish her practice.

She heard Papa's ancient ham radio squawking as she passed through the great room. He'd promised to tinker with it and adjust the frequencies which would lessen that infernal squawking. But somehow, he never seemed to get around to that chore.

Molly's attack was only one of the frightening events that occurred in the last few weeks. The Cuban Missile Crisis had caused the entire country to be in an uproar and a cloud of fear had covered the island. All were relieved when the crisis was resolved. Papa had played a dangerous part in the events surrounding this catastrophic event by stopping mustard gas from being transported to Cuban revolutionists. And this same noisy radio had been instrumental in his intelligence gathering. So, if it squawked a bit, that was probably all right.

Thankfully, that event was over, too, and she hoped the radio would remain mute. Except for those times when Papa's friend, Drifter, called. He was always full of mischief and brought a smile to Papa's face. So, Molly did understand the radio served more purpose than for intelligence gathering and capturing rebels. But that whole event was something she would like to keep far back in the recesses of her memory.

Her keen nose told her she'd find bacon, eggs, and fresh fruit on the counter. Of course, the overwhelming aroma of Cuban coffee all but drowned out other mouth-watering aromas. Looking out the open patio doorway, she saw the two of them. Papa with his newspaper in

10

hand, and Solana placing his breakfast on the table in front of him. Making sure his every need was being met. A habit of long standing.

As Molly approached, the first greeting came from Ensign, Papa's black lab who was growing like a dandelion weed and could be just as irritating with his rambunctious personality. He ran up to her, tongue hanging out and tail swishing like an electric broom, waiting for his now-expected hug and pat on his head.

"Hey, big guy," Molly whispered as she bent down and hugged him quickly.

Then Papa called, "Ah, Molly Mac. Join us. Just on cup number two." Solana stood, reached for a mug for Molly, and began to pour the dark, steaming liquid.

"Thanks, but no coffee for me, Solana. Not today."

Papa lowered his newspaper, "What? You can't start your day properly without coffee. Preferably Cuban coffee."

He stated this with authority as if she couldn't be serious. Solana stopped pouring, set the pot down and, with eyebrows raised, asked, "Can I get you something else? Orange juice? Grapefruit juice?"

"No. I do enjoy your coffee, Papa, but what I truly want is a cup of tea . . . real tea . . . like I used to drink in Baltimore at the little bistro on Market Street. Down on the waterfront. It was run by a sweet old lady from Cornwall. A very proper English dame. And she made wonderful tea. A different variety each day."

Solana nodded. "Then I'll make you a cup right now. I have some Tetley loose tea and some teabags in the kitchen. Just sit still."

"Thanks, Solana, but I think I might go about the island and see if I can find a shop that might sell special kinds of teas. And there are many kinds."

Papa smiled, "Molly, I agree it's time you get about the island and discover what's here. Businesses, people. Whatever. Of course, we don't have everything on this island that you were accustomed to in Baltimore. But if you want a special cup of tea, then I can recommend a place."

"Really? You mean Agnes carries specialty teas at Bailey's?"

"No. Well, maybe she carries tea. But if so, it will be one brand only. And not exactly what you have in mind. No, you should make a stop at Sassy's place. Sassy's Scones and Teas. It's just a few miles from here. When you get to Main Street, go three blocks south, then turn right onto Banyan Way. You can't miss the place." He raised his newspaper higher as Solana stared at him.

"Sassy's Scones and Teas. I've never heard you mention Sassy before, Papa."

"No? She's been here for some time. You probably met her when you were a teenager visiting here."

"If so, I don't remember her. Was she at your resurrection party?"

"No. She's rather a loner. Not much for parties and such."

At that juncture, Solana quickly cleared the cups and coffee pot, her long skirt swishing as she jerked about and returned to the kitchen. Her quick movements weren't missed by Molly.

"Solana not feeling well this morning?" Molly asked.

"Huh? Never know about Solana. She has her moods as we all do," he said as he pulled out his pipe, tamped some tobacco in the bowl, and lighted it. Molly bit her tongue to keep from reminding him the Surgeon General was now confident that smoking caused lung cancer. They'd had that discussion some time ago, but there were some things she'd learned she had to accept. Papa's pipe was one of them.

"Then I'm headed to Sassy's. After that I may make a tour of the downtown businesses. As much as I dislike trying to mingle with the public, I need to familiarize myself with the people who run the businesses. After all, if I'm ever going to practice medicine, I'll need patients. And it occurred to me that I'll need a pharmacist to fill any prescriptions I write. Is there one on the island?"

"Yep. Sure is. Dr. Maxwell. Greg Maxwell. Trained in Gainesville as I recall. Rather young. Maybe in his fifties? Very personable. And his wife, Jeri, is a pharmacist as well. I think she mostly runs the business end of the place, and Greg takes care of medications and other treatment needs. And we have something you probably didn't have in Baltimore. Jeri makes home deliveries of prescriptions and any other items you need. That's quite a help to some of the older folk who don't get about as well as they might have in the past."

"But, with no physicians, how can there be a pharmacy?"

"Well, as it is, Greg's family has pharmacies throughout Florida. His father passed away a few years ago and left his entire estate to Greg, including his pharmacies. He and Jeri decided to come to Cayo Canna where the pace of life is slower than in Miami, where they'd been. So, he started a pharmacy here on our island, knowing it would take some time for island folk to come to him to fill prescriptions from our docs in Fort Myers. Being well-heeled, he charges considerably less to fill prescriptions than most pharmacies, and stocks many cosmetic items, something the women on the island are happy about. And at better prices than over in Fort Myers. It didn't take long for that information to register with the locals. He's been doing fine for some time now."

"And provides delivery service? Huh. Not a bad idea. Well, that's a relief. Maybe those two will be glad I'm here whether anyone else is or not. I'm not known on the island, so it could take some time before my practice gets moving."

"They all will have heard of you, Molly Mac."

"Papa, you know people skills are not my strong point. I'm fine talking with patients about their medical issues, but just chatting with them isn't something that comes naturally to me. And probably what they heard about me was that I stabbed and shot a man in the lighthouse! Which is true, but the story is much more complicated than that."

"Wouldn't worry about what they think, Molly. Most of them are excited to know we have a physician on the island. I think you'll find they welcome you."

"But what if they don't? Then I'll never be able to have a successful practice here. Nor help the people on the outer islands. And what if I come across an illness I don't know how to treat? There are a lot of ifs, Papa."

"That, my dear granddaughter, is a given in life. Even at my age I find myself having to figure out situations that aren't black and white. None of us have answers for everything, and sometimes we have to struggle to get what we want. And that truth will apply to you as well."

"I know. And I want to move forward. I just need to get grounded first."

Papa put his newspaper down, removed his glasses, and gave her his full attention. "You have a very fine brain, Molly Mac. And you've trained at the finest institutions. The only obstacle standing in your way is . . . Molly."

She stared at the ocean for a moment, then bent down once more to scratch Ensign behind his ears. Then—changing the subject—asked a question.

"Papa?"

"Huh?" He looked over his newspaper at her.

"Do you think we'll ever see Patrick again?"

Papa laid his newspaper aside, removed his pipe, and poked at it with a yellow-stained forefinger. "Good question. And one I don't have an answer for. 'Saint' Patrick is quite intelligent, and I expect he's working through a couple of issues. But from what I observed, his head and his heart are sometimes at cross purposes. But I hope we see him again. I miss arguing with him about our political system and world affairs." He smiled and Molly nodded.

"Yeah. I miss him too. And I'm sure he's no saint. He reminded me once that we all have secrets, and I'm sure that includes saints, too. But there was something unique about him. He has the very gift I'm missing. He connects with people. Makes them feel they matter. He's special."

She stood and watched as the ocean water crawled up the shore, leaving behind a fine line of foam filled with bits of seaweed, small shells, and once in a great while, a nine-legged starfish.

Papa looked up at her. "Speaking of missing friends, what happened to your friend . . . the Seminole. Redhawk wasn't it?"

"Yes. Todd Redhawk. He came by a few days ago, but you were out fishing so you missed him. He has a new assignment up in the Gulf waters off Louisiana. Something's going on with the sea life. Dead creatures washing up on shore. But he'll come by when he visits his mother and sister at the reservation. He travels, but this area is still home as far as he's concerned."

"Hmm. Being employed by National Geographic makes for interesting work," said Papa. He returned to his pipe and newspaper. Molly kissed him on the top of his head.

"All right. I'm off. And I'll take the golf cart unless you need it."

"Nope. Don't need the golf cart. Got to catch the ferry shortly. Roscoe's coming to pick me up."

"Oh? You're going somewhere? You didn't mention anything to me."

"Headed to Washington, D.C."

"Washington? Why are you going there?"

"Admiral Whitmore asked Bear Bowen and me to attend a debriefing on the Cuban Missile Crisis affair . . . and the death of Crab and the dispensation of the mustard gas. I'll only be gone a few days."

"Papa, I thought that was all over. Thought you already had a debriefing session."

"Well, completing those details sometimes take days or even weeks," he said turning his attention back to his newspaper.

"Papa? Don't tell me you're still mixed up in that Cuban situation."

Papa laughed, "Molly Mac, once an intelligence officer, always an intelligence officer. But not to worry. This is just routine following such an event."

14

Molly shook her head, knowing she'd not get anything more from Papa Jack.

Chapter 3

From her upstairs apartment Sassy heard the tinkle of the bell over her shop entrance. Then the door slammed. The next instant her ears cringed at the high-pitched screams coming from down below. And to add to the confusion, her oven timer began to screech. Time to take the scones out of the oven.

"Sassy! Sassy! You gotta come. Now, Sassy!" yelled the small, familiar voice.

Wesley? That sounds like Wesley. But she wouldn't be out this early. It's barely daylight.

She hurried out her bedroom door and headed down the stairs. "Goodness me. What is going on? Is that you, Wesley?"

The next moment she was all but knocked off her feet by a small girl dashing up to meet her. The child was in such a rush to get to Sassy she grabbed her by the knees midway up the stairway.

Sassy blinked, then looked at the child. Like the voice, the face was familiar as well. And most times welcomed.

"Wesley? You almost knocked me down. What are you doing . . . "

The child, sobbing with every breath, took both Sassy's hands and began to pull. "Sassy! You gotta come! There's a body under the dock. I think it must have washed up with the tide." She paused just long enough to take a breath, then started crying even louder.

Sassy stared at the girl a quick moment, then took her by the shoulders, "Child, stop this nonsense. You've told so many tales no one believes you anymore. Especially me!" She'd about run out of patience with this little waif. She knew the child's home life wasn't ideal at the moment, but this outrageous behavior was too much.

"Sassy, no . . . it's true! I saw a foot . . . it's a lady . . . and she's wearing a dress with lots of colors . . . and she's laying on the sand . . .

and her foot is so cold!"

Sassy squinted her eyes, "Wesley Laramore, does your father know where you are? How do you know about a body anywhere? You should be home. It's too early for you to be running about this island, going to who knows where."

"He's got a charter today, so he had to leave early. I got bored so I went for a bike ride. But Sassy, we gotta hurry! The tide might come in and wash the body away. Please!"

Sassy looked closer at Wesley's tear-stained face. The child was so adorable with her small elfin face, freckles dancing across her upturned-nose, huge brown eyes, and long dark hair that always needed brushing. Today it appeared she had attempted to clip one side of it back with a sequined, tortoise-shell clip. But it was rather haphazardly placed and beginning to slip down. And she did have a penchant for telling tall tales, which Sassy didn't pay a lot of attention to usually. But today Wesley's cheeks were rosy, her breath coming in gasps as if she had run a long distance, and she insisted she was telling the truth.

Sassy's brain quickly rattled off a dozen reasons why she shouldn't trust this child's story. *But what if she's telling the truth? Whether she is or not, I've got to talk with Adam. I know he has a difficult situation to deal with at home, but something's got to change. This child needs some attention.*

She released Wesley's shoulders and lifted her chin so the child had to look her in the eye.

"All right, ladybug. I'll believe you this time. But if you're making this up, Wesley, then you and I are gonna have a long discussion about right and wrong. And then another one about consequences for lying."

Sassy had to work diligently at keeping her heart strings pulled tight. She was very aware Wesley could step into that secret place where another little girl had lived . . . actually, still lived. A long-ago story. She looked again at Wesley's tangled hair. Just one of many clues that the child's mother was not in the picture. Sassy had asked Wesley about her mother once.

"She's away. For a while. But she'll be back."

She offered no further explanation, and Sassy didn't question her further. Wesley's dad, Adam Laramore, was a fishing guide and from all appearances was on his own with a nine-year-old daughter to care for. He was grateful Sassy had befriended Wesley, and often stopped by her shop for a chat and a couple of her delicious scones. Sassy enjoyed their chats and found him to be quite pleasant, not to mention a feast for any woman's eyes what with his long legs, broad shoulders, dark hair like Wesley's, and a Southern drawl that could melt a girl's heart in one sensual sentence.

"Come on, then. Let's go take a look and get back. I'll have customers coming any minute. And they don't want to wait for their tea."

She took the scones from the oven, unlocked the front door, placed the "Back Shortly" sign in the window, then rushed through the open walk-through to the Writer's Block Bookstore where she heard Luis scurrying about, running the vacuum cleaner and singing one of his ditties in his native language, Spanish. The only words Sassy could understand were *sí* and *corazón*.

A couple of months ago Luis showed up at the bookstore seeking work as a custodian or someone to clean the shop and keep the shrubs trimmed. Since Sassy and Debra, the bookstore owner, shared this building, they agreed to hire him on the spot and were thankful to have him. The vacuuming was easy enough, but keeping the shrubs and trimming the bougainvillea vines over the roof of the shop was a real chore. The warm weather, occasional rain, and constant sunshine meant all things green grew like chamomile in a sidewalk.

According to Luis, he'd come from Nicaragua. The dictator there, a ruthless man called Somoza, treated his people poorly and made their lives so difficult many migrated north feeling living anywhere else was better than being under his rule. At least that was the story Luis told. Sassy had meant to ask Captain Jack McCormick to investigate this tale, but she'd not gotten around to asking him. And now, after Jack had recently "returned from the dead," following what most folks thought was an illness, she thought it better not to bother him. Let him have a rest. Maybe ask him later.

"Luis, when Deb arrives, tell her I'll be back shortly. I have to leave for a few minutes. If a customer comes, please tell them I'll only be gone a moment. There's a pot of tea on the counter. Tell them to help themselves to a cup. My treat."

Luis's English wasn't perfect, but certainly good enough. "*Sí*. Have *té*. *Sí*. I tell."

Sassy and Wesley went out the back door to the small parking pad where Sassy kept her Volkswagen Bug. She didn't use it often, mostly rode her golf cart and occasionally her bicycle. Cars were allowed on the island, but most everyone went about on bicycles. They'd all come here to get away from the hustle-bustle of larger places and liked to keep things as simple as possible. There were golf carts, thanks to Captain Jack McCormick petitioning the local Community Council to allow them. And they did, but with some rather stiff regulations: only duly licensed operators could drive the carts; the cart must be registered with the local authorities; they must not exceed 25 miles per hour; and most important . . . could only be driven from sunrise to sunset.

Sassy started the VW, shifted into first gear, then made a quick turn onto Main Street, but had to slow down to avoid running over a group of bicyclers. She sighed, "More vacationers. Probably staying at the Gasparilla. Wish they would stay up north or take their business to Sanibel or Captiva. Cayo Canna is becoming too popular. Hold on. We'll scoot around them."

They drove a mile or so south on Palm Avenue, then turned left onto Primrose Lane, a small one-lane path made of crushed shells. There were several cottages—vacation places—then the path was very dense with palmetto palms and Australian pines. Thick vines grew up the trunks of these trees which created a canopy over the lane. Finally, Sassy could see the beach front.

"Are you sure this is the right place, Wesley? It's awfully thick back in here."

"Yes, I promise I'm telling the truth, Sassy."

She chewed on the tip of a long strand of hair, trying to control her tears, but she wasn't making much headway with that. Sassy shifted into second gear and crept along, with Wesley sitting on the edge of her seat, hoping the body was still there. Sassy swerved to avoid a fallen palm tree, probably from a storm long ago. Something about the look in Wesley's eyes had her thinking the child just might be telling the truth. If so, then what?

Then Sassy saw the spreading mangrove and the old dock. A few sections of it still ran out into the ocean, but most of it lay in crumpled bits with rotted pilings and slats now overgrown with dune daisies and sea oats standing proudly.

The dock wound itself back up toward a path that led to the cottages they'd passed. Sassy knew the Sandpiper Hotel offered these cottages to its guests that wanted a bit more privacy than staying in the hotel itself. The cottages were still available as rentals, but the dock itself needed major repair and was not a place a child should be messing about. On the right side of the dock there was a path that led from the dock over to The Hook, Line, and Charter, but the path was overgrown now.

"There, Sassy. Over there. See the old dock?" Wesley pointed to the broken-down pier.

"The body's over there. Under the part of the dock where it's not falling."

Sassy's eyes surveyed the area. Two feral cats scampered away as she pulled up. The broken-down dock, shattered beer bottles, and the tattered remains of what must have been someone's sandals at one time told her this area was a dangerous place for anyone.

"Wesley? Whatever were you doing here? There have been reports of a large cat roaming about our island. Some folks think it may even be a Florida panther. But I think it's most probably a bobcat. Maybe just a large one. Either way, you have no business coming here. That old dock is crawling with all kinds of critters. Palmetto bugs, feral cats, ants, and spiders. And probably snakes as well."

Wesley rolled her eyes, "I've never seen a snake here, Sassy. I was just wondering what might be under the dock. Like maybe some pieces of sea glass that could have washed up. I collect it. But I didn't find any glass. Just saw a foot sticking out of the sand."

Wesley didn't think it would help to tell Sassy she'd actually touched the body and seen a fiddler crab running across the woman's face. She was quite sure she was in for a lecture and she didn't want to even think about what her punishment might be.

Sassy got out of the VW and looked about. *I have no business being here either! Especially if there is a body under that dock. Maybe it did wash ashore, but then, someone may have placed it there, too. Sassy you've lost your mind . . . again.*

And that was true enough. She had lost her mind once. Or at least it had stopped functioning for a long time. A full year to be exact. Upon reflection, much later, she decided that was how the brain sometimes deals with a situation it cannot bear. It refuses to entertain coherent thoughts and leaves one in limbo, only able to perform the most basic of tasks. And sometimes even those are difficult.

But she'd survived that ordeal. And today she was able to find a certain amount of joy in life, even though there were still moments when a wave of sadness washed over her, leaving her feeling like a blob of limp, useless, seaweed strewn about the beach. These moments were always cruel and always uninvited.

"Wesley, stay in the car," Sassy ordered in her sternest voice. She was sure the child did not need to see that body again if it indeed was there. She stepped over the broken beer bottles and made her way closer to the dock. The beach was several yards wide at this point, the sand still damp from the early tide washing in. She crept closer and bent down to inspect a folded piece of paper laying in the sand. She picked it up, glanced at it quickly, then placed it back on the sand. Then she slowly let her eyes travel farther. Just far enough to take a quick peek beneath the dock.

This is not a good idea. I'm not any smarter than that nine-year-old! Do I really want to look under there? What if someone's watching? We could both be in danger.

Like Wesley, Sassy also had a curiosity gene that had her on her knees venturing to crawl a few inches farther. She was now completely beneath the dock. She waited a moment for her eyes to adjust to the dimness, then looked about. Straight ahead, a couple of feet farther, she got a close-up view. Closer than she wanted. And like Wesley, she let out a scream that sent several ospreys squawking and seeking the safety of the sky.

"Oh, good heavens! She's telling the truth!" Sassy yelled aloud as she caught sight of a foot. A foot with red toenails. Then, without her permission, her eyes moved on up the body . . . to the colorful dress Wesley had noted, and against her wishes, she took in the eyes that were still staring as if they, too, had been taken by surprise.

No. This can't be happening. Now what? I must report this to Sheriff Rankin. This is a real problem!

She scurried back to the VW and sat for a moment. Contemplating what this could mean.

"Did you see it, Sassy?"

Sassy just nodded. "Yes. You're right. There is a body."

"It was a lady. With red polish on her toes, wasn't it?" asked Wesley, her curiosity getting the better of her. But at least she'd stopped crying.

"What? Oh. Yes. A woman. With red toenails. I didn't get very close, but I saw enough to know we shouldn't be here."

"But don't you think we should find out who it is?" Wesley reached for her door handle.

"Hold on, ladybug. We're not getting any closer. We're going to the sheriff's office. This is a problem for him. Not us."

Wesley was disappointed. She grimaced, "But Sassy, it might be someone we know. Maybe a friend."

"Yes, and maybe the body was left here by the famous Axe Murderer of New Orleans!" Sassy quipped.

She put the VW in reverse and sent dirt and broken shells flying as she sped out of the lane. The sheriff's office was located just down the street from her tea shop. There was no sheriff presently, but rather, a deputy. Cayo Canna was part of Lee County and the Lee County Sheriff's Office had provided a deputy for the island upon the recent retirement of Sheriff Rankin. That meant any incident, such as this one, would need to be reported to the deputy.

The deputy, Ben Harrison, had been assigned to Cayo Canna a few months ago and was in charge until there was a replacement for Sheriff Rankin. He was new but frequently visited Sassy's tea shop. Practically daily. And would consume at least three scones in one sitting.

Deputy Harrison wasn't the best conversationalist, but Sassy observed him talking with Luis, the custodian. The two—neither of whom had a friend or spouse—sensed a common need and worked at forming a relationship. Luis' attempts at speaking English and Deputy Harrison's even more feeble attempts at learning Spanish kept them both laughing . . . and went a long way to furthering a friendship.

Shortly Sassy and Wesley arrived at the sheriff's office. "Stay here. I'll only be a few minutes," Sassy instructed. She hurried inside and found the deputy rummaging through a filing cabinet, mumbling to himself. He didn't appear to have heard her enter.

"Hello? Deputy Harrison?" She drummed her fingers on the counter.

"What? Oh, sorry. Good morning, Miss Sassy . . . and Wesley."

Sassy turned back to see Wesley standing in the doorway, chewing on her bottom lip, and twisting a long strand of hair. Deputy Harrison closed the filing drawer and walked closer. He guessed Sassy to be in her late forties or so and much too old for him. Still, she was a beautiful lady. She was on the small side, with hair that could only be said to be the color of the sunset . . . a mixture of strawberry blond, a few streaks of auburn, a smattering of lighter strands, and always left loose, streaming down her back. She often wore Bermuda shorts or pedal pushers, due to the heat. But then, some days she'd be decked out in a tropical print, floor-length dress—island attire—Ben thought it was called. Whatever she wore, Deputy Harrison approved of her looks.

"Hey, did you bring me some scones? Save me a trip to your place?" he laughed.

"I'm not here with scones, deputy."

"Just kidding. Then what can I do for you?"

"There's a body over beneath the old dock. The one that came down in one of the storms. Between the Sandpiper Hotel and the bait shop. You know the place. Just down from the Gasparilla."

"What you talkin' about?"

"Just what I said. Wesley found a body over there this morning and came to tell me about it. I didn't believe her, so I decided to see for myself. She was telling the truth. There is a body there."

Deputy Harrison took a deep breath and twisted his hands over and over. "You mean a dead body?"

"Yes. A dead body, deputy."

"Oh, Lordy, what do I do now?" he uttered beneath his breath. However, Sassy heard it loud and clear.

"Well, I think you need to get yourself over there and see about it!" Sassy retorted. She had no patience for inept folks, and it was obvious to her this deputy had no idea how to proceed.

"Uh, uh, I'll have to figure out what the proper procedure for this is. I've never had a dead body on Cayo Canna."

Sassy frowned at him, exasperation oozing with each breath. She turned to leave.

"Hold on a minute, Miss Sassy. I'll call the Lee County Medical Examiner's Office. Dr. Strickland's in charge there. He'll have to come over here. And he may have questions for you."

He rang the Medical Examiner's Office, identified himself, and asked to speak to Dr. Strickland. The receptionist responded, " I'm sorry, Deputy Harrison. Dr. Strickland's out of the office at the moment."

"Oh, I see. Well, tell him to call me immediately. It's an urgent matter. A body washed up on the beach here on Cayo Canna. I need him to come before the tide comes in and takes it out to sea again." He was quiet for a second, then nodded, "Okay, just have him call me immediately."

Sassy raised her eyebrows at the deputy, "I've got a tea shop to run, deputy." But as she turned to leave, the phone rang and Deputy Harrison picked it up.

"Cayo Canna Sheriff's Office. Deputy Harrison speaking."

Sassy heard a male voice on the other end of the conversation, but couldn't make out anything being said.

"Oh, hello, Dr. Strickland." Deputy Harrison straightened his stance, then listened a moment. "Yessir, as I told your receptionist, a body washed up on the beach here on Cayo Canna. I need you to come see about it before the tide comes in and washes it away."

He listened as Dr. Strickland spoke at length. The deputy frowned, then grimaced. His mouth dropped open for a few seconds, then he frowned again, took a deep breath, and sighed.

"Yes, Dr. Strickland, sir. I know who she is. That young female doctor that stabbed and shot that man in the lighthouse."

He listened once again, then spoke up, "But, sir, is this woman—this Dr. McCormick—a detective or a medical examiner?" He continued to listen then nodded his head.

"Yessir. I understand. She'll be your representative at the scene. And gather evidence as well. If that's what you want. Yessir. I'll do as you say." Sassy saw him tighten his lips and take a deep breath. "I'll do my best."

Sassy waited for him to hang up. "You don't need to stay, Miss Sassy. Dr. Strickland gave me instructions about the proper procedure I should take."

Sassy sighed, "I've told you several times you don't have to call me 'Miss' deputy. Makes me sound ancient."

"Yes, ma'am. I forget. Just my upbringing in the South. It's meant to be respectful."

Sassy nodded and left with a nagging feeling that wouldn't let her mind rest. When she and Wesley returned to the tea shop, she went across the street to the library, it being one of the few places that had a telephone. She'd requested one herself but still hadn't been given a definite date for installation. Everything on the island moved slowly. Which, again, was why most people came there.

She approached the desk with trepidation. The librarian, Eleanor, wasn't known for her outgoing personality. She ran the library like a general and her word was law. And everyone knew her rules.

"Hi, Eleanor. May I please use your phone? "

Eleanor, in her mid-fifties, quite tall and thin, lowered her large, prominent nose and looked over her glasses at Sassy. "My phone is only to be used when it's absolutely necessary."

"Yes, Eleanor, I understand that. If it weren't important, I wouldn't be asking," Sassy retorted. She could live up to her name when she needed to. But just now she wasn't in the mood to spar with Eleanor.

"Then make it short. And it doesn't always work, you know."

"Yes, I'm aware of that." The persnickety phone system was a joke about the island.

"Do you happen to know Jack McCormick's number?" Sassy inquired.

"I have a phone book here somewhere. I'm sure the Captain's listed. But that doesn't mean he'll answer his phone. You know he can be a bit ornery on occasion," Eleanor snorted. Sassy was also aware of that. But everyone who truly knew Captain Jack also knew what a fine man he was. He was one of the backbones of this community and respected by all.

"Yes, he can be short at times."

She dialed the number for the lighthouse and waited. And waited. It rang six times before a woman's voice answered.

"Captain McCormick's residence."

Sassy recognized the voice. She had been acquainted with Solana for some years and still wasn't sure why the woman gave her the cold shoulder if they happened to meet in town or at the grocery.

"Hello, Solana? Sassy here. I need to speak with Jack. It's rather important, so if you can convince him to come to the phone, I would appreciate it."

"I'm sorry. Captain Jack is away for a few days. When he returns, I'll tell him you called." And she hung up. Sassy stood there staring at the phone in her hand.

That woman is so exasperating. Why does she dislike me so?

There had been a time, years ago, when Sassy would visit Captain Jack and Margaret at the lighthouse. Mostly because Jack was a good listener and Margaret was such a lovely lady. Margaret would often leave Sassy to talk with Jack as he had great communication skills and often helped others sort through their problems. Margaret would serve her a glass of sangria and Sassy would pour out her troubles to Jack. And it was always about the same issue. How she missed her husband, Duncan, and her daughter, Gabby.

After witnessing how inept Deputy Harrison appeared to be, Sassy had hoped Jack McCormick might step in. He was a most capable man and could handle this situation better than that blundering fool, Harrison.

Well, that's that, I suppose. Nothing else to be done.

Finally, she hung up the phone. "Thanks, Eleanor."

The librarian nodded and went back to making sure her Dewey Decimal System cards were in order.

Sassy rubbed her forehead. *What a mess. I do believe this is the first time we've ever had such a crime on the island. And maybe it's not a crime. Maybe the woman just fell off a boat and washed ashore. Right Sassy.*

Of all people, Sassy had first-hand knowledge of that subject—falling from a ship and being lost to the greedy ocean—and that memory sent chills through her body. But she'd not let herself dwell on that tragic story now. She'd reported what Wesley had found and now it was time to get back to the tea shop. And, she'd make a point of having a conversation with Adam Laramore.

She'd talked with him many times, but those discussions always dwelt on his recurring nightmares, which Sassy was sure had to do with his wife, Colleen, being away. But all she could do was be a sounding board. Be someone he could talk to.

But did he know Wesley pedaled her pink bicycle all about the island, sometimes accompanied by two other young girls? These girls had mothers who kept tabs on them, and they had to be home at certain times, forbidden to scoot about the island without supervision. Wesley was not so fortunate.

Chapter 4

Molly hurried to the kitchen, grabbed the keys to the golf cart, then climbed aboard. She was about to back out when Solana came rushing out from the lighthouse, calling to her.

"Molly . . . the phone. It's Dr. Strickland. He says it's urgent."

Molly went back inside. *Dr. Strickland?* A clear picture of a handsome, suntanned face, blond hair falling over his forehead, and smiling blue eyes flashed across her mind.

Why would David be calling me? I had hoped to get to know him better but didn't expect to hear from him so soon after our last encounter.

The last time she'd seen him was when, in his official capacity as Medical Examiner of Lee County, he'd come to the lighthouse and attended the slain body of Sam, her attacker. He'd been so professional dealing with the details of Sam's death and the role she and Patrick had played in it. Still, though, it was only a little after seven in the morning. Rather early for a social call. She picked up the receiver.

"Hello? David?" She waited for what seemed like a long minute before he responded.

"Oh, good morning, Molly. Hope I didn't wake you."

"No, I'm up. And glad to hear from you, but it's a bit early. Is something wrong?"

"Yes, it is early. And yes, something is wrong. Well, not wrong, but it's a sticky situation I need your help with."

"Of course. I can never repay you for helping save Papa's life. What can I do?"

"I got a call from Deputy Harrison at the Sheriff's Office on Cayo Canna. A body's been discovered on the island and the deputy called for a detective and someone from the ME's office to come. I told him we'd send someone, but we've been inundated with a major traffic pileup on U.S. 41, and bodies are coming in as we speak.

"And to add more excitement, two people have been shot over on Matlacha—probably a drug deal gone wrong—and a body was found on a sailboat drifting in Red Fish Pass. That's on Captiva Island. The Lee County Sheriff's Office is running around like three-legged rabbits, trying to manage these situations. Every officer and detective is on duty. That means they can't send a detective out to Cayo Canna so they've asked if I could find someone on the island to help out. I'd send someone from here, but with so many calamities, I need all hands."

"What? Did you say a body? Here on Cayo Canna?"

"Yes, apparently it washed ashore under an old dock about a half-mile south of The Hook, Line, and Charter, a local bait and tackle shop. It appears the dock hasn't been repaired since collapsing during a storm a few years ago.

"Deputy Harrison has only been on Cayo Canno for a couple of months. I believe this is his first assignment after graduating from a criminal justice academy somewhere up in North Florida. Or maybe it was South Georgia.

"The point is, he's inexperienced and will likely make some mistakes. We all do on our first assignments. As I recall, I forgot to put on gloves at my first onsite case.

"Harrison came to the lighthouse during your tragic event and stepped right in to help the EMTs lift the body. But in his desire to be of help, he contaminated a couple of areas where the forensic guys were working. But, again. He's all of twenty-three years old and new at this stuff."

"Yes, I remember him. He's quite large and appeared to be uncomfortable."

"When he called this morning, I reminded him to not disturb the scene, not to touch anything, and to simply cordon off the area. Hopefully, he'll do as I asked."

"So, what do you need me to do?"

"I need you to go to the dock, check out the scene and the body from head to toe. Making note of any markings, bruises, or scrapes. Anything that might suggest how the person died."

"But, wouldn't you think they drowned? I mean, the body washed up on shore."

"Not necessarily. I've seen many bodies that washed ashore, but upon closer inspection, I discovered they were dead long before they were in the water."

"But, David, I'm not a medical examiner nor a detective. I'm a physician. I don't have the training to act in your stead. And I could be just as prone to making mistakes as Deputy Harrison. I've no experience with such as this. What if I miss something? Something important?"

"I realize you're not a medical examiner nor a detective. But you'll do a better job than anyone I know on Cayo Canna. I need you to get to the scene and make sure it's not contaminated by local folks.

"And Harrison will do whatever you ask. He just needs someone to direct him."

"David . . . I don't think I can . . ."

"Molly, I wouldn't ask if it weren't important. A body washing ashore could mean a criminal is lurking out there somewhere. Waiting for his next victim."

She took a deep breath, "I see. But again, I don't feel qualified to do much more than find something obvious. Something anyone could detect."

"You're wrong about that, Molly. As I recall, you figured out it was the ferry captain, Crab, who was transporting sulfur mustard to Cuban rebels. Not just anyone would have made the connection of the chemical property numbers on containers in Crab's ferry. My postmortem will reveal what the cause of death was . . . but not who caused it . . . if it turns out it wasn't an accident."

"I don't know, David. If I could ask Papa to join me, I'd feel better. But he's headed to Washington for a debriefing on that Cuban Crisis assignment he was involved in."

"I have no doubt you're more than capable of handling this problem, Molly. And I'll be out as soon as I can find a moment. Until then, just keep the scene secure and keep your eyes open. Remember that adage about the criminal returning to the crime scene? Well, it's often true. So don't just look at the scene and the body. Pay attention to everyone around the site. And I assure you there'll be spectators trying to find out what's going on."

"All right. I suppose I can't say no. I don't want to think of another criminal on Cayo Canna. It's too horrible to even imagine."

"Thanks, Molly. I'll be in touch. By phone if possible. Glad it was working this morning, but as you know, it's very unreliable. Maybe I should learn to use that ham radio Captain Jack uses. As soon as I can get a breath here, I'll come over. But that could be tomorrow or even later."

31

"But, where do I even start? Do I dare touch the body? What if I contaminate it or the scene myself? What about things like fingerprints? I've never dusted for those before. Where do I even get the equipment to do that?"

"Molly, the body is most likely someone—perhaps a snowbird—who had a heart attack. We see it often this time of the year. But, back to your question, don't worry about fingerprints. You can only do so much. First you secure the scene . . . that is, if Deputy Harrison hasn't. Block off an area larger than the core crime scene by using a physical barrier. You can use tape or even driftwood pieces on the shore. Anything that marks the site. The hardest job will be to keep "nosey Neds and Nellies" from getting too close.

"In your initial walk through you'll be looking for anything that looks out of place. Check the position of the body. Does it look as if it were "arranged," or did it actually wash ashore? Check for blood. Not just on the body, but in the area.

"After you've completed that phase and made your notations and identified any evidence, then you begin to touch stuff . . . carefully. Be sure to collect all potential evidence, tag it, document it, and protect it. Make notations regarding the time of day, any noticeable odors, anything of that nature. If you could take pictures, that would be helpful. If you can't take pictures, then sketch the location, position of the body, and any surrounding area that's pertinent."

Molly let out a sigh and breathed deeply, "David this sounds like something totally out of my expertise."

"Molly, I need you to do this. Find out who discovered the body and ask questions that may shed light on the situation. Often the person is upset and may not recall things exactly as they were. But that's the way it goes. I often have to play "detective" myself when the sheriff's office is tied up. When I arrive, I'll do an in-depth interview with this person and go from there."

If she'd been anxious about going about town meeting the locals, David's request had Molly's anxiety level moving up several notches.

"Then, after I've done my investigation, what then? What happens to the body? I mean, we can't leave it lying on the beach. Can we?"

"That's where Deputy Harrison can be of help. He can have the body removed from the site and taken to the local funeral home. They'll have facilities for holding it until I can get there and do my postmortem examination."

"David, I swore an oath as a physician to do no harm, and I certainly hope this little escapade won't cause me to break that oath."

"You'll do great, Molly. I'll try to call later today or early tomorrow. If I can get caught up here, I'll hop a lift on the sheriff's patrol boat which is faster than any other marine transport I know of. Meanwhile, I'll call Deputy Harrison and let him know you're representing the Lee County Sheriff's Office as well as the ME's Office. You're my partner in crime, so to speak."

"Yes, Dr. Strickland," Molly laughed.

"Thank you, Dr. McCormick," he sighed and the conversation was over.

Papa Jack had come inside during the conversation and heard Molly's half. He detected it was something serious, but waited for her to inform him. If she so desired.

Molly hung up the phone and stared out the window, open today so the breeze could come through. Her highly trained, logical, mind said playing "detective" was not something she should undertake.

Being a physician is not the same as being a detective or a qualified medical examiner. But, when I remember how Lt. Collins, in Baltimore, worked so diligently to find the criminal who attacked me, how can I say no? And even with Lt. Collins' efforts to protect me, I again came close to losing my life a second time. What if the killer is still on the island? If so, he could kill another person. Jeez. How did I get myself into such an untenable situation?

She wandered back out to the patio. Still turning the untenable situation over in her mind and still coming up with the same resolution. She could not say no.

"Papa, I have a problem."

"Oh? What? Living with a grumpy old grandpa and a prickly housekeeper?" He laughed, then gave her his attention.

"Papa, I'm serious. David . . . Dr. Strickland . . . wants me to act as medical examiner and detective for him."

"How so?"

"Deputy Harrison reported that a body washed ashore here on Cayo Canna. David's neck-deep in bodies at his place and can't send someone to come see about this one. And the Lee County Sheriff's Office is dealing with several criminal incidents, so they can't spare a detective. David wants me to go to the crime scene and investigate it."

Papa nodded, "Sounds reasonable to me. A physician would be the best person I can think of to do such."

33

"But, Papa Jack. Being a physician isn't the same as being a medical examiner. Nor a detective."

"That's true. But you're more qualified than anyone else on this island. To my knowledge, we've never had such an occurrence on our little strip of paradise. Did he suspect foul play?"

"He doesn't know anything other than what I told you. I wish you weren't going to Washington. You could help me figure this out."

"You don't need my help for much of anything, Molly Mac. You're perfectly capable of checking out a crime scene and a dead body. Use your brain and trust your instincts."

"But Papa, just this morning I decided to take steps toward getting my practice established. But this request from Dr. Strickland feels like another obstacle to keep me from my work."

Papa peered over his glasses, "Or maybe the first step toward going forward? You'll meet many of the island folk during your investigation. That much I can tell you. It could be a way for you to show off your many skills," Papa grinned at her.

"Yeah, and it could be a way to show I don't have a clue about what I'm doing!" She shook her head, wishing this day had gotten off to a better start.

Their conversation was interrupted by a quick beep of a horn. "That's Roscoe. I've gotta go. The ferry won't wait. The new skipper has that much in common with Crab. Doesn't wait for anyone." He kissed Molly on the forehead and yelled to Solana who was coming through the kitchen door.

"Gone now, Solana. See you in a few days."

"Yes, Captain. See you in a few days."

And she returned to the kitchen where she continued arranging freshly clipped oleander sprigs in a vase. Fresh flowers were abundant on the island, and the lighthouse was always awash in them thanks to Solana.

Chapter 5

Sassy left the library and returned to the tea shop where Wesley had helped herself to a glass of milk and was munching on a blueberry scone. Her usual fare. Sassy hurried through to the bookstore to tell Debra the latest development. Luis was behind the counter, dusting the shelves. He was much more thorough in his cleaning than she and Debra had been.

"Luis, when Debra comes in ask her to step over to my place. I need to talk to her for a minute."

"Sí, Señora. I tell."

The silence of the tea shop was disturbed by the screaming of a siren as the sheriff's office cruiser made its way down Main Street. Deputy Harrison was on the move.

"Oh, that imbecile! Why did he have to use his siren? He's going to have everyone on the island chasing after him," Sassy complained.

Luis came scurrying through the doorway, "Señora? What is this? That noise means something bad, sí?"

"Yes, I'm afraid so, Luis. Earlier this morning Wesley discovered a dead body down at the old dock. The one that runs between the Sandpiper and the bait shop."

"What you say? Body? Dead?"

"Yes. I saw it myself. The sheriff's office will take care of the situation. The best thing we can do is pray it was an accident. Not a crime."

"*Sí. Sí. Accidente.*" Luis mumbled something else under his breath, but Sassy knew very little Spanish, unlike Wesley who, as is common with children, could speak a bit and understand much more.

"I've got to get to the kitchen. Promised Agnes I would bake cinnamon scones today. Her favorite. Don't forget to ask Debra to pop in."

"*Sí. Sí.*" Luis turned back to his dusting and resumed singing his tune.

The tinkle of the shop bell sounded and in walked Vedra, the spiritualist from Mother Nature's Way, the shop next door where one could buy various herbs, natural health remedies, and unusual concoctions for soothing pain. They could also have their palms read and receive "spiritual" advice if they so wanted.

Sassy tried to be pleasant to the woman, but preferred she not visit often. Sassy had no reason to dislike her, but didn't particularly want her blathering about reading palms and holding seances . . . any of that hocus-pocus, mumbo-jumbo stuff.

Of course, Sassy had a few relatives in her home country of Scotland that were said to have "second sight," whatever that was. The only thing Sassy did approve of was the woman's green thumb. Her back-door herb garden put Sassy's to shame. And she grew so many unfamiliar plants that Sassy gave up trying to learn them.

Vedra hurried to Sassy's counter, "What's going on? Do you know what the siren's about?"

She was wearing her usual attire, a loud-colored blouse with a dozen necklaces hanging around her neck, long earrings, a gypsy-type skirt that fell mid-calf, and her heavy makeup would have been ideal for an opera star on stage.

Sassy gave her a short version of the story. "A body washed up on the beach. Deputy Harrison's going to take care of the situation."

"Oh, a body on Cayo Canna. I knew something was going to happen. I felt vibrations all day yesterday. Evil is surrounding our island. We must take care. I feel it still."

Sassy sighed, "I've got scones to make and you've got remedies and potions to stir up."

Sassy then walked back to her kitchen and Vedra, even though hoping for more information, took the hint and went back to her shop.

Relieved that the spiritualist had left, Sassy let out a sigh and smiled at Wesley. "Your chin is laden with 'residue of scone,' she laughed as she went behind the counter and on to the kitchen. Wesley trotted behind her, chatting away as usual.

"Sassy, I think we should go back to the beach. Deputy Harrison might want to ask me some questions. I did find the body, you know."

Sassy had work to do. Scones to be baked. But she knew that little imp sitting here would leave her tea shop and pedal her little bicycle right back to that dock. She needed to come up with a way to keep

Wesley out of trouble and let her get on about her work.

"Tell you what. If you'll help me with the baking, then maybe we'll go by the sheriff's office a little later. After Deputy Harrison's had time to do his work. He doesn't need anyone getting in his way while he's checking things out."

"You mean you'll let me make scones? Really?"

"Absolutely. Come on. Wash your hands and put this apron on."

Sassy tied the apron around Wesley's tiny body. It almost touched her toes, which were bare now as she had been so upset she left her flip-flops on the beach when she ran away from the frightening scene.

Sassy sounded like a drill sergeant, "Rule number one. Always wear an apron. Making scones can get messy."

Wesley stood tall and nodded. "Yes. Always wear an apron."

She watched as Sassy set out flour, sugar, cinnamon, butter, eggs, and currants on the counter. Sassy measured her ingredients and began to stir them with a wooden spoon. Then, without fanfare, she slammed the spoon down on the counter, sending sticky batter flying about the kitchen.

Wesley took a step back from the counter. Not sure what was going on. But a quick memory of her mother throwing a tantrum when Wesley left her wet swimsuit on the bathroom floor came front and center.

Sassy sighed, "No. We've got to go back, Wesley. Harrison doesn't know his head from a melon. And both are full of mush." Wesley stared, not understanding what that comment meant.

"C'mon. We're going to the dock again. You are to stay in the car. You hear me? Stay in the car. I think someone should make sure Deputy Harrison doesn't go trampling across the dune destroying evidence that may tell how the body got there."

They both shed their aprons. Sassy put the "Back Shortly" sign in the window again and looked about for Luis. He must have gone upstairs, so she left the door unlocked and she and Wesley climbed back into the VW and headed to the dock. Sassy so wished Jack McCormick had been home. He'd have known what to do. Or at least he would have kept Deputy Harrison from erasing what could be important clues.

Chapter 6

The screaming siren—which Deputy Harrison felt sure he needed to use—alerted the entire island, and in a few minutes there was a large group gathering at the dock. Sassy parked her VW under a palm tree as Wesley stared out her window at the crowd. Then Sassy turned to her.

"And this time do as I say, ladybug. Stay in the car."

Wesley nodded and Sassy started toward the dock, pushing her way through the throng of people standing about.

Like vultures after a dead seagull, she thought as she got closer.

Sassy was surprised when she spied a familiar face a few yards ahead. Solana. Jack McCormick's housekeeper at the lighthouse. Why would she be here? Sassy knew Jack was out of town, so this was puzzling. Standing next to Solana was a young woman. Not someone she knew. Perhaps a friend of Solana's? A young woman with a ragged scar on the left side of her face. But this scar didn't stop her natural beauty coming through.

Deputy Harrison's booming voice rang out as he strutted about the area, waving his arms and speaking through his megaphone, which wasn't necessary as his voice carried well without amplification. He was quite a large fellow. Behind his back the locals called him "the Jolly Green Giant," and his green uniform added fuel to the joke.

"All right. Ya'll need to stay back. This is a crime scene. No one is to come past this tape I've strung around the area."

The deputy's Southern drawl was another characteristic that marked him as being from someplace much more southern than Cayo Canna where many residents were either from places up North or from South Florida, which is anything but southern!

He stomped about, paying little attention to where he placed his size twelve boots. He hitched up his wide gun holster, making it rest more comfortably beneath his hefty midsection. Some might have called it a "beer belly," but this deputy never touched alcohol. Probably a holdover from his Primitive Baptist upbringing in a small, rural, North Florida town. And even though in the upper part of the state, that region is truly southern, unlike much of the rest of the state.

He'd moved to Lee County only recently, when he was assigned to this post on Cayo Canna. But his childhood years in a rural, southern village left their imprint. And to his credit, having grown up in a small community where strong moral values and ethical behaviors were the norm would serve him well in his chosen profession.

His position on Cayo Canna, a Lee County jurisdiction, was his first assignment upon completing his training at the Florida Criminal Justice Academy a few months ago. To date he'd only had to write parking tickets and arrest an occasional drunk at Timmy's Nook.

But this incident, a dead body on the dock, was his first real chance to use his law enforcement skills. Or would have been if Dr. Strickland hadn't sent that slip of a woman, that Dr. McCormick, to do what he should have been doing. Investigating the scene.

When Molly and Solana arrived, Molly spotted Deputy Harrison easily. He stood head and shoulders above everyone else and wore a regulation, Stetson-style hat which added even more height to his already impressive stature. She walked over to him, nodded, and held out her hand.

"Good morning. I'm Molly McCormick."

"Yes, ma'am. I know who you are. Dr. Strickland told me about you." He stared out, over her head, refusing to make eye contact. Finally, he lifted his shoulders and looked down at her. He took her outheld hand in his briefly, then pulled his hand away.

"Looks like you're in charge of this scene. Instead of me. Hope you know what you're doing . . . ma'am." He glanced away, scanning the crowd which was growing larger. His displeasure at Dr. Strickland having turned the investigation over to this young physician was as glowing as the shiny badge on his chest.

This was Molly's first encounter with "the public." And it had to be a law enforcement officer. One that wasn't exactly happy to see her. Recalling Papa's words earlier—that sometimes one may have to struggle to get what one wants—she sighed and took a deep breath. What she wanted now was his cooperation. And his help.

Then use some of those skills you learned in those psychology courses—those classes you took that were supposed to help you when dealing with your patients—

and pray that they work, Molly told herself.

She walked a step closer to the deputy and placed her hand softly on his forearm. "I'll do my best, Deputy Harrison. But I would appreciate having you at my side. I have no doubt your training will have prepared you for parts of this investigation that will be foreign to me. And, likewise, my training as a physician has prepared me to examine a body and perhaps see clues that would not be readily seen by someone without my medical background."

"Yes. I have had extensive training in such situations," he retorted, again looking over her head as if trying to ignore her presence.

"That relieves me greatly, deputy, as I have no training whatsoever in law enforcement. This is my first exposure to such," Molly commented.

What she refrained from saying was "Yes, we're both educated in our fields, but neither of us knows what the hell we're doing at this point."

Deputy Harrison was not expecting to have this civil, almost friendly, conversation. And besides that, he wasn't expecting her to be so attractive. She'd been sitting outside on the porch when he arrived at the lighthouse following the event there a month or so ago . . . the event where this woman, this doctor, killed a man. All he'd seen was her leaning her head on a man's shoulder. That priest fellow. And he appeared to be comforting her. But the deputy certainly hadn't forgotten the bloody, almost decapitated body he'd seen in the kitchen. The one Molly had stabbed and shot. The one the priest unloaded his Walther PPK on. Yes, he was aware she was a unique woman.

"I . . . uh, yes. I've taped off the crime scene area starting down at the far end of the dock close to the water. And be careful down there. There are places where the dock's caved in. Then I taped along each side of the dock leading up to the rear of the Sandpiper. I think that should cover the area pretty well. And I'll be standing by. Right here. If you need my assistance, Dr. McCormick."

"Thank you, deputy. I believe two brains are better than one and teamwork always produces better results. And it's Molly, please."

"Yes, ma'am. Uh, Miss Molly."

He looked around and stood taller. She'd asked for his help. He stepped forward and once again called out, cautioning the onlookers. "As I said, keep your distance. We've got a lot of work to do here."

Being sure to include him in her initial moves, Molly called out to him, "Let's start with the grounds first. Then we'll move on to the body."

She donned gloves and began to make her way inside the taped area, taking great pains to look carefully before she stepped in any direction. The first picture she took was of a footprint very close to the dock where the body lay. It was a very large footprint just inside the tape . . . and a matching one just outside it. At least a size twelve. Molly smiled, knowing it could only have come from Bigfoot or her latest acquaintance, Deputy Harrison. But still, a photo should be made.

A quick visual of the area told her a lot. In addition to the size twelves, there was another set of prints leading from the walking path directly to the part of the dock where the body was located. They appeared to have been made by a much smaller person. Perhaps a woman. With flat shoes. But, of course, anyone from the beach may have walked to the dock and had nothing to do with this event. Still, another photo.

There were also prints made by a bicycle tire. And a long line of very small footprints leading from the beach directly alongside the dock, starting at the beachfront and leading to the body itself. Prints made by tiny, bare feet. Could only have been made by a child. More photos.

Deputy Harrison stood at the entrance to the cordoned-off area, legs spread wide, arms folded across his broad chest. No doubt sending a non-verbal message about entering his area. It had not occurred to him to wear gloves, but once he saw Dr. McCormick wearing them, he hurried to his vehicle and put a pair on as well.

The young physician walked about the area, stopping occasionally to take photos, make notes, and take measurements of various angles from the dock. She then got on her knees and appeared to retrieve something from the sand and place it in a bag. After quite a while in which she bagged several items, she took more pictures and walked over to consult with Solana.

Then she called out, "Deputy Harrison, I've pretty well covered the crime scene grounds and I'm ready to check out the body now. I need a flashlight. Do you have one?"

"Yes, ma'am. In my car. What do you need a flashlight for?"

"The body's beneath the dock, so it'll be darker under there. A flashlight would be helpful."

"Oh, okay. I'll get it," he responded. But Molly wasn't sure she wanted him to leave the scene. Many people were milling around and his presence did lend an air of authority.

"No. Let me get it. You stay here and make sure no one touches anything. I think they may be more inclined to listen to you as an official. They may not pay much attention to me."

Deputy Harrison nodded and Molly hurried to the cruiser. She looked in the front seat, where she spied a notepad, a couple of empty, paper coffee cups, half of a leftover scone, and several cans of cat food.

But the backseat was much more interesting. There was indeed a flashlight laying on the seat. And, in addition, there were several books. All of them classics. Two of which she'd read, and another she intended to read one day: Ulysses, Great Expectations, and Moby Dick. Somehow this was not what she expected.

Well, then, perhaps there's more to my new friend than his size twelve feet.

She grabbed the flashlight, hurried back to the scene, and began to gather information as best she could. Examining a body was not new, but gathering evidence of a possible crime was.

Deputy Harrison observed Molly took a long time to cover the grounds, made a lot of notes, and bagged many items he couldn't see the reason for . . . bits of paper, something shiny that he couldn't identify, and a handful of seaweed. And she appeared to take photos of everything. But she had acknowledged he knew some things she didn't know and that, in his opinion, showed she was at least intelligent.

While Molly went about doing her investigative work, Solana took note of the people gathered about the scene. She could call most of them by name but there were a few she didn't know. But, as she'd said to Molly, if they had come to the island in the last couple of months, then she would not know them. She was a bit surprised at the size of the group but then again, finding a dead body on the island was a first.

She recognized Sean Feherty, the bartender at the Temptation. A fellow in his sixties. Warm, friendly. She recalled Captain Jack saying Sean had a history, but nothing the Captain was worried about.

Standing behind him in the next row was Antonio Carlucci, the desk clerk at the Sandpiper Hotel. Solana also knew his secrets. He had several, but Captain Jack decided he passed muster. Solana knew many things about many people simply because she worked for Captain Jack who made it his business to check out everyone who moved to Cayo Canna. What a former intelligence officer would do. But whatever secrets Solana knew stayed in the lighthouse.

Over to her far right she saw Dr. Greg Maxwell, local pharmacist, and his wife, Jeri. Also a pharmacist. They were near the dune talking with a few other residents. Perhaps they thought they might lend a hand if needed. Even Eleanor, the librarian, had shown up. She would have learned from Sassy about the body, of course.

But the one person Solana would have expected to see was missing. Joe Stanhope (Kokomo Joe), Adam Laramore's manager at The Hook, Line, and Charter, the nearest shop to the dock. She'd have thought he would be the first one to arrive. Having a body wash up fairly close to his establishment couldn't be good for business.

Then she spotted Harold Snow who ran Snow's Liquors. His place was one frequented by many on the island, except Captain Jack. He still ordered his Glen Fiddich special malt whiskey from Scotland as he always had. Solana made sangria, using her personal recipe, so she occasionally dropped by Snow's Liquors to purchase red and white wine for her concoction. Other than that, she had no need of Harold's supplies.

Standing next to Harold was Vedra, the spiritualist. Captain Jack had checked her out, but Solana had her own suspicions about this lady. Something in the way she stared at Molly didn't sit well with Solana who had seen such people as Vedra in her home country of Cuba.

Out of the corner of her eye, she caught a glimpse of long, strawberry-blond hair blowing in the breeze coming from the ocean. She didn't have to look closer to know it was Sassy. She didn't particularly like Sassy, though she couldn't verbalize exactly why. Just didn't like that the woman would drop by the lighthouse and take up the Captain's time bothering him with her troubles. But Solana did acknowledge the woman had reason for grief. Even these many years later.

Sassy walked over to Solana who tried to look busy writing on her notepad. She was doing what Molly wanted, listing everyone she saw, listening when she could, and watching for anyone who might appear to be too interested.

"Good morning, Solana. Guess you heard the news?" she asked.

"Yes, early this morning."

"Too bad Jack isn't here. He'd have been a great help to Deputy Harrison. And he could use help for sure," remarked Sassy.

"Yes, but Molly will do a fine job. She's rather like the Captain in that respect. Very accomplished and skilled in many ways."

"Molly?"

"Yes. Molly. Dr. Molly McCormick. She's in charge of this investigation."

"Oh? So that young woman is a physician?"

"Yes. That's Molly. She's a physician. And a very talented one at that." Solana spoke as if Molly were her own daughter. Someone she was proud of.

"Molly McCormick . . . then she's related to Jack?"

"Yes, she's the Captain's granddaughter."

"I see. So, is she also a medical examiner or investigator? Or maybe works for the police? She seems to be making notes and surveying the scene."

"No, she's neither, but she's acting as representative for Dr. Strickland, the Medical Examiner for Lee County. And the sheriff's office in Fort Myers has asked her to assist in the investigation as well."

"But, why didn't they send someone over?"

"It seems there are several incidents over on the mainland and some criminal activity on Captiva. Everyone is tied up, so Molly agreed to help them."

"Then I'm glad she's here. Any granddaughter of Jack would likely have inherited at least some of his genes. And we all know Deputy Harrison is great for writing parking tickets, but I fear this is beyond his abilities."

Solana nodded. "How did you come to know about this situation?"

"My young friend, Wesley Laramore, found the body. She came to my place and told me about a body washing up on the beach. Of course, she's known to tell some tales occasionally, so I didn't believe her at first. Glad I did finally check her story out, though. Otherwise, the body may not have been found for some time."

"At least not until the vultures got scent of it," remarked Solana, with a slight smile. Might be she'd have to revise her opinion of Sassy. But she'd not get in a hurry about it.

Chapter 7

Baltimore, Maryland

As the two disembarked from the plane, Captain Jack McCormick buttoned up his Navy peacoat, turned the collar up toward his neck, and wrapped his wool scarf tighter. And his friend did likewise. They'd completed their debriefing in Washington, D.C., and were ready to complete one last task in Baltimore, Maryland.

Jack stomped his feet, "Damn this cold. I'm ready to go back to Cayo Canna. Don't know how I ever stood living up in this part of the country. Thought D.C. was cold, but Baltimore feels even worse."

Admiral Theodore (Bear) Bowen stood next to Captain McCormick, feeling much the same. These two old Navy warhorses, Bear and Casper, had long ago retired. At least officially. But the military officials in Washington always managed to find them when they were needed.

Their latest assignment, the Cuban Missile Crisis, had been a real challenge. It had brought many retired officers back from their retirement ease, and these two intelligence officers had played a significant role in stopping arms shipments to Fidel Castro. More importantly, they had prevented a very large shipment of sulfur mustard from being sent to rebels in Cuba. Sulfur mustard which would have been turned into mustard gas and dispersed across a very large area, causing great illness and death to many. Both Captain McCormick and Admiral Bowen were relieved to have that assignment behind them and looked forward to getting back to a more relaxed life. Sort of.

Bear Bowen piped up, "A few hours in D.C. are enough for me. I'd say the briefing went well and yeah, I didn't miss Admiral Whitmore's comment about needing a couple of intelligence guys to spy on Castro in-country. But let 'em find some others. We've done enough, Casper.

What you say?"

"I say we lay low . . . and keep our powder dry!" Jack smiled at his friend. He knew as well as Bear that if they were called for another mission, they'd go without question. But it would be nice to sit in his ivory tower on Cayo Canna and paint again a bit. He was close to finishing a painting he knew was going to please the person to whom it would be given.

Today, however, this last task he had to complete was an easy one. He'd told Molly he was going to Washington, which was true. But he "forgot" to tell her he was also going to Baltimore where she lived before coming to Cayo Canna recently.

"So, what are we doing here in Baltimore? I'm sure you told me, but hell, my memory is about as useless as my new knee. The docs repaired it the best they could, but it's still a problem some days."

"We're going to pack up Molly's things in her apartment and have them shipped to the island. She doesn't need to come up here and be reminded of that bastard who tried to kill her. She doesn't say much, but I know her. She still has him running around in her head. I hope if she gets her stuff back and knows there are no ties to Baltimore, she'll rest easier."

"Maybe. But an experience like that . . . some psychotic idiot torturing you and then trying to kill you not once but two times . . . that stays with you for a lifetime, Casper."

"I agree. But it's worth a try. If she would just get her practice up and going, she'd be too busy to think about that sorry bastard."

"So, she's going to stay on the island?"

"Yeah. That's what she says. But I have yet to see her making any moves toward getting herself settled to begin working as a physician. However, as I was about to leave for this trip, she was telling me about a task she'd been given. And one I think could be helpful."

"What's that?"

"You remember David Strickland, Dr. Strickland, Medical Examiner for Lee County?"

"Yeah. He was at your resurrection party. Nice fellow."

"He called asking Molly to stand in for him on a case on Cayo Canna. A body washed up on shore, and he was tied up and couldn't come over. Asked her to investigate the case."

"Well, now. That could keep her busy for a few days." The Admiral shuffled his feet, scratched the back of his head, and looked at Jack.

"So, that's why we're not going back today. You sneaky old devil. If you were there, she'd turn to you to help her. But, with you gone, she'll have to figure things out for herself. Right?"

Jack grinned. "You always were quick to pick up on my convoluted plans. Yeah. I'm going to let her find her way through this maze. She doesn't need me, but she doesn't know that yet. This assignment will be good for her."

"Uh-huh. Just don't expect her to thank you for not returning and helping. Something tells me she may appear to be Molly-Meek-As-A-Mouse, but a lady who stabs and then shoots a man is a strong, resourceful woman. Wouldn't want her to turn her wrath on me."

Jack chuckled. "I agree. That wouldn't be my first choice. Come on. Let's get a cab to the Monaco Hotel. It's a bit on the fancy side, but the food is quite good. We'll go to the apartment tomorrow and get that place squared away."

As they approached the front door of their hotel to go to dinner, the doorman held the door for them and, at their request, hailed a taxi. In a second a Yellow Cab swerved to the corner and they got in.

"The Monaco," Jack called from the back seat.

"Yessir. Right away. It's the best place in town."

Jack had no argument with that statement but didn't particularly like being back in Baltimore. The memory of Molly lying in a hospital bed with her head bandaged, looking half dead and vulnerable—was one memory he wished he could erase.

Chapter 8

Agnes Bailey, the proprietor of Bailey's Island Grocery, heard the screeching siren as the police cruiser sped past her store that morning.

"Damned nuisance. That deputy needs to learn not to set that irritating siren off at every little incident on the island."

She muttered to herself, probably to hear a voice if for no other reason. Today she wasn't in the best of moods. At sixty-two years of age—a confirmed maiden—she was still spry, stayed active by walking the beach every day, and her daily schedule kept her on her toes.

As well as being the only grocery on the island, Bailey's was designated the official U.S. Post Office and Agnes, therefore, the official postmistress. She enjoyed having a bit of official status, plus she knew a lot about everyone simply by seeing the mail they received.

She spent the first part of each morning sorting the mail and placing it in the appropriate boxes located just inside her establishment. On the right wall as you entered. That way customers could get their mail but did not necessarily have to come on farther into the store. Unless they needed groceries. Which most of them did, but some just came on back to speak with Agnes.

Today she slapped envelopes into their respective boxes, swatted at a no-seeum buzzing about, and shoved aside a box of postal flyers sitting on the floor. Those flyers were to have been disbursed in each mailbox. And as she knew, postal rules were to be followed explicitly. But Agnes made her own rules.

She kicked the box of flyers a bit farther down the hall, muttering to herself as she did so. "This morning I'm not in the mood to accommodate a whim by some pompous-ass official in Washington who wants all post offices to put these flyers in all mailboxes. It's a stupid announcement anyway. So what if postage is going to five cents next year? I don't give a hoot if you increase it to fifty cents. I don't write anyone anyway!" she called as she picked up the box and tossed the flyers into her trash bin.

What she did object to was the postal service wielding authority over citizens. For some reason which she hadn't yet acknowledged, she felt out of sorts today.

She straightened the canned goods on their shelves and began to inspect her vegetables. She hoped a couple of customers would buy the remaining three heads of lettuce and a couple of mangoes, or she'd be forced to discard them. But there should be a fresh shipment coming from the mainland tomorrow on the ferry, the *Calypso*.

Following the disaster with the death of Crab, the former ferry pilot of the *Calypso*, Agnes had found it necessary to approach the new ferry pilot about bringing her vegetables over from the mainland. He refused on the spot.

The new pilot, Skip Wainwright, looked down his aquiline nose at her and snorted, "What? You expect me to bring vegetables over to Cayo Canna on my ferry? I've never transported perishable goods. This is a ferry, not a damn grocery store," he said with a dismissive wave of his hand.

But Agnes stood her ground and continued her argument. "Crab always brought my vegetables. How else are we folk on the island to have fresh ones? Or you either as far as that goes?"

Skip (whose given name was Louie) was from a long line of ferry pilots, all of whom ferried travelers on the St. Mary's River between the cities of Sault Ste. Marie, Ontario, and Sault Ste. Marie, Michigan—the two Saults. But Skip left the area recently as the ferry service would be non-existent as soon as the International Bridge was completed.

He saw the writing on the wall and began to make plans for the future. Plus, he needed to find a warmer climate as he had recently begun to suffer from a condition his doctor called Raynaud's Disease, a disease process that affects one's fingers and sometimes toes. Blood vessels in the hands and feet overreact to cold temperatures or stress. Skip didn't feel particularly stressed as he was a single, middle-aged man with no particular problems. However, the cold weather in that part of the country was a factor, and he didn't relish the pain that it brought to his fingers and toes.

When he spied an advertisement in the local Ferryman's Journal seeking a ferry pilot for a small island off the coast of Florida, he applied. With his experience he was a perfect candidate, and now he resided on Cayo Canna. If you asked him, he'd say he hadn't found time to pursue any personal (meaning female) relationships. Besides, his life revolved around keeping his ferry in tip-top shape and reading his many history annals. His one vice—gambling—was one he watched carefully; but he did so enjoy a good poker game.

After the unpleasant interchange with the new pilot, Agnes had a few words with Captain Jack. A few days later, Jack invited the new pilot to the lighthouse for one of Solana's scrumptious dinners on the patio. By the end of the evening, Skip realized he'd perhaps been a bit hasty in his refusal to assist Agnes. Somehow, he and Captain Jack had much to talk about. Politics, military issues, the state of affairs in Europe. The pilot was delighted to find a man so well-versed in world history, one of his favorite subjects. And Solana's *tapas* made with fresh vegetables from the mainland were delicious!

Still grumbling, Agnes finally admitted why she was so irritated this morning. More than usually, that is. She'd been "stood up" by her friend, Lizzie. They were to have gone to the Historical Society Meeting last evening. But Lizzie never showed to pick her up as they planned. And now Agnes was in a real snit as to how she should feel about that situation.

Yesterday Lizzie had come by as she did most every day. Even if she didn't need any groceries, the two women enjoyed a daily chat. Agnes greeted her as always, "Lizzie? My, but it's early for you to be out and about, isn't it?"

Lizzie Strafford had moved to Cayo Canna in the last year. Her husband died of a heart attack at an early age and left Lizzie with more than enough resources to live well. She decided to come south, to Cayo Canna where they vacationed a few times in years past. She and Agnes struck up a genuine friendship based on the fact they were both alone and lived close to each other. Lizzie was a bit younger than Agnes, but they enjoyed sharing reading materials. And Agnes was teaching Lizzie to knit. Or trying. Lizzie didn't seem to have a knack for working with her hands. But it gave them something to do when they talked together over a glass of wine in the evenings.

Lizzie responded, "Hi, Agnes. I'm trying to get my errands done early."

"Good idea. It'll be ninety degrees by noontime. Unusually warm for December. But just wait until tomorrow. It'll change," she laughed.

Lizzie smiled and Agnes came from behind the counter and walked closer, "I'll be getting fresh vegetables tomorrow if you need anything.

So, what can I get for you this morning?"

"Just some milk and bread. I'll drop those off at my cottage then I'm headed to the beauty salon."

"Oh, your hair always looks lovely. And Bertha is a fine hairdresser, which is a good thing since she's the only one on the island." They both laughed. Lizzie always brought out the best in her.

"Well, I've got a date as it turns out."

Agnes raised her eyebrows, "Still seeing Raphael?"

Lizzie nodded, "Yes. Nothing serious. We both enjoy dancing, so we're going to Timmy's Nook tonight. They've got a great dance floor. And you should see Raphael dance! He's a regular Lawrence Welk."

Agnes laughed, "Good for you. Keep busy. Speaking of keeping busy, why don't you come with me to the Historical Society Meeting tomorrow evening? We've got an author coming to speak."

"Oh, my. How did we get so lucky?"

"Debra Morris invited her. You know Debra. She has the Writer's Block Bookstore on Banyan Way. Right next door to Sassy's place. The author is a friend of hers. Lived in the same place . . . maybe Newport, I think. The author has visited Florida several times and has started writing novels set in our fair state. Sometimes a real place, sometimes a fictitious one. Haven't read her latest novel, but I understand it has a lot of early Florida history in it."

"Then maybe I should go. I don't know a lot about Florida even though I live here now. I suppose you do, what with your penchant for reading every night."

"Yes. Juan Ponce de León and I are some of the earliest settlers," Agnes chuckled.

"Of course, he brought more than just soldiers with him. He brought Florida a number of diseases that the local Calusa Indians could have done without. Practically wiped them out."

"Really? Sounds like I've got a lot to learn. All right then. It's a date. What time?"

"The meeting starts at seven, but we have a few minutes of social time at about 6:45, then the speaker takes over."

"Where do you meet?"

In the Pirate's Nest at the Gasparilla Inn. Last Friday of every month. All the rooms are lovely in the Inn, but the Pirate's Nest was named for a Spanish pirate, José Gaspar, who plundered treasure that was thought to have been buried on our island. The room is especially appealing with its pink and green decor. And it's large enough for a group meeting."

"Then I'll pick you up about six o'clock, and we'll go together. I know you're not keen on driving at night."

Agnes nodded, "Yes, my eyes aren't quite as good as they once were. I need to get over to the mainland and see Dr. Hernandez. He keeps telling me I'm developing cataracts. Not sure there's anything to be done. But I'll see him soon."

"Then I'll see you Thursday evening."

But, Thursday evening, last evening, had come and gone and Lizzie still hadn't shown up.

"She could at least come by and offer an apology. Maybe she's not such a good friend after all," Agnes mumbled and swatted at that same no-seeum that kept buzzing around her head.

Chapter 9

Deputy Harrison handed the flashlight to Molly and started back to stand his watch at the staked-off area. Molly called out, "Would you please walk with me to the body, Ben? That's where we'll both need to have our senses on alert."

The deputy was at least six feet five inches and looked more like a linebacker on a professional football team than a local deputy who spent his time writing parking tickets and hauling in an occasional, inebriated customer from one of the local bars. But, in sharp contrast to his he-man body, he had the face of a young boy, rather ruddy-cheeked with thin lips and a small nose that seemed out of place in such a large face.

"Uh, uh, yes ma'am . . . Miss Molly. We both need to pay close attention to all details. It's easy to miss something important."

Molly smiled at him and they walked toward the area where the body was resting. She bent down and took a quick peek beneath the portion of the dock that was still standing. Deputy Harrison got down on one knee which was as far as his large midsection would allow. It was obvious, even to him, that the space beneath the dock would be far too small for him to crawl into.

Molly had not particularly enjoyed the required psychology classes she'd taken, but some of the techniques she learned in them were coming in handy. So, calling on those techniques again, she took care of the situation.

"I think there's probably only room for one of us under there, Deputy Harrison. I would appreciate you shining the flashlight while I make my way closer to the body."

"Sounds like a plan."

Molly had only gone a short way under when she saw one important clue. Several large green flies buzzing about. Then she saw a foot. And

toes with bright red polish. "Hold the light a little higher, please, Ben."
"Yes, ma'am."

When Molly crawled a foot closer, she halted and swatted again at the flies. As soon as one dropped to the sand, she carefully picked it up and bagged it. This scene was not at all what she expected to see. The body before her was a rather petite, middle-aged woman clad in a colorful, floral-patterned dress that Molly felt sure was a Lilly print. Very expensive. She was fully clothed and a long string of pearls was draped around her neck. And she wore matching pearl earrings.

Molly stopped for a second. *No, that's not right. There's only one earring. In her left ear. Where is the right one? Did she lose it earlier in the evening? Or perhaps it's in the sand here? Better check carefully. Could be important.* She didn't voice her thoughts to the deputy. Not yet anyway.

The woman was lying on her left side with her left arm pinned beneath her body. She was wearing one red, spiked-heel shoe and the other one was snugged up next to her body, partially buried in the sand. Then something got Molly's attention. Something caught a ray of sun that crept between two boards on the dock. A hairclip . . . with rhinestones that winked in the tiny slit of sunlight. Another item for her bag.

The woman appeared to be smiling. Her eyes open as if in a trance. Her lipstick had been applied carefully and Molly could smell her perfume as she got closer. It was one she'd smelled before, but couldn't place at the moment. The fact that she could still smell her perfume told Molly something—the woman hadn't been dead very long. Molly knew it took roughly twenty-four hours to three days after death for a stench to develop, and there was none yet.

She reached her hand behind her, "Let me hold the flashlight, Ben. I need to take a closer look."

Deputy Harrison reached as far as he could, passing the flashlight to Molly. "Can you tell much about the body? Whatcha seeing there?"

"Body is female. Approximately fifty-plus years of age. Caucasian. Fully clothed. Wearing spike-heeled shoe on right foot. Hair held neatly by a rhinestone clip on right side, but falling free on left side. No sign of blood anywhere. I may be able to tell more once we remove the body from this space. She's in rigor mortis, but from what I see she's been here less than twenty-four hours. But a closer inspection will need to be done to tell the exact stage of rigor mortis. When oxygen is no longer present, the body may continue to produce ATP via anaerobic glycolysis, but when the body's glycogen is depleted, the ATP diminishes, and the body enters rigor mortis."

"I see, " replied Deputy Harrison . . . even though he didn't understand any of the science she'd spouted. He was beginning to appreciate this young woman, this physician. He'd struggled to get through some of the complicated studies at the Academy, but Molly appeared to know a sufficient amount of material relating to time of death circumstances.

Molly called to him, "Give me another minute. I don't want to miss anything. What I can tell you is that she did not wash up under this dock. Her clothing is damp, but not soaked. The sand beneath this section of the dock is only slightly damp. I would think the high tide had come ashore shortly before she got here. Not sure though. From the marks in the sand, it appears she may have crawled here. Or maybe was placed here by someone?"

She was quiet for a couple of minutes, thinking. She had made notes of the area and had taken several photos. This Polaroid camera was turning out to be quite a useful item. She never would have expected to use it as a tool for investigating a crime. Now it was time to move on to the next phase of her assignment.

"I think you can call for the ambulance to take her now, Ben. Once they remove the body, I'll have one last look at the space under here and then inspect her body at the funeral home."

Deputy Harrison got off his knees and let out a sigh of relief. That position had been most uncomfortable. He couldn't have gotten under that dock if his life depended on it. Once again he made a mental commitment to lose weight. Even he realized he would have been in real trouble if this slim physician hadn't been here.

When Molly crawled from beneath the dock, Deputy Harrison took charge. "I'll call the guys at Clovis Funeral Home. They'll keep her on ice until Dr. Strickland can get over here."

The deputy was in his element now. He was on the phone, glad to finally have a chance to take care of some of the details himself. He called the funeral home and asked them to send an ambulance. Filling out paperwork was his forte, so he got busy with that.

Molly felt she'd covered the area well. Now she took inventory of every bit of debris she could see under that dock. She bagged a few more items and made numerous notations. Not sure any of them would be of help to Dr. Strickland.

Solana stayed put near the taped-off area, taking note of residents she recognized and also noting there were a couple of people she didn't know. She walked over to Sassy who had her hands full trying to keep Wesley from tearing off to view the body.

"Sassy, I think Molly may want to ask the young girl a few questions if you could wait a few more minutes."

Sassy stared at Solana, "Questions? Oh, yes, I suppose she might want to do that. I don't think she can tell you anything, though. She was quite upset when she arrived at my place. But I wonder if you and Molly could come by my shop? We'll have a cup of tea and a scone. Think it might be better for me to take Wesley away from this scene."

Solana nodded, "Yes, that would be better. I'll tell Molly."

Another obnoxious siren—again unnecessary—announced the arrival of the ambulance from the funeral home. Deputy Harrison led the attendants to the dock and gave instructions. "Be careful when you move the body. Please wear these gloves and don't touch it any more than absolutely necessary."

While the ambulance attendants were preparing the body for transport, Molly caught Solana's eye and motioned for her to come over.

"Solana, I know this won't be pleasant, but I wonder if you would mind looking at the body? See if it's someone you might recognize."

Solana walked closer to the gurney where the body lay and Molly turned back the sheet to expose the head. Solana looked for only a moment then turned to Molly.

"Do you know her?"

"No. She's not a local. But then, it could be someone who has moved here very recently."

"I see. There's no identification on the body. Nothing. So, we now have a dead body and no clue as to who she is."

Solana started to walk away but turned back. "Greg and Jeri Maxwell, our pharmacists, are over by the taped area. Greg knows more people than I. I'll ask him to step over here."

Molly nodded. That seemed like a reasonable idea, so she waited as Solana hurried over to speak with Greg who started making his way over. A few seconds later his wife, Jeri, followed. He stopped, turned back to her, and put his hands on her shoulders.

"No, Jeri. You don't need to see this. Go back to the shop. This body won't be a pleasant sight. Go on. I'll catch a ride with someone."

"But . . . I might be able to . . ."

"No. Dead bodies have a repulsive odor and I know how sensitive your nose is. Go on. I'll see you in a few minutes."

60

Jeri nodded and patted her hair which had blown slightly in the breeze. Then she left for the pharmacy as there was a recent shipment of medications that must be checked in properly, a new line of makeup to arrange on her shelves, and she needed to start taking her monthly inventory. She had a daily and monthly routine and did not like anyone to disturb it.

Greg walked up to Molly and smiled as he reached out his hand "Hello. I'm Greg Maxwell. My wife and I are the local pharmacists. Solana tells me you're our new physician. I can't tell you how pleased Jeri and I are to have you join this island family. We've needed a doc for ever so long."

Molly reached her hand out and Greg took it, holding it in both of his. Molly waited for a second, then pulled her hand back. She was surprised at a pharmacist with such a warm personality and way of greeting a stranger. He was middle-aged, with a comb-over hairstyle and a twinkle in his eye as he looked her over from head to toe.

"Thank you. I'm very excited about getting a practice started, but at the moment I've been asked to assist Dr. Strickland with this incident. But I only know a couple of people on the island and I wonder if you would mind looking at the body. Solana didn't recognize the woman, but feels you might know more people than she."

"Of course. She's right. In my line of business you do usually meet most of the locals. They will either need to fill a prescription or get some toiletries. So, what can you tell from your initial assessment?"

"Not much. But I'm sure David will be able to tell a lot more from his autopsy and toxicology report."

"Certainly. All right, let's take a look."

Molly walked with him and pulled back the sheet again as she had done for Solana. Revealing the head only. Greg stared at the body and stood still for several moments. Then he looked down at his feet and tapped his forefinger on his chin . . . as if thinking.

Molly waited, then he spoke. "Yes, I do know the woman. Or at least I know who she is. She's not local, though. Her name is Gillian Hartwell. She's a writer. She was the guest speaker at the Historical Society meeting last evening. Jeri and I have read all her books and were excited when we learned she was going to make a presentation."

Molly sighed, "That's a relief. Having an identity for the body. That will be the most helpful information I can give Dr. Strickland. He'll at least have a starting place. But why would she have been out on the . . ." She stopped. She was about to discuss the situation with him but thought better of it. She didn't know the protocol for such a situation but felt sure she should keep all details to herself.

"You've been very helpful, Greg. I'll stop by and meet your wife. Papa Jack speaks of you both often. And he depends on you to fill his prescriptions."

"Glad to help. If I can be of assistance in any other way, please let me know. You can always find me at the pharmacy. And Jeri would love to meet you."

She said goodbye, then spoke to Deputy Harrington who was still standing by. Maybe waiting for his next instructions?

"Ben, I think we can let the guys take her away now. Then I'll go back under the dock and see if I missed anything." The deputy walked to the attendants, said a few words, and they loaded the body into the hearse. Once the body was removed, Molly crawled back under the dock once again.

Wearing one sandal and the other partially buried close by. A pearl necklace with matching earrings. Or earring. One missing. And a Lilly dress. No external signs of trauma. Did she just wander here after a few drinks at one of the several watering holes close by? Something's not right here.

Molly scanned the sand where the body had been lying. At first she didn't see any other clues but watched a small fiddler crab as he skittered across the sand, leaving his telltale mark behind. Then as she turned slightly to her left next to the post where the body was lying, she spied a small scrap of paper. She carefully picked it up with her gloved hand and looked closely. The paper had partially disintegrated apparently from the water coming in. White paper. Too thick to be newspaper, but there were a couple of letters visible and what appeared to be a drawing of bits of leaves in the upper left corner. But she wasn't sure about that. The letters she saw on the paper didn't help any either. Were the letters A and C? And was the last one W? No. Maybe it could have been a Y? Too difficult to know. But was it even important? The paper could have been laying here for several days. It may have nothing to do with this event.

It occurred to Molly that this line of work was even more challenging than figuring out disease processes. Diseases and illnesses could be difficult to diagnose, but they could usually be cornered if you looked hard enough and had the proper training to understand the clues they left along the way. She laughed to herself then.

Yeah. Just the same as a medical examiner or detective would do in this case. But since I'm neither of those, I have no idea if any of these items I collected are clues or not.

Perhaps David Strickland had known all along what he was doing. Asking a "disease detective" to help him out. She smiled when she remembered, a couple of months ago now, sitting with him under the umbrella at the Tiki Hut on the mainland, waiting for the ferry to bring her and Papa's "ashes" back to the island. David had been in on the plan for Papa to "die" and had played an important part in returning him to health. She owed him a favor. But she did hope today's task would cover that debt. She was even more anxious to begin her practice on the island. To get on about her life.

Molly felt she'd covered the scene at the dock. She looked around, again noting she knew no one in the group of islanders that had gathered. She quickly took a couple of photos of the group, thinking that perhaps Solana would have taken careful notes and could identify the islanders. Maybe add some knowledge Molly might find helpful. Before moving on to Solana, however, she walked over to Deputy Harrison as the ambulance attendants loaded the body and pulled away.

"Ben, thank you for keeping that crowd at bay and being close as I crawled under that dock. I have to admit I was a bit anxious about what I might find. But your presence made that task somewhat easier."

"That's my job, ma'am . . . uh . . . Miss Molly."

"And now I would like to follow the ambulance to the funeral home and take a closer look at the body. Would you mind escorting me there?"

"Of course. My pleasure. Just fall in behind my cruiser. We'll be there in a few minutes."

Solana had witnessed Molly's careful handling of the deputy and couldn't refrain from making a sly comment.

"Looks like you made friends with our deputy."

"What? Oh, maybe. He had his nose out of joint when we first met. But hopefully, he realized I was just following orders from the ME. And don't let his Southern drawl and quaint manners mislead you. The valedictorian in my graduating class at Johns Hopkins was a young woman from a small town in the Florida Panhandle. Her classroom presentations made the rest of us look like simpletons."

Solana nodded, "I rather doubt that. But I'm familiar with that particular assumption. Believing people are not as intelligent as others simply because of where they come from. There are folks here on Cayo Canno that feel that way about folks, like me, who come from the islands.

"But, whatever. If you can make friends with the deputy, I think you can manage to make a few more in the community. Didn't look like you had any trouble to me. Don't think I believe that nonsense you go on about. That you don't particularly have 'people skills.' It's just that. Nonsense." And she turned, swished her long skirt about swiftly, and walked toward the golf cart.

Chapter 10

Before Molly joined Solana in the golf cart, she took one last look at the scene. Most of the folks had moved on, back to their homes or their businesses she assumed. However, one person appeared to be hanging back, near a large stand of palmetto shrubs. From this distance she saw he was dark-haired, tall, and muscular. He was wearing shorts and a long-sleeved tee shirt which she thought rather odd since it was at least eighty-five degrees at the time. And she couldn't miss seeing his biceps pulling at his tee shirt fabric. His face was practically hidden behind large sunglasses, so she couldn't tell much about his facial features. She wondered if perhaps he was from Cuba, or somewhere south. Either that or he had a great tan. What she could see was that he had a strange gait to his walk . . . not exactly a limp, but perhaps one leg or foot had been injured. He appeared to drag it ever so slightly.

She removed her gloves and placed her bagged specimens in a large Tupperware container and put a lid on it. When she looked up again, the man had disappeared. Where had he gone? He'd have needed to come by her on his way to the street. But he hadn't. She couldn't dwell on that at the moment.

Deputy Harrison was sitting in his cruiser, waiting to escort her to the funeral home. Granted, he wasn't the most sophisticated, experienced officer, but Molly sensed there was more to him than she had originally thought. He had a strong moral compass and she was glad they'd buried the hatchet. No doubt they would run into each other frequently on the island. Better to be friends than enemies.

The sound of the deputy's wailing siren had both Molly and Solana smiling. "Well, you did ask for an escort," Solana laughed.

As soon as they arrived at the funeral home, Deputy Harrison opened the back door and stepped back for Molly and Solana to enter. The strong scent of lilies was overwhelming and Molly pinched her nose for a moment. She'd seen many dead bodies during her training but still preferred seeing them in a hospital setting rather than a funeral home. Something about these places felt so impersonal to her. She turned to Solana who was right on her heels.

"Solana, you might want to stay here in the reception area. A dead body isn't the most pleasant thing to view."

Solana nodded, "I've seen my share of dead bodies, Molly. If you would like me to wait in the reception area, then I will. Otherwise, I'll go with you. Who knows? As you told Deputy Harrison, two brains are better than one. Likewise for two sets of eyes."

Molly nodded. "Good idea. Come along then. Let's get this done."

Then Molly called to Deputy Harrison, "Ben, would you mind standing near the door? Don't need any curious onlookers peeping through the glass before I take another look. It shouldn't take me long to complete my examination."

Deputy Harrison, still wearing his Stetson, nodded and took his position at the door, legs spread wide, arms crossed over his chest. Apparently, he felt this stance was as appropriate here as it had been at the crime scene. Molly smiled her approval at him and began to pull on her gloves.

Solana gloved also and stood by Molly's side watching every move, but remained quiet. Then Molly began describing her findings, beginning with the time and date of this examination. As if she were presenting a case to one of her professors in medical school:

"The body is in rigor mortis, with the hardening of body muscles resulting from the body's loss of adenosine triphosphate which is a substance that gives energy to the muscles. The muscles of this body are completely stiff which indicates that death occurred within the last eight to twelve hours. Of course, other factors will potentially slow down or speed up the rigor mortis process. And certain drugs and disease processes may increase body temperature which could be different from the temperature of the body at the time of death. So, that's something Dr. Strickland will check out."

She continued her assessment and head-to-toe examination, making note of various scars, moles, a birthmark, and pointed out that the body had several bite marks, probably mosquitoes or no-seeums. Her forehead was swollen, but the skin was not broken. She noted the woman had undergone a facelift at some time as evidenced by minuscule lines behind her ears. Whoever had performed the surgery had done a superb job. She also observed and noted the woman had a small tattoo on her left ankle. So small it would have been overlooked by a less observant examiner. The tattoo was a tiny candle with a flame that appeared to flicker when Molly moved the foot. Molly made note of the small tattoo, then turned to Solana.

"I need to turn the body over and examine the other side."

Solana stepped forward, but Molly shook her head. "Let's ask Deputy Harrison to help us with this detail."

She lifted her chin, caught the deputy's eye and called out, "Ben, I need to turn the body. Could you give me a hand, please?"

Deputy Harrison stood still for a long moment. Then he adjusted his heavy gun holster and slowly walked toward the examination table. When he got within two feet, he halted.

"Okay then. We need to turn the body," he said.

Then he walked closer and for a moment stood next to the table and stared at the body. But didn't touch it.

Molly waited, then looked at him. "If you'll lift her shoulders, I'll do a cursory exam. David will do a more thorough one. But I do want to check her spinal column for bruising and such."

The deputy nodded that he understood. But still didn't make a move to touch the body.

Molly then took a look at him. A close look. He was as white as the Stargazer lilies that filled the reception area.

Hmm. I thought this might give him a chance to participate in his first exposure to dealing with a dead body. But perhaps we'd better let him off the hook before we find him on the floor.

With a straight face, she turned to him. "Ben, I just saw a couple of people staring through the glass portion of the door. Perhaps you should return to your position. Solana has done this before. She'll lift the shoulders." He nodded his head rapidly, and before Molly could turn back to the table, he made tracks to the door. Molly was not sure he'd still be standing when she looked again.

Solana carefully lifted the woman's shoulders and Molly quickly scanned the back. "A couple of bruises here at the base of her skull. But no scrapes. A few areas where sand has stuck to the back of her arms. Nothing else." Solana was about to lay her down again when Molly stopped her.

"Let me check the cranium and her spinal column."

Molly ran her fingers along the skull, from top to bottom and around the sides. Nothing to note. But when she placed her fingers behind the head to lay the body back down, she felt a small area where the tissue was soft. Just below that she discovered a two-inch jagged-edged cut at the base of the skull. A small bit of dried blood there, but nowhere else. She made a note of this. David would have to pay attention to that detail. A quick check of the woman's lower backside revealed nothing noteworthy. So Molly pulled the sheet back over the body.

"I think that's it, Solana. A swollen forehead and a small jagged edge at the base of her skull. Not much to go on. But I'll get this information organized and ready for David. Then I suppose you and I should take a look at the photos of the crowd. I'm depending on you to identify people and provide any information you can."

"I knew most everyone. There were a few I didn't recognize, but then the Captain may know them."

"Well, yes, he would know them. And for that matter, could have helped with this investigation. If I didn't know better, I'd think he just made up this trip to Washington."

Solana smiled. "He always has your best interest at heart, Molly." But she grinned as if she too may have similar feelings about that trip.

Molly returned all utensils to their proper place and turned to the deputy. "Ben, I think we're finished here. Is there anything else you think we should do? I told David I'd do my best, but I'm sure more guidelines should be followed, and I don't have a clue about those."

"No, Dr. McCormick . . . Miss Molly. I think you've covered everything. I'll get these guys to put her on ice and Dr. Strickland can take it from there."

Molly reached out her hand and this time he took it without hesitation.

"You've been so patient with me. You could have finished this job in no time, I'm sure. But I do appreciate your letting me put my knowledge to work. Maybe our work will help Dr. Strickland figure this out."

"He's the best. I've seen him in action," said Ben.

"Yes. I'm sure he is. Then Solana and I have to talk to some of the spectators. As I'm sure you would want me to do. And one more thing. I need to talk to you about getting a driver's license. I've just never gotten around to getting one, but I read somewhere that you must have one to drive a golf cart on a public highway with a speed limit above 25 miles per hour."

"What? You're driving without a license? But . . . that's breaking the . . ." He stopped then.

"I can help you with that."

He nodded and held the door for the two women to exit.

Chapter 11

Sassy parked the VW behind the shop, then she and Wesley entered through the back door. She hoped she might find Paul Thornton poking about the Writer's Block. He was an interesting man and Sassy enjoyed chatting with him. He was well-read, had traveled extensively, and was easy on the eyes. But he wasn't around and the bookstore was without a customer, which was fine since neither Debra nor Luis were anywhere about.

"Deb? Luis? Where are you two?"

She removed the "Back Shortly" sign from her window and opened the door wide. Perhaps someone from the bookstore would wander in for a cup of tea and a scone. Sassy's business was steady, and even if it weren't, she was financially secure. Her husband, Duncan, had been the proprietor of a hunting lodge in the borderlands between Scotland and England, a lodge she sold for a hefty sum after he had been declared deceased following their disastrous event.

When Duncan wasn't hunting, he could be found puttering about on their 65-foot sailboat. But he hadn't been the one who insisted they make the voyage across the Atlantic to America. It had been Sassy. The truth was she hadn't been so keen on the idea, but knew he had dreamed of making such a trip as long as she could remember. That was before Gabby had come along, and they'd had to revise their thinking in a number of ways. They knew several couples who had made the trip and had come back with stars in their eyes. Of course, none of them had the misfortune of an out-of-season hurricane to deal with. A long-ago event now.

Wesley had already donned her apron. Ready to pick up where they left off. "Sassy, can we finish making the scones now?"

"Why not? I've got to finish the cinnamon batch at least. Agnes will be upset if I don't have these ready when she comes by."

Wesley picked up the wooden spoon and began to stir. Just this little act, stirring a spoon, brought back a flood of memories of making Christmas cookies with her mother. But Wesley knew there wouldn't be anyone making cookies this year.

"Let's pop these into the oven."

Sassy set the temperature on the oven and reached for the sheet of scones, but stopped when she heard the tinkle of the bell at the door. She turned around to see a very handsome face that looked just right on his equally striking body.

"Ah. A customer at last. Do come in. Wesley and I were just about to stick these scones in the oven. But I have some fresh ones here on the counter."

Adam Laramore nodded, "Thanks. I believe I'll try one."

Wesley turned at the voice.

"Daddy? What are you doing here? I thought you had a charter."

"Yep. Charter was cut short. Nothing biting today."

"Oh. Too bad. But that gives you some free time, right?"

"No such thing as free time, Wes. Just time to do something else I've been putting off."

"But you said we could go shopping for new Keds for me."

"We've got plenty of time to shop for Keds. And, yeah, I remember. You want red ones. Right now you and I need to grab some lunch. Sassy's got work to do."

Wesley bit her lip and began twisting her hair around her finger.

"Wes, go on now. Grab your bike. I'll meet you at the shop then we'll grab a mushroom burger at Timmy's Nook."

Wesley turned to Sassy, "See ya, Sassy. Maybe tomorrow." Sassy smiled at her. Such a special little girl.

When Wesley departed Adam sat at one of the small tables. He waited as Sassy poured him a steaming cup of Earl Grey, thinking maybe it would be one he may have heard of. Without asking, she placed a fresh blueberry scone on a plate and served it with the tea.

Sassy knew from the look on Adam's face that he had come here with a purpose. So, in her customary fashion, she jumped right in.

"Guess you heard about Wesley finding that body under the dock."

She sat down and sipped at her cup of Keeman, a tea imported from central China. Its slightly sweet flavor was interesting and it didn't need sugar.

"Yeah. Joe radioed me when he heard about it, so I brought the charter back in and followed the crowd over at the scene. I saw Wesley

70

was with you, so I stayed back. There was a lot of activity there. Thanks for being with her. She's a handful sometimes. Got a mind of her own. I hope she hasn't been a bother."

"No, she isn't. She was very upset when she got here. Then, after I checked out her story, I notified Deputy Harrington about the body, then thought I should go to the scene. Don't know what good I could have done, but felt I should be there. When I arrived, I learned the medical examiner in Fort Myers asked Captain Jack McCormick's granddaughter to investigate. He couldn't spare a man, so he called on her."

"She's a law enforcement officer?"

Sassy shook her head, "No, but she is a physician, so I can see why he might ask her to help."

"Didn't know we had a physician on the island. Guess I better tune in a little more to local gossip," he smiled and Sassy heard that slow, Southern drawl wrapping around his words. Not often did one hear such on Cayo Canna.

"She only came a few months ago. I met her today. She's called Molly. Seems very capable, if a little standoffish. I don't know the whole story, but today I overheard a couple of people saying she was attacked by a man, and that she stabbed and shot him in the lighthouse."

Adam nodded, "Oh, yeah. Heard something about a death in the lighthouse a while back. That was her?" He sipped his tea and bit off a chunk of the scone.

"Believe so. She's quiet. Maybe like her grandfather, Jack. He keeps his business to himself. But he's a most gracious, intelligent man. He's been a great friend to me. I'm expecting Molly any minute. She wanted to ask Wesley some questions, so I'll tell her to come by the bait shop. I think you should be with Wesley when she questions her. And no worries about Wesley, okay? She comes by occasionally and waves when she goes by on her bicycle with her friends." Sassy smiled.

"That's going to come to a screeching halt here shortly. Riding by on her bike, I mean."

"She doesn't bother anyone. She's just a child. A very curious child," she smiled.

"Yeah. Tell me about it. But it's not that. I'm going to have to send her to my sister in Fort Myers after the holidays. Wesley and several other youngsters have been going to school over on Sanibel for a couple of years now. Wiley Duncan takes his granddaughter and

71

several other children over on his cruiser. But his health has taken a downturn and he's going to move back to Fort Myers shortly. So, I have no choice but to send Wesley to school on the mainland. I can't take time to run her over to Sanibel every morning. Most of my charters begin at first light."

"She's not gonna like that. She loves being here, " Sassy inhaled the aroma of her Keeman brew and took another sip.

"Yeah. You're right. She won't like it." Adam placed his cup on the table, and stood, towering over Sassy as she held the door for him.

"Adam, how about your nightly visitors? Are they still coming around?"

"Yeah. Every night."

"Nightmares seem to have a mind of their own. Come when they please. Believe me, I know. I've been there, but now I only have one occasionally."

Adam stood then and smiled at Sassy, "Thanks again. Tea was great." Then he smiled, "Almost as good as coffee."

There it was again, that soothing, teasing, Southern drawl. And Sassy was beginning to think he knew exactly when to exaggerate it.

Chapter 12

As Adam walked out the front door, a bedraggled Debra walked from her shop into Sassy's. She was without jewelry, her hair was held back with a headband, and she had no trace of makeup. And most telling of all, she was wearing a plain cotton shift and flip-flops. Most times she was decked out in a Lilly dress with designer sandals, fine jewelry, and perfectly applied makeup.

Sassy knew a hangover when she saw one. But Debra had been in the shop next door for a couple of years and Sassy had never seen her in this condition. She'd been late on several occasions recently, but Sassy had never even seen her having a drink. But then, Sassy didn't frequent the local bars very often, so she wouldn't have known if Debra had imbibed.

"How about a cup of tea?" Sassy asked. She bit her tongue to keep from asking the obvious question . . . how are you feeling? Debra nodded and took a seat at the same table where Adam had sat.

"Got fresh cinnamon scones. Care for one?"

"No. No scones. Just tea, please," she mumbled. Sassy served her a cup of Earl Grey and had another cup herself. She'd never thought of herself as a good listener, but today she seemed to be everyone's listening post.

"Sassy, I would like to say it's not what it looks like. But I'm afraid it is. It doesn't happen often and I suppose I should have told you my 'secret.' But, like all alcoholics, I thought I had it under control. And it's not good for my diabetic issue. But I have a new medication for diabetes. Thanks to Greg Maxwell. He's been such a dear. It helps keep me on an even keel and helps with appetite control as well. He's so kind and thoughtful. " She was on the verge of tears, her lips quivering as she spoke.

"We all have secrets, Debra. One day I'll tell you mine. But today, let's just agree we're all human and make mistakes."

"Thank you. Trouble is, Gillian is not as understanding as you. She was feeling no pain either when I left her last evening. Well, except for complaining about feeling a headache coming on. But then, she can afford to drink when she wants to. Doesn't appear to affect her the way it does me. She'll have a headache, then sit down and write another bestseller an hour later."

"Gillian?" Sassy frowned, then remembered the name.

"Oh, yes. Your friend, the author. I'm sorry I didn't make it to the Historical Society meeting. I was exhausted from standing on my feet all day. I fell asleep on the sofa and woke up with a crick in my neck. Maybe I can meet her before she leaves the island. She staying at your place?"

"No. She's at the Sandpiper. She got her nose a bit out of joint about not being able to stay at the Gasparilla—they were booked solid—only the best for Gillian—famous writer. You know? And the Sandpiper is just as beautiful as the Gasparilla. Just not as well known. We learned a long time ago we can't spend much time in the same house. She's a bit of a slob in my opinion. And I can't bear it when she lets papers fly all over the floor when she's writing. Plus, I get tired of her hounding me about my diet. Never lets me forget I'm diabetic. She's always after me to eat better. Just because she's slim doesn't mean she eats well herself. She's just one of the lucky ones that inherited skinny genes." She smiled at her own pitiful joke.

"And, of course, she never fails to remind me that I owe her money. A lot of money, in fact. If my ex hadn't taken my good jewelry, I'd have had enough funds to open Writer's Block without her help."

She quit talking then. She knew her tongue was getting way ahead of her brain, else she wouldn't have divulged so much personal information.

Just as Sassy got up to pour Debra another cup, someone came hurrying through the walk-thru. Sassy turned to see who had arrived, "Oh, hi, Jeri. Don't see your face here very often. Would you like tea? Scone?"

"Hi, Sassy. No, I'm just looking for Debra." She turned then to see Debra holding her head in her hands.

Jeri frowned, bent down, and put an arm about Debra's shoulders. "Debra? Are you all right? Did you forget to take your insulin?"

Debra looked up. "What? Oh, no. Just not feeling up to par today."

"I'm sorry. Maybe tomorrow will be better. I must tell you that both

Greg and I enjoyed your friend's presentation at the Historical Society meeting last night. I've read all her books. She's quite a talented lady."

Debra nodded, "Yes, she is. And I know she went by your pharmacy yesterday. To pick up a few items she just couldn't do without. Her Maybelline makeup and Adorn hair spray. And knowing Gillian, I'm sure she picked up a few more 'necessary' items. She wanted to be perfectly turned out for her speaking event. She was low on cash, so I told her to have Greg put whatever she needed on my account. I'll come by tomorrow and settle up with you."

"Yes, I got a few things together for her. She was quite pleasant. She indicated she's thinking of buying a place here. Greg says she was taken with our island haven. Would be nice for you to have a friend nearby."

"Yes. That would be nice. But Gillian talks a lot. Doesn't always mean what she says."

"Well, then. No need for you to come by tomorrow. I'll send you a bill. Since I was coming this way, I brought a refill of your migraine supplements. Greg said it's time. Saves you a trip to the pharmacy.

"You know, Greg follows the latest information on clinical trials and keeps up with the new supplements and medications that he feels his customers may benefit from."

"Thanks, Jeri. You're a lifesaver. As it is, I gave Gillian my last three migraine tablets last night. She felt a headache coming on, so she seemed to need them more than I did. But this morning I need some myself. Lately, I've had a few episodes of stomach ache, fatigue, and muscle aches. And I do believe I'm losing some hair. Getting old I suppose."

Jeri handed her the medication which she promptly dropped into her large purse.

"Now, don't forget. Rest is the best medicine of all," smiled Jeri.

Debra nodded. "Of course. And thanks again."

"Hope you feel better. Gotta run. Have a couple more deliveries on the south end of the island."

Sassy watched as Jeri patted her hair down after breezing through the door. Jeri was a fairly attractive woman who always wore a white lab coat, sensible shoes, and kept her light brown hair neatly trimmed. Never a hair out of place. Of course, she didn't wear perfume. She believed it was inconsiderate to spread scent about the room where others may not particularly enjoy it. Sassy thought she was 'wrapped a bit too tight,' but kept that opinion to herself. Jeri was always talkative.

Sometimes so much that Sassy wondered if she was lonely. But she was with Greg all day, so surely not.

Sassy had known Debra had migraines, but had no idea of the alcohol problem. She never appeared to be having any difficulty. Until today. And Sassy assumed that was from whatever she had drunk the night before.

"That's one thing I do like about living here. Having a delivery service for medications. Sometimes when you're under the weather, it's nice to know Jeri will bring it to you."

Debra nodded in agreement, and from the look on her face, was still feeling the effects of last evening's cocktails.

Sassy decided to come to her rescue. "Why don't you go home? I'll look after the shop. Luis is upstairs. I'll call on him if I get too busy. His English may not be the best, but it's better than my Spanish. I'm sure between the two of us we'll manage."

Debra nodded and stood, took one last sip of tea, and let herself out the back door, carefully avoiding trampling through Sassy's flowerbed where she grew various varieties of mint for her tea. A little farther over, behind the next shop, Vedra also had a flowerbed where she cultivated various medicinal plants that she used for her herbal remedies. No one seemed to know exactly what, however.

She got into her golf cart, wondering just how much she would owe Maxwell's pharmacy after Gillian had made a turn through there.

Chapter 13

Solana stood by the golf cart, waiting for Molly to finish up with Deputy Harrington. She'd been thinking about Sassy's request for them to come by her shop where Molly could ask the little girl whatever questions she felt were pertinent. But she wasn't at all sure she wanted to accompany Molly to that meeting.

Molly placed her medical bag in the cart and hopped on. "All right. Looks like maybe I won't get a ticket for driving without a license. At least not today." She smiled at Solana. "So, we've covered the dock. We've checked out the body. Now we should ask questions, I think." Molly shook her head back and forth.

"This is not the way this should be handled. I am quite sure of that." She looked at Solana who sat quietly.

"I wanted to speak to the child that discovered the body. Ask her a few questions. But apparently, she left. Do you know who she is? Where she lives?"

Solana nodded. "Yes, I know who her father is. Adam Laramore. He's a fishing guide. Owns the Hook, Line, and Charter Bait Shop."

"Do you know where that is?"

"Of course I do. But Sassy has asked that we come to her shop to see the child. She thought she should remove her from the scene, so she left."

"I see. That was good thinking. Then we'll go there."

"If you would, please, drop me off at the lighthouse first. I've got several chores I need to attend to. You go on to see Sassy."

"But, Solana, I don't even know her."

"She knows who you are. She's expecting you to come by."

Molly didn't question Solana any further. She was learning there were some things she still didn't know about Solana. But she took care of Papa Jack and that's all that mattered to Molly.

After leaving Solana at the lighthouse, Molly headed to Sassy's. She didn't know exactly what she was expecting but was pleasantly surprised. The aroma of freshly baked scones and brewed tea saturated her nostrils the moment she entered.

Oh, what a scrumptious smell. Smells just like the bistro in Baltimore.

Sassy met her at the door and held out her hand, "I'm Sassy. Good to meet you. I've known Jack for many years and I've heard about you." Sassy again took note of the scar on the side of Molly's face. She also noted, as she had earlier, that it didn't detract from her beauty. And the soft brown, doe eyes that tilted up at the outer corners were sparkling. She was quite a lovely girl. Jack had always spoken about her intelligence, but he'd not mentioned how attractive she was.

"Here. Take a seat."

Molly sat down and Sassy started right in, "That was quite a scene at the dock. And I for one am glad you took charge. Ben Harrington is a pleasant enough guy, but I feel sure your investigation of the scene was much better than what he would have come up with."

"Don't be too sure. I admit that I'm flying by the seat of my pants and I'm in over my head. Being a physician prepares you for many things, but this detective-medical examiner business is foreign to me. And don't let the deputy fool you. He's got more going for him than meets the eye."

Sassy lifted her eyebrows. "Interesting. Solana tells me the medical examiner in Fort Myers asked for your help?"

"Yes. Dr. Strickland. A friend. In Florida, he's called Medical Examiner. Other states have coroners. He helped get Papa Jack back on his feet. And I owe him."

Sassy nodded, "So, I assume you're here to talk with Wesley?"

"Wesley. That's her name?"

"Yes, Wesley Laramore. She found the body early this morning and came over to tell me about it. But, as much as I enjoy her stopping by, she does stretch the truth sometimes. Nothing to make a fuss about. Until this morning. Unfortunately, this time she was telling the truth. So, I'll give her a little slack. And maybe this will teach her a lesson."

"May I speak with her? I don't even know what to ask, other than the obvious questions."

"You just missed her. Her father, Adam, came by a few minutes ago. He would prefer that he be with her when you ask your questions. Just being a protective father, I suppose," she smiled.

"Of course. Where can I find him?"

"He runs the Hook, Line, & Charter Bait Shop . . . on the beach side . . . behind the Gasparilla Inn. Not far from the scene."

"Then I'd better get going. I promised David, Dr. Strickland, I'd talk to as many people as I can. Maybe someone will have seen something. Or heard something."

Sassy grimaced, "Maybe. Afraid I can't add anything. I just took a peek under the dock and confirmed what Wesley had told me. Then I hurried back to the sheriff's office to tell Deputy Harrison about it."

"Ah, so that would be your footprints alongside the very small ones that had to have been made by Wesley. Those two sets were the only ones that I found at the site. I'm glad you had the foresight to check out the child's story. The body could have lain there for some time if the she hadn't found her."

"Yes, but it did upset Wesley. Glad it wasn't someone she knew. Perhaps fingerprints or photos will help identify the woman."

"Thanks to the pharmacist . . . oh . . . Mr. Maxwell, I believe?" responded Molly.

Sassy nodded, "Yes, Greg. Greg Maxwell. He and his wife, Jeri, are both pharmacists."

"He identified the woman. It seems she was the guest speaker at the Historical Society Meeting last night. A writer he said." She looked at her notes quickly. "Gillian Hartwell. Greg and his wife went to hear her speak."

Sassy's mouth dropped open. She stared at Molly.

"Oh, no. She's Debra's friend . . . or was Debra's friend." She pushed her hair back from her forehead and sighed. "Dear me. I'll have to tell Debra before she hears it through the local gossip grapevine."

"Who's Debra?"

"Debra Morris. Owns the Writer's Block Bookstore next door. She was just here. But I sent her home. She wasn't feeling well." Sassy kept her other observations regarding Debra's condition to herself. She was savvy enough to realize this situation could get very complicated.

"It would be most helpful if you could arrange for me to talk with her. Dr. Strickland will need as much information as he can get, and the sooner the better. If you would call me at the lighthouse, I'll meet her at her convenience. But it needs to be as soon as possible."

"Yes, of course. I'll go to her place now. And if the phones are working, I'll call you."

Molly nodded, "Meanwhile I'll try to find Wesley. And thanks. I'm sure a real detective would have a dozen more questions, but I can't think of anything else to ask you. Other than what time do you open in the morning? I would so love a cup of tea and a scone at this delightful tea house. The aroma that grabbed me at the door will stay with me until I find time to come back."

Sassy smiled. *Not so standoffish after all.*

She observed that Molly worked at keeping the scarred side of her face turned away when she spoke. Sassy was sure there was an interesting tale behind such a mark. Maybe she'd learn about that later. But now, she closed up her shop and hurried out the back door to attend to a most difficult task.

Chapter 14

The dining room at the Monaco Hotel looked like a setting from a Hollywood movie. Captain Jack McCormick fully expected to see Humphrey Bogart and Ingrid Bergman come waltzing across the floor. Low lighting—from small suspended lights over each table—would have been perfect for a romantic dinner for two. The waiters were attired in tuxedos and shiny black shoes that shone in the dimly lit room. The pianist was playing a slow, jazzy piece and the lush, intoxicating sound of a tenor saxophone was wailing in the background.

Jack and Bear looked about the cozy room. Neither of them needed to voice their thoughts. With a nod to the maître d' they exited without a word. Next minute they were standing on the corner, tugging at their peacoats as a blistering wind screamed across the harbor.

"Don't think that's exactly what we had in mind. Margaret would have loved it, though." Jack laughed and threw up his hand. A Yellow Cab came to a screeching halt, and the two hurried into the warm interior. That wind with its ice shards blowing about was too much to bear.

"Take us to the waterfront. Someplace nice. But not too fancy. We just want a good dinner and a decent bottle of wine."

"Know just the place. Bernardo's. Best Italian food in Baltimore. I should know. Bernardo's my cousin." He grinned and a couple of minutes later he let the two old seadogs off in front of the restaurant. Huddled beneath a couple of huge Thuja trees, the old brick building looked inviting. A long green and white awning strung with white fairy lights stretched from the doorway to the street.

Bear nodded, "Yeah. This is more what I had in mind. And I can smell garlic and tomatoes even before we enter!"

Jack was quite fond of Solana's tasty island dishes, but once in a while a great plate of spaghetti and meatballs was exactly what he wanted. Along with a good bottle of pinot noir.

Dinner hit the spot, and now the two were back at the Monaco sitting in a quiet corner of the bar. It was rather late, so most customers had gone their way, except for one young couple sitting across the room at a table for two. Jack saw Bear smiling as he took in the view.

"We were that young once, Casper, remember?"

"What you talking about? We're still young. Did you forget we just helped prevent a major calamity from happening in our country?"

Bear nodded, "We did. We did. That was an important operation."

He took a sip of his pinot noir and felt it slip smoothly across his tongue. Then taking a deep breath, he rested his elbows on the table. "So why do I still have this feeling in the pit of my gut that something's not quite right . . . that there's something missing . . . unfinished business?"

Jack kept quiet for a moment and looked across at the young couple who were now leaving the bar arm-in-arm. For one quick second, he let his memory recall another young woman . . . her laugh . . . her perfume . . . and how he and she had often walked just that way.

"You too, huh? Bear, we've been at this game most of our lives. And we know by now that when nothing else tells the truth, your gut will. I was hoping it was just my displeasure at being here in this place. Baltimore. Where Molly's life was changed drastically. But I've got that same itchy, irritating feeling in my gut too."

Bear nodded, "Then we've got a problem. If only one of us is feeling like there's an unfinished, unsettled situation, that's one thing. But if we both are experiencing queasiness of the gut, that's another."

"I agree. We've got a problem. Let's get some sleep. We'll have all day tomorrow to mull over our feelings while we pack up Molly's things. Then we'll head back to Cayo Canna. I'd wanted to stay away another day or so and give Molly some time to take care of her assignment. But I think you and I both know our "problem" lies closer to home . . . off the coast of Florida."

"Sometimes I think you've got built-in radar, Casper. But if you recall, we said the Cuban Missile Crisis would be our last operation."

Jack nodded, "I do recall that. Yeah. And it was. But maybe we have a few more details to clear up."

Bear shook his head. "Casper, we agreed at the briefing with Admiral Whitmore. We'll not volunteer to participate in any in-country shenanigans in Cuba. You remember that part, too, right?"

Chapter 15

Agnes never approved of gossip and didn't engage in it herself. Well, not very often anyway. But as she looked up from counting her cans of vegetable soup, she was glad to see someone to whom she could confide her latest problems.

Bertha Holland, the island's only hairdresser, came through the door, stopped to check her mailbox, and came to the counter. She closed her shop one day a week and that day she spent doing her errands and grocery shopping. Being the hairdresser, Bertha was privy to the secrets of most every customer. Some secrets she wished she didn't know.

Agnes greeted her friend, "Bertha. Glad to see you out and about. What you hearing from that grandson? He went on to college somewhere up in Alabama, didn't he?"

"Yes, he wanted a little distance from his mom and dad, but after one semester in Alabama, he transferred to Florida State in Tallahassee. Seems he missed his home state. But, that's still a bit of distance. Always was an independent little character. Full of mischief from day one. But Carolyn and Mark miss him."

"Making good grades? University life is quite different than high school."

"Well, I'll probably never know. But I can tell you he's more interested in playing football than he is in studying physics or Western Civilization." They both laughed at that remark.

"Are you doing all right, Agnes? I missed you at the Historical Society meeting last night. And the speaker was great. It was that author. Oh, what's her name? Gillian something. Wrote several books set in Florida."

Agnes never forgot a name and knew this one. "Yes, Gillian Hartwell. Well, I had planned to go, but my "date" didn't show up, so I stayed home and nursed my anger with a couple of glasses of sauvignon blanc. Didn't ease my anger, but did help me go to sleep.

Did you have a good turnout?"

"Oh, my, did we ever. All the regulars were there and we even had a number of men. Guess the author is well known in the state."

"Did you know she's a friend of Debra Morris?" asked Agnes.

Bertha raised her eyebrows, "Really? Aren't we just the lucky ones. I wonder if Debra had to twist her arm to get her to come over here? Goodness knows Debra's bookstore can't hold a candle to those bookstores in larger places, like Tampa or Miami."

Agnes nodded in agreement. "Maybe Ms. Hartwell was just being generous with her time. And they've been friends for a long time. But I am sorry I didn't get to hear her speak. Did she have an interesting topic?"

"Yes, yes. Ancient Florida history. She kept the group entertained and afterward a goodly number of them went to The Temptation for a drink and dancing for those who like that sort of thing."

"Then I did miss something."

"Oh, did I forget to mention that she not only writes but is quite an attractive dish? Hair to die for. There were several men at the meeting and she certainly caught their eye. But, back to you, whatever got you so angry? That's not like you. I might have seen you cranky a few times, but never angry. A date you say? Who was the lucky man?"

"Just kidding. My date was Lizzie Strafford. You know her. She moved here a while back. Her husband died of a heart attack and she relocated to the island. They'd vacationed here several times, and she thought it would be an ideal place for her. But she seems a bit antsy these days. Anyway, I asked her to join me and attend the Historical Society meeting. She seemed happy to do so and was to pick me up. But she never showed, and I still haven't heard from her. Guess she'll have a good reason."

"I'm sure she will. I styled her hair a couple of days ago. She was excited about a date. I believe it was with Raphael. She has lovely hair and wears beautiful hair clips most of the time. She would have been a good hairdresser herself."

"Yes, she's always well turned out." Agnes bagged the groceries and held the door open for Bertha.

"See you later," Bertha called out and went on her way.

Less than an hour later, Agnes heard the squeal of brakes and the sound of shells being crunched in the parking lot as a car came to an abrupt halt. Seconds later Lizzie came rushing in through the door, her hair flying about and talking rapidly as she entered.

"Oh, Agnes. I am so sorry. Please forgive me. I don't usually behave in such a manner. But, to be honest with you, when Raphael dropped by unexpectedly, I completely forgot about our plans. He is such a charmer . . . and insisted on taking me to dinner at the Temptation. Then he had to leave me for a few minutes to pick up two customers. Well, when he returned to the Temptation with his customers, Debra Morris and her friend, the writer who was the guest speaker at the Historical Society Meeting, I remembered our arrangement.

"But, Agnes, there were more people at the Temptation than I've ever seen. Raphael said they had been to the Historical Society meeting, and the speaker was buying drinks for everyone. Anyway, the Temptation has a great dance floor, and Raphael knows the bartender. Sean something. And he kept serving us his special drink . . . something called Long Island Tea. And we danced until our feet hurt. 'Course Raphael never drinks, but he kept them coming for me."

"Then later, things got a little out of control, and one thing led to another . . . and the next thing I knew it was morning, and I was not in my own bed!" Lizzie hushed then. Not sure what she should say now. So, Agnes gave her a smile that relieved any worry about missing their date.

"Well, then. Maybe I will forgive you. I had no idea you and Raphael were on such 'intimate' terms. And I'd say you had a perfect evening," laughed Agnes. She'd never had such an evening herself, but loved hearing about Lizzie's.

"But, Agnes. There's just one problem with my perfect evening."

"What? Didn't last long enough?" Agnes grinned even larger.

"No. The problem is I can't remember anything except the dancing. I don't remember leaving the Temptation. Nor getting in Raphael's car. Nothing. And then this morning I woke up in Raphael's bed, but he wasn't there. I've no idea where he is. He mentioned he was going to take the ferry to the mainland. Something about needing supplies for his new project. Maybe life jackets? I can't remember. But I don't know how I ended up at his place. And that is just a bit scary."

Agnes put an arm about her shoulders, "Come on back behind the counter. I've got some coffee brewing. Some of that rich stuff Captain Jack gave me. He gets it from Cuba. Or did. Not sure if he can get it anymore now that Crab's dead. Getting anything from Cuba is almost impossible these days."

Chapter 16

Finding the Hook, Line, and Charter Bait Shop was not difficult. Most of the businesses were located within a two-mile radius of the Gasparilla Inn which sat practically in the middle of the island. There were several restaurants as well as bars. All of them served good food, and there seemed to be an ongoing contest to determine which establishment would receive the "Island Favorite" ribbon each year.

Molly left Sassy's shop and followed her instructions for getting to the bait shop. She parked the golf cart in the angled-parking space and entered. The door was standing open and a breeze coming from the ocean flowed within. A pudgy, middle-aged gentleman wearing long shorts and a blue striped tee shirt greeted her.

"Morning, miss. What can I help you with?"

His customers were mostly men coming to purchase bait, a new rod and reel, or wanting to book a charter. But this gorgeous lady didn't fit his idea of a woman who would be interested in fishing. She was looking about the place, taking in the various items he had on display.

"My bet is you're not wanting fish bait." He smiled at her and she returned it.

"No. Not fish bait. I'm looking for Mr. Laramore. Sassy said I would find him here."

"Yep. Most of the time he's either here or out on a charter. But at the moment he's got a date with a lovely young lady."

"Oh, I see. Then perhaps I should come back tomorrow. Don't want to interrupt a date."

The man reached out his hand. "I'm Joe Stanhope. Most folks call me Kokomo. I keep this place running while Adam goes about his charters. He's just a block down the street. At Timmy's Nook. Having lunch. He won't mind you joining him. Go on. But when you do need bait, come back by."

Molly was surprised that everyone was so friendly. Papa had said they would be glad to have a physician on the island, but so far no one had questioned her about such details as that. Maybe getting to know the locals wasn't going to be so difficult after all.

With that confident thought she walked into Timmy's Nook. This place would be appealing to anyone. Someone had strung colored lights all about the room, from side to side. On the left side of the room, a large wooden dance floor took up most of that portion of the place. There was a spot for a live band to set up. Across the room, on the right side, was a curved bar with padded stools. It would seat at least fifteen to twenty people Molly thought. And at the back of the room, was a doorway that opened to another room, which must be where food would be served. Or perhaps that was where the famous "prayer meeting" took place?

She watched as a couple of young women rushed about, calling out to someone in the kitchen as they bussed tables, removed empty beer bottles from the bar, and giggled as they worked. Happy. This was a happy place. And now at lunchtime, there were several customers, some at the bar and others in the dining room. She wasn't sure exactly how she would know Adam. She'd not asked Sassy to describe him, but surely one of the wait staff would know him.

She stood for a moment, then approached a young, bleached-blond girl wearing short shorts and a tee shirt that emphasized her "assets."

"Excuse me. I wonder if you could help me?"

"Sure thing. What you need, hon? Table? Or you wanna sit at the bar?"

"No. Neither. I'm looking for someone and Kokomo, at the bait shop, said I would find him here."

"Yeah? Who you wanna to talk to?"

"Adam. Adam Laramore. Is he here?"

The girl looked at Molly. Head to toe. Then cocked her head to one side. "Yeah, he's here. Who are you?"

"I'm Molly McCormick. I'm new on the island."

"McCormick. Related to the Capt'n?"

"Yes. He's my grandfather."

"Oh yeah? So, you're the new doc. The one that shot the man in the lighthouse . . . and stabbed him too, I heard."

Molly stood quietly. This was exactly what she feared would happen. Her reputation was established before she even had a chance to get her practice started. She hardly knew what to say, so she kept quiet.

The young woman placed a warm hand on Molly's arm, "Good for you, girl. Sounds as if he needed somebody to kick his sorry ass. Looks like you took care of that."

She laughed and pointed Molly to the dining room to the right of the bar. "Adam's in there. Can't miss 'em. Best looking man you'll ever see." She laughed again and began bussing another table.

Molly walked into the dining room and looked about. Three men were at a table up front, a business lunch she assumed as they appeared to be pouring over some kind of contract. There were two tables of women. Most likely ladies' bridge club she figured. They were all dressed casually, and all talking at the same time. Molly never had experienced that kind of relationship with women. She usually only had one or two friends. And that was enough for her. Then, back in the rear of the room, she saw a man with his arm around his date's shoulder. His date leaned into him and smiled up at him. Molly started to turn around and leave but remembered that she had a job to do.

She walked over and stood at his table. The waitress was right. He might actually be the most handsome man she'd ever seen. And the body matched the face. For a moment her tongue felt glued to her palate. Eventually, she began to introduce herself.

"Excuse me. I'm Molly McCormick. Are you Adam Laramore?"

The man looked at her for a long moment. Before he could answer, his date looked up. "Yes, he's Adam Laramore. And I'm Wesley Laramore." Molly smiled and the child cocked her head to one side, "You've got a scar. I have one too. See here? Here on my chin. I fell off my bike."

Molly reached a hand to her cheek as if to hide it. But she didn't respond to the child's 'unfiltered' comment. She took in the tiny face, long dark hair (somewhat matted) being loosely held by a clip, freckles across her nose, and eyes that were entirely too large for her face. Molly thought she looked rather elfin . . . and angelic at the same time.

"Wesley, eat your burger." The man stood and reached out his hand.

"Yes, I'm Adam. You must be the doctor who investigated the murder scene."

"Yes, but I don't know that it was a murder scene. It may have just been an accident. That's why I'm here. I'm trying to gather information for the Medical Examiner, Dr. Strickland, to make that determination. I understand Wesley found the body this morning."

Wesley nodded her head up and down as she took a bite of her burger. "It was just lying there. Under the dock. And her toes were painted red. Did you see them?" Molly squatted down so she'd be at eye level with Wesley.

"Yes, I saw her red toenails. Was anyone with you when you went to the dock?"

"No. Just me."

"And what were you doing at the dock?"

"Nothing. Just looking for sea glass."

"I see. Did you see anyone else when you were there?"

Wesley nodded as she slurped from the straw in her Coke. "There was a man with a dog and a few other people walking on the beach. Maybe they collect sea glass, too."

"So, then you went to tell Sassy about what you found?"

"Uh-huh. But Sassy didn't believe me at first."

"Why did you tell Sassy instead of going home to tell your mother?"

Adam slammed his hand down on the table and glared at Molly.

"Hold on a minute. What exactly do you want to know, Dr. McCormick? Wesley's a child. A little girl. She just told you what she saw. I don't think taking her through the experience again is very helpful. Her well-being is more important to me than you getting information for some medical examiner. She told you she saw a body under the dock. And toes with red polish. Nothing else. There's nothing more to tell. She'll answer no more questions." He grabbed Wesley by the hand, practically dragging her from the table.

"But, Daddy, I didn't finish my mushroom burger!"

Molly stood back and watched Adam walking hurriedly, his limp a bit more exaggerated as he pulled Wesley along. Presently, Molly was wishing she could crawl under a dock herself.

Guess I didn't handle that inquiry very well. Looks like I asked something he didn't like. But what was I expecting? If I had a child, I'm sure I would be just as protective as he is. So now what? Tell David that in addition to failing Medical Examiner class, I also failed Detective Class 101?

She straightened her shoulders and fingered the scar on the side of her cheek. An unconscious habit she'd developed since the attack. One that came into play whenever she was anxious about something. She looked about. It would be dark soon and the golf cart had no lights and wasn't to be driven after dark.

Molly decided to get back to the lighthouse. This day just needed to end. She hopped aboard the golf cart and sent bits of shells flying as she sped off. Her brain was so tired but refused to stop churning.

For a quick moment, Molly recalled how easily Patrick always put others at ease. His ability to relate to people . . . no matter their status in life . . . was certainly an asset in a priest. Or anyone. If he were here, she would have asked him to assist in this investigation. But they hadn't heard from him since he left Cayo Canna weeks ago, presumably to return to Ireland. Would he ever come back to Cayo Canna? If so, would that have any bearing on her life? After all, he was a priest and she was aware her feelings for him could not be reciprocal. Today, however, she would like nothing better than to talk with him.

She arrived at the lighthouse, slammed on the brakes, and jerked the golf cart to a halt, her brain on fire with questions for which she had no answers. One thing she did know, however, was that she was fairly angry at David Strickland for asking her to assist. And her brain was still churning as she muttered to herself.

David Strickland, my debt to you has been paid in spades. I've plunked about a crime scene not knowing a clue from a gecko, then I crawled beneath a dock that could have fallen on me any second, then I assessed a dead body and had to swat at green blow flies, and then I badgered a young girl with questions she should never have had to answer! If I ever wanted to be a medical examiner, this has cured me of that disease!

Chapter 17
Patrick's Dilemma

Father Patrick O'Brien had placed his Walther PPK next to Sam's head, pulled the trigger, and finished off what Molly had started. This deranged man, this Sam, had attacked Molly in Baltimore, then again at the lighthouse on Cayo Canna. Patrick also knew there were other issues he also needed to finish off as well.

Following the smashing "resurrection party" for Capt. Jack—who had been presumed dead—but was alive and well—Patrick took his leave of the island. Before leaving, he had a conversation with Captain Jack about some "unresolved issues" and now was taking the first step to resolve them. He promised to return to Cayo Canna. But no idea when.

With a heavy heart, he left Cayo Canna and made a trip to Baltimore to see his good friend, Paul. The priest he'd been friends with for ages. The same priest that had been sexually abusing young men in the church where Patrick was pastor.

No matter how he tried, Patrick couldn't forgive his friend for such heinous behavior. So, he'd met with Paul and told him his feelings regarding the issue. His suggestion was for Paul to get on his knees and ask for forgiveness from the Almighty. As for Patrick, he simply couldn't forgive such an evil act. He departed Baltimore having expressed his feelings to his friend—now former friend—and headed home to Ireland. There were issues that still needed to be addressed there as well.

The moment the plane landed on Irish soil, Patrick breathed a sigh of relief. He had always hated flying and the flight from Boston to Dublin seemed to get longer every time he made the trip.

But the minute he stepped out of the plane and scurried down the steps to the tarmac, he forgot about that particular problem as another more imminent one hit him in the face. Literally.

Jaysus, Mary, and Holy St. Joseph! Damnation! I'd forgotten how raw the Irish weather is in November. Maybe I should have given that some thought before I hopped across the Atlantic Ocean.

Moving along toward the terminal, his thoughts returned to Cayo Canna, where he was sure the weather was warm and inviting. For a moment he recalled sitting on the patio with Molly, consoling her after her second near-death experience with that lunatic, Sam, who had carved her face and tried to kill her not once, but two times.

Patrick was glad he'd been able to finish that fiend off and still had no qualms about taking that vile man's life. But would the Church see it the same way? Maybe not. But Molly was alive and that was justification for his actions in his mind.

He pulled his greatcoat tightly about his body and entered the car rental building. He'd need transportation and didn't want to ask his aging parents to pick him up at the airport.

The drive to the Lime Kiln, the bed and breakfast his parents owned, was a two-hour trip. But Patrick loved driving along, seeing the countryside. This place was home, no matter how many years he'd spent away from it. But this trip might not be a pleasant one.

As he pulled up the long lane that ran between the limestone walls that led to the Lime Kiln, snow covered the countryside as far as he could see. Smoke billowed out the chimney and the sheep in the pasture stood huddled together in an attempt to keep warm. To Patrick, this could be a postcard setting and he smiled as he walked up the walkway to the front door.

Running a bed and breakfast meant Mum had already decorated the large, wooden front door with a seasonal "fall" wreath made from pine cones and greenery from fir trees that were part of the landscape. She had a real knack when it came to placing the colored ribbons into the greenery. Patrick remembered gathering pine cones and bits of greenery in his childhood. Mum always had decorations for whatever season and delighted in making the Lime Kiln an inviting place to spend some time.

He rather hoped his folks would close the B&B, but they had hired several workers in the last few years, which meant the two of them didn't have nearly the workload of earlier times when Patrick had been a lad working alongside them. He had learned to cook by spending an inordinate amount of time in the kitchen with his Mum, and cooking was still his favorite pastime.

Patrick didn't ring the bell. Just opened the door, stomped into the hallway, and called out, "And is anyone home? A cuppa with a touch of Jameson would go well about now!"

Mum came rushing from the kitchen and squealed with delight. "Patrick! And what a grand surprise this is!"

Da heard the commotion and wandered to the hallway as well. "Ah. Shoulda known it was someone special. Your Mum never greets our guests with such a smile and joy on her face."

Patrick gave both a big hug and found his way to the kitchen, where something enticing would always be simmering on the stove.

Mum hurried about making him a cuppa with a touch of Jameson to add a bit of warmth on such a cold day. Of course, she placed a plate of scones within his reach.

"Well, lad, despite the fact we didn't know you were coming, we're delighted to see you. I know there must be a reason for such an unexpected visit. What's it been? More than a year?"

"Aye. And you're right, Da. I should have come long before now, but sometimes time gets away from you and it's later than you think. But, yes. I've come back to settle some unfinished business. Still not sure how I'm going to do that, but I thought I'd talk with Angus. He's always been tuned in to my issues and usually reads my mind as well." He smiled at his own comment.

Da came closer and put his arm around Patrick's shoulder. "Then, you'd better get on about seeing him, lad. I was at the Druid's Fountain a couple of weeks ago and stopped by the pub. Just for a word with Angus. He came down from his rooms above the pub, but when he tried to go back up, one of the lads from the kitchen hurried over to help him. He's a bit frail, lad. I believe it's something about his heart. Plus, he's not getting any younger."

Patrick stared at Da. "But . . . I've corresponded with him numerous times over the time I was in Baltimore. He never said anything about a heart condition."

"No? But then none of us "elder" ones want to tell the world about any problems we might be having. Just some things we keep to ourselves."

Patrick finished his cuppa and downed two scones. He stood, started for the front door, then looked at Mum and Da.

"Then I'm off to see Angus. I had planned to spend a few days here before I went to visit him, but I think I'll go on now and come back here later if that's all right with you two."

95

"Of course, lad. We'll be here. Do what you must now. There's always a bed for you in this B&B," Mum smiled and hugged him once again.

Chapter 18

After leaving Sassy's shop, Debra went directly home, then parked her golf cart in its assigned place. Then she entered through the back door to the kitchen. She retrieved her purse and quickly put the insulin in the refrigerator. This medication was a life-saver. She'd not forgotten the time she decided to stop taking this particular medication. She hated giving herself injections every day. As it was, about two days later she went into a diabetic coma and spent several days in the hospital. That experience left a lasting impression.

She quickly downed one of her migraine tablets and lay on her bed. It'd been a long time since she had suffered such a hangover. Yesterday had been a long day, and the evening even longer. The Historical Society gave Gillian a fine welcome and she charmed them as she always did. But the latter part of the evening had taken its toll and Debra was now paying the price of her overindulgence.

She lay on her bed, but sleep wouldn't come. For a brief moment she thought about having 'a hair of the dog' that bit her the night before. But she nixed that idea. It was time she regrouped and got herself back together. She was relieved Jeri had brought a refill of her migraine medication, else she might never get relief from this insane pounding in her head. And presently she made a vow to never drink again . . . a promise she had made many times before.

She lay on her bed recalling the events of the last couple of days. Yesterday she had waited for the ferry from Fort Myers to bring Gillian over to Cayo Canna. She'd been glad to see her as it had been some time since their last reunion. Some years ago the two had met in a bar in Newport, Rhode Island. Two women sitting alone at the bar, sharing stories of painful divorces, rotten men, and in Gillian's case, a grown daughter that had been a problem from day one. Of course, what they most had in common was loneliness.

Gillian, still well-kept and attractive at fifty-six years of age, was only a year younger than Debra, but with her "facial touch-ups" as she called them, passed for a younger woman. Debra might have envied Gillian's "touch-ups," but was the first to admit she was a talented writer. So, when the Historical Society learned that Debra had a friend who was an author, they leaned on her to invite Gillian to come as a guest writer and speak to the group. Debra was delighted, though a little surprised that Gillian accepted the invitation. She had many invitations to speak, and Cayo Canna was rather a remote island where she would not likely sell many books.

Debra waved as Gillian disembarked from the *Calypso*, looking as if she'd loved every minute of the trip from Fort Myers. She simply beamed.

"Hello!" Gillian called out as Debra waved from the ferry dock. The ferry was early, which was most unusual. But today Debra was glad. Now they would have plenty of time to get Gillian to her hotel and then change before they headed to the Historical Society meeting.

They embraced and chit-chatted a few minutes . . . about issues they always shared, such as their latest diet, special men in their lives, Debra's bookstore, and Gillian's latest novel.

"This island living is agreeing with you. You look thinner than when I saw you last. Dieting again?" Gillian asked.

"No, but after the Thanksgiving dinner I ate I probably should! But I am watching what I eat. Greg . . . that's our pharmacist . . . he suggested a couple of supplements that may help me. So I'm trying those."

"What about the headaches? And weren't you having a problem with allergies?"

"Everything's fine. No complaints about the allergies. Under control. Still have headaches, but Greg has recently given me a new supplement that helps those. All in all, I'm doing well."

"Oh, good. Medical issues can be such a nuisance."

Gillian smiled then and asked, "Any special male companion these days?"

Debra laughed, "Not unless you include Luis. My new gardener. A gentleman from Nicaragua. Very pleasant. Great gardener. And at least eighty years old!"

"And what about you? I see a sparkle in your eye that tells me something good is happening."

"Yes, you're right. It's called antidepressants. Wonderful

medication."

Debra smiled, "Well, they seem to be working. So, are you still seeing the same guy? Fella from Newport, wasn't it?"

"Uh. No. That's been over for a while. No one special in my life. At the moment."

Debra raised her eyebrows, "Speaking of health issues, as I recall, you were having difficulty with . . .what was it . . . depression and blood pressure issues? And wasn't there an issue with heart failure, or was it heart palpations?" Sometimes Debra's ability to remember even the smallest details irritated Gillian to no end.

"I'm fine. And, yes, I have medication for the blood pressure problem. And that one incident they called 'heart failure' was a misdiagnosis. A couple of days in the hospital and I was good as new. I've some medications and haven't had any problems with my heart since then. Actually, it got better the moment Mr. "Newport" left!" That remark had them both giggling like two teenage girls.

Debra had arranged for Raphael, the local cab driver, to pick them up at the ferry dock. Raphael was very conversational and Debra saw him occasionally at Timmy's Nook, where he was usually out on the dance floor with whatever woman he was "escorting" at the time.

Raphael zipped the two women over to the Sandpiper Hotel where Debra had booked a room for Gillian as the two didn't do well if they spent too much time together. When Raphael carried Gillian's bags inside the hotel, Gillian immediately went to the desk counter and rang the bell. Vigorously.

A moment passed and the desk clerk, Antonio Carlucci, came forward. "Good afternoon, ma'am. May I help you?"

"Gillian Hartwell. Checking in."

"Of course."

Then he looked past the woman and saw Debra. "Hello, Debra. So, is this the friend you told me about? The writer?"

"Hi, Antonio. Yes, this is Gillian."

Gillian quickly completed the registration form and handed it to Antonio. He smiled and held out her room key. "Room 115. Two doors down the hall on the left."

"What?" She turned to Debra. "First you book me in a second-rate hotel and now you have me staying close to the lobby?" She turned back to Antonio, "I can't stay in that room. I need something at the far end of the hall."

"Let me check my reservation chart."

Antonio looked over his glasses at Debra, and she rolled her eyes and shook her head, wishing Gillian would treat Antonio with a bit more courtesy.

"I'm afraid we're booked completely. There's a convention going on. All rooms have been booked for weeks."

"Then I'll just have to find another place." Gillian lifted her chin and headed for the door.

Antonio called to her, "Just a moment."

He looked down at his reservation book once more, then turned back to the women. "Seagull Cottage is available. I think you might like that. It's only a short distance from here . . . down a path to the dune. It's lovely if I do say so. The hotel usually reserves it for special guests . . . and I feel sure you would fall into that category, Ms. Hartwell."

"A cottage. Yes. That's more like it."

Antonio retrieved the key and escorted Gillian and Debra out the rear door. Down a path a few yards from the Inn was a Key West Style cottage with a tin roof and island-colored exterior . . .hidden in a cluster of tall Australian Pines and oleanders that dripped with blooms. Like a postcard. So inviting.

"Oh, yes. This will be just perfect."

Gillian loved that it was private and well-appointed. And indeed, she should be considered a special guest. It wasn't every day that she accepted an invitation to speak at such a small place. But Debra had helped her out with her wayward daughter on occasion, so she felt some obligation.

After Antonio got Gillian settled in the cottage, he left the two women. They were pushed for time, so Debra helped Gillian change to what she called her "evening outfit," which was much more elaborate than was necessary to speak at the Historical Society meeting.

"It's a regular meeting. No need to dress in such finery," Debra said.

"I understand. But this is what I'll wear," quipped Gillian.

As soon as Gillian had put the last touches on her makeup, the two walked up the path that led back up to the hotel. From there it was just a short walk to the Gasparilla Inn. The meeting was to be held in The Pirate's Nest, a meeting room that Debra assured her would hold a large crowd.

As they walked along, Debra couldn't resist asking, "Why did you need a cottage? You going to bring in a 'man of the evening' for midnight entertainment?"

Gillian gave her a small smile. Debra had a problem with alcohol.

Gillian had a problem with men. She thought nothing of bringing home a different one every night of the week.

"They provide fodder for my novels." Debra had heard that many times. That was always Gillian's response when she brought up the subject.

The meeting room was perfect. Gillian dazzled her audience with her presentation and the speaking event was smashing. It was only later in the evening that things began to deteriorate.

~ ~ ~

When Debra left Gillian late last evening, long after the Historical Society meeting, they had agreed to spend today together, and then have dinner at one of the local restaurants. Jeri coming by Sassy's and bringing her migraine medication was a Godsend. So, hoping her migraine medication would kick in, Debra took a shower, put on a pink sundress, and worked on her makeup. But one could only do so much about bloodshot eyes with dark bags beneath them.

Gillian denied ever having had facial surgery, just insisted that she'd only had a couple of "touch-ups." Debra was sure she'd had more than that. But she also knew that if she had the funds Gillian had, she'd do the same thing.

It was now almost noon. Gillian still hadn't come by and Debra's headache had not abated. An hour later Gillian still hadn't shown up. Debra was so irritated with her she swore she'd never invite her to Cayo Canna again. But then her memory scratched at something.

What did Jeri say this morning at Sassy's? Something about Gillian talking about buying a place on the island? Oh, heavens I hope not.

Their friendship fared better when they only saw each other occasionally. Primarily because both women knew something about the other that kept them from severing the relationship.

Debra's father once told her something he'd read that she thought was applicable in this case: keep your friends close—and your enemies closer. Well, she didn't think of Gillian as an enemy, but still. Gillian did know some history Debra would just as soon keep hidden.

Now, with her head still threatening to explode, Debra picked up the phone and was glad to hear a dial tone as you never knew if the blasted thing would work or not. After a couple of rings, a clear female voice answered, "Sandpiper Hotel. How may I direct your call?"

"I'd like to speak to Ms. Hartwell. Gillian Hartwell. She's staying in one of your cottages." There was a momentary silence, then the voice returned.

"I'm sorry. The cottages don't have phones, only our rooms in the hotel."

Debra shook her head. There were a few things on Cayo Canna that she did find annoying. The telephone situation topped the list. "I see. Thank you." She hung up and looked one last time in her full-length mirror. She decided she'd done all she could about her appearance. And did it matter? Gillian had seen her looking much worse than this. She plopped down on the sofa, totally exasperated with Gillian and her escapades.

It's so like Gillian to be so self-absorbed and not give a thought to the fact that we were planning to spend the afternoon together and then have dinner. Some things just never change. Then I'll just wait for Princess Gillian to arrive, but it will be a cold day in hell before I ask her to visit again!

Having not gotten any relief from her throbbing head, she popped another migraine tablet and a Xanax pill, something she only used when she had difficulty sleeping. She promptly fell asleep, her last thought being something about convincing Gillian to not buy property on the island. After all, their friendship was only possible if they kept some distance between them . . . a great distance.

Chapter 19

Sassy wheeled her VW out of the parking pad, shifted gears, and sped along. Hopefully, Debra would not have heard about her friend yet, but Sassy didn't look forward to being the bearer of such gruesome news. Debra always appeared to be balanced, intelligent, and pleasant. But she did have a problem Sassy had been unaware of. And now? Would this latest tragedy have her going 'round the bend?

When she arrived at Debra's she knocked at the door. After waiting a few moments and no answer, she walked around behind the bungalow and saw Debra's golf cart parked in its usual place. But if she was home, she wasn't answering the door or the phone.

After knocking several times again, Sassy decided Debra may have left with someone, or was possibly sleeping. So she got back into her VW and headed back in the same direction she had come from.

Think I'll go to the Temptation. Sean will have heard about the dead body, and if there's any gossip or any new information, he'll be the first to know.

Sean Feherty grew up in Ireland, just a hop and a skip from Sassy's home country, Scotland. They had talked many times about things they missed in their home countries. Sean was a good listener and people told him things they wouldn't divulge to anyone else.

Guess that's why I come by occasionally, too.

The Temptation was always busy, so Sassy wasn't surprised to see a crowd. And the snowbirds were as thick as the no-see-ums this time of year.

Sean was behind the bar, filling frosty beer mugs with draft beer, laughing with his customers, his Irish brogue still as rich as when he left Ireland some years ago. He was around sixty or so Sassy thought. A divorcee. Two grown sons still in Ireland. As much as he listened to others, he didn't reveal much about his own life. Sassy never pressed him, but did wonder what brought him to America in the first place.

Sean saw her come in and motioned for her to come to the bar. "Sassy, lassie!" He called to her across the busy room.

"Hello, Sean. Got a minute?"

"Sure thing. Sit down at the end. Be with you in a sec. Glad you stopped by. Always like having a beautiful lass sitting at my bar."

Sean was a flirt, but a harmless one. He and Sassy were neither looking for a romantic interlude. Sassy's Duncan had been the love of her life and she knew no one else could fill those shoes. As for Sean, his situation was the opposite but led to the same conclusion. His wife had found every man appealing and gone to most of their beds. That being the case, Sean was content to stay single and occupy himself with a good book at night. That was just so much easier than getting involved with another woman who might be the same as the last one.

Sassy slipped up on a high-top stool and looked about. The food here was quite good and Sean provided an ear. But the thing most folks liked about the Temptation was the live music and a grand dance floor. Sassy smiled when she saw Raphael spinning a young woman about, her laughing up at him and him grinning back. Raphael stopped by for scones about once a week or so. And Sassy had recently seen him about the island with Lizzie Strafford in tow. But tonight, he was with someone else. A younger woman she had seen, but didn't know her name.

Sean placed a sparkling glass of white wine in front of her, "Best in the house . . . a sauvignon blanc from France."

"Thanks, but I can't stay. I'm looking for Debra Morris. Have you seen her?"

"Not today, no."

"Sean, I'm sure you will have heard about the body under the dock."

"Oh, yeah. It's the talk of the island. And some tall tales are already spreading about."

"Really? Well, it would have to be "tales" as not much is known about the woman yet."

"Yeah, but that doesn't stop some loose tongues from wagging."

"What are you hearing?"

"The wagging tongues are saying the woman under the dock was murdered. By a local. It's a lot of nonsense. But I can tell you she was here last evening. A large group of folks came over after the Historical Society meeting. Sounds like she was the guest speaker."

"Yes, a writer. And a friend of Debra's. Debra Morris from The Writer's Block."

"Yeah, I know Debra. She was here as well. It was quite a happy group and the writer bought drinks for the house. After that, the dancing got into full swing and lasted into the late evening. And you know Raphael. He dances as long as he can get a partner. But he drinks nothing. The strongest thing he'll touch is a virgin vodka tonic."

"Did you see anything to make you think someone wanted to harm her?"

"No. She danced with Raphael . . . as did all the women. And the crowd began to thin out about ten-thirty or so."

"Did you see her leave?"

"Uh-huh. She and Debra came to the bar before leaving. Said they were headed to Timmy's Nook for one last drink. Seems the writer is acquainted with Will Johnson, the bartender over there. He's a friend of her daughter."

"So . . . they all drank and danced and the writer and Debra left, headed to Timmy's. Did you know how they were getting about?" Sassy asked.

"No. But I hope Raphael took them. Neither of them was in any condition to be behind the wheel."

"I see. So what else are the wagging tongues allowing?"

"Oh, the tongues say the writer left Timmy's with a young man. Not sure who it was. But Debra wasn't with them. Don't know any more than that. But you know how tales travel on the island . . . probably not a dram of truth to any of it."

"I must say it gives me an unsettled feeling. If she was murdered, then we've got a killer roaming about. But I don't think we should jump to conclusions yet. A young physician is conducting the investigation. Jack McCormick's granddaughter, Molly. She seems to have a good head on her shoulders, so maybe she'll figure out what's happened."

"Yeah. The locals have been telling me about a young female physician they're calling 'Dr. Mac.' Since she's the Captain's granddaughter, I suppose that moniker is appropriate. Heard she was running the show at the scene. Bet that must have scalded Deputy Harrison's arse!" He laughed.

Sassy lifted her eyebrows, "He's young. Got a lot to learn. But a true Southern gentleman. Dr. Mac, huh? I talked with Dr. Mac a few minutes ago. She'll most likely come by your place once she learns the writer was here. She's pleasant but intense. I'd suggest you be open with her. Got a feeling she's a chip off Captain Jack. Don't think much will get by her."

105

"Thanks for the heads-up. I'll be waitin' for her."

"Thanks, Sean. Gotta run."

"Try the Sandpiper. I heard the writer talking about staying there for the night. Maybe Antonio might know something."

Sassy said goodbye to Sean and headed to the Sandpiper. She was surprised Gillian wasn't staying at the Gasparilla Inn as that would be where a famous writer would stay. The Inn was the pride of the island. Folks from all over the country would book a reservation weeks in advance to make sure they had a place during the season. It was a classy hotel, and Sassy would occasionally go there for dinner just to experience the taste of fine food and excellent wine. As she and Duncan would have done were he here.

Antonio was off duty when Sassy went by the Sandpiper. And discussion with the staff turned up no news of Debra's whereabouts. Sassy had made a diligent effort to find Debra and inform her of Gillian's death, but now it was time to get home. Tomorrow would be here shortly and she would once again start her search.

Chapter 20

Sassy rose early and brewed a fresh pot of strong Scottish tea. A tea that's stronger than some like. But this morning Sassy felt she needed a bit of a pickup. Yesterday had been a very busy day and she knew today might be as well. She would head to Debra's place shortly. Maybe she was just asleep yesterday when Sassy knocked several times. Whatever, Sassy still needed to tell her about her friend if she hadn't learned about her already. Still not a task she relished doing.

A few minutes after seven she heard the tinkle of the bell on The Writer's Block next door. That would be Luis. He always got to the shop early, wiped down the countertops, and tidied up the place before Debra came, which was usually around 9:00. Luis stuck his head in Sassy's place, as he did every morning, and greeted her. Their morning ritual so to speak.

"*Buenos días, Señora.*"

"Good morning, Luis. Care for a cup of tea? Or a scone?" Sassy gave out more tea than she sold, but that was her nature. Giving to others satisfied some unmet need, but she wasn't sure exactly what that need was.

"*Sí, Señora. Gracias.* Scones and *té.*"

Sassy placed a cup of tea and a cranberry scone on the counter in The Writer's Block. "Luis, the body of the woman . . . the one that washed up on the beach yesterday . . . it was a friend of Debra's."

Luis dropped his dusting cloth and grabbed hold of the countertop. "¡Dios! ¡No! A compadre?"

"Yes. A woman Debra has been friends with for a long time. It's after seven now and I need to check on Debra. If anyone comes for tea, tell them to have a cup on me. I shouldn't be too long."

"*Sí, Señora. Sí.* Is trouble for Señora Debra? *Sí?*"

"No, I don't think so. There are a lot of unanswered questions at this point. But Dr. Mac said the sheriff's office on the mainland will send the investigator and medical examiner. Maybe we'll know more today."

Luis nodded and murmured under his breath. "No is good. No is good," then continued with his dusting.

Just as Sassy was about to leave, someone pounded on the shop door. She opened it and a breathless Vedra pushed her way through, her many bracelets jingling as she pushed her wild, windblown hair from her eyes.

"Sassy! Did you hear the latest about the body under the dock? The woman had been killed and dragged there. And she was seen at Timmy's Nook the night before! And earlier that same evening she was the hit at the Temptation Room. Dancing and drinking and . . ."

The look on Sassy's face halted any further ranting by the gossipy spiritualist. But, to her credit, Sassy held her tongue. "Vedra, go back to your shop. There are many unknowns about this poor woman's death. You don't need to spread more gossip."

Vedra shook her finger in Sassy's face. "I told you. I felt strong vibrations that day. And they continued all day yesterday. And the wind . . . did you hear it whispering last evening?"

"Goodbye, Vedra."

Vedra stared at Sassy for a long moment, then left with her long hair flying out behind her. Sassy closed the door, exited her shop out the back entrance, and got into her VW Bug. Vedra could be most exasperating, and the last thing the island needed was her spreading even more tales.

Sassy arrived at Debra's bungalow and knocked once. When she knocked again and still got no response, she tried the back door. The door swung open and Sassy went in.

"Debra? Are you here?"

She heard someone cough. Maybe in the kitchen. She headed in that direction. Debra was sitting at her kitchen counter, nursing a cup of strong coffee. A special coffee Luis had insisted would help her headaches.

She had awakened this morning, still in her clothes. But at least she felt better than last evening when she fell asleep after a Xanax pill. But what she called a "shadow of a headache" still hovered close by. She tried to avoid taking more migraine medication unless she really needed it, so she decided to start her day with Luis's coffee.

She looked up, surprised to see her friend and shop mate. Sassy was wearing a pair of island-print pedal pushers and a matching sleeveless top. Her strawberry blond hair was hanging loosely down her back. Debra always dressed exceptionally well but felt like an Amazon Priestess compared to Sassy who barely stood five feet tall and was thin as a marsh reed.

From the looks of Debra's face, swollen red eyes, and bags beneath, Sassy knew Debra had heard about Gillian. So, that was that.

"Hi, Debra. Sorry to barge in. I came by yesterday and knocked several times, but I guess you didn't hear me. I thought I'd come by this morning and see how you're doing. Losing a friend is difficult. I know."

Debra teared up but didn't break down into heart-wrenching sobs as she had earlier when she learned of Gillian's death last evening.

"Oh, Sassy. I've never experienced anything like this. I waited for her for the longest time. We were going to spend the day together and then have dinner. When I couldn't locate her, I decided to just stay home and wait for her call. A call that never came. If I had only gotten in my golf cart and driven around, I would certainly have seen the commotion at the dock. But my head was in no condition to do anything but try to keep from bursting.

"At least I heard of Gillian's death from a friend. Margot, one of the waitresses at the Temptation, heard about it and stopped by to check on me late last night. She remembered seeing Gillian and me at the Temptation and knew I would be upset. She was very kind to come over after her shift. But I was in no condition to do more than stay in bed.

"Oh, Sassy, I still can't believe Gillian's dead. I mean, why would someone want to kill her? She didn't even know anyone on the island."

Sassy pulled up a stool next to Debra. Perhaps if she could get Debra to talk about what happened last evening she might learn something that could be of help to Molly and Dr. Strickland. But she needed to be careful not to upset Debra even more than she was already.

"What happened following the meeting of the Historical Society?" asked Sassy. Debra shifted on the stool and shook her head as if to clear her brain, which presently seemed to have some empty spaces in it.

"I can remember most of it. It was like most other evenings Gillian and I have had over the years. Guess I hoped this one might be different. Looks like I was wrong about that."

Then the tears started. Sassy quickly decided it was just too much for Debra to go through this so soon. Plus, she would just have to rehash the scene for Dr. McCormick when she interviewed her.

Sassy had no words of wisdom to ease Debra's emotional pain even though she had ample personal experience with that particular ailment.

"I tell you what. Why don't you come to the shop with me? I'll get in touch with Dr. Mac and she can meet us there. No sense in going through these details more than once.

"Who's Dr. Mac?"

"Oh, she's a local physician who went to the scene yesterday and made a preliminary investigation. She's not a medical examiner nor a crime detective, so I assume the mainland sheriff's office will eventually send some qualified people to follow up with her."

"I didn't know we had a doctor on Cayo Canna," responded Debra.

"Yes. She's new to our island. And she's Captain Jack McCormick's granddaughter."

"I see," Debra said, then looked at Sassy. "Would you like a cup of this special coffee? Something Luis brought to me. It's delicious. And it's got a kick."

"No, thanks. Already had some Scottish tea. It's a wake-up necessity sometimes."

Debra proceeded to pour herself a second cup. "The Captain's granddaughter, huh? So you know her then?"

"Not really. I've heard Jack speak of her but I'd never met her until yesterday. She appears to be quite intelligent and very skilled. At least according to Solana. She was filling in for Dr. Strickland, the medical examiner for Lee County. She gathered evidence and examined the body." At that juncture, Debra did begin to sob.

Sassy put an arm around Debra's shoulder. "I'm sorry, Deb. That was not very tactful of me. But Dr. Mac asked me to have you call her. I know she'll have questions. So, if you'd like me to be with you, I can be."

"This physician, this Dr. Mac . . . she wants me to call her?"

"That's right. She needs all the help she can get and we do need to know what happened to Gillian. We don't even know if it's an accident or a crime. If it's a crime, then the culprit could still be out there. Waiting for another victim."

Debra gulped the last swig of coffee. "Oh, dear me. I hadn't thought of that. Then I must get myself organized. Maybe you could take me to your place and ask her to come there. That way I can keep an eye

110

on The Writer's Block. "

"That sounds like a good plan. Then, if she needs to question others, they can join us at the shop. Maybe if we talk to everyone who saw Gillian Thursday night we might learn some facts we don't know at the moment."

Debra excused herself and returned shortly. Like Sassy, she had to meet the public in her shop, so she dressed in her usual attire: a Lilly sun dress with matching sandals. She'd clipped her hair up and applied a light coat of makeup. But the makeup didn't quite cover the dark circles beneath her eyes nor the pain on her face.

She and Gillian had their squabbles and spats, but they always managed to repair any emotional damage that may have come from such. She would truly miss her friend.

Chapter 21

Dr. David Strickland climbed aboard the patrol boat and held on as the wicked craft did a stomach-flipping twist that had it circling on its side, headed out to sea. Getting a lift on the patrol boat from the Lee County Sheriff's Office was a much more convenient way of getting to Cayo Canna than coming either by ferry (the Calypso) or by your own watercraft . . . even though the craft could turn one's stomach with its quick maneuvers. Today David needed to make as much time as possible. His to-do list was a mile long.

When he'd received a call from the deputy sheriff on Cayo Canna reporting that a body had washed ashore on the island, he already had too many incidents to deal with. There were three unidentified bodies in his morgue, a child had been grabbed by an alligator in the backyard of his home on Matlacha, a sniper was holed up in a bar on Sanibel, and a huge pile-up had occurred on U.S. 41. But, as Lee County ME, he was required to at least view a body before it could be moved from any outlying islands to the mainland. So, today he would get through this business on Cayo Canna and hurry back to his morgue and try to get things under control.

The fact that he was looking forward to seeing Dr. Molly McCormick made this trip at least one he wasn't dreading. She was a most impressive young physician . . . and her natural beauty was a breath of fresh air. And the fact that she didn't know she was beautiful made her even more appealing.

When the knock on the lighthouse door came, Solana called out from the kitchen, "Molly? Will you get that, please? My hands are covered in batter. I'm making coconut flan for the Captain."

Molly was coming down the spiral staircase and wasn't in any mood to listen to some door-to-door salesman make his spiel. She usually supported kids selling magazine subscriptions for their school or even donated to the various religious groups that might need a handout. But today, she was inclined to send them on their way. She was too tired to do anything more than that.

"I'm sorry, I can't . . ." Molly stumbled backward as the face that greeted her was not one she was expecting. This face was suntanned, smiling, and quite handsome. Dr. David Strickland reached forward and embraced her as if they were old friends.

"David?" I wasn't expecting you today. But am I ever glad to see you. Come in, please."

David stepped in and followed Molly to the dining table where she had laid out all the crime scene photos.

"Molly, I can't thank you enough for taking charge of this investigation. I was, and still am, so swamped I can hardly breathe. It appears this is the season for drunk drivers, hungry alligators, and insane criminals to gather in our area."

"I wouldn't thank me so quickly if I were you, David. I have no idea if I did what you wanted, or if I just ruined the investigation for someone who would have known what to do."

He just smiled. "I am quite sure you did a superb job. I wouldn't have asked if I had any qualms about your abilities."

Molly indicated he was to sit, so he sat next to her and it was as if they had always worked together. Both were comfortable with the other and so they began.

"So, let's take a quick look at these photos." David picked up one photo which showed several people standing in the foreground. At that juncture, Solana quietly placed a plate of warm muffins and a pot of coffee on the table.

"Good morning, Dr. Strickland," Solana said with a smile. David nodded, "And to you. Solana, isn't it?" Solana smiled and left them to their discussions.

"This man looks familiar. The one with the gold chains around his neck. Do you know him?"

Molly took a look. "Let's see. I know his name as Solana went through the photos with me. I made a list of names and indicated something about them to help me identify them. This man is Antonio Carlucci. He's the desk clerk at the Sandpiper Hotel."

"Sandpiper Hotel. Isn't that near where the body was discovered?" David asked as he looked at Molly.

"Yes. It was lying beneath an old dock that partially washed away during a storm a few years ago. The portion where the body was found is still standing, but probably not for long."

"Okay. Let's move on through the photos. I'll take some notes. Then we'll look at whatever items you collected that could be clues."

Molly raised her eyebrows, "David, I'm not sure that anything I collected is a clue. A couple of items I can add a bit of clarification to, but you may wish you'd let Deputy Harrison conduct this investigation."

David smiled, "I rather doubt that. And besides, if the body was beneath an old dock, I'm fairly sure he couldn't have gotten under there to check it out."

"Well, yes. That would have been an issue. I crawled under the dock, and it was strange. I could still smell her perfume. Something I've smelled before, but can't recall."

"You could still smell her perfume? That's a clue for sure."

"Well, at least I got that part right. It's just some indication of the state of rigor mortis she was in. But, David, she was exposed to changes in temperature overnight, and who knows how long the high tide lasted. Her dress was still slightly damp. Wouldn't all that, the temperature changes and the tide coming in, have some bearing on the state of her body?"

"Correct, but I'll learn more about those issues when I see her body. Think I have to call you Dr. Mac, Medical Examiner Du Jour!" He laughed and Molly let the sound find a place in her memory. A memory she could access when she needed.

After reviewing all the photos of the scene, David nodded. "Those are great, Molly. All right, then. That covers the photos from the scene. They may be very helpful to the criminal investigator. Perhaps you and Solana could go through them again with him as you did with me."

"Of course."

"Then let's take a look at any other clues you may have collected," said David, reaching for muffin number two.

"I did collect a few bits of interesting paraphernalia under that dock. One thing I do know for sure. It wasn't a robbery. She was still wearing a pearl necklace with matching earrings. One, that is."

"Anything else of interest?"

"Uh-huh. She had a rhinestone hair clip holding her hair. On the right side only. The left side had nothing. I'm not sure, but I think I've seen that kind of clip before. But, perhaps not. The most interesting item, however, is this." She used her tweezers to reach inside the plastic bag where she'd placed a small bit of thick paper that he'd found in the sand once the body had been removed.

"Look at this scrap of paper. It's too thick to be newspaper. Maybe more like stationery. And see here? There are a few letters. Can't tell what they are. Maybe this one is A? Or C? And in the upper left corner it looks like drawings of small leaves."

"Ah. Yes, and sometimes it's the smallest items that provide the most clues. Looks like you've collected items that may prove to be helpful. I'll ask you to keep the photos and items for the investigator. I know a lot about dead bodies, but as for looking at a piece of paper or a hair clip and figuring out its significance, I'm not your guy.

"Seeing the body will provide even more information. Once we know what killed her, we can better zero in on these items you've gathered."

"Deputy Harrison had the body moved to the local funeral home. Clovis I believe is the name."

"Yes, I'm familiar with the name. They also have a place over on the mainland. All right, then. Let's run over there now. I'm required to take a look at the body before it can be taken to the mainland. Make sure we're not bringing in a corpse with some contagion or dangerous disease.

"If you have time, I'd like you to join me at the funeral home. Perhaps you can add some details while I take a quick look. Sometimes when a body is moved, new clues are exposed that weren't there when they were discovered. So, I'll take a quick look and then be off. There's a patrol boat waiting to take me back to the mainland. No, that's not right. I believe we're headed to Sanibel from here, then back to my place. We sure could use you at the morgue. Someone with your credentials would be a Godsend today."

"Uh, no thanks, But I'll go to the funeral home with you. I'm not sure I can add anything, but I made a few notes when I examined her. I'll go over those with you."

"I assume you've seen any number of dead bodies before?"

"Uh-huh. Many. Dead bodies are part of our medical training. Not a particularly pleasant part, but necessary. I'd like to watch you examine the body if you don't mind."

"Sure. And, if you like, maybe you can come to my place on a day I'm doing an autopsy. Perhaps you'd like to assist me. See what goes on in the world of crime."

"Yes. I think I would like to do that. Let me know when that's scheduled and I'll get over to the mainland."

"Let's go then. See if we can't get this body to talk to us."

Molly groaned and then gave him a slight smile.

"Sorry. Medical Examiner humor," he grinned. He didn't need Molly's help, but he figured they made a great pair. She was an interesting woman and every time she smiled David felt that dimple in her cheek winked at him.

Chapter 22

Capt. Jack and Admiral Bowen arrived at Molly's apartment in Baltimore. The weather alone was enough to cause Jack to be in a foul mood. He stepped up on the porch, inserted the key, opened the door, and looked about the room. Then he hesitated a moment as he tried to block out the images his brain was sending . . . Molly being tied to a chair . . . her attacker holding a lighted cigarette to her breast . . . slamming her head with the butt of his pistol . . . then carving into her face . . . her lying in the closet . . . crying on the ham radio . . .'Help me, Papa!' All the horrors that had happened to her in this apartment.

"Damn him to hell!" Jack muttered under his breath.

"What's wrong, Jack?" asked the admiral.

"Huh? Oh, nothing. Just wish I could have had a hand in eliminating that bastard who hurt Molly."

"Yeah, that would have been satisfying. But from what I know, sounds like Molly unloaded a couple of shots into his abdomen and stabbed him before the priest came in. And I understand he did quite a number on him. I'd say the moron got what was coming to him."

"I know. Just wish Molly hadn't had to go through that experience. She's spent years learning to save lives, and whether she'll voice it or not, I know that killing this man bothers her."

"We both know about that, Jack. Killing anyone, even an enemy, leaves psychological scars. You and I made a career of stopping foes, so we learned to deal with it. Give Molly time. She'll find a way to get past this chapter in her life."

"Yeah, you're right. I'm sure she will. Once she gets her practice going, she'll be too busy to spend much time thinking about that experience."

"You think she's going to do that? Have an office on Cayo Canna?" Bear asked.

"Yep. She thinks she can put her skills to good use on the island. But she's taking her sweet time about finding a place for her office and getting it set up. Sometimes she can be as stubborn as a jackass. Does things her way and in her time."

Bear laughed. "Wonder where she learned that?"

Jack grinned back at him. "All right. Let's just pack up the essentials and have them sent to the lighthouse." He opened a large cardboard box and handed one to Bear.

"Something tells me what you and I call essentials won't be the same as what Molly would," commented Bear.

"Uh-huh. We'll pack her clothes, whatever trinkets she's put about, and her books. She's got two cabinets full."

Bear spotted the bookcases. "That shouldn't take too long. I'll start with the books and you pack her trinkets and clothing."

A couple of hours later and the essentials had been boxed, ready for shipping to Cayo Canna. Bear looked around, "I think we're done, Casper. Books, clothing. Trinkets and photos."

Jack nodded. "Just one more item. We gotta pack Nancy. That's the most important item of all. If I leave her behind Molly will hang me by a couple of very sensitive parts of my anatomy."

"Nancy?"

"Yeah. She's in the closet in the foyer."

"Molly's keeping a woman in a closet? Sounds interesting."

Jack smiled. "Nancy is what she calls her ham radio. Long story. I'll tell it to you some time."

When Jack opened the door of the closet, he took a deep breath and bit back a string of expletives that were burning his tongue. There, on the floor, was a large dark stain. Blood. Molly's blood. That discovery brought even more hideous images to his already active imagination.

He checked his emotions and called out, "Come on Bear. Let's get this done. I've had enough of this place."

Once the radio was packed, Jack called a shipping service to retrieve the packed items and have them delivered to the marina in Fort Myers, Florida. Then the ferry, the *Calypso*, would bring the packages from the mainland to Cayo Canna.

Jack grinned at his mate. "Skip, the pilot of the *Calypso*, won't like bringing this stuff on his ferry. But he'll do it anyway. Of course, I'll have to promise him another of Solana's dinners to appease him."

Jack liked this new ferry pilot, even if he was a bit obsessive-compulsive at times. He was also highly opinionated, but then so was Jack.

Bear stood and stretched his back. "I'm with you, Casper. Let's get back to our warm tropical world. Then I suppose we gotta made some decisions. We agreed we wouldn't volunteer to be undercover in Cuba. But we both know Admiral Whitmore is not going to let us just "retire" again. He needs experienced men and he's short on those. Yep, as sure as my name is Bear, he'll be calling. But, Jesus, do we have to think about going to Cuba? Thought that affair was over."

"Any affair having to do with Cuba is never over. At least not as long as Castro's alive," Jack stated.

As soon as the shipping service retrieved the boxes, the two mates hailed a cab and headed to the airport. Fort Myers sounded awfully good at the moment.

Chapter 23
Ireland – The Druid's Fountain

Entering through the front door of the Druid's Fountain, the noisy pub where the locals were having their supper and a pint, Patrick took the stairs two at a time and headed to Angus's apartment on the second floor. The blare of Celtic music from the pub below filled the air, and this particular piece was a foot-stomping, bagpipe-swirling tune that would even make Patrick want to dance an Irish jig. He gave one knock on the door, pushed it open, and stood in the doorway waiting. For what he wasn't sure.

The lively Celtic music from below was incongruous with the sight before him. His eyes sent a message he didn't want to believe. Angus is dead. He refused to believe this visual message and stepped forward, closer to the bed. Angus was lying in his bed with several papers strewn about the bed and more on the floor. He was snuggled beneath a heavy woolen blanket, his few sprigs of gray hair plastered to his head. He looked frail and had lost weight. His sunken cheeks, ashen skin, and weathered face sent another strong message to this priest who had seen his share of illness and death.

There was one uplifting sight, however. The bedside table was stacked tall with Angus's favorite books and what appeared to be a small glass of Jameson, his favorite Irish whiskey. Patrick reached down and placed his finger on Angus's wrist and smiled when this touch was answered with flickering eyelids, then two piercing blue eyes staring at him.

Angus coughed, then cleared his throat. "Took your time about gettin' here, lad. Thought I might have to ask Father Matthew to administer last rites before you arrived." He squeezed Patrick's hand then.

"Glad to see you, my lad. Aye. Glad to see you."

Patrick gathered up the papers on the bed and floor and sat in a small chair next to Angus's bed. "Angus, we've corresponded for years, talked on the phone many times, and when I visited a year or so ago, not one damn time did you mention a heart condition."

"Aye, then. I see your vocabulary is still limited. But, about the heart condition, it didn't seem worth mentioning, you kin? And besides, lettin' you know about my heart attack would only have had you flyin' across the Atlantic for no reason."

"That's a pretty sorry excuse for not letting me know you're sick, you old gobshite."

"Aw, now, no call for such a reprimand, Father O'Brien. You're here now. That's what counts."

Angus looked at Patrick again. "What? No collar today, Father O'Brien?"

Patrick pulled his chair closer. "No. Traveling incognito as it were," he smiled.

"And now that I'm here, bring me up to date. What does your doctor say? Are you taking the proper medications? Do you need to be in hospital?"

"Hold on, lad. Dr. McRae is a fine gent and the best doctor in this area. He's kept me kicking along for years now. He thinks I should rest a couple of days and then he might consider a new drug. Something called Warfarent? Or maybe it's Warfarin? Can't recall exactly. But he thinks my blood is probably too thick and this new medication will do the trick. So, no. No hospital needed."

Patrick's thoughts turned to another physician. Dr. Molly McCormick. If she were here she'd know about this medication. But Molly wasn't here. So, he'd have to trust that Dr. McRae knew his business. Angus didn't appear to be concerned, so perhaps everything was under control.

When he'd gone on sabbatical recently, Patrick had thought about going home, to Ireland, but had opted to go to Cayo Canna instead. He'd returned home several times during his tenure at St. Marks, but there was something inside that still wanted to keep a bit of distance from Ireland. No, that's not exactly right. Not Ireland. What he wanted to distance himself from was memories of events that had happened there. In his country.

But today he was back home again. And Angus was still his mentor. His confidant. Being with Angus was much like being with Captain Jack McCormick. Both would listen with an open mind. And, even if it were painful, would offer their opinion of whatever issue he might be struggling with. Neither would handle him with kid gloves.

Angus pushed the blanket down and sat up a little higher in his bed. "Now. Enough about me. What brings you to our shores? Thought maybe you'd decided America was going to be your home. Huh?"

Patrick leaned forward, still holding the papers he'd collected from the bed and floor. He sighed and leaned back. "Ah, Angus. Sometimes I'm not sure where I belong. I've got such happy memories of this place. My home. This Ireland. But as you well know, there are some painful ones as well. Presently I have a situation in America that's got me so frustrated I can hardly think."

Angus scratched at his chin and looked directly at his young friend. "Must be something pretty awful then. Thinking is one of your best qualities," he grinned.

Patrick shook his head. "The problem is simple. The solution isn't."

"Then give me the rundown. Maybe you haven't forgotten everything I tried to teach you. Like how sharing your troubles with a friend can be helpful."

Patrick sighed and continued, "I haven't forgotten. But that's part of the problem. Being unable to forget . . . or forgive either. It seems that for some time now my best friend, a fellow priest, has been abusing young boys in the parish. Right under my nose, apparently. And I've been oblivious to the entire affair."

"Ah, yes, I can see where that might be problematic," responded Angus. "And what else?"

"When I took the issue to Bishop O'Malley, he instructed me to keep the information to myself. It seems the Church is aware of the problem and, according to him, is dealing with it. But that isn't true. The Church's solution is to move an offending priest from one parish to another. Of course, the abuse then begins all over again. Nothing changes except the names of the young, abused boys."

Angus opened his mouth, but Patrick stopped him before he could say more. "And yes, I know that sexual abuse has been going on since the first popes and bishops, but I don't think I can be part of such an organization that refuses to stop such heinous behavior in this day and time."

Angus watched Patrick's face as he told his story. He saw a sadness that he'd seen in that face once before. Just before Patrick took the collar.

Patrick laid the papers on the bed, then put his hands together—in a prayerlike fashion—and proceeded, "I'm thinking of leaving the priesthood."

The room was quiet for a long moment in which neither man uttered a word. Finally, Angus nodded, "So, then, you've given your situation a lot of thought. As always. And I don't have to tell you that leaving the priesthood is a grave undertaking, lad. Folks, maybe even some of your friends or family, will come out of the woodwork to flay you for such. Many will call you a "deserter" and some will call you by much worse names, I fear."

"Aye, I'm sure you're right. But this decision has come after some long, hard, examination of my life, my grievances, my sins—which are many—and my conviction that the Almighty has a hand in all our decisions. Leaving the priesthood doesn't mean I've abandoned the beliefs and values the Church has instilled in me. Some things stay in our hearts for a lifetime. And I pray the Almighty will forgive me if this decision is a mistake . . . one of many that I have made."

Angus cleared his throat, "So, then, have you come up with a solution or a plan of what you should do?" He figured Patrick would get around to telling him, but sometimes he had to be prodded a bit.

"Yes. I've done nothing but think about this problem for six months now. I've just come from Boston where I've made my feelings known to Paul, my friend, former friend, who is abusing the lads. There is no room in my heart to continue a friendship with him, so that issue is settled. And I'm at peace with my decision. But there are a few items of unfinished business I have to attend to here in my country as well."

Angus was aware of Patrick's empathetic nature. For him to severe a friendship was indicative of how strongly he felt about his friend's behavior. There would be no excuses for that as far as Patrick was concerned.

"So, you've severed a friendship. And now? What is this unfinished business here?" Angus asked. He knew the answer to his question, but asking it would help Patrick verbalize the issue.

"There's nothing to be gained by continuing to swirl the same arguments around in my head any longer. Whatever decision I make, it's bound to not meet with approval by some."

"And since when did you care about meeting anyone's approval? 'Cept maybe mine," smiled Angus.

Patrick offered a small grin. "Leaving the priesthood is a big step. Even bigger than entering it, perhaps. But that's what I'm struggling with, so there you have it."

"Hmm. I can remember when you were struggling with the opposite problem. Entering the priesthood. And as I recall, that decision was also difficult."

"Aye. But I was a different man then. I'm not sure I would even recognize the young man I was then."

"Well, lad, it's not been all that long ago. But I agree. You are a different man today. Time has a way of changin' all of us. But, if I may, I'd like to remind you of that young man. "

"Angus, I came to check on you. But, yes, I would like to hear anything you have to say. You've been a guiding light for me. I don't think you'll lead me astray now, even if you are an old gobshite."

Angus pointed to his nightstand. "If you'll look inside, you'll find another glass. Perhaps we could have a wee taste and I'll bend your ear. Just a bit."

Patrick found the extra glass, poured himself a small taste of Jameson, and refreshed Angus's glass. "Does Dr. McRae know you're drinking this whiskey?" Patrick quizzed.

"Who do you think that other glass is for?" Angus laughed and took a sip.

"'Tis good to see you, lad. Feels like old times. I remember when your mam threatened to skin you alive when she discovered you were coming to my pub. 'Course, you were only fifteen, so I guess she had grounds!" Both laughed at that memory.

"So, let's take a trip down memory lane. Mind you, a short one. Don't want to drag this out."

Patrick smirked, "Your memory is probably better than mine. I spent a lot of time trying to forget a lot."

"Yes, lad. But it's those "forgotten" memories that we need to bring back. And I know how painful they are. It was a bad time for you. For our country."

"Angus, I can't say I'd change anything about that time, though. Ireland was going through a rough patch and I was young and full of myself. Thought I could change the world."

"And I have no doubt you did, Patrick. If we all would do one good thing in our lives, then this old world would be a better place. And, as I recall, you did rid our lovely *Eire* of a few less than desirables."

"Yeah, but at what price? The enemy was a group of young men exactly like me and my fellow rebels. And they were fighting for their cause as I was fighting for mine. So, what did any of us accomplish in the end? Pain? Sorrow?" Patrick slumped in his chair and took a sip of his whiskey.

"'Tis the way of humankind, Patrick. We've been fighting since Adam and Eve bickered over who would take the first bite of the apple. We have to hope that, eventually, we'll become less human and more humane. In the animal world, the creatures only fight when they're either being preyed upon, are hungry, or someone is trying to steal their mate.

"But don't be so sure that what you fought for wasn't worth the cost. Catholics and Protestants have been at each other's throats ever since Henry VIII informed Pope Clement VII that he, Henry, would be the final authority in matters relating to the English church. And that battle will rage on forever. You and your group of rebels kept your district from being overrun by a rather nasty group of zealots who threatened your people. That says a lot about commitment and courage."

"Yes, but in the process I lost someone very dear to me. A special woman. A woman I loved with all my heart. A woman that a part of me still loves."

Angus nodded his understanding. "Claire, yes, such a loss. But you must remember, Patrick. Claire chose to be part of the rebellion you were involved in. She knew the dangers of sneaking behind enemy lines and the possibility she could be caught. You couldn't have stopped her if you tried."

"But, Angus, she was so young. Only nineteen years old. And, like me, full of energy and lofty ideas of how to change our world. She had promised she'd not leave our compound without one of us being with her. She said she'd keep out of harm's way. But the minute I turned my back, she left and crept into the forest, found her way to the enemy stronghold, and snuck into the back entrance.

"She'd always had a plan. A plan to set the place afire, then hurry back to our safe house. But, of course, they had men planted all along the path she took and they grabbed her the minute she got within a few yards of their place. When I realized she was gone, I knew where to find her. Without a moment's thought, I took off in a huff, and like her, was captured quickly.

"But they didn't want to kill me. They wanted to show me how futile it was for us to continue our campaign. No, they didn't kill me. Instead, they tied Claire to a post and set up a firing squad. A firing squad made up of young men, some as young as Claire. Then they held a gun to my head and forced me to watch as they riddled her young body with bullets.

"I'd seen men killed and had done my share of killing as well. All for 'the cause.' But I was unprepared for such cruelty. I stood planted to the ground and stared at them. Then, to make sure I couldn't retaliate anytime soon, they tied my hands behind me and each of them battered me to their heart's content. Then they dragged me deep into the forest and tossed my crippled body into a deep pit. The last thing I remember about that day is their laughter. Killing Claire had not affected them whatsoever."

"Aye, lad. I know the story," Angus whispered.

"By then I was so tired of seeing young men—and women—die that I lost all reason to live. Shortly thereafter I left the group as I was no good to them any longer. It was an effort to put one foot in front of the other. Eventually, I sought a way to have peace in my life. To erase those images of Claire's bullet-ridden body slumping on a post. The priesthood has provided that peace, but now I'm not sure it's the place for me. I feel I've "used" the Church and the priesthood as a place to hide. To be safe from the outside world. I'm not proud of those feelings, but that doesn't make them go away."

Angus was quiet for a minute before asking his next question. "So, what is this unfinished business you have here, lad?"

"Not long after I left the group, the fighting fizzled out. Both sides were ready to stop the insanity, I suppose. And even though I wanted to, I never sought out Claire's family. Never told them I was the reason she joined the rebellion. Never told them how special she was to me. I never asked their forgiveness because I felt, and still feel, my actions were unforgivable."

Angus nodded, "Forgiveness. Yes. But to need forgiveness, one has to have committed an offense. Anyone who joins a rebel group will eventually have to admit their part in taking someone's life. And often more than one life. Perhaps you weren't ready to make such an admission then, Patrick."

"I don't know, Angus. I thought I had put all those memories and desperate feelings behind me. But that's simply not so. Lately, after learning about Paul's deception and abuse, I realize I must clear my conscience, and must own up to the fact that I was responsible for Claire's death. I must find her family and tell them the story. The whole story."

Angus shifted in his bed, finding it impossible to get comfortable. "You're wrong about being responsible for Claire's death, lad. She might have joined the rebellion because she wanted to be near you, but that was her choice. And as I recall, this was not the first time Claire involved herself in dangerous situations. Her death is not on your shoulders. And as for feeling that you have used the priesthood, the Church, as a way to find peace, I remind you that like any shepherd, the Almighty finds many ways to care for his sheep. Perhaps he decided Claire was better off in his pasture. Perhaps he gave you a place of solace in the priesthood. For a while. And perhaps now he thinks you're ready to take a new path. Who are we to question his wisdom? I believe the Almighty speaks to everyone. Of course, not everyone opens their ears. But when we do, his voice is usually quite clear."

"What would I do without your wisdom, Angus? Should have come here long ago. I'll find Claire's family. Do what I have to do. But first, I'll make sure my ears are wide open and make sure I don't miss any messages coming through."

Angus drained his glass and snuggled back down in his covers. "Then, I'll see you tomorrow?"

"Yep. Better get home now. Mum's keeping a dish of cottage pie warm for me. But I'll come by in the morning. By the way, the pub downstairs is standing room only. What's going on with that?"

"Got a new cook. She's very talented and the fact that she's a lovely, Irish lass doesn't hurt either. Makes me wish I was a frisky, young lad again."

Patrick laughed and headed for the door. "Oh, here. I picked these papers up from the bed and some on the floor. I was about to take them with me. And they appear to be rather legal looking. What are they?"

"Oh, just some documents. Laying here gave me time to put a few things in order. My last will and testament . . . instructions for who's going to say grace over this ancient body . . . where to bury this pile of bones . . . those kinds of issues."

Patrick came closer, "What? You just told me Dr. McRae said you're doing well. But if, so, then why hurry with a will and all that other business?"

"Well, since you're here, let's take a second and look at these papers. A few things I want you to know about them."

"Angus, that's your business, not mine. See you in the morning," he said as he pulled the door closed behind him.

Chapter 24

Once their flight landed at Page Field in Fort Myers, Jack flagged a cab and he and Bear scooted over to the marina. The old Chris-Craft Cobra was waiting in her berth and Jack had them underway in a flash. They had both had enough of cold, bitter weather. East coast weather.

"Ah, eighty-eight degrees and ninety percent humidity. My kind of day," laughed Jack as he steered the Cobra south. Toward Cayo Canna. Toward home.

"Yep. I know some folks think the humidity aggravates my arthritic knee," said Bear. "But I'll argue with them on that front. It feels better now than it has since we left here." He dug into his coat pocket and brought out one of his Cuban cigars. "Would you care for one, Casper?" he asked.

"No. I'm not much on cigars. I'll stick to my pipe. Of course, I may not be able to get my favorite tobacco anymore. Crab always kept me supplied with Cuban tobacco and Cuban coffee. Not real sure how I'm going to get those now."

Bear grumped, "Well, maybe we should go undercover to Cuba as Admiral Whitmore wants us to. We could do our covert business and steal some tobacco and coffee while we're there." Bear laughed and Jack grinned at him. They rode along in silence for a short while, enjoying the salty mist that clung to the humid air. And the cries of gulls and waterbirds trailed them as they made their way to the island.

Jack had the Cobra moving along at a brisk pace and liked his old "girlfriend." She was kinda like him . . . getting older, but still relevant. Bear's exquisite craft, the *Admiral's Lady,* was moored in Cayo Canna at the moment. Bear would board her and return to his place in Placida as soon as they got to the island.

"Our island is hard to beat, you know. Even if the no-seeums eat you alive at times. Patrick used to swear he'd wake up one morning and find himself in Mosquito Lagoon." Jack smiled just thinking about Patrick.

"Patrick is a most unusual man. And certainly a most unusual priest," offered Bear.

"That he is. He's quite a fine fellow," Jack said as he altered his course slightly.

"Have you heard from him since he left?"

"No. But I really hadn't expected to. He's got a few issues to work through . . . and they're difficult to say the least. But I expect he'll find a way to deal with them. He's much more capable than he lets on."

"Yep. He certainly took charge of the situation at the lighthouse. That was the work of someone who had executed that kind of intervention before. I'd say almost like a professional. A military man."

"Uh-huh. I agree. He's not told me anything about his life before he became a priest, but I'm sure it's an interesting story. Maybe he'll tell me one day. Or, there may be some secrets he keeps to himself."

"Yeah. Well, Casper, we all have secrets," said Bear.

Chapter 25

David looked once more at the photos and items Molly had procured from the scene. "I think I've seen everything. It's probably better that I leave these photos with you, Molly. When the investigator comes over, he'll want to see these first thing. The way my office is running these days, they could be lost in a stack of unsolved crime clues and never found again. So, let's get to the funeral home and see what the body can tell us."

"When is the investigator coming over?" asked Molly. "I've done all I'm capable of but there must be some protocol for interviewing locals and that sort of thing."

David sighed, " I'm not sure when an investigator will get over here. It's tourist season, the snowbirds are down here and the sheriff's office is overwhelmed. There's a sniper holing up in a bar on Sanibel, a gator snatched a small child and disappeared into the lagoon behind the child's home, over in Matlacha. There's been another crash on U.S. 41, and at the moment, there are three unidentified bodies in my morgue. All of them migrant workers who have no external wounds.

"Every agent has his hands full, so it could be several days before someone gets over here. They'll need to talk to the person who found the body, anyone who saw her the evening before her death, her friends . . . anyone who might give us something to go on."

"I see," responded Molly. "I made a couple of inquiries yesterday after I completed my initial investigation and assessment of the body. But I'm afraid I didn't get very far. But I think if they ask Sassy, a local who knows everyone, she can help facilitate the interview process."

"Great. Perhaps you could assist them? You've done a great job, Molly. Now, let's see what the body reveals. If the cause of death is obvious, that's great. If not, then I'll perform an autopsy where I can dig further. And I think I'll call Deputy Harrison. Have him meet us at the funeral home. He may have some new information."

Molly nodded, "Come inside. Sometimes the phone works. Sometimes it doesn't." David dialed deputy Harrison's number and after a couple of rings someone picked up.

"Sheriff's Office. Deputy Harrison speaking."

"Deputy Harrison, David Strickland here."

"David?"

"Dr. Strickland, ME from the mainland."

"Oh, yes. Yessir. How can I help you?"

"I wonder if you'd meet Dr. McCormick and me at the funeral home? I'd like to examine the body of the woman that washed up beneath the dock."

"Uh, yessir. I suppose I can do that. But I think Dr. Mac already made a thorough check. She covered that crime scene like an expert. And she examined that woman from top to bottom. I bet she didn't miss anything."

David smiled at Molly, then continued, "I'm sure she did a superb job. Then we'll see you there shortly." He hung up the phone. "Looks like you've got a fan in the deputy. He thinks you're a top-notch investigator." He laughed at Molly's expression.

"But there is one more problem," David continued.

"What? Did I forget to do something important?"

"No. It's just that I don't have transportation. The driver from the Gasparilla brought me here."

Molly smiled, "I have the latest in dependable transportation."

"Oh, a new model Cadillac?"

"Not exactly. Come on." She escorted him outside to the golf cart. "Here you are. Papa actually has a car . . . somewhere. It's in storage on the mainland. I think. But he prefers to use this golf cart. It's a bit slower. But it's quite fun, actually."

"Sure thing. Great for an island."

"But there is one other problem still. I don't have a driver's license. So far Deputy Harrison has looked the other way, so maybe he'll give me a few more days before he starts writing me tickets."

When they arrived at Clovis Funeral Home, Deputy Harrison was standing at the door, His arms were crossed over his huge chest and his holster rode low on his hips. David walked up to him, "Deputy Harrison," and reached out his hand.

The deputy nodded, "Dr. Strickland," and shook his hand briefly.

Then Molly followed. Deputy Harrison quickly removed his hat and smiled, "Dr. Mac. Good to see you. Follow me." Molly returned his smile and followed through the door he held for her. David had to catch the door before it hit him in the face. But he just smiled to himself. He could understand how a fellow could fall for Dr. Mac.

David and Molly donned gloves, and David performed a cursory exam but found nothing that jumped out at him. "There are no overt marks to indicate she was attacked, no defensive wounds. No bleeding."

"If I may point out one thing . . ." Molly started. She was afraid she might be overstepping her bounds. After all, she was only a physician, not a ME."

"Absolutely. I'll take her to the mainland and conduct a number of tests, but if you found something that may point me in the right direction, then let's hear it."

Molly went to the head of the examination table. She stood behind the woman's head. "Feel here. Just at the base of her skull. Across the top of her neck. A small area. I think I feel a jagged edge. So, perhaps an injury here at the back of her head? But look here. Her forehead is slightly swollen, suggesting an injury on the front of the head as well. I'm not sure, but I think I remember one bit of information from studying fractures."

"Yeah?"

"Something about . . . uhm . . . coup and contrecoup injuries. . . coup refers to damage directly under the spot of impact, and contrecoup refers to brain damage on the opposite side of the brain from where the impact occurred. But she has damage to both the back of her neck, and on her forehead. Do you think her death could be the result of a head injury? And maybe that caused brain injury as well?"

David was grinning from ear to ear. "Dr. Mac, that's good thinking. So, her most obvious injury is at the back of the skull, so most likely she was sitting, or lying. Maybe not moving, or if so, not quickly. Maybe she was even stationary. This jagged edge that you feel here is most likely a fractured cervical vertebra. And most probably what caused her death. I see victims with broken necks more often than you'd think. But what caused it to be broken? She may have been struck at the base of her skull . . .or . . . perhaps she was lying face down and someone applied pressure to her neck . . . or . . . maybe she fell and hit her head on the dock. But the swollen forehead must also be considered. So, first things first. What often looks like the obvious cause of death can be misleading. And I can tell you that many of these snowbirds die of cardiac arrest. They come down here and live it up, ignoring the fact that their hearts can only take so many "mojitos or margaritas" and fried fish platters. Ah, a lot of unknowns."

He was interrupted by Deputy Harrison as he announced, "I'll just wait in the foyer. Keep the peeping toms away."

Molly nodded as he walked away. Then she smiled at David, "Deputy Harrison's not too fond of being in a room with a dead body."

"Really? Dead folks are the safest folks of all. I've never been attacked by one."

She laughed. "I know. More ME humor. But I believe there might be more to our deputy here than we're giving him credit for. Don't know much about him yet, but I do know he reads good literature."

David raised his eyebrows . . . then went on with his examination of the body. He took numerous blood samples, oral swabs, swabs from all orifices, and then took her fingerprints and cut a lock of her hair.

"Hair sample, too? What will that tell you?"

"Maybe nothing. But may contain some chemicals that may be involved. Hair can tell us a lot. And I also need her clothing. Clothes always provide a lot of information."

Molly retrieved Gillian's clothing which had been placed in a sealed bag. She handed it to David. "These are her clothes, but her shoes are at the lighthouse. I forgot to show them to you. Sorry."

"No worries," David replied as he packed all his samples in a container with dry ice and placed them in his bag.

"Okay, then. We've done all we can here. I'll take her to the mainland as I go back. After I'm completed my work, I'll call you. Meanwhile, I'll leave these photos and other items with you. You can discuss them with the investigator."

"You're returning to the mainland now?" Molly asked.

"Yeah. After we go to Sanibel. I've got dead bodies all over the place. Kathi keeps telling me we've got to hire another lab tech. She's working overtime as it is. The patrol boat's waiting at the ferry dock. It's a lot faster than any other boats."

"I see. Then I'll wait to hear from you and the investigator."

"Right. I'll have these Clovis guys take me and the body to the ferry dock and I'll be on my way."

"You're going to take the body with you?"

"Yeah, it will save the sheriff's office a trip. As I said, they're shorthanded at the moment. Perhaps I can come back over when I finish my report. Maybe we could grab a bite of dinner somewhere?"

"I'd like that—several great restaurants on the island."

"And, Molly, you've been a lifesaver. Having you on Cayo Canna is such a help. I promise not to abuse our friendship, but I hope I can call you again."

"Of course. Then I'll head to the lighthouse and wait to hear from you." She walked to the foyer and Deputy Harrison held the door as she exited.

"Thank you, Ben. Dr. Strickland will finish up here. I'll see you soon."

"Yes, Miss Molly . . . uh, Dr. Mac." And he watched until she was out of sight. Still driving that golf cart without a license.

Chapter 26

When Molly arrived at the lighthouse her brain neurons were firing like fourth of July firecrackers and she was running in circles trying to decide what, if anything, she was supposed to do next. David would complete his autopsy and review the labs and with that knowledge be able to tell them the cause of death. But there were other questions Molly felt were as important given that she, along with David, Papa Jack, and Deputy Harrison, all had a gut feeling Gillian was killed. Questions like who killed her? Why did they kill her? And was the killer still on Cayo Canna?

As she pulled the golf cart into its space, she took a moment to reflect on her time with David today. She was disappointed he wasn't staying the night on the island as she would have liked to have had dinner with him. Maybe discuss other topics than medical issues. He was handsome, intelligent, kind, and interesting. What every woman was probably looking for in a mate. Her thoughts came to a screeching halt.

What? Am I looking for a mate? I really do want to get my practice established before I think about anything else. And once I begin seeing patients, my time will be limited. No. The time's not right for seeking a permanent relationship. What was I thinking?

She gathered her photos and the various bags of items she hoped would provide information. Then one more thought wormed itself through her convoluted brain. And this thought—unbidden as it was—added more turmoil.

And what about Patrick? Is he ever coming back to Cayo Canna? Do I want him to?

She walked on toward the lighthouse, watching the waves as they rushed to shore. An osprey sailed high in the sky, squawking his message to anyone listening. And her own, internal message squawked as well.

Yes, yes. I want Patrick to return.

Upon entering the lighthouse, she heard voices coming from above. Papa Jack and Solana appeared on the spiral stairway. Papa had changed from his Navy dress uniform to his "island uniform" as he called it . . . khaki shorts and a golf shirt, along with a pair of ancient dockers that were so scruffy and salt-weathered Solana had threatened to toss them.

"Ah, Molly Mac. Glad you're here. Thought David Strickland would be with you," said Papa as he descended the stairs and gave her a quick kiss on her cheek.

"Hey, Papa Jack. Glad you didn't stay in D.C. As to David, he had to take the body of the deceased woman to his morgue on the mainland. Some sort of state requirement regarding corpses having been at least seen by the ME before entering the mainland.

"Plus, there's so much going on in Fort Myers, Sanibel and Matlacha. He can hardly take a breath; he looked pretty ragged today."

"So, did he learn anything from his examination of the body?"

"Not much. There were no outward signs of a struggle. No defensive wounds. But it was a very cursory examination. He collected some specimens from various orifices, along with several vials of blood. Also took fingerprints and hair samples. But we're no closer to solving this crime than we were when you left for D.C."

"Did the investigator make any progress?" Papa inquired as he wandered outside to his seat under the gigantic, banyan tree. Molly and Solana followed and sat across from him.

Molly shook her head. "They haven't sent one yet. David says it may be several days before someone can get to the island. The Sheriff's office is shorthanded and they don't appear to think our crime on Cayo Canna warrants stopping their work on other "more important" ones on the mainland."

"I see," said Papa. "Guess they have their reasons, but time is of the essence. It's important to talk to everyone who has any information. Anything that will provide a place to start looking for the person who killed this woman."

"I know, Papa. I tried but I didn't get very far. I think I have to wait for the investigator to make any headway."

"Do you think that's wise? To wait longer?" Papa quizzed as he chewed on his pipe, unlit at the moment. He really did try to avoid actually smoking it in Molly's presence as he knew her feelings about that subject. To her credit, however, she didn't harp on the lung cancer issue.

"No, but I really don't know what more I can do. It's obvious I'm not good at interviewing those who may have knowledge of the woman or some helpful information. So, that's where I find myself," Molly responded.

"Huh. Unlike you to give up so easily," Papa stated, looking over his half-glasses at her.

Molly stared at her grandfather. He of all people knew she never quit on anything important. She continued to stare as Papa poked at his pipe again. She could count on one hand the number of times she and Papa Jack had crossed swords. But, today, she found his comments irritating. So, knowing she'd probably regret it, she took the bait he just threw out.

"You're right. I don't give up easily. That being the case, I'll be resourceful and go in a new direction."

"That's the spirit," Papa quipped. "Like Churchill. Never, ever, ever, give up."

Molly then stood and walked to stand in front of Papa Jack. Hands on hips.

"Then we'll begin right after lunch. As I recall, *Casper,* you have experience in this kind of situation. So, I'll expect you to lead the way and I'll follow."

Papa Jack laughed aloud. "Thought you'd never ask. Then, after Solana's lunch—which just happens to be paella—we'll take a look at what you've collected. There's bound to be something in there that can get us started on the right tract.

"And before I forget to tell you, your belongings from Baltimore will arrive on the *Calypso* tomorrow and Raphael will deliver them to the lighthouse for you."

"What? But how? I haven't had time to go back and pack everything up. It just seemed like a chore I wasn't quite ready to undertake."

"Yeah. Well, Bear and I had nothing better to do so we got everything packed and ready for shipment. Of course, I had to bribe Skip to bring them to the island on his ferry. He's persnickety about what he allows on that old tub. But I promised he'd be invited to dine on one of Solana's scrumptious meals. That sealed our deal."

"But what about my medical books and journals? Did you pack those also?"

"Yep. All three hundred of them!" He laughed.

"And did you . . ."

"Yes . . . we packed Nancy up as well."

"Thanks, Papa. I may never use the ham radio (Nancy) again, but I didn't want it to be left in Baltimore."

She headed from the room as Papa's ham radio once again started sending out squelching noises and unintelligible sounds.

"Speaking of radios, Papa, that's the second time this morning I've heard that radio squawking. And it's been totally quiet since that disastrous event when you were trying to stop the Cuban rebels. Is there something going on? Something you're not telling me?"

Papa had heard the static and noise as well. "Nah. Probably just a new kid learning to use the radio. Remember when you first started? You were quick to learn, but had a few trying experiences with the ham."

Chapter 27

The Lime Kiln – Ireland

Patrick crawled out of his cozy bed at the Lime Kiln, dressed warmly in a woolen overcoat, and wrapped a scarf about his neck. He opened the front door with care, hoping to ease out without waking Mum or Da. It was still dark as he stepped out and headed to the cliff about a mile down the lane from the Lime Kiln. As he had done many times over the years, he wanted to watch the sunrise over the Irish Sea. With the strong east wind blowing this morning, she'd be pitching and howling like a lonely wolf, sending wild plumes of foam spraying high into the air.

He wrapped his scarf tighter as he stood close to the edge of the cliff and looked down to the craggy beach below. Over eons of time, a small inlet had caused a spit of land to form between the mainland and the sea. Patrick had read that the ocean floor has faults, and these faults often shift, causing small islands such as this one to form.

When he was a lad, he spent countless hours exploring the spit. He'd climb down the vertical side of the cliff, hanging on to small branches of gorse that provided a handhold. After numerous trips down, he carved footholds into the face of the cliff and after that he fairly flew down. Of course, the trip back up took a bit of work.

He'd learned to swim in this inlet, with its violent waves crashing in from the Irish Sea, resulting in his becoming an excellent swimmer. Of course, Mum forbade him to climb down the cliff side lest he "fall into that bottomless pit that's just 'waitin' to swallow you up, lad," she'd say.

As he continued to breathe in the salty air, the slightest hint of pink peeped over the horizon, the sun being ever so gentle in awakening this slumbering island in the North Atlantic. Patrick looked out as far as he could see. Scotland lay across the water. In the early morning light the water appeared to be a deep blue, and even deeper shades of green shone through when the waves withdrew and returned to the depths. A beautiful sight to his eyes.

But appearances can be deceiving. The Irish Sea had a reputation for being a bloody nightmare to cross and Patrick could attest to that being true. He'd made many a trip across her in the dark of night. In another lifetime—or so it seemed.

This same sun would be making her appearance across another body of water also. This water would show her colors as brilliant aqua with areas of darker turquoise in its depths. And when the sun was at her peak, golden shades of light would bounce off the waves as they came to shore.

This body of water, the Gulf of Mexico, had a place in Patrick's memory also. He'd spent the last six months on Cayo Canna, an island off the coast of Florida, that was surrounded by this Gulf, with its shallow coral reefs and sprawling beaches along its coastline. During those months, he brooded about a problem he was only now coming to grips with.

The wind whipped about the top of the cliff and brought sparkling daggers of sea spray to Patrick's cheek. This place, this Ireland, was embedded in his soul. He'd left her, but perhaps it was time to return for good.

He smiled, remembering his visit with his old "mucker" last evening. *Should have known Angus would understand my problem. He's always understood me better than I understand myself. He's never minced words. Always leveled with me. Even when he knew it would be painful. And I know he's right about what I must do now. And I will. I will.*

The sun crept higher, struggling to claim its dominance over the darkness. Finally, she burst over the horizon and spread her kaleidoscope of colors across the earth. Morning had broken.

Patrick's heart was full. The beauty before him had him repeating his favorite verse: *This is the day that the Lord hath made. Let us rejoice and be glad in it.*

After stuffing himself on Mum's full Irish breakfast and listening to Da's latest tales of the "troubles" in Ireland, Patrick took himself off to see Angus. He'd made his decisions and wanted to tell Angus his plans. These decisions called for actions that would be difficult. Painful even.

A couple of hours later he scurried up the stairs at the Druid's Fountain which was rather quite this time of the morning. A young woman was busying about the kitchen, but Patrick didn't stop to talk.

He wanted to get on about his mission now that he knew what it was.

He knocked on Angus's door but didn't wait for an invitation to enter, simply strode over to the bed and gently touched Angus on the shoulder. The oldster opened his eyes and grunted, "Back again are you? Two visits in two days is a record, lad." Patrick took note of a tremble in Angus hands as he raised himself up in bed and leaned against his pillows.

"I had nothing better to do, you see," smiled Patrick as he pulled the small chair closer to the bed.

"Thought you'd be hightailin' it to the golf course. It might be a bit nippy, though. I can hear the wind through these stone walls. She must be blowin' all right."

"No. No golf for a while. I'm on my way to Derry. That's where Claire's family lives. Or at least where they lived the last of knew of them. I'll start there. Then I'm off to Belfast. To see the bishop. It's time for me to make a new life. One in which I'm no longer hiding behind a collar seeking peace. I believe the only way I can truly get peace is to face up to the issues that wake me at night and keep me in limbo. Thanks to your counsel, dear friend, I have at least voiced those issues and am determined to deal with them."

Angus shifted in bed and turned to face Patrick. "Well, then. But you're young. Got plenty of time to figure out what you should do. I know you, Patrick. You'll find a path that will lead you to continue what you've always done . . . help others. There are other ways than the priesthood to do that."

Patrick nodded, "So, when do you see Dr. McRae?"

"Oh, he comes by every day or so. He's a lot like you, now that I think about it. Sticking his nose in places where it might not be needed," he smiled. Patrick was Angus's idea of what a son should be. Even though he had none.

"I should be back in a few days. Derry first. Then Belfast. Then back here. Not sure after that. But I'll drop in here. Maybe we'll have a wee dram of Jameson. Like old times."

"Aye. That could be arranged."

Patrick leaned over the bed and gave him a hug. "And listen to Dr. McRae. Do what he says. As ornery as you are, I don't think a heart attack can get the best of you."

"Go on with you. I'll get us a tee time at the Curragh Club. Hope ye've kept up your game. Nothing worse than playing with a duffer . . . especially a young one."

Patrick stood and headed for the door. "We might make a small wager?"

"Uh-huh. Might make the game a bit more interestin'."

"The loser buys a round and dinner to boot!"

Angus shifted in bed and grunted, "I'll get us a tee time. You just show up and take your beatin' like a man."

"Aye, aye," said Patrick as he hurried towards the door with a smile on his face.

"And we need to look at my papers when you come back, lad. They're important—at least to me," Angus called out.

"Golf first—then papers," laughed Patrick as he scooted out the door.

Chapter 28

Molly applied the last of the topical antiseptic to the scar on her face. It would always be there, of course, but she knew if she kept applying the ointment, it might not be the most blaring feature of all.

Perhaps I should think about seeing a plastic surgeon in Fort Myers. See if he thinks surgery would improve the appearance of the scar. Maybe I'll do that.

But something kept her from acting on that thought. Removing the scar, that is. The scar marked an event she could never forget. And it changed her outlook on life. Patrick had once referred to it as her "badge of courage," and had remarked on more than one occasion that "the scar does not detract from your beauty, Molly. A scar is only skin deep. Your beauty goes much deeper than that." As always, thinking about Patrick brought confusion to Molly's usually ordered mind.

He's thousands of miles away and I rather doubt he thinks of Cayo Canna and his friends here. But he did bring such life and exuberance to this place. This island. Was that because he was a priest? Or was it just who he is? Just Patrick. Whatever. He's not here and I am.

She was relieved Papa had gone to Baltimore and removed her belongings from her apartment. *Now I don't have to return to that place. That place where my life was almost taken from me. That place where my world changed forever. And now that chapter of my life is truly over. Cayo Canna is my home now.*

She sat there another moment, then heard Papa's voice calling from the great room, "Molly Mac! We need to get on about going through these clues and photos you collected."

"Coming, Papa," she replied and joined him. Knowing he was giving this situation his attention eased Molly's apprehensions about the whole ordeal. She tried to not think about this event as being a crime, but no matter how hard she tried, her brain kept telling her it was. After all, it didn't make any sense to believe that an intelligent woman—as that writer must have been—would crawl under a dock during the night and go to sleep!

"Alright, then. Tell me about these clues. What do make of them?" Papa asked as he chewed on his unlit pipe.

"I don't know what to make of them, Papa. Here. Look at this. A bit of paper was at the edge of the dock. It's sort of heavy—maybe like stationery? There are a couple of letters on there, but none that I can decipher. Maybe this one is the letter a? Or maybe c? And, look here. Drawings of leaves in the upper left corner."

"Uhm . . . somehow that looks familiar. Can't recall where I might have seen it, though. What else?"

Molly picked up the next item. "This is interesting. A rhinestone hairclip. It was in the sand next to the body. Somehow it looked a little out of place with her other adornments. An expensive pearl necklace and matching earrings. Or rather, earring. One was missing. Oh, and this item."

She held up a small, amber colored plastic bottle.

"This may be an empty plastic medication bottle . . . but it doesn't have a top. These small ones are used for many purposes. Not just for medications."

Papa took the bottle and held it up to the light. "Uhm . . . pretty common. Anything else?"

Molly reached into her bag on the floor. "Just these. Her shoes. Again, very expensive. I'd say designer made."

Papa took one in his hand and looked it over. "Yep. Fine leather. And I'd say they're practically new. The soles are hardly worn at all." Molly looked at the shoes again.

"Oh, yes. You're right. I hadn't noticed that. As I told you Papa, assessing bodies is a skill I possess, but deciphering clues at a crime scene is not," she sighed.

"Enough of this, I think. Who've you interviewed?"

"Only one person. The child that found the body. Wesley Laramore. A nine-year-old with an angelic face and inquisitive mind. I could tell that from just a few minutes with her."

"What did you learn?"

"Not much, I'm afraid. Her father, Adam Laramore, took offense at a question I asked and refused to let me continue. He stormed out of the restaurant and that was that."

"Adam, huh. I see."

"Well, I don't. You know him?"

"Yes, of course. He's been here a number of years now. A Southern boy. Comes from somewhere around Cedar Key—a coastal town a bit north of here. He's very likeable and appears to be good at his job. Fishing guide. What did you ask that was so irritating to him?"

"Wesley said when she found the body she ran to Sassy's to tell her about it. I simply asked why she didn't go home to tell her mother instead. And that seemed to set Adam off like a lighted firecracker. For a quick second I thought he might actually get violent."

Papa chewed on his pipe a bit, then looked up to the ceiling . . . apparently trying to remember something. "Yeah, well he had good reason, I suppose."

"What? You think he had reason to be angry with me?"

"Molly Mac, there are some things you can't possibly know about people on the island. Things that I know because that's what I do. Make sure I know about people on our island. Not everyone is as law abiding as we might wish. Or think. In this case, Adam is not one of those, but he's in a difficult position. About a year ago his wife, Colleen I believe, had some serious mental issues. Clinical depression as I recall. After seeing a number of physicians, psychiatrists etc., in Fort Myers, the consensus was she needed some in-house treatment as she was becoming suicidal. So, Adam admitted her to a psychiatric hospital up in Sarasota. One that was highly recommended. That, my dear, would be reason enough for him to respond in such a manner."

Molly stared at Papa, "Yes. I see. Of course. That would be upsetting to anyone. And I would never have asked had I known his situation."

"No matter. Comes with the territory. Part of gathering information. Trust me. I've made more blunders than you would believe. Part of being in intelligence or gathering evidence of any potential crime. And the more I think about it, the more I lean toward this being a crime."

Molly nodded, "At least I'm not the only one."

"All right then. You've told me Debra at The Writer's Block was a friend of the deceased."

"Yes, Sassy told me that when I was over there yesterday. She was going to find Debra and tell her about her friend. She couldn't find her yesterday, but did see her earlier this morning. She called and said she and Debra would be at the shop later today."

"Good. Then let's take ourselves over there and ask a few pertinent questions. I know Debra casually, but we need to remember she may be quite fragile after having lost a friend."

They both rose and started for the door. Then, for the third time this day, the ham radio raised its noisy head. Papa tossed Molly the keys to the golf cart.

"Get the golf cart started. I'll be right with you."

Jack walked over to the radio. "K4ELD here. Go ahead, Drifter."

A few minutes later, Papa Jack came outside and climbed in the golf cart. Molly was the designated driver it seemed.

Molly smiled at him, "You know, Papa. I don't have a driver's license. Deputy Harrison has let me get by for a while, but I think I better put some priority on getting my license."

"A driver's license, huh. Well, yes, it took some doing for me to convince the Community Council to allow golf carts on the highway. And they insisted on some rules for driving them. Guess you can blame me for that little complication." He laughed then and off they went.

When they arrived at The Writer's Block, Debra and Sassy were sitting at a table in the rear of Sassy's shop. Sipping yet another delicious cup of tea. Sassy grinned from ear to ear when Jack and Molly entered.

"Jack!" She hurried over and the two hugged—maybe for just a longer bit than was necessary.

He held her at arm's length and stared for a long moment. "Sassy. Haven't seen you for some time. Molly tells me you two have met."

Sassy nodded to Molly. "Yes. We had a conversation yesterday. I know she has a difficult job trying to gather facts about Gillian's death."

She then directed her questions to Molly. "Did you find Wesley and Adam?"

"Yes, but I didn't learn much. Adam really wasn't keen on me interviewing Wesley."

Sassy lifted her eyebrows. "I see. Well, I can't tell you much more than I did yesterday. Although I did talk with Sean at The Temptation. He reported someone saw Gillian leave Timmy's Nook with a young man. But no one seems to know who."

They approached Debra and Jack held out his hand and greeted her. "Debra. Good to see you again. I wish it were under better circumstances. I'm so sorry about your friend. That's a difficult loss."

"Thank you, Capt. McCormick. Yes, we've been friends for a number of years now. I will miss her."

Jack pulled Molly by the hand, "Debra, this is my granddaughter, Dr. Molly McCormick. She's been asked to assist the medical examiner with gathering facts surrounding the death of your friend."

Molly reached out her hand, "I'm so sorry you've lost a friend. That's such a terrible loss for you, I'm sure."

Jack stepped in then. "Debra, I'm trying to help Molly with her inquiries. I wonder if we could have a few minutes of your time? I know talking about this incident will be difficult, but we must find out what actually happened to Ms. Hartwell."

Sassy brought them back to a table in the far corner of her shop. "Come. Sit here. It's the quietest place in the shop. You'll not be bothered." She left them then and continued clearing tables from customers who had their afternoon tea earlier.

Sitting across from Capt. Jack, Debra took a deep breath. "I hardly know where to start, Captain. It all seems so strange—like a dream that couldn't possibly be real."

"Just take your time."

Debra began and once she did, the story came flooding out. As if it wanted to be told. Needed to be told, even.

"The speaking engagement at the Historical Society was a success. Gillian has a way of making her audience feel she is speaking directly to them personally . . . treating each one as if they were a character in one of her novels. She was in her element now. She'd captured her audience with her words and was reveling in their applause.

"She smiled at them, telling them what a terrific audience they'd been. Then she suggested they join the two of us for refreshments at the Temptation. I'd told her about the place. The good food. And how Raphael always talks about the grand dance floor there.

"The applause continued as we made our way through the door and on to Raphael's cab. He had agreed to pick us up after the meeting as I figured Gillian wouldn't be too excited about riding in my golf cart."

Jack nodded and smiled, chewed on his pipe, listened, and watched Debra's face as she told her story. He believed faces often tell you more than any words.

"We headed to the Temptation. The evening progressed with much laughter, drinking, music, and dancing. I'd forgotten how engaging Gillian can be when she so desires. And she was in rare form, drinking more than she probably should, and dancing with Raphael. I took a turn about the floor with him and returned to sit with Gillian. Then, as the evening was wearing down, Gillian announced she would like to go to Timmy's Nook. 'Why do you want to go there?' I asked. 'The Temptation has everything to offer that Timmy's does. And we're already here. And, anyway, it's almost time we thought about calling it an evening.'

"Gillian would have none of that. She wanted to talk with the bartender at Timmy's. Will Johnson. She asked if I knew him. I nodded, 'Only slightly. I go there occasionally. But I don't go out at night much. Running a business means I stay home a lot and try to stay out of bars.'

"She insisted she wanted to meet him. It appears her daughter, Christina, and Will were friends at one time. Close friends according to Gillian. Well, that comment had my antenna shooting straight up. If Gillian's daughter, Christina, was close friends with him, there would be a story I didn't want to hear. Trying to understand that girl is like trying to follow a hurricane's path. You think you have it mapped out, but it always veers at the last moment, throwing everyone into a tizzy."

"So, you know Gillian's daughter, but you didn't know about her relationship with Will?" asked the Captain.

"Yes, I know Christina, but had no idea she and Will were acquainted. I asked Gillian if Christina and Will had gone to college together. Gillian shrugged her shoulders and said, 'For a short while. Then he dropped out and left town. But they got back together when he returned to Tallahassee and began working as a barkeep at the Duval Hotel.'

"I tried to ease away from the conversation. Christina's friendships don't last long as I recall. Gillian said she wasn't worried and that the relationship is over. Or the boyfriend thinks so. She then dropped her bombshell of the evening. 'But, you see, he left Christina with a little going away package.'

"What does that mean?" I asked. "Then I stopped asking questions and stared at her as she sat there with a diabolical smile plastered on her face. She hadn't seen Christina for several months. Then, a few weeks ago, the girl showed up at Gillian's door looking like The Great Pumpkin ready for Halloween.

"I was floored. Then I asked her what she was going to do about the situation. She continued smiling and said, 'Not much I can do. Too late for an abortion. Stupid girl should have told me right off. Now I have to convince the father to own up to his obligations—send money in other words.' The she lifted her glass and finished the last of her cocktail."

"Mercy me. So, agreeing to speak at the Historical Society was just an excuse for her to come down here?" Molly interjected.

Captain Jack sat quietly. He'd checked out Will Johnson when he arrived, but nothing showed up except a couple of speeding tickets and a landlord tossing him out for lack of rent payment up in Tallahassee.

Debra took a sip of her tea and began once again. "Yes, I think you're right. She said something about killing two birds with one stone—and suggested I not take it personally as she was happy to speak to my group.

"Then I stood and gathered my purse and called Raphael to take me home. I didn't think I needed to participate in her conversation with Will. I suggested when she was done talking with Will that she call Raphael as he would still be at the Temptation. Still dancing most likely. He would take her to her cottage at the Sandpiper.

"She assured me she would find a way to her cottage, and mumbled something about having to clean up another of Christina's problems. Then she told me she had the damnedest headache just thinking about dealing with Will Johnson.

"I rummaged around in my purse and came up with my migraine medication. Something Greg, my pharmacist, gives me. Jeri had just brought it to me that morning. It's better than any aspirin and won't leave you feeling groggy. I gave her several and told her to take one just before she went to bed as it might make her sleepy."

"What kind of migraine medication?" asked Molly as the mention of medication for migraine had her ears on alert.

Debra thought for a moment. "Don't know the proper name just now. Just something Greg puts together. Works really well, too." Molly nodded but didn't quiz Debra further. Maybe later.

"Then we agreed she would come to my place today and we would spend the afternoon together, then have dinner later. I guess that was yesterday. Then she confirmed she was still going back Monday morning as planned."

Jack made a mental note to ask Skip, the pilot of the *Calypso*, if he could add any information relating to Gillian as she had taken his ferry to the island. Skip had a keen eye and intuition about people.

"So, Raphael dropped her at Timmy's Nook and I waved to her as she entered. Glad to be going home alone. From past experience, I was quite sure Gillian would find a way home, and it wouldn't be with Raphael."

She stopped abruptly then. When a couple of minutes passed and

153

she didn't continue, Jack then asked only one question. But one he felt was important. "And you never heard from her again?"

Debra shook her head, "No. I waited and waited. But the call never came." Then she broke down in heart-wrenching sobs again.

Jack leaned back in his chair and called out, "Sassy? You got anything stronger than Scottish tea? I think this would be a good time to share it if so."

Molly reached out and placed her hand over Debra's. Saying nothing. Knowing that sometimes a touch says more than words anyway.

Sassy emerged from the kitchen with four glasses and a bottle of Glenfiddich—the special libation she knew Jack drank.

Jack nodded, "I think that's just the ticket."

Chapter 29

Back at the lighthouse, Molly and Papa Jack sat at his desk in the great room. Where he always sat when he had important decisions to make. Ensign was in his usual place—sprawled at Jack's feet. Molly had her notebook that contained information about the scene she and Deputy Harrison had covered. They had interviewed Debra, now she waited for Papa to tell her the next steps to take in her project. This investigation.

Jack picked up a pencil and began doodling across the top of a piece of paper. "All right. Let's dissect what we learned from Debra. She did a fine job of recounting events. I sensed a very organized mind that could almost remember verbatim the conversations she and Gillian had. Great asset for someone who runs a bookstore."

Molly agreed. "Yes, I was a bit surprised. I thought we might have to dig the information out of her. But, is any of it helpful in deciding whether Gillian's death was accidental or criminal?"

"Can't know that yet. First, we list out what facts we learned. Who, what, where and when will sometimes lead you to a suspect. Always start with those questions in mind."

Molly jumped in, "Ok. Let's start with who. Debra. Long-time friend with Gillian. She did seem genuinely upset, but I sensed an underlying current of anger. Maybe they aren't as close as we might be led to believe."

"Bingo, Molly Mac. You read that right. I think there's some history we aren't privy to that may have bearing on this case. We need to find out more about that. Sometimes friends become enemies. But there are some other "whos" we need to learn more about first."

"Right. I suppose I need to interview Will Johnson, the bartender Gillian wanted to meet with. Then I think I'll talk with Sassy again. She was actually the one who Wesley went to first. Then they went to the site. Maybe she saw something. And, she mentioned she spoke with someone named Sean?"

"That would be Sean Feherty. Tends bar at the Temptation. He has the "heartbeat" of the island better than anyone. Definitely need to talk with him."

"But, Papa, if these interviews don't go any better than the one with young Wesley, I won't know any more than I do now. Maybe I'll just leave everything to the investigator—the one who's going to come eventually."

"That wouldn't be my first choice, Molly Mac. Evidence and memories have a way of getting stale. Best to learn what you can and do it quickly. So, we can learn something from the interviews, but what else did Debra tell us?"

"Umm . . . the presentation at the Historical Society was a success . . . they celebrated at the Temptation . . . she didn't want to go on to Timmy's as she felt both had too much to drink . . . she had a conversation with Gillian regarding a daughter . . . a pregnant daughter . . . apparently from a relationship with Will Johnson . . . Gillian had a headache thinking about a confrontation with Will . . . Debra came home alone . . . never heard from Gillian."

"Good. Good recall. Now you might want to . . ." He halted mid-sentence as the ham radio screeched and squawked. Again. Molly sighed. Something not right about that.

"Papa, that infernal radio is screaming just like before."

Papa answered immediately. "K4ELD here. Go ahead K6DNB."

"Casper, switch to my code," said a familiar voice on the other end. "Will do K6DNB."

That instruction "switch to my code" had Molly's ears perking up. She recognized that call sign. And the voice. That would be Drifter. Former intelligence mate of Papa's. Still in active service with the U.S. Navy. Stationed at Key West. He, Papa, and Admiral Theodore (Bear) Bowen were instrumental in preventing mustard gas from getting into the hands of the Cuban revolutionaries during that Cuban Crisis a couple of months ago.

Molly was adept at using Morse Code. In fact, it was required for anyone wanting to be a licensed ham radio operator. But that was the only code she knew. Drifter had developed a code the intelligence mates used. Solana had learned it in a couple of days, but then Solana seemed to have a real knack for learning codes . . . a skill that appeared to be a holdover from her time with Fidel Castro and Che Guevara.

Now Molly wondered if she shouldn't give Drifter's code a try also. If Papa needed her help, then she was game in spite of her desire for him to truly retire.

Drifter's message to Jack was an important one. "Admiral Whitmore needs you and Bear. I know Bear can't participate as much as he has in the past, but the special equipment on his *Admiral's Lady* may come in handy. And he knows how to use it. That being the case, a Navy SEAL, Lt. Jim Carrington, will rendezvous with you in the waters close to Cuba. He'll assist you with getting inside the Cuban compound and taking photos of whatever you find within those hatches that appeared on the aerial photos taken by one of our spy planes. And, Casper . . . no heroics. Just get there, get your photos, and get your ass back home!"

After a couple of minutes, the two intelligence mates signed off. Molly didn't need to ask any questions. Papa simply stood and addressed her. "Molly Mac, I have to leave. Now. Admiral Whitmore has requested my assistance in an operation that's urgent. A national security issue."

"Oh, Papa . . . but . . . " She stopped then.

There was no point in begging him to refuse. He would never do that. And if it involved national security, how could anyone refuse when a senior officer called on you to come to the aid of your country?

"Are you flying to your destination?"

"No. *Admiral's Lady* has a few special instruments and equipment on board that may be of use to us. Bear will pick me up at the ferry dock at 18:00 hrs."

Solana stood in the doorway. She had heard the radio also. Like Molly, she didn't make a fuss. Rather, she did what she always did. Supported this intelligence officer to whom she owed much.

"What do you need me to do for you, Captain?"

"Get my small, leather travel bag ready. And my frog gear. I'll pack any other items I need."

For a moment he considered keeping all information about his assignment to himself. He so disliked having Molly and Solana worrying about him. But Molly was not a child any longer and didn't need to be shielded from happenings in the world. As for Solana, her time with Castro and Che had left her with invaluable skills and Jack knew she always had his back.

"I thought about keeping you both in the dark about this assignment. To keep you from worrying. But that would make you worry even more."

"What can you tell us, Captain?" Solana asked.

"Apparently the latest aerial photos of the Cuban missile sites, where Castro had amassed his nuclear arms, indicate he has removed the missiles as he promised President Kennedy. However, these photos also show several doors, or maybe hatches is a better description, along the outer edges of each of the missile sites. Since we only have Castro's word that he's removed all nukes, Admiral Whitmore needs someone to go in-country and see firsthand what the hatches contain . . . if anything. Kennedy removed the quarantine on the island on Nov. 20, which means he believes all missiles have been removed and all is well. But we have to know what's in these hatches. With Castro, nothing is as it seems."

"You mean you're going to Cuba?" Molly dreaded to hear his answer.

"That's my assignment. Don't ask any more questions. Just know I've conducted many such operations in my career. That's what "spooks" do.

"I have a couple of requests. Solana, please stay close by the radio. Your coding skills may be needed once more. And, Molly, I have to ask you to do the same. I hope to not involve anyone else, but I don't know what may happen once I get to my assignment. You may be called upon again."

"Of course, Captain," Solana remarked and started toward the spiral staircase that led to the lantern room, the Captain's quarters. The small bag the Captain referred to was the one with a hidden compartment where he kept not one, but two, pistols. And on occasion even more lethal items. Solana knew more than she would ever divulge to anyone . . . except the Captain.

Molly took her clue from Solana, even though she didn't like hearing Papa was packing his frog gear. That meant he would be engaging in something dangerous. But she kept her thoughts to herself.

"Well then, Papa, looks like Ensign and I will be the investigating team. He can assist me when I go on my interviews," Molly smiled when she really wanted to do nothing but cry.

"Molly Mac, you'll do a fine job with this investigation. Trust yourself. You have talents you aren't even aware of yet. Let them come to the surface." With that he bounded up the spiral staircase to the tower. Time to engage.

Chapter 30
Ireland

Patrick felt as if an elephant had been removed from his shoulders. An elephant he'd been carrying for years now. And one that apparently didn't need carrying. It was only a figment of his imagination.

He was taken aback when he saw Claire's parents. They seemed much older than he remembered. But then, Claire was the youngest of their five children, so perhaps they were older than he had originally thought.

The death of their daughter had taken a toll on both, of course. As it had on Patrick. After a few minutes of pleasantries, Claire's father finally asked, "So, Patrick, surely you had better things to do than come all the way up here to visit two old folks who sit about reading the Daily Herald and sipping tea. What's on your mind?"

Patrick explained his reason for coming. Explained that he needed forgiveness for a grievous sin. The two listened quietly, then Claire's da folded his hands together, rested them in his lap, and looked Patrick in the eyes.

"Oh, Patrick, my lad. Claire was a headstrong, independent, lass from the day she was born. We loved her dearly. Still do. But in spite of our teachings, our prayers, and our pleading with her to refrain from participating in those rebellious groups that cause trouble, she always went the way of a wild wind. Blowing first one way, then another. Never knowing where she would end up.

"Nay, Patrick. You're not responsible for her death. Claire resides in a better place now. Of that we are certain. And she would not wish you to carry this unwarranted burden of guilt. Lay it down, lad. Get on with your life and when you think of her, remember her lovely face and her caring heart. That's what she would have wanted."

After tears and hugs, they said their goodbyes and Patrick left. With a much lighter heart. Yes, it was a relief to know Claire's parents never blamed him. In their minds Claire was responsible for her own disastrous ending. Any forgiveness that was to be extended would be for Patrick to forgive himself for not leaving the group earlier. And maybe Claire would still be alive.

But Patrick knew from experience that forgiving yourself is often more difficult than receiving forgiveness from others.

With this issue settled the best it could be, he would now undertake his next one. Resigning from the priesthood. Angus had helped him see the Almighty sometimes has plans for us that we may not understand yet. But, if we follow our hearts, they usually won't lead us astray. And his heart had told him for a long time now that his time as a priest had come to an end. And, if so, then he had to trust that the Almighty would present another path to him. In His time, of course.

The meeting with Bishop Dunne was just as freeing as his conversation with Claire's folks. The moment Patrick and the bishop greeted each other, Patrick noted that the twinkle in the bishop's eyes was still there.

"Ah, Patrick. 'Tis you, is it?" He embraced Patrick and held him close for a moment, then pulled away, and smiled.

"You know, I remember the first time we met, Patrick. 'Twas at St. Bartholomew's . . . my very first assignment. As I recall, I caught you and young Danny McDowell smoking in the acolyte's closet."

Patrick grinned. "Yes, I do believe you did."

"And now here we are. Still connected these many years later."

Patrick presented his case quite well as he had given much time to this decision, this new direction. And, to his great relief, Bishop Dunne didn't question him about taking more time, or other questions along those lines. The bishop had known Patrick long enough to know he would have asked himself more questions than anyone else could have even thought of. Instead, he leaned forward in his chair and looked eye to eye with Patrick.

"Leaving the Church is a difficult decision. Not to be taken lightly. But the Church teaches us that we are all called for a particular purpose. And I believe that to be true. I also believe our Lord and Savior would not wish one to continue in His service as a priest if his heart feels it has another calling. I've known you for years, Patrick. From the time you were an acolyte in our diocese. You are an intelligent man and I know this decision is one you would have struggled with long before coming to me. My advice is to keep counsel with those who have your best interest at heart . . . the Almighty being at the top of that list. And one final thought . . . one can serve Him without wearing a collar."

Patrick walked away feeling his decision was absolutely correct. And was relieved the bishop gave his full-hearted support and prayers for a future in which Patrick would play the part the Almighty intended.

Today he was headed back to Dublin. To tell Angus about his meeting with Claire's parents. Dublin was festive this time of year. First would be Thanksgiving feasts and then Christmas would be fast upon them. When he arrived, people were walking the streets, greeting each other, and ducking into their favorite pubs and restaurants. When Patrick entered The Druid's Fountain, the place was quieter than he could ever remember. Most times Celtic music would be bouncing off the rafters and laughter would fill the air. But today there was soft Celtic music humming in the background and a few customers chatting at the bar. A pretty lass was serving a table in the corner and turned when Patrick came through the door.

"Ah, you're Patrick, aren't you?" she called out.

"Aye. That would be correct. And I gather you're the new cook Angus told me about. And he was right. Lovely lass, just as he said," he smiled at her.

She placed the food on the table then came closer to Patrick. "Come with me to the kitchen. I have something for you."

"Can it wait? I need to see Angus first, then I'll stop by the kitchen."

"No. I think you better come with me first."

She started for the kitchen and Patrick hesitated a moment, then followed. The aromas in the kitchen were much like those in Mums' kitchen. Mouthwatering. A couple of other girls were stirring pots on the stove and smiled at him, but said nothing.

"I'm Grace. I run the pub for Angus. And today I'm doing a favor he asked of me. He asked me to give you a letter when you next came in."

"The old reprobate can give it to me himself. I'll just run up and . . ."

Grace sighed and folded her hands beneath her chin in a prayerlike fashion, "Angus passed away sometime during the night, Patrick. When I took his breakfast up to him, he was already gone. He gave me the letter yesterday afternoon, so I believe he had some inkling that his time was near."

Patrick stared at Grace for a long moment.

"But . . . that can't . . . I was just here a couple of days ago. He assured me he was getting better. He . . . but . . . no . . . that can't be . . ."

"I know. It seems impossible to not hear him calling for his tea or asking for a taste of Jameson . . . his preferred medicine."

Patrick stood as if rooted to the floor. Grace took him by the elbow and ushered him to a table in the rear of the pub. She was thoughtful enough to bring a bottle of Jameson and a glass, then left him to come to grips with the situation and to read his letter privately.

After the third reading of the rather long, but clearly written epistle, Patrick poured a large drink for himself. And another. Then, struggling to get through the fog of his aching heart and troubled mind, he stood and clinked his glass with a spoon from the table.

The groups at the tables and the customers at the bar turned in his direction. Patrick walked to the center of the room and without any more fanfare, called out in his deep, booming voice:

"A toast to Angus. The epitome of a true friend. May he rest in the warm bosom of the Almighty."

Everyone raised their glass and toasted their friend. And they were all friends with Angus. He gathered friends like flowers gather bees. Without effort.

Having given Patrick time to digest the letter, Grace appeared at his table.

"I was told you would have some business to discuss with me. But Angus didn't give any more information than that. So, when the time is right, I'm here every morning at 6:00 a.m. getting ready for the day. I'll make time for you whenever you need it."

"Oh. Yes. I . . . it's . . . it's complicated. Give me a couple of days to do what has been asked of me. The first request being that I preside over his funeral mass and lay him to rest."

Grace smiled, "And I'll make sure we have all the proper food and refreshments to follow. The Druid's Fountain will host the finest "going away" party you've ever seen!"

Patrick tried to smile through his pain. "Yes, Angus would like that. Thanks, Grace."

What he didn't tell her . . . at least not yet . . . was that the letter she'd handed to him was more than just a letter. It was Angus's last will and testament along with a couple of other legal documents as well.

Angus had bequeathed The Druid's Fountain to Patrick. Sole owner. And that was a reasonable bequest. In Patrick's mind. The other bequests, however, were totally unexpected and he was trying to get his head around them.

The first instruction was for Patrick to see Sean MacDuff, the solicitor in charge of Angus's affairs, and ask him to explain any details that might be confusing. But even Patrick could read legal papers and know that in addition to ownership of The Druid's Fountain, Angus had left him his investments, and any and all monies deposited in the bank—which was about £15,000.00, give or take a few shekels.

Jaysus, Angus! Where in hell did you get so much money?

Patrick racked his brain. He recalled Angus talking about a couple of investments he'd made . . . but that was years ago. Had they been more profitable than he expected? Or had he made others? Or perhaps a family member left him funds?

And the last bequest was the most surprising of all. Patrick read the sentence again. Now for the fourth time.

"I, Angus Conor O'Neill, being of sound mind, do hereby bequeath to my loyal, beloved friend and companion, Patrick O'Brien, my estate, *Hawk's Nest*, located in Northern Ireland."

Patrick's mouth dropped open.

Hawk's Nest? The large estate set aside as a sanctuary for hawks, eagles, kestrels, goshawks and any raptors or birds of prey? I've been there a hundred times. My favorite place in Ireland. And Angus first took me there when I was a delinquent-in-making. Taught me about nature. Kept me busy coming here . . . to 'commune with the birds' he would tell me. Anything to keep me out of trouble. And he sensed I would love the sanctuary and the birds. But I had no idea he owned the place!

He had a lot to think about. But at the moment, profound sorrow ruled his world and he was only able to register one thought.

I'll never have another friend as special as Angus. No. Of course I won't. There is no one else like Angus. A friend like that only comes once in a lifetime. If we are lucky.

He put the letter back in the envelope and placed it in his coat pocket. Certain to read it many more times. Now, however, he had other issues to deal with.

Then it looks like I'll don the collar one last time . . . and it's an honor to do so.

Chapter 31

Molly stood on the dock and watched in silence as Papa Jack tossed his leather bag to Bear Bowen and boarded the *Admiral's Lady*. She bit her tongue to keep from saying the obvious *be careful* to these two "retired" intelligence officers. The next instant they were underway and Molly threw up her hand as they entered the channel and Bear opened the throttle, leaving a gigantic fishtail behind. Time was of the essence.

And, so that's that. Castro and Cuba raise their ugly heads once again. And it looks like I have no choice but to follow Papa's suggestions to get on about my investigation. By myself. And to do it quickly. If his thoughts are correct, that this is a crime and not an accident, then some unhinged person is still on the island.

Early the next morning, Molly started the golf cart and reached over to pat the head of her companion, Ensign. He had hopped on the golf cart the minute she started it. Papa and Ensign were a well-known pair about the island and Ensign got treats at most every stop.

"Well, I'm not so sure you and I will be as welcome at places as you and Papa. But it really doesn't matter. I gotta get these interviews done. And I've got to ask some questions that may ruffle some feathers. So don't expect to get many treats when you're with me, little buddy."

First stop was Sassy's. The shop opened at 7:30 a.m. which was good as many of the retired folk on the island were early risers. Molly wanted to see what else Sassy might know. Papa said "She's as aboveboard as they come. She'll tell it like it is—or at least the way she sees it. You can trust her, Molly Mac."

She wheeled the golf cart into the parking lot, spraying a scattering of crushed shells in the process. Upon entering Sassy's shop, Molly almost forgot what she came for. The scent of cinnamon and citrus filled the air.

Sassy smiled when she saw Molly. "Ah. Dr. Mac. Hello again. Come on in. Got some freshly baked scones just out of the oven."

"Then I'll have one. And a cup of whatever tea you've got brewing. It smells divine."

Sassy brought the scone and tea and pulled up a chair. "I assume you've got more questions?"

"Well, yes, actually I do. I was wondering if you learned anything more from Debra. She was quite adept at recalling events, but I felt something was left unsaid. But I'm just guessing. Could be nothing."

"No, you're right. I think there was something about the relationship between Debra and Gillian that wasn't exactly warm and cozy. They go back a long way. And my sense is they have had some disagreements over the years. But, again, I don't really know. Debra's business helps my business and likewise. Folks come looking for a book and end up in here for a cup of tea and a scone. And sometimes they stop here for tea and mosey into Debra's and leave with a book or two. The arrangement works for both of us."

"Wasn't there a Hispanic gentleman in Debra's shop when Papa and I were here?"

"Yes. That would be Luis. He's our gardener-custodian. He's new. A few months now. Comes from Nicaragua. Keeps both places cleaner than Debra and I did. I meant to ask Jack to check him out, but his illness and other events at the lighthouse have kept him busy. I'll ask him about it later."

Molly stopped herself before blurting out "he's gone again." This spook business was as irritating as the investigative business. Medicine was still more appealing.

Molly took the last bite of the delicious scone and gulped down the tea. "Then I've got some other stops to make. Thanks for the delicious tea and scone. Knowing your shop is here makes me like this place even more."

"So . . . you thinking of staying?"

"Yes, I am. I'm planning to open a family practice office. But this bit of investigative work has halted my progress on that front. Hopefully, a real investigator will get over here shortly and relieve me of these interruptions."

She said goodbye and walked outside. A second later, Sassy dashed out the door, headed to the golf cart. "Almost forgot. Here you go, Ensign." And she held out her hand for him to scoff up a small scone tidbit.

Molly grinned and shook her head. Ensign licked his chops and sat

166

upright in his seat. Looking very much like he belonged there.

Chapter 32

Deputy Harrison sat behind his desk. A few minutes earlier he'd debated stopping at Sassy's for a couple of scones and tea. But he'd had to struggle to fasten his uniform belt this morning, so perhaps he'd leave off the scones. For a couple of days, anyhow.

His desk was littered from one side to the other with various papers. Most of them were items to be filed. But a couple of them were notes he'd prepared after attending the scene at the dock. With Dr. Mac.

After reviewing them, he thought he would call Dr. Mac. Or better yet, run up to the lighthouse and talk with her. He strapped on his holster, grabbed his Stetson, locked the door to the office and headed to the lighthouse. He'd only gone as far as Periwinkle Way when he spotted Capt. Jack's golf cart at The Island Pharmacy. Easy to spot as the Captain's dog was sitting in the front seat. As if waiting for someone.

As the deputy approached the golf cart, Ensign wagged his tail and stood in his seat. Guard dog he was not. Harrison rubbed Ensign's head then looked about. The Captain had been ill recently, so perhaps he needed medication. Hence the reason he was at the pharmacy.

But he learned it wasn't the Captain in the pharmacy as a few seconds later Molly came walking toward him.

"Oh, Deputy Harrison, Ben, good morning."

"Dr. Mac." He quickly removed his Stetson and nodded, still not terribly comfortable in her presence. In fact, anytime she was around his tongue and brain seemed to have no connection whatsoever.

"I needed a couple of items from the pharmacy. But I'm a bit early. Looks like they open a bit later on Saturdays."

"Yes, that's right. But they deliver if you really need it."

"Right. That's a very nice service."

"Dr. Mac . . . I was just thinking about the body. The dead body we attended. And the more I think about it the more I feel this death wasn't an accident. I can't quite put my finger on it, but I just don't believe a woman walks on the beach and crawls under a dock and dies."

"Yes, I know what you mean. Let's hope we hear from Dr. Strickland. Once he completes the autopsy, we'll know a lot more. And the lab report will give us important information. Labs are always the first thing a physician wants to see before coming to any conclusion regarding a disease process. I would assume that same thinking applies here."

"This whole affair is keeping me awake at night, I can tell you. I mean . . . what if we have a serial killer loose on the island? He could have come by boat, or on the ferry . . . or maybe he's one of those Cuban rebels . . . one of those that tried to kill Captain McCormick."

"Oh, well, I suppose that could be, but I think those guys are long gone. They wouldn't be inclined to stay around following what happened to Crab. Surely."

"Maybe not. But I hope Dr. Strickland lets us know something soon. Meanwhile, I'm combing every street and path looking for anything suspicious. Someone knows something."

"And I'm headed to interview Sean Feherty at the Temptation. Papa says he often knows things before others. Guess that's what all bartenders do. Listen. I'll let you know if I learn anything from him.

"And, about your being awake at night . . . sleep is important. Has a definite purpose. It's the time our body replenishes itself and keeps us functioning properly. You might try relaxing with a good book and a glass of warm milk before going to bed."

"Oh. Okay. I've got a couple of books I've been wanting to read. Maybe I'll try one of those."

Molly smiled. "We'll talk again soon. If I learn anything from Sean, I'll stop by your office and fill you in."

Deputy Harrison just nodded. Several times. Brain and tongue still tripping over each other.

Chapter 33

Dr. David Strickland walked into his office, plopped down into his chair, and ran his fingers through his thick blond hair. "If those damn snowbirds would just stay home until after the holidays maybe I could get a handle on all this . . . chaos!"

Kathi, his long-time radiology technician, smiled at him. "Yeah. We appear to get more behind every day. But a bit of good news. The new rad tech, Lynda something . . . hmmm . . . Lynda Gentry? She'll be joining us the week after Christmas. Relocating from Nashville, as I recall. Comes highly recommended by the head of radiology at Vanderbilt."

"Great. Wish we could drum up another ME, too. I'm sinking fast around here. Can't even take time for a haircut."

Kathi noted dark circles under his eyes and knew he was more than overloaded.

"I know the feeling. Having Ms. Gentry will be a welcome late Christmas gift for me. Don't think I can look at another X-ray. I'm seeing them in my sleep."

"At least you're sleeping. Not sure I know the meaning of the word. And if one more person on Matlacha attacks or kills someone, I will walk out into the Gulf of Mexico wearing galoshes filled with cement so I can swim with the fishes forever.

"The traffic on Sanibel is worse than ever and we have some kind of accident every day. Yesterday someone plowed into the rear of a truck taking supplies to The Lazy Flamingo. The driver was killed instantly. Now I have to see if alcohol or any other intoxicating chemical shows up in his blood work. Seems the Lazy Flamingo is talking about suing for damages."

Kathi was aware this time of year everything was a bit hectic. The economy depended on visitors. Particularly the snowbirds who stayed for several months. But this year it felt like there were more calamities than usual.

"And what about the body on Cayo Canna? Did an investigator get over there yet?" Kathi asked.

"No. And I've got to call Dr. McCormick. She's probably pulling her hair out by now. It may be a week or more before he can get there."

"Have you done the autopsy yet?"

"No. I went over and took a quick peek at her. Middle aged woman . . . Caucasian . . . around sixty years old. A writer from up North someplace. She's still on ice. I'll put her at the top of my list . . . tomorrow. But there's no real hurry about her actually. We already know what killed her.

"Really? What?"

"She has a broken neck . . . or at least one or more fractured cranial vertebrae. Can tell more when I open her up tomorrow. The labs are back, but I haven't had a chance to look at them yet."

With that he headed to the "inner sanctum" as he so affectionately called his morgue, where he needed to take a careful look at the body the sheriff's office had delivered earlier this morning. He needed to remove a couple of slugs and help define the caliber of bullet. Could be the same weapon used in another case that was getting high priority.

Kathi appeared in the doorway holding an envelope. "Just one more item to add to today's agenda . . . Memorial Hospital says these slides take priority over everything else. Slides taken from several patients on the second floor. According to the nursing notes, 'all four patients presented with extremely elevated temperatures, nausea and vomiting, sensitivity to light, and altered mental state. One experienced hallucinations and had to be put in four-point restraints.' They want you to take a look at the slides and share your information with the pathologists and docs."

"Great. Just what we need. Hallucinating patients and an unknown disease process . . . and four patients have it already . . . then I'd say that looks like it's contagious.

"I was over there yesterday. Actually, on the second floor. Checking on Mrs. Stoutamire. She lives in the same condo building as me. A couple of doors down. Her atrial fib is under control and she's scheduled to go home today. Which is good considering there may be a contagious issue on that floor. But I'll bet a silver dollar this problem is nothing more than the flu." Which was another one of those irritations that David associated with the annual influx of snowbirds.

172

"Just wish the snowbirds would leave the flu up north instead of bringing it down here."

Kathi couldn't resist chiding him, "Now, really, Dr. Strickland. You do go on about the snowbirds. But don't I recall that you moved here from Maine some years ago?"

"Yep. And that's what gives me the right to complain about them."

He laughed and took the envelope of slides and placed it by his microscope. He'd look at them a little later. Right now he needed to complete the autopsy he started earlier. One the sheriff's office was hounding him to complete.

He walked to the exam table and looked at the corpse lying there. Then he took a deep breath and spoke aloud . . . or maybe to the body lying on the table.

"Nope. These slides can wait and so can you. You aren't going anywhere. I'm going to call Molly. Right now. I should at least let her know I'm still underwater over here."

But the phone at the lighthouse wasn't cooperating with Dr. Strickland on this day. But then, neither was anything else. Molly would have to wait until the moon and stars lined up and the phones worked again!

Chapter 34

Sean Feherty did a double take when Molly walked in around noontime. He usually knew any and every one that came through his door. But it was the season, and snowbirds were arriving daily. When she came and sat at the bar, he approached with a smile.

"Good day. What can I get you?"

"Oh . . . just a . . . a glass of orange juice."

"Allrighty. Orange juice coming up."

Sean brought the juice and began the usual questions he posed to newcomers.

"You here for the holidays?"

"Uh, no. I live here. Now."

"Oh, well then. I'm Sean Feherty. Glad to meet you Mrs. . . . ."

"It's Miss. Molly McCormick."

Sean nodded, "Then you would be Captain Jack's granddaughter, I assume."

"That's right."

"I heard we have a new physician on the island. And I'm glad of that. Going to Fort Myers for every little ailment gets old."

"Yes, I suppose it does. Once I get my office established, I hope to be able to alleviate some of that inconvenience."

Sean smiled again. Molly wasn't sure how to approach him with her questions, so she just jumped in feet first.

"I've been asked to investigate the event on the beach. At the old dock. The dead body."

"Ah, of course. That's something new for the island. A death and no explanation so far. Have you learned anything?"

"Not much. But Papa Jack says you're a good source for information. He suggested I ask you to recall whatever you can about that evening. I understand the deceased and Debra Morris were here that evening."

"Yes. That's correct. Debra and her friend, along with others from the Historical Society meeting, came here. They all had drinks, danced a bit, and most of them left about 10:30. All except Debra and her friend, that writer lady."

"Did the women appear to be enjoying the evening? Or were they perhaps arguing?"

"They both had enough to drink, certainly. At one point they appeared to be having a serious conversation, with Debra continuing to shake her head as if to say "no" or at least in disagreement with her friend. I asked if they wanted another drink, but they said they were headed to Timmy's Nook. Apparently, the friend knows the bartender over there. Will Johnson. Raphael, the local cabbie, agreed to take them. That was the last I saw of them. But, from what I hear, the friend went to Timmy's Nook . . . without Debra."

"I see. What about this person, Will Johnson. Do you know him?"

"Bartenders know everyone, Dr. Mac." Sean smiled at Molly, enjoying meeting this new physician he'd heard about. Didn't expect a physician to be quite so attractive.

"We've met. Believe he came to our island from Tallahassee. Originally from up North someplace. Maybe Philadelphia? Likeable fellow. Only been here a couple of months or so. But I don't know anything about him personally.

"There were rumors that the writer left Timmy's Nook with Will. That's just hearsay. But you might check with Antonio at the Sandpiper. He may know more than anyone as the writer was staying there. At least that's what I heard."

"Antonio, you say? Then, I'll go by the Sandpiper next. Maybe he has some information that may help."

"Come by anytime. I'm usually here."

Molly didn't care much for hearsay, but that's all she had to go on yet, so she headed to the Sandpiper.

If only you were here, Papa. You always check out anyone new coming to the island. My bet is that you probably know more about Will Johnson than anyone. But, looks like Fidel Castro trumps Will Johnson at the moment.

Ensign was sitting in his assigned seat on the golf cart. Waiting. Molly hopped on and pulled up at the Sandpiper before dinner time. Several couples—dressed to the nines—were entering the large front doors where the doorman welcomed them. She waited for them to enter, then followed a few moments later and made her way to the reception desk where a middle-aged man with dark hair and wearing gold chains around his neck was standing. He greeted Molly with a smile and she noted a bit of an accent . . . Italian she thought.

"Hello. I need to speak with Antonio Carlucci if possible."

"I'm Antonio. What can I do for you?""

"I'm doing a bit of investigation for the Lee County Sheriff and Dr. Strickland, the medical examiner. Gathering information related to the body that was discovered on the island a couple of days ago."

"Yes, then you would be Captain McCormick's granddaughter . . . Dr. Mac."

"Yes. I am. Could you tell me anything about the woman, Ms. Gillian Hartwell, who apparently booked a room with you?"

"That's right. Well, actually Debra Morris booked a room, but when Ms. Hartwell arrived, she insisted on a room some distance away from the door. Said she didn't like to be annoyed by others coming and going. I didn't have another room, so I suggested she stay in one of our cottages. They're every bit as nice as our rooms, of course. So, I took her to Seagull Cottage and she was happy with that arrangement.

"She and Debra came to the lobby here a little later and Raphael picked them up as she was giving a presentation to the Historical Society group. I didn't see her again. That is until the wee hours of the next morning. Very early—about 1:30 a.m."

"Oh, you saw her then?"

"Yes. She came by the front desk to ask for a wake-up call. I informed her that the cottages do not have phones, but if she liked, I would send one of the bellhops to wake her. She complained about our hotel not having a phone, but left then and I suppose she was headed to her cottage."

"She was alone when she came to your desk?"

"Yes. Alone . . . but . . ."

"But, what?"

"We don't normally discuss anything about our guests; however, I realize this is a different situation. What I was about to say was that as she left, I came over to lock the door again, and I noticed a man standing outside the front door. Waiting for her I suppose. But I didn't watch to see if he went with her or not."

"Did you know this person. This man?"

"Well. It was dark. He was tall and thin. But I couldn't really see facial features. There's a rumor already going around about someone seeing her leave Timmy's Nook with Will Johnson, but I couldn't swear that's who it was.

"Of course, being the bartender, Will would have worked until at least 1:00 a.m. or maybe even later. So, I can't say it was him."

"Did you see the man again . . . maybe later?"

"No. I work various shifts, depending on who shows up for work. Michael called in sick, so I was working the late shift that night, and I often work the morning shift. Again, depending on who shows. We're short staffed and even those we employ don't always show up. But no. I didn't see the man outside nor the writer again."

Molly thanked Antonio and headed home. Having used the last of her antiseptic cream this morning, she decided to stop by the Island Pharmacy again. The posted hours were 7:00 a.m. to 8:00 p.m. so it should still be open.

When she entered the shop she was surprised at the number of over-the-counter medications, supplements, first-aid supplies, perfumes, and even several items of beachwear hanging in one aisle.

The next moment she felt a hand on her lower back.

"Ah, Dr. McCormick. Nice to see you again," said Greg Maxwell. He held out his hand and Molly took it . . . and once again, he held it between both his. A bit too long for her comfort.

"Greg. Good to see you again, too."

"What do you need, Molly. May I call you that?"

"Of course. Uh . . . I need some antiseptic ointment if you have any. I used the last of my supply and need to replenish it."

Greg looked at her, scanning her face; The he lifted his forefinger and carefully traced the "S" scar on her left temple.

"Ah, I see. Nasty scar, that. What happened?"

"Uh . . . it's nothing . . . just an accident."

Molly removed his hand, then started toward another aisle. But not before Jeri Maxwell witnessed the scene. She was coming through the doorway and quickly came to where Molly and Greg were standing.

"Jeri, come meet Molly McCormick. Our new physician," Greg called out.

Jeri gave Molly a quick head-to-toe look as she approached them. Greg had told her the new physician appeared to be intelligent and perhaps a bit high strung. What he didn't tell her was how attractive the woman was, in spite of that scar on her temple.

"Molly. Yes, Greg told me he met you at the dock. Terrible tragedy. So sorry you had to be involved. You'd think the sheriff's office on the mainland would have enough employees to send someone over."

"Yes, but that didn't seem to be the case, so I suppose it was the best they could do."

"What brings you to our little shop? We have quite a supply of medications, etc. We do try to keep items our customers need. Or want."

"Just some antiseptic cream today."

"Of course. Just a sec." Jeri hurried to an aisle on the far side of the store. She returned with the cream in a bag and handed it to Molly.

"Here. This should do quite well. And, you know, I'll be happy to deliver anything you might need. You don't have to trouble yourself to come by here. I know you'll be one busy physician as soon as everyone knows you're available. And, speaking of that, have you established your office yet?"

"No. Not yet. I'm scouting the island, looking for a place. But I haven't had much time to find one yet."

Jeri took her arm and escorted her to the front door. "Thanks for coming by. I'm so glad to meet you. Don't worry about payment. We'll send you an invoice. See you soon."

Molly was relieved to return to the golf cart and her companion. She patted his head, "Ensign, you're better company than most people."

Chapter 35

Casper and Bear pushed the *Admiral's Lady* hard. Needed to get to the waters off Cuba as soon as possible. With the calm waters they made good time, but shortly they would have to cease such and engage in activities that required other skills. And between the two they had an abundance.

"Casper, it irks the crap out of me, having a Navy SEAL help with this operation. And why did Kennedy think we needed a new branch, these SEALS? What was wrong with frogmen? Like us?"

"These fellas are exceptional, Bear. Their training is even more difficult that what you and I went through. And, from what I've read, these guys are highly intelligent as well. Not just a bunch of hard bodies with no brains. And their equipment is first-rate. Underwater guns and attack rifles. Unbelievable stuff."

"Well, our weapons have served us pretty well. We also have underwater guns, dive knives, and spearguns. Think I'll stick to those."

"Yeah, but I might like to check out these new weapons . . . you know. Just to understand what they're capable of doing. In case we might need to use one sometime."

"Casper, let me remind you. This is our last mission. The very last."

"Right. It is. The SEALs have the latest weapons, but what we have that they don't is years of experience. And our intelligence officer training. So, sometimes age is an asset, Bear."

"Yeah, SEALs, frogmen. Whatever. But you know I can't be much help to you with this bum knee. I'm not sure surgery helped at all. Blasted thing still aches and I couldn't run if a bear was after my ass. Keeping my *Lady* waiting offshore is easy enough, but if you should get into any tight situations, let us say, I may not be of much use to you."

"No worries, Bear. We've conducted a number of operations just like this one. You keep our transport ready and Lt. Carrington and I'll return before you know it. From my experience with the rebels that worked with Crab, I don't think these guys are the sharpest foes we've ever faced. All I need to do is get a first-hand look inside one of those missile launch hatches and take some photos. That's all."

"Yeah, and you need to remember Drifter's instructions . . . just get the photos and get the hell out of there. No heroics, Casper."

"I remember. And that SEAL will be a great asset. He can stand watch as I move inside. Drifter's gonna keep in touch on the radio. So, it's not like we're without assistance if we need it. He's promised there will be several "fishing boats" in the area . . . and the fishermen will be navy types with plenty of firepower."

"Then, if one SEAL is joining us, why the hell didn't Admiral Whitmore just send several SEALS instead of two old fossils like us?"

"Well, there are only two SEAL groups as yet. Kenney commissioned them in January. And with the conflicts brewing in South Vietnam, Yemen and Central America, there aren't enough SEALs to cover all necessary sites. That's why they called on us. And, Bear, we can still play a necessary part. Plus, thanks to Solana, my Spanish is probably better than what most folks speak. Could be useful if I should encounter a watchman.

"And, if needed, these fishermen will provide a diversion so that Carrington and I will be able to slip in and out unnoticed. At least that's the plan. And once we get the photos, we'll return. Then you and I'll beat it back to Cayo Canna."

"Sounds a bit iffy to me," grumbled Bear.

Casper continued, "The fishermen will have orders to carry out long after you and I have disappeared. So, keep the volume up on the radio, listen for Drifter, and be ready to pick us up when we give you the signal."

"Yeah, yeah, Casper. I know we've done this before. But we were a bit younger then. And I didn't have a damn useless knee!"

Casper went below to retrieve his underwater gear. Bear turned to the radio to check the volume, to be sure he would hear it. When he turned back to the helm, he was struck in the face by a blinding light that had him raising his arms in defense and forcing him to close his eyes.

"Holy shit!" he yelled as he reached for his 9mm Sig Saur which was always strapped to his side. "What the hell . . ."

A loud, firm voice called out, "Hold, Admiral, sir. Just a SEAL coming up for air. Lieutenant Jim Carrington. Reporting in."

Bear let out a deep sigh, "Jesus, Carrington. You just about gave me a heart attack!"

"Sorry, sir. Just doing my job. Reporting as per my orders. I was told to assist Captain McCormick and Admiral Bowen. Didn't mean to upset anyone, but sneaking in is what I do best."

"Yeah, well, you did that alright. But, now you're here, let's get a few things straight . . . like not shining your beam in my face again. Just send a radio message. Or something like that."

"Aye, sir. No more bright beams," grinned the lieutenant as he held onto the swim platform at the stern of the boat, with only his head sticking out of the water.

Bear didn't know whether to be relieved or scared. Where had the SEAL come from? Bear never heard nor saw a fishing boat. He had to admit it looked like these guys were top notch. Even so, he felt uneasy. Finally, he lifted his night binoculars. There, some fifty yards off his port bow, were three small fishing boats. That looked exactly like so many others fishing off the coast of Cuba.

Casper came topside, dressed in his frog gear. He also had a special underwater camera, the latest toy the Navy used for taking pictures underwater or otherwise. It was so small it fit inside his dive belt. The same belt that also held his 12-inch diving knife, and a special Navy issue underwater pistol . . . both of which had come in handy when dealing with Crab on the night of his demise. And, as always, his speargun was attached tightly to his left side. That was a lethal weapon when it needed to be.

Adrenaline flooded his system and he was itching to get this assignment underway. He had to admit he was pleased to have a SEAL going alongside. Most times he preferred to act alone, but a SEAL wasn't just another helper. He was someone who knew what he was doing.

Then Bear began with his usual questions, "Casper, you got your camera? Your knife? What about your speargun? If you should get caught, you'll need them."

Casper sighed, "Bear. Relax. You can't see a ghost. If you can't see him, then you can't catch him."

Bear turned to the cockpit. "Yeah, but let me check water depth and winds." He looked at the instrument panel, then turned to Casper, "Water depth here is . . ."

He looked about. Carrington and Casper were nowhere in sight.

Just gone. Both had disappeared without a sound. Into the inky darkness of the night. Like a couple of eels slithering through the water. And Bear was left staring out into a dark ocean.

"Damned old fool. You never think we're beyond carrying out a black ops. Hope you're right."

Less than three minutes later, Bear's radio came to life. He hurried over to answer it, hoping the "fishermen" and Drifter were checking in with him.

Chapter 36

Officiating at a mass for the deceased was part of any priest's duties. And Patrick had officiated at a number of masses for his deceased parishioners. But never had he had to say final words over a friend. A very dear friend. It was most difficult. Even so, he'd been honored to do so. And now, the group at The Druid's Fountain were giving Angus a sendoff unlike any Patrick had ever seen. Angus wouldn't have missed it for the world!

It seemed everyone in the pub wanted—or needed—to say a few words about how they met Angus and what an influence he'd had on their lives. Patrick himself refrained from making any comments. He didn't have a need to share his experiences with Angus. He'd keep his memories within and visit them frequently.

If it hadn't been for Angus, Patrick may well have gone the way of many young lads in Ireland during that time . . . toward a life of delinquency and trouble. His folks had given him guidance, but he chose not to listen and began hanging out with some less-than-desirable types and showed up at The Druids Fountain one day. Why Angus had chosen to mentor him was a question he would never know the answer to. Whatever the reason, Patrick sent a prayer of thanksgiving for this special man having come into his life. Angus had cared for him when Patrick was sure he was far from being worth caring for. If he ever wondered what a blessing truly was, he now knew.

And Angus was still caring for Patrick. Even from the grave. Patrick had met with Angus's solicitor and after a short conversation, understood what he already had figured out. Angus had left him his investments, his funds, and yes, an estate called Hawk's Nest.

In the style of a solicitor, Mr. MacDuff took a moment to read from a document he thought might be of assistance in Patrick understanding Angus's family.

"Sir Michael Alexander O'Neill, Angus's father, founded Hawk's Nest when Angus was but a lad himself. Sir Michael saw a need for a sanctuary for what he called 'those magnificent creatures that grace the sky.' He was an educated man, knighted by the Queen, (a difficult feat for an Irishman) and knew the history of raptors on the emerald isle. In the 1700 and 1800s, humans persecuted raptors extensively. The raptors were killed for sport because it was thought they preyed upon domestic chickens and ducks. This resulted in a massive reduction in all species of raptors on the island and outright extirpation of four species. Sir Michael took it upon himself to do his part in rectifying this situation. Thus, Hawk's Nest was his contribution to preserve the magnificent raptors."

Patrick shook his head as the solicitor explained this situation.

"But, *Sir* Michael? It's quite a feat to be knighted if you're an Irishman . . . but it does happen, apparently. I never knew Angus was so well connected. He never even talked about his father. He was just gone and Angus never mentioned him. As far as I knew, Angus made good investments and bought The Druid's Fountain years ago . . . from a fellow in Belfast as I recall."

"Aye. That would be like Angus. Kept his business to himself. But he was determined to have these papers drawn up, and that's where I come in. So, you are now sole proprietor of The Druid's Fountain and Hawk's Nest. Two very fine establishments I must say."

"Aye. Aye. And I know nothing about running either establishment. Jaysus, Mary and Joseph! What am I going to do?" That was a question he would utter many times in the next few days and weeks.

The solicitor spoke up then, "Angus knew what he was doing. He had all the confidence in the world in you, Patrick. Spoke of you often. So, my advice as an older solicitor is to enjoy your windfall. And put it to good use."

They shook hands and, having concluded the evening at the pub, Patrick headed to the Lime Kiln. He'd spend a few days with Mum and Da, but then what? They had listened without interruption as he told them his decision regarding leaving the priesthood. Da had only one comment:

"If the Almighty led you to that decision, then who are we to question it?"

That had been a couple of days ago, and now he was at his Mum's kitchen counter again, sipping his Jameson. He now had another situation to inform them of. His latest "windfall" as the solicitor had put it.

Da listened, then had a few words he felt needed to be said. "Then, lad, you've got some hard thinking to do. I've always heard that for those to whom much is given, often much is required."

"Aye. I think that's probably true," responded Patrick.

Mum kept stirring her stew, but finally put the wooden spoon down and came and took both Patrick's hands in hers.

"Patrick, you've lost a dear friend. One that will always be with you. But Angus would tell you to get on with your life. Live it to the fullest. Make every day count. And just because you've left the priesthood doesn't mean you don't still love the Almighty and he still loves you. You can still pray, my lad. And I will tell you to pray and follow your heart."

Patrick took another long swallow of Jameson. *Follow my heart. Do I dare do that? From past experience I know what the heart wants sometimes leads to unforeseen complications and may not necessarily be a smart decision.*

Chapter 37

Kathi wasn't surprised the lights were already on when she arrived at the morgue. That meant Dr. Strickland was already here, hard at work. Even though she knew he probably didn't leave here until late last night.

She went to the kitchen and poured herself a cup of coffee. Strong. Dark. She headed to David's office to see what he wanted her to work on first. There were so many issues that needed attention. Bodies still parked on slabs in coolers. Paperwork overflowing on desks. Unanswered phone messages.

She picked up the newspaper on the counter, reading as she scooted down the hall to the "inner sanctum" where she knew David would be. She called out as she moved along the corridor,

"This stuff has enough caffeine to make a corpse jump off the examining table. Shall I bring . . ." She stopped.

Yes, David was there. Sort of. It appeared he never went home last evening. Just fell asleep on the job as it were. Literally. Presently he was lying on one of the exam tables. As quiet as the bodies in the coolers. She rushed to his side and lay a hand on his forehead. But one thing was different than the other bodies. He wasn't cold. She could feel his body heat the moment she touched him. When he felt her hands on him, he greeted her. His voice barely audible. Then he started trying to give instructions.

"Kathi. You're here. Good."

"David! What's wrong?" She had never seen him in such a state. Straining to speak, trying to sit upright, but unable to.

"Not sure. But at this point I think you better call an ambulance. I don't think I can get off this table without help."

"David . . . you're burning up. How long have you been like this?'

"Not long . . . and Kathi, get this envelope to Dr. McCormick . .

.make sure she gets it today . . . tell her I haven't looked at the toxicology on her body on Cayo Canna . . . I'm just too tired to . . ." Then he drifted off into oblivion.

She called for an ambulance and stood by holding David's hand, knowing there was nothing more she could do. The EMTS were there shortly and had him on their stretcher in minutes.

"Hurry. Get him to the ER now. He needs help," cried Kathi. She debated going with them, but her duty was to keep the morgue going. There was still a lot she could do to move things along.

She hurried back to the table where she had found David. There was a large envelope lying on the table. He must have been lying on top of it. Must have been something he was working on before he passed out.

Attached to the envelope was a note to her, which didn't surprise her. He often wrote notes to her in case he was gone when she came to work. This one was rather short, but to the point. "Kathi, get these lab reports to Dr. Molly McCormick on Cayo Canna. The body over on the island had two fractured cervical vertebrae, but I'm just too tired to wade through the entire toxicology report . . . not feeling so well. See that she gets them STAT."

It was so unlike Dr. Strickland to not carefully comb through any report. If nothing else, that was an indication to Kathi that he was indeed sick. She was even more concerned now, but got about her work.

Mailing the lab reports will take several days. Come on, Kathi. You can be more resourceful than that.

She grabbed the envelope, hurried to her car, and made a beeline for the ferry dock. The ferry would leave this afternoon and have the envelope on Cayo Canna today. She would call Dr. McCormick and let her know to expect the report. That is if the phones were working. As it was, they were not working, so she instructed the ferry pilot to make sure the envelope was delivered to Dr. McCormick at the lighthouse and he agreed, since he would be going that way himself as he left the ferry for the evening.

She headed back to the morgue. But first, she stopped by the ER to check on David. The bodies in the morgue would still be there when she got back, and her X-Rays would still reveal the same results in a few hours as they would if she processed them now.

Getting information out of ER nurses wasn't the easiest task she'd ever had. They all knew Dr. Strickland and fell over each other trying to be at his bedside. At the moment, however, several physicians were standing around him, comparing observations and thoughts. They came to a most alarming conclusion. Dr. Strickland appeared to have the same symptoms as the four patients on the second floor.

Dr. Lloyd Massey—a rather gruff fellow but excellent emergency room physician—gave an order. And his orders were always followed without question.

"Nurse Jenkins, have Dr. Strickland placed in isolation on the second floor. Same as the other four. We may have an epidemic on our hands."

Kathi shoved her way through a throng of people and was close enough to hear that statement. She obviously wasn't going to be allowed to see him, so she returned to the morgue and sorted through his calendar and agenda log. She'd send her latest X-rays to the radiologists then file some papers that were piled on her desk. She hoped someone would call with a status report. But that might not be today.

Chapter 38

At their meeting in Washington D.C., Admiral Whitmore reported that aerial photos revealed activity around the missile hatches on Cuba. Hatches that must lead to underground storage of some kind. What was inside them? Maybe nothing. Or maybe something the Navy needed to know about. Either way, finding out what was in those hatches was Casper's assignment. The Admiral's actual words were, "Casper, get inside one of those holes, take some photos and report your findings. And do it ASAP. And, oh yeah, don't get caught."

Casper had spent hours poring over the many aerial photos and maps of the missile launch pads and hatches on Cuba. Which meant he had a good mental picture of the base and where he and the lieutenant needed to go. The aerial photos pinpointed the exact location of several launch pads that had hatches. His targets . . . or target. He decided to go to the hatch on the west periphery of the base . . . a bit away from the others that were located in a section of the base that was heavily guarded. He only needed to get inside one to get photos of the contents. In fact, if you hadn't looked closely, you wouldn't even know the hatch was there. It appeared to be at the edge of a marsh, camouflaged by sugarcane stalks and thick growths of mangrove swamps.

Taking a deep breath as he crawled ashore, Casper had to admit swimming from the *Admiral's Lady* to the island was a tad more taxing that it had been at one time. Getting onto the island and then the base meant getting past security guards, an electrified, concertina fence, and dodging search lights. None of which was particularly difficult for a seasoned intelligence spook and a Navy SEAL.

They snuck ashore in the darkness, stowed their underwater gear beneath a large mangrove close to the shore. They would need that gear for their return trip. They now had to make their way on foot and evade being caught by the roving security officers on watch.

As they began to make their way closer in, Lt. Carrington whispered in the darkness, "Damn! These sugarcane stalks cut like a razor!"

"Yep. But they do come in handy for "unwanted" visitors like us," said Casper.

Like all the islands in the Caribbean, Cuba had numerous species of palm trees. And tonight, Casper and Carrington were thankful for the trees and the sugarcane as they provided great cover which allowed the two of them to get within a few yards of several concrete buildings next to the hatch. The one Casper needed to get into. Captain Jack was the ranking officer, so he issued commands as he always had—with authority.

"These trees are good hiding places, lieutenant. Keep yourself hidden and be ready to take out anyone coming my way."

"Aye, Captain. Will do."

Then a rustling noise in the sugarcane had both men lifting weapons and standing back-to-back. The next moment a large, black animal made a loud, snorting noise and came running from within the sugarcane, scrambling past them as if he didn't know they were there.

"What the hell was that?" asked Lt. Carrington as he lowered his weapon.

"That would be a wild hog. Almost as many of those on the island as there are people. The Spanish brought them over when they conquered the island. Long time ago." But Lieutenant Carrington may not know the history of the island. Something Casper had made a point of learning.

Lieutenant Carrington was one of the very first Navy SEALs, an elite maritime military force designed to conduct unconventional warfare—a group established by President Kennedy. One group was based on the East Coast. In Little Creek, Virginia. And a second one was based on the West Coast, in San Diego, California. This assignment, stealing inside a military compound crawling with enemy combatants, was Carrington's first.

As they moved forward again, Lt. Carrington stopped abruptly, and turned to Casper.

"Did you hear that?"

"What? I didn't hear anything?"

"Something just squished under my foot."

Casper grinned in the darkness, "That would be *coquis*. Frogs." There are about fifteen or so species on the island. Harmless. But there

194

must be thousands of them here."

"Oh, great. Don't like snakes . . . or frogs. Slimy little bastards."

"Just ignore them. They're everywhere."

Casper laughed to himself. Here was a SEAL. A hard-as-rock man known to be able to kill a hundred ways and to have the mental fortitude to do so. But was afraid of snakes and frogs.

Casper needed to make his way closer to a concrete building some fifty yards away. Only problem was he would have to travel over an open field to get there. And the moon goddess must not have heard his prayers for a dark night. Normally he would have planned this escapade on a night when the moon wouldn't be so glowing as it was tonight. But he couldn't wait for the moon to accommodate him as Admiral Whitmore made a point of the urgency of this assignment.

"Lieutenant, stay here in the mangrove until I get across the yard. Then join me if the coast is clear. Just watch for the security guards. My plan is to be in and out without anyone knowing we were ever here—but take the guards out if you must." When on assignment, Casper was *all* Navy Intelligence Officer.

Casper patiently squatted beneath three palm trees. Getting his bearings. Then he darted across the field, quiet as the ghost he was. Finally, he flattened himself against a wall behind a large metal container—a large box-like affair that had a noisy engine running.

I'll take that as a good omen. Finding a large, noisy box to hide behind.

But even before he completed that thought, he heard voices. Voices getting nearer and nearer his position behind the metal box. Two men appeared shortly. Both were tall, one thin and the other rather large about the middle section—both wearing olive-drab uniforms and carrying automatic weapons. Security guards making rounds. The two stopped in front of the metal box behind which Casper was standing. Holding his breath at the moment.

The tall, thin guard reached inside his jacket and removed a flask . . . then took a long swig and handed it to his fellow guard. The two talked for a couple of minutes, both took another swig and then, following an exchange of laughter, moved on.

Carrington's young. Hope he doesn't get trigger happy, but he might have to take these guys out.

Casper couldn't hear everything the guards said, but heard enough to tell they'd been partaking of that flask for some time how. Which rather surprised him. The Cuban Missile Crisis was over weeks ago, but he would have expected Castro to still have competent men guarding

195

the base. Maybe because this hatch was so far away from the center of the activity it wasn't too much of a concern. A couple of moments later, the guards moved on and Casper breathed a sigh of relief.

So far so good.

He moved slightly to his right in an effort to reach a doorway a few yards away. The hatches were difficult to see even in the daytime as they were camouflaged to be the same color as the ground in which they were placed. And these hatches had large lids that Casper knew would be difficult to lift.

Just as he bent down and grasped the handle on the hatch, the engine on the large metal box began an erratic humming noise, skipped a few beats, then sputtered and came to a complete stop. No longer producing the noise that was providing cover for him.

Guess that was too good to last very long.

As he expected, opening the hatch—which was much larger and heavier than he would have thought–was extremely difficult. The handle was covered with a slightly sticky substance and as Casper lifted with both hands, the hatch slipped from his grip, slamming shut. Of course, the noise it made was a rather loud, clanging sound of metal on metal.

Damned arthritis! Never know when my fingers are gonna let me down.

He waited a moment and listened. Total quiet. Believing all was well, he tried once again to lift the hatch. The next moment he heard running of feet. Apparently, the clanging had been heard and someone was coming to investigate.

Casper hurried back to his secluded place behind the machine, praying he hadn't been spotted. But, as he well knew, even the best of plans often go awry. Any experienced intelligence officer knew that. And he'd learned long ago that learning to get out of a compromising situation was the real key to being a successful spy.

"Did you see anyone?" A security guard called out to a second guard as they hurried past the metal container, weapons held at the ready. The security guards had heard the noise, but apparently did not see Casper as he again took refuge behind the machine.

"No, I didn't see anyone. It's probably nothing. If we report a noise, we'll spend the whole damn night chasing ghosts. Let's walk the perimeter again. Our watch is over in a few minutes. If there is anyone close, the flood lights will show us where they are.

"This situation with America, Kennedy, and Russia has had all of us on alert for weeks now. But that's over. We don't need to jump every time we hear the slightest noise. Come on. Let's head back to the barracks. We get off duty shortly. Maybe we can sneak a couple of cervezas from the cantina."

The guards spoke Spanish, which was fine with Casper as his Spanish was more than adequate, thanks to Solana who corrected him when he made a linguistic mistake. He was expecting the guards to be Russian, but not so. He'd learned a smattering of that language long ago, but whatever he knew back then was what he called "fugitive information" today.

As soon as the guards were a distance away, Casper was on his knees. If he could get inside for a quick minute, he could get his photos and be back in the water with Carrington.

With the guards moving along at a fast pace, Casper went back to his task. This time he pulled the hatch cover slightly to the side, rather than lifting it. That appeared to be the proper way to open it as it slid along with ease.

He climbed inside the hatch and stood for a few moments, allowing his eyes to adjust. Then he switched on his flashlight. The room was immense. It was an underground storage bunker half the size of a football field.

"What the hell? This is unbelievable!"

When his shocked brain finally registered what he saw, Casper closed his eyes as if he no longer wanted to see what was in front on him. Then he bent his head for a moment . . . as though a quick prayer must be needed.

God help us. The nightmare is not over.

It only took a few minutes to get oriented to the scene before him—the scene he wished were not true. A stash of weapons . . . tactical nuclear weapons . . . stacked carefully from floor to ceiling filled the gigantic room. It was nothing short of an arsenal.

He quickly identified short-range missiles, artillery shells, land mines, depth charges, and torpedoes . . . all of which were equipped with nuclear warheads. There were others he couldn't readily identify, but he had no doubt they were as lethal as the others.

The aerial photos he had seen in D.C. had been taken sometime earlier, about November 6. According to intel from Washington, the agreement between Kennedy and Kruschev called for all nuclear weapons to be removed and returned to Russia "within a few days" following the conclusion of their negotiations. Early in their negotiations, Kennedy had placed a naval blockade—a ring of ships—

around Cuba. The aim of this quarantine was to prevent the Soviets from bringing in more military supplies.

The most recent photos that Casper viewed showed missiles being removed, sites being destroyed and dozens of Russian seamen scurrying about loading guidance packages, launching equipment and dozens of crates of carbines, handguns, and ammunition. Three Russian ships, Arkhangelsk, Indigirka, and Aleksandrovsk, were loaded between October 30 and November 3, which was in compliance with the agreement. Subsequently, Kennedy had removed the quarantine on November 20 after witnessing the Russian ships being loaded and missile sites being removed.

But today is November 28, and this stash of nukes is still on the island. Which means we are nowhere near being finished with this crisis. Jesus, we've got to get back ASAP. Every second counts.

Casper took a number of photos, scanned the room once more, then made a decision. A decision he would question more than once later.

I'll report my findings to Admiral Whitmore ASAP. But I'll keep knowledge of these weapons to myself. No point in telling Molly or Solana what I've discovered. Sometimes ignorance is better than knowledge.

Castro, you arrogant, ignorant bastard! You apparently have no concern for your own people nor any others either. And my gut tells me you never intended to send all the nukes back to Russia. Thought you would keep a few for future use? Thought the U.S. wouldn't know? Well, Señor, this ghost will haunt you and change your plans.

There was no need then to penetrate another hatch. No matter what was in them, there was enough weaponry in this one underground warehouse to annihilate anything and anyone within 1000 miles of the island.

Casper killed his light and climbed back out of the hatch. Hoping Carrington was close by. As he closed the hatch he stepped down to the ground and headed for the metal box where he could hide again. A couple of seconds later, he heard a squishing sound followed by a whispered "damn frogs!" Carrington was waiting for him behind the box.

"And? What did you see, Casper?" Carrington asked as he cowered behind the box.

Casper took a deep breath, "There are enough nukes in that underground facility to destroy this island, Florida, and most of the East Coast as well. Always thought Castro was a madman. This proves

198

it. He would sacrifice his own people to wipe out anyone who opposes him."

Carrington sighed, "Then I presume we better get moving. This mission has turned into a most important black ops operation. Never thought I'd be involved in anything of this magnitude so early in my career. Which could be a short one if this issue isn't resolved."

"Lieutenant, this is information only you and I will know about. You can't even tell your fellow SEALs. Admiral Whitmore will know what we know as soon as I get back aboard the *Admiral's Lady*. She's got equipment that allows us access to the Admiral when needed. You'll find keeping secrets is part of your job. Learn to do it well. It might just save lives."

"Yessir, Captain. Understood. You go first now. I'll follow up behind you. But I'll be glad to leave this blasted frog-infested island."

Casper nodded and hurried across the open space back to the mangrove on the marsh. As he reached for his underwater gear, however, he heard a short scream, then silence. Then, one moment later, another short scream. Then silence again.

Two screams. The same two guards returning?

A couple of minutes later he felt a hand on his shoulder. Standing perfectly still, he waited . . . then rapidly turned with his 12-inch diver's knife pointed at whomever had tapped him.

Even in the dark he could see Carrington's white teeth grinning back at him.

"Jesus, Carrington! That's a good way to take an early trip to your next life."

"Sorry, sir. Didn't think coming to your front would be very smart. I've seen how quickly you draw that Sig."

"So, what happened back there? I heard two short screams, but nothing more."

"Well, sir, two guards started following you as you made your way across the open space. So, I just gave them both a tap on the head. One that will keep them unconscious and out of commission for a number of hours. Didn't think it was necessary to permanently do away with them as they appeared to be extremely inebriated as it was. They could barely stand. Either of them."

Casper nodded, "Probably the same two I saw earlier. My bet is they'll be reluctant to report seeing anyone. If they even remember the event. If they do report seeing us, they would probably be accused of neglect in performing their duty and be subjected to some unpleasant consequences, shall we say. But I agree. No need to cause more trouble than necessary. As I said, get in, get out, and leave no trace of your having been there."

Carrington took a step back from the Captain then and in the process found another "slimy bastard" beneath his right foot. He wiped the ground with his boot and uttered what sounded like a groan.

"Can we go now, Captain? I have squished at least a dozen of these "*coquí*" critters tonight."

Casper laughed. "I do believe you have just earned your military moniker. It fits."

"Sir? I know you are called Casper. . . a ghost . . . something about you being able to go in and out of a combatant's place without being seen. Which I have just witnessed."

"That's right."

"So just what did you have in mind for me . . . sir?"

"Oh, that's easy. You'll be "*Coquí.*" Fits in more ways than one!" laughed Casper.

Carrington shook his head. "Let's get out of here . . . sir."

They put on their gear and began to crawl through the mangroves to the edge of the water. They'd been able to avoid that infernal searchlight so far. No need to get spotted now. As they entered the water, Carrington stood for a brief moment, trying to get his mask situated properly. At that juncture, two bullets zipped past him and entered the water near his legs. Then a third one found its target.

"Holy shit!" he groaned as he grabbed his thigh which began to ooze sticky, warm blood.

"Come on, lieutenant. Move it!" yelled the Captain as he shoved Carrington farther into the water. He came up behind him as several more bullets came screaming across the water in their direction.

"Move your ass, Carington! We gotta get in deeper water. That search light only shines about a hundred feet out. We can be gone before it makes another round in our direction."

Carrington gave a thumbs up and both men were out of sight in seconds. After a couple of minutes passed, Casper surfaced and looked over to see Carrington who had just surfaced himself.

"What's your status, Carrington?"

"Caught one in the left thigh, sir."

"I assume that fishing boat I see fifty yards ahead of us is your mates?"

"Yessir. I signaled them already. They're waiting for me."

"Can you make it that far?"

"Yessir. Can do. We've got a medic on board. He'll fix me up."

Casper sighed, "Damn sorry this happened, Lt. I've had a couple of incidents over the years. Nothing to stop me, though. If you're sure, then I'll head on out. Bear Bowen will be waiting for my signal."

"Yessir. It's been a pleasure working with you, sir. Hope we meet again."

"Oh, I feel sure we will, *Coqui*."

They went their separate ways then. In a matter of moments Casper saw a quick blink of light coming from the fishing boat. Carrington had made it aboard. Then, after a few minutes swimming at a brisk pace, Casper spotted the *Admiral's Lady*. Just where he left her. When he got a bit closer, he signaled he was at her stern and Bear came back to help him aboard.

Casper tossed his fins up first, then his mask and snorkel, and finally he pulled himself up. Slowly.

Bear was relieved Casper had returned from this insane mission. But that relief was short lived when he saw his mate struggling to get aboard. Since when did boarding become difficult?

"Casper?"

"No theatrics, Bear. Bring me the medical kit. Just a flesh wound. Need to clean it and then make my report to Admiral Whitmore. And we need to let Drifter know our status."

"What the hell? Where is this flesh wound, you damned old fool! Still think you can do what you did at thirty!"

Bear helped Casper to a seat and brought a towel to lay his leg on. "Jack. Listen to me. This is not just a flesh wound. There's too much blood flowing for that. We gotta get you back to the lighthouse. Molly will need to attend this."

"No, Bear. First things first. We gotta call Whitmore and report what I found."

"What did you find?"

"In a few words, Castro is holding enough nukes to wipe Cuba, Florida, and most of the East Coast off the map."

"Damn his sorry ass!"

Once again, the equipment on the *Admiral's Lady* was a key element in this operation. They radioed Admiral Whitmore and Jack made his report. Whitmore instructed them to keep all knowledge to themselves, which wasn't necessary. These old seadogs knew exactly what they should and shouldn't go in a situation like this.

Admiral Whitmore spoke quickly, "Jack, Ted, your country is in your debt. I'll be in touch. Meanwhile, stay tuned. May need to call on you again."

The call to Drifter, whose ship was somewhere out in the Caribbean Ocean, close to Cuba, was short. To the point. "Drifter, Castro's one crazy bastard. He's got a hatch full of nuclear weapons. Bear and I have reported our findings to Admiral Whitmore. We're depending on you guys from here. Over and out."

Drifter responded, "Message received. We're here and ready for whatever the Admiral needs. Out now."

Jack saw no reason to report any difficulties to the Admiral. Some things were not as important as others. After they disconnected with Whitmore, Bear put a second tourniquet on Jack's wound, then took his place at the helm.

"Hold on, Casper, we're headed to Cayo Canna. And we're gonna be flying."

Chapter 39

As Molly began to pull away from The Island Pharmacy, she stopped when she saw the ferry captain, Skip Lawrence, waving to her as he pulled up next to her in his golf cart.

"A moment, Dr. Mac?" he yelled. Molly halted, then waited as he hurried over.

"I've got an envelope for you. The woman said it was from Dr. Strickland. Said you would know who he is. Must be important. Said it was urgent that I get it to you today."

"Yes, I know Dr. Strickland," she said and reached out as Skip handed her the envelope.

"Then, I'm off. Meeting a couple of fellas at Timmy's Nook. It's prayer meeting night. Hope to play a few hands of poker," he smiled and sped away.

Molly opened the envelope and read: Autopsy Report, Lee County, Fort Myers, Florida. Deceased: Gillian Hartwell.

"Oh. Good. Maybe David found something that'll help me with this blasted investigation.

She tore into the envelope and glanced at the report, looking specifically for the "cause of death." David had performed all the required toxicology tests, drug screen, pharmacological report, diagnosis of diseases by examination of body fluids and tissues, as well as hair samples. All items she would have expected in the report.

But, in the block where the cause of death would be indicated, he had hand-written a note that stated: Most *probable* cause of death: Two fractured cervical vertebrae."

Then he had written a personal note in pencil: "Molly, I didn't get to complete the . . ." and then the sentence stopped. This was confusing. That David didn't complete the report. Particularly one that involved a possible murder?

What did he not complete? Was it something important? Something I need to know? Doesn't sound like the David I know.

She reached over and began to rub Ensign's head while her brain whirred at high speed. *"Ensign, something is bothering me, but I'm not sure what. What was it that David didn't complete?*

She chewed on her thumbnail . . . a habit of long standing when trying to solve a problem.

If I were having difficulty figuring out what is going on with a patient, I'd start over. Do another head-to-toe examination and work from there. Maybe that's what I should do with this investigation. Start from the beginning and work from there. Papa's not here so I've got to figure this out myself. And David must still be swamped with cases, or he'd be here. So, he can't help.

"Looks like you and I are on our own, pal. All right then. Let's start at the beginning. The scene of the crime."

With that she started the golf cart and headed to the dock where Gillian's body had been found. Crime scene tape was still in place and presently there were no gawkers as there had been when she made her initial investigation.

Carefully walking about the perimeter marked by the tape, she recalled taking various photos of a very large footprint . . . probably size twelve . . . which she was sure belonged to Deputy Harrison. She remembered retrieving a small bit of paper and placing it in a bag, along with a hairclip. For a moment she tried to imagine how this woman, or any woman, could have gotten beneath the dock.

Surely she wouldn't have crawled under there . . . had to have been placed there by someone. She was a petite woman, but still it would have been difficult to place her body under the dock. Perhaps whoever she left Timmy's Nook with put her there? If so, why isn't there another set of footprints? All I found were those made by Sassy and Wesley. And none by shoes with spike heels like the ones Gillian was wearing. So, did someone attack her and then place her under the dock? If so, why aren't there are prints to show she was dragged or carried?

She walked around the tape to the opposite of the dock to see the view from that angle. And, as she recalled on her first visit, there were no prints on this side of the dock, other than those made by the deputy.

So, if there are no prints on this side either, then again, how did the body get there?

She then walked a few feet beyond the dock, to the well-worn path leading to the Sandpiper. Presumably the path Gillian would have used to get to Seagull Cottage. She saw a line of shrubs planted several feet from the walls of the hotel.

That's interesting. The space between the tall shrubs and the walls of the hotel is quite large. It could have easily been a place the body could have been stashed and later placed beneath the dock.

She got on her hands and knees and within minutes discovered a most important fact she had overlooked earlier. Like the area on each side of the dock, this area behind the shrubs was very clean. No leaves, no palm fronds, no debris. It was perfectly clean and —most interesting to Molly—she could see streaks in the sand where the gardener had raked the area. Raking was a crucial part of the gardeners daily routines at all the hotels on Cayo Canna as they were noted for their pristine appearance. That meant gardeners were forever keeping the grounds in tiptop shape.

So, any prints of a body being dragged would have been raked over very early the morning that I carried out my investigation. Erased before I got here. Oh, Molly! Why didn't you think of that? What a mess you have made of this whole investigation. David will rue the day he met you.

She walked farther down toward the water, which she had not done at her initial investigation either. However, Deputy Harrison had apparently thought he should cordon off the access to the beach at this area, so had extended his tape to include the beach front. At the juncture where the dock had collapsed years ago.

Now she stopped abruptly. Just beyond the edge of the tape along the waterfront was a set of prints . . . certainly made by a woman as they were small . . . and very different from the prints made by Wesley and Sassy. But then, a day had passed. These prints could have been made since that time. And one other new find brought a smile to her face: a tiny pair of pink flipflops which she was sure belonged to Wesley.

What? How did I miss that? Why didn't I think to walk down closer to the water where the dock had collapsed? And these small shoes were flat . . . not spike heels like those worn by Gillian. So . . . female . . . or perhaps small male, wearing flat shoes? But many people walk the beach daily. These prints could be from anyone . . . not necessarily anyone connected with this horrendous event. And the prints stop at the edge of the dilapidated part of the dock. Did the person step up on the dock even though it would have been dangerous to do so? Or did they just move on down the beach?

After walking the entire perimeter once again, Molly made one last inspection of the grounds behind the shrubs next to the walls. But this time, she pulled back the lower limbs on one of the bushy Coontie shrubs. When she did, she was so flabbergasted she opened her mouth to say something. But nothing came out.

It appeared that the gardener doing the raking in this area did not rake beneath this particular shrub, which meant several clearly defined footprints—that looked just like the size twelves she found during the first investigation—were easily seen. Plus, prints of small shoes . . . with spike heels . . . were right there next to the large prints.

But look how close the prints are. They're toe to toe. Facing each other. Could they have been embracing?

The prints of the small shoes with spike heels were directly in front of the large prints. So close Molly felt sure her thoughts were correct. This couple was embracing. And closer inspection showed a small area where the sand was pushed up against the Coontie shrub.

But pushed up by what?

She got down on her knees then and pulled another Coontie limb back.

Oh, good heavens! How could I have been so stupid?

Laying close to the base of the shrub, partially covered with sand, a heavy gold chain sparkled . . . and next to it lay a small, black evening bag . . . one a woman would have used for an evening out. Molly's mind spun in circles for a moment.

Where have I recently seen chains similar to this? Too heavy for a woman. Had to belong to a man. Oh, think Molly! Think!

She placed the gold chain—which was broken—and the evening bag in a plastic bag, then took several photos of the Coontie shrub, the marks made by a rake, and the shoe prints. She then looked behind several more Coontie shrubs. But found nothing more. With this new information, however, she was even more confused.

At the first investigation she noted two large footprints . . . roughly size twelve . . . which she assumed to be Deputy Harrison forgetting where his feet were. Then smaller prints. And even very small ones. She'd learned that these smaller prints were made by Sassy and Wesley. Now she had discovered several more large prints beneath the shrub . . . and they looked exactly like the large prints at the scene. Maybe those large prints weren't made by Deputy Harrisons after all.

Oh, Molly, you have just flunked the first test of Private Investigator and Papa Jack will hang you by your toes. That is if David doesn't beat him to it.

She took one last walk around the perimeter of the crime scene and was at a loss as to what to do now. If David were here she would just fess up and tell him what a mess she'd made. But he wasn't, and neither was Papa Jack.

As if sensing Molly's distress, Ensign loped over and stood next to her, offering a quick, wet lick to her hand, then leaning into her with his warm body.

Molly had been tutored by the best teacher, Papa Jack, and his words of wisdom often echoed in her head. "Molly Mac, never quit on anything that's important to you. You can learn from many teachers, but ultimately how your life turns out will be determined by your decisions and your commitment to making it what you want it to be. Give it all you've got, my girl."

She knew exactly what Papa Jack would do were he in her shoes. With that thought still ringing in her head, she started home. She'd go to Papa Jack's lantern room in the lighthouse and stare out over that great Gulf and figure out her next steps. Papa always swore you'd find answers to most dilemmas if you stared at the Gulf long enough. And, to her thinking, she didn't need to take steps. She needed to take leaps. It was time to make some sense of this senseless situation. She sat quietly, making mental notes to herself.

So, the footprints down on the area closer to the water were made by a woman, but that could have been anyone coming from the beach. But I have trouble thinking a woman could have dragged Gillian's body beneath the dock. Perhaps Gillian's friend, Debra, had accompanied her to the hotel. But according to Sean Feherty at The Temptation, Debra left Timmy's alone and someone saw Gillian leave Timmy's with a young man . . . not sure who it was . . . and apparently Gillian is acquainted with Will Johnson, the bartender at Timmy's . . . seems he's a friend of her daughter.

Okay. So perhaps Gillian took a young man back to the hotel with her? But, if so, then why wouldn't they have gone into the cottage? Why would they go to the dock? Okay.

Let's look at another angle. The autopsy report. David states probable cause of death as "fractures of cervical vertebrae." I recall there was a cut on her neck, but very little bleeding, and a slightly swollen forehead. There were no defensive wounds, no broken fingernails, no torn clothing. But one rhinestone hairclip was laying in the sand, and one pearl earring was missing. Does that mean there was some kind of altercation? Or disagreement?

She stared out at the Gulf, which was now spouting white caps and bringing in clumps of seaweed with each wave. The many moods of the Gulf were so interesting. Sometimes it was smooth as a porcelain vase, then in a matter of hours, it could bring angry waves crashing onto the shore.

I've never been so lost as to what to do next. Think I'll head back to the lighthouse and climb that infernal spiral staircase to the lantern room. Maybe what Papa Jack says is right. Maybe if I stare at the water long enough, I'll come up with some kind of plan for what step to take next.

Ensign stood in his seat, his tail switching back and forth. Molly patted his head, sat for a moment, then stretched her arms over the steering wheel and rested her head on them. Ensign whimpered as though he shared Molly's feelings of despair.

Chapter 40

If I never travel on another damn plane, it'll be too soon! Some people sleep the entire trip when flying across the ocean. I've never developed that particular skill. It's six hours into the trip and I'm counting the minutes 'til we land. At least today I'm not headed to Boston. That part of my life is over.

The plane ride from Ireland to America was nerve-racking as always. Patrick's ultimate destination would be Miami, Florida. From there he would rent a car and drive to Fort Myers. Finally, he would catch the ferry, the *Calypso*, to Cayo Canna.

He was aware his anxiety wasn't coming entirely from the flying. Some of it came from wondering exactly why he was returning to the island. No, that's not correct. He knew why he was returning, just didn't know if returning was a good idea. As with most of his decisions of late, he struggled with this one as well.

But his decision to leave the priesthood was a decision he was at peace with. Having done that, there were so many more decisions to be made that he hardly knew where to start. Leaving one life behind meant starting a new one somehow, somewhere.

The last few days in Ireland were spent arranging for the workers at the Druid's Fountain to meet with him so he could explain the new arrangements for the pub. The new lass Angus had hired, Grace, agreed to keep things functioning and he promised he'd keep in touch.

The Hawk's Nest was presently being cared for by a young couple from Belfast. Patrick explained to them what had transpired regarding his being the new owner. The couple agreed to stay on as care keepers until such time as Patrick could decide what he ultimately would do with the sanctuary.

Not knowing what would happen tomorrow was a new experience for Patrick. He'd been accustomed to a routine schedule for some time. Until he went to Cayo Canna. There he'd had the freedom to walk the beach, visit with Jack McCormick, swim in the lagoon . . . and talk with Molly.

Molly was at the top of his list of reasons to return. But would she welcome him? Or, would she wonder why he had come back? Surely, she must have sensed his attraction to her. But, then, during the time he was on Cayo Canna Molly was in the middle of a personal crisis. Her days were spent wondering if Sam, the crazed patient who had attacked her in Baltimore, would find her again. And, as promised, he did.

Of course, Patrick also recalled he had played a crucial part in saving Molly's life when that deranged imbecile tried to kill her in the lighthouse. She had shot and stabbed the fiend, but Patrick stepped in and finished the lunatic off with a shot to his head.

All these memories ran through his mind, and he still came to the same conclusion. He spoke aloud, as if to confirm his decision once again. "Yes, that was exactly what needed to be done. Taking a life is not something I wish to ever do, but in this case, there was no choice. At least that issue has been put to rest. Maybe now she can move forward."

He tried to relax by reading the latest novel by James Michener, *Hawaii.* After he reread the first paragraph for the third time, he put the book down knowing it was useless to try to read when his brain was on fire with questions. Questions for which he had no answers.

What will Molly think when I show up? Will Captain Jack understand my decision about leaving the church? And what will I do with myself once I'm there? What was it that Mum and Da advised? Oh yeah, 'do some hard thinking, pray, and follow your heart.'

Simple. Right. Jaysus, Mary and St. Joseph!

Chapter 41

Molly hurried across the small porch at the lighthouse. Solana's sandals were in their accustomed place, next to the entry, an idiosyncrasy that Molly always found amusing.

When she first arrived at the lighthouse a couple of months ago, she'd asked, "Solana, why do you leave your shoes on the porch and go about barefoot?"

Solana smiled and said, "Oh, just something my *abuela* told me when I was a small girl. She said, 'Solana, never wear shoes in a house. Your feet have great powers. They can sense the soul of the house and you'll always know if something is wrong. Or, if something is pleasing to the house.'"

"And do you think that works? Do the soles of your feet tell you anything?" Molly grinned as she asked.

Solana gave a small smile, "Oh, *abuela* was a bit of a character. She was full of life and understood many things others do not. She often knew when something bad was going to happen. She once said to me, 'One day our homeland, our Cuba, will be ruled by an evil man,' and we can see her prediction was correct.

"But, as for my feet talking to me, I will tell you that the first time I entered this lighthouse, the soles of my feet tingled and I sensed this was a place of refuge. A sanctuary of sorts. And, I believe *abuela* had a gift only a few people are given. It's not for me to question."

Today, Molly didn't have time to engage in such discussions. Today she called out as she entered, "Solana! I'm home."

There was no response, so she knew Solana was probably over in Keeper's Cottage tidying up. She forbade Molly to do any cleaning in the cottage. Taking care of Captain Jack, his lighthouse, and Keeper's Cottage was her domain and she refused to share it.

Molly scampered up the spiral stairs with Ensign at her heels. She sat at Papa's desk, then laid the broken gold chain and the black evening bag on it. And looked out at the Gulf. But at this time, it didn't offer any suggestions or solutions to her issues.

So now what? This gold chain is an important piece of evidence. And the prints look as if two people were standing very close . . . perhaps embracing. And the black evening bag? Maybe I should ask Debra to take a look at it to see if it belonged to Gillian? But it might be that the chain and the bag have absolutely nothing to do with Gillian's death. Good heavens. What a mess!

Papa told me to question anyone involved with Gillian from the time she arrived on the island to the last time she was seen. So, I think I'll follow up once again on the "gossip" I learned from Sean Feherty at the Temptation . . . about Gillian having been seen leaving Timmy's Nook with Will Johnson, the bartender, or someone else? Maybe. But when I talked with Antonio Carlucci at the Sandpiper, he said Gillian came in about 1:30 a.m. . . . .and he might have seen a man outside the door as she left the lobby and walked outside.

Maybe he's remembered something since I talked with him. Gillian would have had to walk past the front door of the hotel to get to the path leading to her cottage. Someone has to know something. Then I'll call Debra and ask about the black evening bag. Although I really dislike having to disturb her again. She appeared to be struggling with this whole ordeal. As anyone would.

Down the spiral staircase she dashed, with Ensign bounding down also. Ready for their next adventure.

"Solana! Be back later," she yelled as she hurried out the door.

Once again they were off, arriving at the Sandpiper in a few minutes. This hotel was quite a place, even though it didn't quite have the reputation the Gasparilla Inn did. Still, a very fine place to spend a few days when visiting Cayo Canna.

When she entered the lobby there was no one at the desk. She waited a moment then rang the small bell. In a moment Antonio showed up, smiling as he approached her.

"Ah, Dr. Mac. Two visits in a couple of days. What brings you to our hotel today?"

"Hello, Antonio. I'm sorry to bother you again. But I'm still trying to trace Ms. Hartwell's movements from the time she left Timmy's Nook and ultimately came here to your hotel. There has to be someone who knows something and if I keep asking questions, hopefully I'll get some answers that help me know what happened to her."

"Ah, yes, Ms. Hartwell. She was not the most pleasant guest we've ever had. But we try to accommodate to the best of our ability."

"So, tell me again, please, when did you last see her?"

"As I told you earlier, Ms. Hartwell returned to our hotel about 1:30 a.m. And again, I'm only revealing information about a guest because of the unusual circumstances we find ourselves in. That being the case, I should tell you she was stumbling along, barely able to walk. It would appear she had more alcohol than she could handle.

"She was slurring her words and it was difficult to understand what she needed, but I finally realized she was asking for a wake-up call. I informed her that we do not have phones in the cottages, but I would arrange for a bellhop to come to her cottage and awaken her. She was quite upset with that information, then stumbled out the door, heading to her cottage, I believe."

"But you mentioned a man standing outside the door. Is that correct?"

"Yes. It was dark, but I think there was a tall, thin man standing at the corner of the hotel. I cannot tell you who it was."

"And did he walk along with Ms. Hartwell when she left?"

"I don't know. As soon as she left I locked the door and continued with my duties, closing all drapes, making sure everything was in order for the next shift."

Antonio bent over to retrieve a coffee cup that had been left on the small table in the lobby. As he leaned forward, something shiny sparkled in the light coming in from the window. When Molly realized what was sending out such a dazzling light, she held her breath— unable to take another one.

Chains. Gold chains. He's wearing gold chains. But . . . no . . . that means he maybe . . . oh . . . not . . . no . . . maybe he's who I'm looking for . . . Oh, Jesus. I've got to get out of here!

Antonio picked up the cup, wiped the table with his cloth and then looked up at Molly. "That's all I can tell you, Dr. Mac."

"Yes. Yes. I see. Then I'll move on. And thank you."

With that she hurried out the door, grabbed the steering wheel of the golf cart with trembling hands and found herself hyperventilating . . . something she knew a lot about from textbooks, but had never experienced personally. She backed out of the parking lot and Ensign quickly lay down as he felt the golf cart swing about in a tight circle almost throwing him off his seat.

What should I do? Papa's not here. Maybe I should call David. Yes, I'll call David. She pulled over to the side of the road. Think, Molly. David needs to know.

Yes. Call him. Or should I let Deputy Harrison know? Would he know what to do? Something has to be done.

When she got to the lighthouse, she ran up the steps, across the porch, with her ever-present shadow, Ensign, hugging her heels.

"Solana! Where are you?"

Solana appeared at the top of the spiral staircase. "I'm here, Molly. What's wrong? Why are you yelling?"

She came down the stairs, slowly as always. Solana was not one to get panicky, even when a disastrous situation occurred. Her time "running" with Castro had taught her that a clear mind and calm emotions led to better outcomes than thoughtless, emotional responses.

Molly took a deep breath, then began. "He was wearing chains, Solana. Gold chains."

"Who was wearing chains?"

"Antonio. At the Sandpiper."

"Antonio was wearing gold chains. Ah, yes. Now that I think about it, I believe you're right. I think he's Italian. Looks like he's fond of flashy jewelry." Solana looked closely at Molly who was obviously still in a state of excitement.

"So, he wears gold chains. Many men do today."

"But, Solana. I found a broken gold chain in the shrubs next to the Sandpiper. And a small, black evening bag. I think the bag belonged to Gillian Hartwell . . . and I think the chain belongs to Antonio." She let out another long sigh.

"What? You think Antonio had something to do with the woman's death?"

"Uh, huh. And I found footprints in the shrubbery . . . prints I didn't see on the first day. Large shoe prints and prints made by small heels. The prints were facing each other. I think whoever made these prints may have been embracing."

"What? Antonio has a bit of history, but I don't think he's a killer. Molly, we need to think this through."

"Right. Oh, Solana. I wish Papa were here. He'd know how to handle this."

"Of course he would. But, as you say, he's not here. So that leaves the two of us. And Deputy Harrison, I suppose."

"Solana, I don't know that the deputy would know how to handle this either. He's so new at his job. He's only arrested a couple of drunks at The Temptation and written parking tickets."

"I see. Well, what about David Strickland? Can he handle this situation?"

"I think I should call him first. See what he thinks."

Solana nodded her agreement. Molly went to the phone and dialed David's office. This was one of the better days when her call actually got through.

"Dr. Strickland's Office," a voice on the other end answered.

"Oh, hello. This is Molly McCormick. I need to speak to Dr. Strickland, please."

"Hello, Dr. McCormick. This is Kathi, in Dr. Strickland's office. I'm sorry, but David is in the hospital. He and four other patients have contracted some kind of virus, or pathogen, and are hospitalized. So far it's just the five of them. But at this time the nature of the illness is still a mystery. Is there anything I can help you with?"

"Oh, dear. Would you please keep me informed about this illness? Sounds like it may be contagious. Hope we don't have an epidemic. We've got enough problems without that."

"Yes, of course. I'll let you know as soon as I hear anything. At the moment, I can't even visit him. You did get his autopsy report I sent by the ferry pilot?"

"Yes, and thank you for that. David had written a partial note . . . something about not being able to complete something on the report . . . any idea what he was referring to?"

"No, but he was coming down with this illness during the time he was working on the report. He always checks everything twice. Maybe he didn't do a second review?"

"I see. Okay. Thanks Kathi. Please let me know how David's doing."

"Of course. We'll talk soon."

Molly shook her head, "Looks like David is unable to help. He's contracted an illness and is hospitalized. Along with four others. Some kind of contagion obviously. So, that just leaves Deputy Harrison. Let's go see him and see where that takes us."

"We have no choice, Molly. But I don't think Antonio would commit such a crime. If memory serves me, he's actually part owner of the Sandpiper. I've known him for some time and Captain Jack checked him out early on. If he were a danger to the island, he'd be long gone. Trust me. The Captain has "arranged" for more than one person to find another place to reside."

Molly and Solana drove in silence to the deputy's office. When they entered, they were greeted by a very young lady, perhaps in her teens.

"Hello. Is Deputy Harrison in?" Molly asked.

"Yes, ma'am. I mean no, ma'am. Well, he's in. But he's out at the moment."

"I see. When do you expect him to return?"

"Oh. I'm not sure. I'm just here to take any messages and he'll be back maybe tomorrow. But it might be longer. He didn't know exactly how long he would be gone."

"Is he on the island?" Molly asked.

"Oh, no ma'am. He's been called to Fort Myers. He's providing an escort for Governor Bryant who's making a speech at the new Edison Junior College. Today is the first day it will admit students. "

"I see. Having a junior college in the area is a good idea. Then, if you hear from him, tell him to call Molly at the lighthouse. It's important."

"Yes, ma'am. I'll tell him." She smiled and resumed chewing her wad of gum.

Molly and Solana left and sat for a moment in the golf cart. Molly blew out a long breath, "So, we may have a killer on the loose and no one to deal with him. Somehow, I don't think two women and a shaggy dog are capable of bringing him in and putting him in that cage that Deputy Harrison calls a jail."

Solana agreed. "Let's go home and have dinner and let this sink in. Captain Jack would not want us to put ourselves in danger. We'll come up with something. We will."

Molly bit at her thumbnail, "I find myself wishing Patrick were here. He seems to take these kinds of problems in his stride. Without his help, I might not have survived the attack in the lighthouse. And, you know, he never seemed afraid or uneasy. Almost as if he'd been through similar situations before."

Solana nodded, "Yes, I think there's much we don't know about Saint Patrick. What we do know is that he's an intelligent, caring man. But, like all of us, he has issues."

Chapter 42

Solana stayed the night at the lighthouse, as she often did when the Captain was gone. She had no children herself, but Molly came pretty close in her mind. Solana so wished Molly could get her life back on track. Start her practice. Find a young man to begin a family with. All the things Solana had wanted for herself many years ago. But her time with Castro and Che had changed her life and now she was content to be here, at the lighthouse, with Captain Jack, looking after him, and now Molly as well.

The time when she was in league with Castro was a time of great excitement, and great despair as well. When she discovered Castro's true nature, she'd managed to leave . . . with the help of Che Guevara. Like Castro, Che was a rebel and revolutionary. But he had a soft spot for Solana, and it was through his scheming and efforts that she was able to escape and ultimately found her way to Cayo Canna. She pondered those memories for a few moments.

Is this problem Molly and I are experiencing any more difficult than those I had to overcome back then? The problem today being how do we bring Antonio Carlucci to a place where he can be held until such time as a law enforcement officer can take over? Maybe we just bide our time until Deputy Harrison returns. But that means we could have another death if Antonio is indeed a killer.

Solana fell asleep on the small cot in the lantern room, which suited her just fine. She'd spent many nights there over the years. Molly never did fall asleep, but lay awake most of the night in Keeper's Cottage. She opened the windows and listened once again to the Gulf. If it had any answers to her problems, it was keeping them to itself. Perhaps she wasn't listening as well as she might as her mind flitted from one problem to another.

But perhaps she had jumped to her conclusion about the Gulf not offering any suggestions to solve her issues. For now, early next morning, as she got up and dressed she made a decision.

I'm quite sure Solana will not agree with my plan. But I can't sit here waiting on Deputy Harrison to return. If Antonio is responsible for Gillian's death, then how do we know he won't kill someone else? No. I've got to do something. But if he's actually not a dangerous person—not a killer—as Solana suggests, then it might be a good idea to have one more discussion with him. Try to see if he knows something he's not telling me.

Molly loved living in Keeper's Cottage. It was private, being just a short walk from the kitchen in the lighthouse, through a breezeway . . . and close to Papa Jack if she needed him. And, most days, she felt she did. As she entered the kitchen, the aroma of Solana's coffee was a treat to her olfactory membrane. She went to the patio where she found Solana sitting beneath the glorious banyan tree, looking over Papa's morning paper.

"Solana, I'm going to put all this business about Gillian Hartwell on the back burner. Hopefully Deputy Harrison will return today. Even if he isn't experienced in this kind of problem, he's more qualified than you and I are. Meanwhile, I'm going to ride about the island and see if I can find a place to have an office. It's impossible to begin a practice if I don't have a place to work from. So, I'll take Ensign with me and we'll be back this afternoon."

"Wouldn't you like a cup of coffee? And I've got some Cuban pastry in the kitchen."

"No, thanks. Think I'll stop by Sassy's and have one of her Scottish scones. Papa keeps reminding me that Scots blood flows in my veins, so maybe I should listen to him," she smiled.

Solana agreed that was a good idea . . . leaving the Antonio problem to the deputy. But she sensed something was off about Molly. She wasn't one to leave anything "unfinished" as it were . . . and to accept that Deputy Harrison could handle everything? Still, Solana would trust Molly to use her very fine brain and not do anything foolish.

I do wish the Captain would get home. He'd have this situation under control and we'd be done with this whole affair. And I refuse to think he won't return. He's been on many dangerous missions before. This is just the latest one.

And she truly didn't think the Captain wouldn't return. It was simply not an idea she would ever consider.

Molly and Ensign headed to Sassy's Scones and Teas. This time of the morning there were a few people about, some walking their dogs or strolling the beach, some pedaling bicycles along the sidewalk, and others sipping coffee at Java Jane's Express, an outdoor restaurant with small tables sitting under one of the banyan trees. This tree was much smaller than the one that wrapped itself around the lighthouse, but beautiful just the same.

Molly smiled as she patted Ensign's head. He had freedom to run on the beach next to the lighthouse, go for a swim if he wanted, and Solana saw to it he was well fed.

"Somehow, I don't think you'd care for being put on a leash and 'walked' every day. Papa taught you to run without a leash and return when he whistles for you. The only problem is that I can't whistle! Hope you come when I call you."

Entering Sassy's shop was a treat. "Oh, goodness me. If I come here every day I'll have to get a larger golf cart." Molly smiled as Sassy opened the door for her.

"Dr. Mac, Molly, come in. Blueberry scones specialty of the morning. Take a seat. I'll bring them out. Tea? Coffee? I just brewed some Scottish black tea . . . it's on the strong side, so I brewed some Earl Grey as well."

"Some of your Scottish black tea would be great. Sleeping seems to escape me at the moment, so perhaps that will get me moving."

Sassy brought a plate of scones, a cup of steaming tea, then took a seat next to Molly. Molly hadn't missed there was something special about the relationship Sassy and Papa had. Whatever it was . . . she was not privy to that knowledge.

"So, how's the investigation going? Learning anything important?"

"Only a smidgen here and there. Nothing that tells me anything yet. But as I've admitted, this investigating business is not something I've been trained in. So, I'm trying to figure out things one step at a time."

"Yes, I wouldn't know where to start either. It's such a tragedy for Debra and for our island. People have never been afraid to come here. I hope this incident doesn't ruin our reputation. Some businesses on the island depend on the tourists traffic. And though I have daily customers, tourists play a role for me as well."

"Yes, I suppose they do. Speaking of Debra, I need to ask her a question. Is she coming to the shop as usual? Or maybe I should just run over to her shop?"

"I think I heard her enter just before you came in. She's determined to come to work every day. To keep moving. To deal with this death.

But it's wearing on her. However, I agree coming to work as usual is a good thing. Come on. We'll step over to her place."

The two walked over to The Writer's Block and found Debra dusting bookshelves and sipping a cup of Sassy's tea. She looked up as they came closer.

"Oh, Molly, hello. I was hoping to see you today. Have you learned anything more about Gillian's death?"

"Hi Debra. Not exactly. But we have discovered a few clues and Dr. Strickland has assured me a real investigator will be here soon. Today, however, I need to ask you to identify something if you can."

"Identify what?"

Molly reached into her large purse and pulled out the plastic bag with the small, black evening bag inside. She held it out to Debra.

"Do you know if this evening bag might have belonged to Gillian?"

Debra reached out to take the plastic bag, then quickly jerked her hand back.

"Oh, yes. Gillian has a dozen or more evening bags. One to match whatever color outfit she would be wearing. Yes. I am sure it belonged to her. I saw her open it when I gave her some medication for her headache. She placed it in that very bag."

"I see. Well, that's one issue that may help us find whoever committed this crime. I'm sorry I had to bother you with it, but it is important."

"Please, don't hesitate to ask me anything. I don't think any of us will ever feel safe until you find this monster." Then she returned to her shop as if she needed to get away from anything that reminded her of Gillian.

Sassy waited until they got back to her shop, then asked questions as well. But hers were directed to Molly.

"Where did you find the evening bag?"

"Sassy, I'm sorry. Papa instructed me to keep all information to myself and I must follow his advice. He knows a lot more about these issues than I will ever know."

"Oh, yes, of course. I should know better than to ask. If Jack says keep it to yourself, then that's exactly what I would do. He's a special man and a good friend to me. Let me know if there's anything further I can do to help."

Molly took her leave and headed to the Sandpiper, knowing full well that Solana, and Papa Jack as well, would skin her alive for engaging

Antonio again. But something had to be done and it looked like she was the only person around to handle the task.

As they were about to pull off, Sassy scooted out the door with a treat for Ensign. He wagged his tail and gobbled it down immediately. Then he resumed his position as navigator and off they went to the next stop.

The groundskeepers were already at their task, which was raking the sandy areas about the hotel. This was what Molly decided had happened on the day of the discovery of Gillian's body. She felt sure many prints and possibly other bits of evidence had been raked away. But, after she found the gold chain and the black evening bag, she had to press Antonio even further. After all, it appeared he was the last person to see Gillian alive.

Molly checked her watch. Nine thirty. Perhaps because he was part owner of the Sandpiper, Antonio was willing to work when other staff didn't show up. So, if he wasn't here now then she'd have to return later.

She got off the cart and looked toward the front door of the hotel. Suddenly—actually in the space of a heartbeat—she felt her pulse begin to race, and her breath felt trapped in her chest, then came rapidly and shallow. And sweat poured from her hands. At the same time, her brain was on fire. But her feet seemed planted to the ground and her hands trembled, so she put them together thinking that would help. Her brain then made a leap from sizzling to "medical mode." She tried talking to herself. Anything to help relieve these staggering physiological symptoms.

Okay, Molly. You know what's happening here. This is nothing more than a fight or flight response. Your sympathetic nervous system is simply sending out adrenalin, epinephrine, and several other hormones, responding to what it senses may be a dangerous situation. But you know it's probably not. So, take a few deep breaths, relax, put your brain in charge, and let your parasympathetic nervous system do its thing . . . mainly get your body back to homeostasis. No need to have a full-blown panic attack. This is just your body trying to take care of you.

She stood next to the cart for a minute, tried to calm her breathing and held her hands together again. But no matter how hard she tried, her body had a mind of its own and continued to dump even more hormones into her nervous system in order to do what they were designed to do—take care of a dangerous situation.

With more willpower than she'd ever exerted previously, she took a step forward, then another. Then just before she arrived at the door,

221

her brain made a leap onto an even higher plane, sending its own version of the danger it sensed, inundating her with questions she couldn't begin to answer.

What if Antonio IS the killer? What if he realizes I suspect him? Then he would have to get rid of me before I tell the authorities . . . and what if he attacks me . . . and what if no one ever knows what happened to me . . . and what if he . . .

Jesus, Molly! Get a grip. Solana believes it's highly unlikely Antonio is the culprit. And if he is, it's early morning with guests in and out the lobby. I don't expect he'll do anything to cause a scene. So, now. Just get on with it!

Presently her heart still raced and she was certain her blood pressure was high enough to cause cardiac arrest. She opened the door with trembling hands. When she stepped in, Antonio was walking through the lobby carrying an armload of linens. He stared at her for a long moment, then greeted her.

"Dr. Mac. Good morning. Another visit? So soon?"

"Good morning, Antonio. If you would give me a few minutes of your time I'll be on my way. But an issue has come up that I hope you can help me with."

"Sure thing. Just give me a minute to put these linens away. Be right back," and he disappeared down the hall.

When she looked up a couple of minutes later, Antonio was returning from his task. Molly watched as he came forward, his large feet moving slowly toward her.

He's a very tall man . . . and his feet . . . his feet are so big . . . just like . . . like the prints behind the shrubbery . . . maybe they were his?

Antonio walked to the front door, opened it, and looked about for a moment. Then he closed the door and turned to face Molly, his back toward the door.

"So, what is this new issue you need help with?" He stared down at Molly from his much greater height.

"I was wondering if you would tell me once again about seeing Ms. Hartwell when she returned to the hotel on the evening you last saw her."

"What else do you need to know? As I told you on both your previous visits, she came to the front desk asking for a key as she had misplaced the one I gave her earlier when she checked in. Then she left by the front door. I saw a tall, thin, man standing out by the edge of the building. But it was dark, so I couldn't see his face."

"And you said earlier she appeared to have had too much to drink? Is that right?"

"Yes. She was having difficulty speaking and was unsteady on her feet."

"Did you think she was able to get to her cottage without help?"

"It occurred to me she might have trouble walking through the path. Yes, I did think of that."

"And you say you couldn't see if the man outside went with her to her cottage?"

"As I told you, Dr. Mac. I don't know if he did or not. I had other business to attend to. This hotel has to be tended to and I went about doing my evening chores."

"But, if Ms. Hartwell was in such a state, did you not think it would be a good idea to call a bellhop or someone to assist her? Or may you've remembered something more to tell me?"

Antonio stepped closer. His face registered his frustration with answering the same questions for the third time. He took several deep breaths, then continued.

"There's nothing else to tell."

"So, you watched her leave, staggering, and still you didn't offer any assistance?"

"I've already told you everything. Several times now."

Molly saw the look of exasperation on his face. But it was time to press him a bit farther as she had an inkling there was something he wasn't telling. So she continued her probe.

"Antonio, there are some new clues I've just become aware of."

"Oh, and what might those be?" he asked as he eased closer, his six-feet-three body towering over her. He was standing so close Molly could feel his breath on her face as she reached into her large purse and pulled out the black evening bag . . . and the heavy gold chain.

"Do you recognize either of these items?" She lifted the evening bag in her hands, then dangled the broken, gold chain in front of his face, demonstrating that it looked much like those he wore around his neck at the moment.

Antonio exploded! He grabbed Molly by her shoulders with such force that she felt her feet leave the floor. Then his fingers were digging into her upper arms sending pain throughout her arms.

"Stop, Antonio! You're hurting me!"

Molly's already-pounding-heart pumped even harder, and her endocrine system released a deluge of even more hormones that

223

further accelerated her pulse, her breathing, and caused her brain to scream again—GET OUT OF HERE!

Antonio reduced the pressure of his threatening grip, but kept his hands on her shoulders.

"All right then. The truth is that yes, I did help her to her cottage. She could barely walk in those ridiculous spike heels, so I held her up and we walked behind the shrubbery where the sand is not so soft. She kept stumbling and it was difficult to keep her standing. So, I put my arm around her waist in order to hold her upright.

"Then she turned to me and grabbed me around my neck, yanking me closer. She mumbled something unintelligible, then wrapped her arms around my waist and pulled me closer still. I thought she might be trying to kiss me. When I tore her away from me, she grabbed at my neck and broke one of my chains. She gasped loudly . . . and fell backward . . . I couldn't hold her . . . and she fell to the ground . . . I shook her and checked for a pulse . . . but couldn't find one . . . I tried to revive her several times . . . then I realized she was dead . . . so I placed her under the dock because I knew I would be blamed for her death."

Then he yanked Molly by the shoulders again and leaned into her face, his breath coming in gasps. "I'M TELLING YOU I DIDN'T HURT HER!"

"Antonio, let me go!"

Paralyzing fear now raised its ugly head. The same fear she'd felt when Sam attacked her. She was aware fear was nothing more than the body reacting to danger. But it also put a screeching halt to her ability to think. All she could do now was respond.

Antonio eased his hold on her, mumbling "You don't understand. You didn't see . . . she was . . ." But still he didn't remove his large hands from Molly's shoulders. She stared at his face, so full of hatred. Veins in his forehead standing out. A moment passed and Molly prayed he was regaining his composure. But no. He tightened his grip and began shaking her harder.

"You've got to understand! I never wanted to hurt that woman!" He jerked her even closer to him. Molly squeezed her eyes shut, not wanting to witness whatever injury Antonio was planning on delivering.

A door slammed behind Antonio and the next instant he felt a large vice going about his neck, squeezing him so hard he couldn't breathe.

He gasped as he struggled to get even half a breath. But the pressure from that vice about his neck became more intense.

A deep voice attached to that vice—which was actually a large, hairy arm—spoke calmly. "I think you might want to let the lady go. Or I might be inclined to finish what I've started. Killing you, you spawn of Satan!"

Antonio immediately let go of Molly's shoulders. "But, I nev…" Then things began to go black, and he fell to his knees . . . but still that breath-stealing vice never released its pressure on his neck.

Molly's brain, still in chaos from the frightening situation, filtered out this latest input of information.

That voice. I know that voice. I would know that voice anywhere!

When she opened her eyes she stared into a face she'd pictured a thousand times since she'd last seen it. The same face that had always been too handsome for any priest, with its square jaw, straight nose, scar on chin, and piercing eyes that held you in place. And that same dark hair that could use a trim. Without warning, her body decided a good cry would be in order.

"Patrick! Oh Patrick, you always appear in my darkest moments!"

She was unsure what to do now. Her first impulse was to embrace him but he was rather busy keeping Antonio in a headlock.

Patrick nodded to her, still holding Antonio in a death grip.

"Molly, this man needs to take a seat. He's too heavy for me to keep in this position for long."

Molly put her hands on her cheeks, brain still in limbo. She nodded, "Oh, yes, of course. But Patrick, I think he may have killed someone."

She couldn't stop staring at Patrick. *How had he happened to be here? Just at the right moment again?*

Patrick released his grip slightly and Antonio shook his head back and forth, then whispered as his vocal cords had been damaged by that vice called Patrick's arm.

"Dr. Mac. No. I didn't mean to kill that woman. She just fell and hit her head on a coquina rock laying in the sand. It was an accident . . . just a terrible accident, I tell you."

Patrick pushed Antonio into a chair nearby. "Sit. Don't move. If you do, I'll do more than put a chokehold on you."

He then turned to Molly, "What the hell is happening here?" He, too, didn't know whether to pull her closer or stay put. So he remained where he was.

"It's a long story, Patrick. But I know Papa Jack would tell me to keep Antonio someplace where he can't hurt anyone else."

"Where is Jack? Is he on the island?"

"No. That, too, is a long story."

"Then, where's that local deputy? The big guy. Looks like this is a job for him."

"He's gone, too, so I'm the only one who knows the details of this case. And I don't know much either. But I do know that Antonio appears to be the prime suspect for having killed a woman, a Ms. Hartwell."

Patrick looked back at Antonio. He took in that the man was tall, rather thin, and had feet as big as Patrick's own. But something about his face told a different story. If there was one thing being in the priesthood had taught Patrick, it was how to read faces. And this wasn't the face of a killer. However, Molly didn't usually make decisions that were not based on good information or facts to support them.

"So, when will the deputy return?"

"Probably today. But maybe not. He's in Fort Myers escorting Governor Bryant to the opening of the Edison Community College. But that should be over by now. So perhaps he'll return this evening."

"I see. Well then, I suggest we take this 'gentleman' to the deputy's office. I assume the deputy has some sort of lockup, or detention center. A place to hold those who break the law?"

Molly looked dumbfounded for a second. "Uh, well yes. I know there is a small area in the rear of the office. Looks like a small cage to me. But, yes, I guess that is a lockup compartment."

Antonio whispered as loudly as he could, "Dr. Mac, no, you can't put me in that place. Everyone on Cayo Canna will hear about it. Please, I'm not likely going to leave the island. The ferry is in for the night, and there's no other transportation to the mainland. Somehow, I've got to prove to you her death was an accident."

Molly looked at Patrick, hoping he would have something to offer in the way of dealing with this "suspect."

The door of the hotel then shot open, slammed against the wall, rattling the windows in the process. Antonio, Patrick, and Molly turned quickly toward the door.

A huge man, every bit of six-foot-six filled the doorway. His Stetson made him appear even taller and more menacing. And the fact he was holding a loaded and cocked .357 Magnum made him look very dangerous. In fact, he looked downright sinister.

His booming voice filled the lobby, "All right, Antonio! You've killed your last woman! Get out of that chair! Now!"

Antonio opened his mouth, but then decided to keep quiet as he was sure his voice wouldn't cooperate with his brain, which was reeling presently. Deputy Harrison came closer then, still brandishing his weapon—which was still pointed at Antonio—then grabbed the man by his collar, lifting him completely out of his chair and depositing him on the floor.

"Dr. Mac, you all right?" He stared at Molly as if she might disappear any minute.

"Yes, Deputy. I'm fine. Antonio was just telling me his story. There are some new clues since you and I have talked. I need to fill you in on this information. Antonio insists this was an accident. But we need to talk to Dr. Strickland and others in authority before we take further steps."

"Yes, I agree. Lucy, the young clerk in my office, said you needed to talk to me so I went by the lighthouse. Solana told me about the evening bag and the gold chains. And I know Antonio always wears chains. Seen them many times. Looks like he's wearing them now, actually."

Antonio spoke then, his voice barely audible, "I can explain. It's complicated, but if you'll just let me tell the whole story, I know you'll understand."

Deputy Harrison grabbed Antonio by the collar, "At the moment you'll be coming with me. I'll get in touch with those that need to know. Dr. Mac looks like you've turned out to be rather good at investigating."

He turned his attention to Patrick. "I believe I know you. You're the priest, aren't you? Father Patrick? I remember meeting you at the lighthouse when Dr. Mac was attacked."

"Uh, yes, I'm Patrick. We made our acquaintance at the scene at the lighthouse. And we're glad you came today. Weren't sure what to do with our suspect. But if you'll take him from here that would be helpful. Dr. Mac has had a frightening experience. I think I should get her home and let her take it easy a bit."

Deputy Harrison nodded, "10-4. He's going with me. I'll be in touch with authorities in Fort Myers."

Molly let out a breath. One of relief. "Thank you, deputy. Ben. We'll talk soon. Let me know what you learn from the authorities in Fort Myers. I'm not sure what the next measures should be."

"Yes ma'am . . . uh, Dr. Mac. I will."

He jerked his prisoner toward the door. "Let's go Antonio. You can tell your story to the Lee County Sheriff. And a judge I imagine."

Antonio squeaked out, "But, Deputy Harrison, Ben, You know me! You know I wouldn't do such a . . ."

"Come willingly or I'll put you in cuffs."

"No. That's not necessary." Antonio looked at Molly once again. "Dr. Mac. I promise I didn't do this. Please believe me."

Molly nodded, but didn't respond. Patrick came over then and took her by the hand.

"Let's go. We're finished here."

Deputy Harrison walked Antonio to his vehicle and placed him in the front seat. The Lee County Sheriff was trying to get barriers installed in patrol cars, so those being taken to jail couldn't attack the officer driving the vehicle. But local communities didn't want to pay more in taxes which would be needed to pay for them. So, at the moment it often meant two officers had to make the arrest, one to drive and the other to keep the arrested person in check.

Antonio looked once more at Molly, as if he wanted to say something more. But presently, Molly was being led to the golf cart by Patrick, neither of them looking in his direction.

Deputy Harrison got behind the wheel. "Antonio, if you make any attempt at getting away, I'll stop, run you down, and put cuffs on you so tight you'll wish you never thought about escaping."

"I'm not going anywhere. Even if I try to hide, this island's got eyes everywhere. And, as soon as the gossipers get talking, I'll be judged before I even get a chance to explain what happened."

At the last moment, Molly hurried to the window of Deputy Harrison's vehicle.

"Oh, Ben. I think it would be better to take Antonio in quietly. Maybe no siren this time? Let's allow the Fort Myers authorities to do their job. Meanwhile I'll continue to ask questions and see if I can find any more clues."

"What? No siren? Well, okay. Yes, Dr. Mac. Whatever you say."

Chapter 43

The *Admiral's Lady* pulled into a berth next to a smaller vessel, a Boston Whaler, which belonged to a friend of Captain Jack's. This friend had passed away recently, but the craft was still moored here.

Bear was still in charge. "Casper, you stay put in your seat. I've called Raphael. He'll be here momentarily and take us to the lighthouse. Molly will have you back in shape in no time. "

"Bear, this is nothing more than a minor incident. We need to keep this issue to ourselves. No one on the island needs to know about our latest escapade. And we're not going to tell Molly or Solana about our findings. There's no point in getting them upset about Castro's horde of weapons."

"Yeah, well, keeping anything from either of those two will be quite an undertaking. Molly is no fool. She'll hound you to heaven if she thinks you're not telling her everything. And Solana can read you like a book. Don't forget. She's as good a spy as either of us ever have been. I say you better tell it like it is."

Jack sighed, "Yeah. You're probably right. But let's agree we won't go into any detail. Just the facts. We completed our assignment. We discovered Castro still has weapons and Admiral Whitmore has been informed. What happens from here on is up to the officials in Washington. We're done. Maybe."

Bear just grunted, "Yeah, and Molly's gonna have a field day learning how you just happen to have been shot!"

"Bah, it's just a flesh wound. No big deal."

Raphael arrived and sprinted over as he saw Bear supporting Jack, helping him walk down the dock.

"What's happened? Boating accident?"

"Something like that, Raphael. No problem. Just help me into the car and get us to the lighthouse if you will."

"Yessir, Capt. Jack. Have you home in a sec."

Raphael knew not to quiz Capt. Jack about much of anything. If it weren't for Jack, Raphael might not have been allowed to stay on the island. His past wasn't one he necessarily wanted everyone to know about, and the Captain was responsible for his being part of this community. The Captain believed in giving second chances to those he believed deserved it. And it was his opinion that Raphael fit into that category.

When they arrived at the lighthouse, Raphael and Bear helped Jack to the door. As they neared the entrance, Jack heard Ensign give a short bark and laughter filled the air. Then a deep voice called out, "Solana, you wouldn't know where Jack keeps his ration of Jameson would you?"

"Jameson? Oh, you mean that Irish whiskey he keeps in the bottom of his liquor cabinet? I expect it's just where it's always been. You're the only one that drinks it as I recall." She smiled, then went to the cabinet, poured a small amount in a tumbler, and handed it to Patrick.

"Ah, the only thing missing now is Jack," said Patrick. "So, where is he? Or do you know? He's got more secrets than anyone I know."

The front door opened then, and Jack entered with Raphael on one side and Bear on the other.

Captain Jack spoke up, "You're right about that. We all have secrets, Patrick. And I see you've made yourself at home with my Jameson." He smiled then and Patrick hurried over, then stopped short when he realized Jack was being assisted to stand.

"What the hell?"

Molly and Solana rushed over and Ensign chimed in as well, pushing his way through to place his nose on Jack's thigh. Molly stared at the blood-soaked dressing on Papa's calf and performed a quick head-to-toe assessment looking for any other injuries.

"Papa? What happened?"

She immediately slipped into her physician-in-charge roll, directing Raphael and Bear to bring Papa to the sofa where she knelt down and began asking one question after another, never waiting for an answer.

"What happened? Who dressed this wound? When did it happen?"

"Hold on, Molly Mac. It's nothing more than a flesh wound. Sometimes happens in my line of work."

Molly called out, "Solana, will you get my bag from the cottage? And bring some towels, too. I need to inspect this wound. See if it is just a flesh wound. Somehow, I rather doubt that."

Solana returned with Molly's medical bag which was Raphael's clue to step outside. He never did care for anything having to do with blood. As soon as Raphael stepped out, Bear—ever mindful of Solana's majordomo position—asked if she would mind bringing out a taste of Jack's Glenfiddich whisky. "I've seen that stuff work wonders at times like these," he suggested.

"Would be my pleasure, Admiral Bowen. That is if the attending physician approves," she smiled. Molly nodded, "That might be a good idea, Solana. This wound needs cleaning properly and Glenfiddich might serve as anesthetic."

Papa Jack looked up at her, "What? Bear and I cleaned that wound. It's perfectly fine and it'll heal quickly."

Molly looked down at her grandfather, "When you have MD after your name you can decide what medical treatments are in order. Until then, I'll take care of those issues." She bit her tongue to keep from asking how this injury occurred. But Papa Jack had specifically said no one was to know about this latest mission. So, if he wanted to let Patrick in on the latest happenings, then that would be his decision.

Patrick stared at Molly, then looked to Jack, then back to Molly. It was obvious to him there were some events and information he was not privy to. Not yet anyway. He'd bide his time until the proper moment, then he'd ask Jack to give him a rundown on what was going on. He was very certain it was something to do with the Cuban Missile Crisis situation. Even though the world thought the issue had been settled, Patrick knew there would be details that not everyone needed to know about. And Captain Jack McCormick would be right in the middle of them.

Once Molly cleaned the wound, she looked into Jack's eyes. "Papa, I've cleaned the wound, and I'm afraid you're wrong about it being just a flesh wound. But you're fortunate that the bullet passed completely through your calf. From the angle of entry, it appears you were shot from behind, which tells me you were probably escaping from some place where you shouldn't have been. Does that about cover it?"

Papa stared at her, "As I said, Molly Mac, just a minor problem. Now, I want to know details about your investigation. But first of all, how is it that I find my very expensive Jameson being served to some Irishman who just happened to stop by?"

Patrick chuckled, "Well, being that I'm the only one on this island that drinks the stuff, I thought it would all right."

Jack grinned at his friend. He'd missed Patrick and was glad he'd returned. Did that mean he'd dealt with his demons? Jack wondered. But, not knowing exactly the nature of these demons, he would wait until the right time to ask him about those problems.

Molly, satisfied she'd done all that was needed, put her medical bag away and sat next to Papa Jack on the sofa. "Papa, there have been a couple of developments in the investigation."

"That's good to hear. I don't particularly like thinking a murderer is running about on Cayo Canna."

"Well, there's a lot I haven't figured out yet. But it appears Antonio, at the Sandpiper Hotel, may be our man. He's certainly involved and I have proof he was at the scene of Ms. Hartwell's death."

"Antonio? Really? And what makes you think he's involved?"

"It's a long story, Papa. I interviewed him once I learned Ms. Hartwell had booked a cottage at his hotel. When we talked, he stated Ms. Hartwell had returned to the hotel about 1:30 a.m. and came to the lobby asking for a key to her cottage as she had misplaced the one he gave her when she registered. He said there was a man standing outside the front of the hotel, but it was dark and he couldn't see his face. I asked if the man walked Ms. Hartwell to her cottage and Antonio responded he didn't know as he walked away and went on about his evening duties.

"So, still having no real clues, I made one more inspection of the crime scene. This time I discovered footprints . . . very large footprints . . . behind the shrubbery at the hotel. When I looked beneath the shrubs, I found a small, black evening bag tucked beneath one of them. And I also found a broken, heavy gold chain next to it."

"So, what did you do then?"

"I went to see Debra at the Writer's Block. She confirmed the small evening bag did belong to Gillian Hartwell. But that left one of the clues still unaccounted for. The broken gold chain. At this point I was grasping at straws. There was gossip that Ms. Hartwell left Timmy's Nook with a man. But no one knew who. So, I thought maybe I'd see Antonio once more and hope maybe he'd remembered something since we last talked. So, I went to the hotel and talked with him again. He gave me the same answers as before. He'd given Ms. Hartwell a key, she went out the door headed to her cottage and he didn't know if the man outside went with her.

Papa looked at her, "But he still didn't give any new information. He hadn't thought of anything he forgot to tell you?"

"That's right. But as I was about to leave, he leaned down to clear a coffee cup from the table in the lobby. When he did, something sparkled in the light coming from the window."

"Something that got your attention?"

"Yes, the spark came from one of several heavy gold chains hanging around his Antonio's neck, Papa."

Papa nodded, "Ah, yes, Antonio always wears chains."

"As I was about two seconds away from having a panic attack, I left as quickly as I could, trying to keep myself together enough to get back here and talk with Solana. You weren't here, Deputy Harrison was in Fort Myers, and David Strickland was in the hospital. So, I had no one to give this information to. Solana and I decided we'd keep quiet about the clues and give them to the deputy when he returned to the island.

"But, after thinking about it overnight, I decided I had no choice. If Antonio is the killer, then we're all in danger. It was with that thought that I visited him a third time."

Molly waited for what she knew was coming, namely, Papa telling her how dangerous that action was and that she should never do such again.

But, to her surprise, he said nothing. Just listened intently. Waiting for her to continue with the story.

"So, at this visit, did Antonio change his story?" Papa took a sip of his Glenfiddich, and continued to listen.

"Yes, Papa. He finally admitted Ms. Hartwell came into the hotel at 1:30 a.m. needing a key. But this time he told me details he'd left out the first times I talked with him. It seems Ms. Hartwell was unsteady on her feet, stumbling, slurring her words, and Antonio could barely understand what she was saying. According to him, when he saw the condition she was in, he thought it best to escort her to her cottage. Along the way, however, she had difficulty walking in her spike heels, and that combined with too much alcohol made it difficult to keep her upright.

"He then walked her over to a path behind the shrubbery, where the sand is not so soft, hoping that would help her walk. But, for some reason she turned to face him, grabbed him around the neck and almost choked him. The chain broke in that instant and she sagged against him. He tried to lift her up, but couldn't. He says she then fell backward and hit her head on a large coquina stone laying in the path.

He checked her breathing, two or three times, tried to resuscitate her several times, then finally realized she was dead. It was at that point that he lifted her, trudged through the shrubbery and sand and deposited her body under the old dock. Hoping it would go unnoticed. He was afraid to report it as he felt he'd be blamed for her death."

"That's quite a story. So where is Antonio now?"

"Deputy Harrison has him in custody. He's holding him in the jail here on the island. He's to get in touch with officials in Fort Myers and I suppose we'll go from there."

"You're telling me that Antonio willingly went with Deputy Harrison. Just like that? He didn't put up a fight or protest, make some kind of scene?"

Molly fidgeted in her seat, "Uh, well, that's not exactly what happened, Papa. When he and I were discussing the new clues I had discovered, he became rather upset. He grabbed my arms and . . ."

Patrick stood and walked closer at that juncture. He had no desire to rile Jack up any more than necessary. He'd give him the facts, but not necessarily all the gritty details of Molly and Antonio's altercation.

Patrick addressed Jack, "I arrived today and came immediately to the lighthouse, thinking to find you and Molly here. After Solana told me Molly was out scouting a suitable place to have an office, finding her was easy as there's only one golf cart on the island that has a dog riding shotgun. So, after greeting Ensign, I went inside the Sandpiper. First glance told me the situation I walked in on was getting a bit testy, so I stepped in and convinced Antonio he should take a seat and calm down."

Jack looked at Patrick, knowing this young man would go to any lengths to protect Molly . . . and anyone else he thought was in danger. And the fact that he didn't give any details of "convincing Antonio to calm down" told Jack the situation must have been dire.

"I see. Then I'm glad you happened along, Patrick. I know a bit of Antonio's history, but there are probably some incidents I don't know about. So, the deputy will take over from here?"

Molly shrugged, "I don't know what else we can do, Papa. David says a real investigator will come over, but he's not shown up yet. And, with David still being ill, who knows when someone will come."

Papa stared at his granddaughter. The daughter of his only son. A son who was missing in action and had never returned from combat. The older Molly got, the more like Tom she became. And that was a good thing. Of course, Tom had been a younger version of Jack.

"Molly Mac, you've done a great job of investigating this event. I'm beginning to think you've chosen the wrong profession. Most folks would have run away from confronting a possible murder suspect. But you ran directly to him. That speaks of great courage, fortitude, and a bit of fire in your soul. Like your Scottish ancestors. Couldn't have done better myself."

Molly hardly knew how to respond. So, she kept quiet and let her mind have a moment of rest and relief, something it hadn't had for some time now.

Papa then inquired, "So, you say David's ill? What's he got? Some kind of stomach bug? Happens a lot this time of year down here. I always swear the snowbirds bring it with them."

"No, Papa. Actually, the physicians at Lee Memorial don't know what he and four other patients have. Whatever it is appears to be contagious, so no one is allowed to see him. His rad tech, Kathi, has promised to let me know how he's doing. I hope to hear from her later today, maybe."

Jack took a deep breath, "So, if Antonio is telling the truth as he insists, then there could still be someone out there. And that means we've got to dig deeper. But this day has been long enough. I'm ready for my bed. We'll comb through all this tomorrow. When my brain's had a chance to decompress. And, Solana, if I could have just a taste of your coconut flan that I smelled the moment we entered, I think I would sleep the night through."

Solana smiled. Just as she'd thought, the Captain had returned and was his usual self. Obstinate, inquiring, and ready for whatever came next. Yes, he was still the Captain. And in spite of his wounded leg, he insisted on sleeping in his lantern room.

"That will be more healing than any medicine you might pour down my throat, Molly Mac."

Bear stood up and looked over at his friend. They'd had so many escapades together that he could hardly remember all of them. But he really did hope this was the last.

"Looks like you're in good hands, Jack. And I agree with you about this being a long day. That being the case, *The Lady* and I are heading to Placida," so he said goodnight to all, then went outside where Raphael was waiting to take him back to the marina.

Patrick assured Solana he would get Jack up to the lantern room, so she took her leave as well. Now that the Captain was safe and home, she went to her own bungalow just a short walk down the road. She'd lived here for a number of years now and it suited her well. Her time with Castro and Che, in which they would move from one place to another, bringing chaos and havoc wherever they were, gave her a new appreciation for her life today. Caring for Captain Jack, the lighthouse, and now Molly, gave her purpose and as far as she was concerned, her life was more than she ever hoped for.

After a few bites of Solana's dessert, and with the help of Patrick, Captain Jack was settled into his lantern room, with Ensign in his assigned place at the foot of his bed. He felt immediate relief being in his favorite room. Then he cracked open a window so he could hear, smell, and feel the healing power that he knew resided in that great Gulf.

Chapter 44

With Solana and Bear leaving at about the same time, and Papa settled in his lantern room along with Ensign, that only left Patrick and Molly. Without preamble, Patrick took Molly's hand and they walked outside and down to the dock where Papa's old Chris-Craft boat was moored.

"You know, I think I might need to get a boat. Something like this. Something with character. Nothing fancy. Just something for me to run back and forth to the mainland, and maybe over to Sanibel or Captiva," said Patrick looking down at Molly as they walked along the dock which was quite visible in the bright moonlight.

Molly stopped and looked up at Patrick. "Patrick, I don't know what would have happened if you hadn't come along. Antonio was so very angry. He was not himself . . . he . . . "

Patrick took both her hands in his. "Molly, it's over. Don't think about it anymore. He's not going to hurt you or anyone else." Then he pulled her closer and placed a soft kiss on her forehead.

Molly put her arms about his waist. This man had saved her from danger and when she was near him she felt that's where she belonged . . . where she wanted to be . . . near him . . . with him. But, was the feeling reciprocal? If not, then why had he returned?

It was only a kiss on the forehead, Molly. Don't go reading more into this than it probably is. Just Patrick being Patrick. It's his nature to protect others. Not necessarily just you. And, don't forget . . . he's a priest . . . though I recall from conversations with him that he's unsure about that calling.

He smiled at her then, "But somehow, I think if I hadn't come along you'd have managed just fine. Jack was right about you. There's a bit of fire somewhere inside. As he said . . . some of that Scot's blood he's always talking about."

"Papa's proud of his Scots blood. Guess I should research family history a bit. But I'm afraid of what I might find," she laughed and they continued walking down the dock to the boat. The moment of closeness helped break the ice of Patrick's return. But now what?

They sat side by side on the edge of the dock. "I know you're right, Patrick. Antonio isn't in a position to hurt anyone. But something about this entire situation, this murder of Ms. Hartwell feels off. I can't explain it. But I know something isn't right."

Patrick smiled down at her. "Well, Mum would tell you, 'then ye must give it more thought. Listen to yer intuition. It won't lead ye astray, lassie.'" Molly returned the smile,

"I think that's exactly what I should do. Give it more thought. And hopefully David will send that investigator soon. But, now that Papa's back . . . and you're here . . . I have help with working through this investigation. Someone to make sure I don't miss something important. And, speaking of important issues, do you need a room tonight? There's an extra guestroom in Keeper's Cottage."

"Thanks, but I made arrangements to rent the same bungalow, down close to the lagoon, where I stayed when I was here before. The real estate agent had a cancellation on it and so I took it for a three-month period."

"Ah, so maybe you're staying awhile on Cayo Canna?"

"Yes, I do believe I will. Might even think about getting a small place of my own since I'm not obligated to any particular place at the moment."

"So, you're not returning to Baltimore? To your church there?"

"No, Molly. I've left the Church. I have my reasons and I'm at peace with my decision. For the time being I'm putting one foot in front of the other and I'll see where that takes me."

"Then that makes two of us. I've decided to start my medical practice on Cayo Canna. I just have to find a good location. But, I'm knee-deep into this murder investigation and hardly know what day it is."

"Since Jack is back, I feel sure he'll help complete this task. Something tells me he's done a lot of this sort of work."

"Yes, but that leg is going to keep him from moving at his usual pace. He's not gonna like that for sure. But he'll be better now that you're back. He's missed his political discussions with you," she smiled and they began to walk back to the lighthouse.

Patrick turned again towards the water, "You know, that sound, the water breaking upon the shore, is as old as time itself. I never tire of hearing it."

When they reached the lighthouse, Molly waved goodbye as Patrick left in his rented golf cart. Getting about the island demanded either a rental car or a golf cart, and Patrick choose the later.

"See you tomorrow."

"Yes, tomorrow. And Patrick . . . thank you for everything."

Chapter 45

Even though she'd not slept the night before, Molly had another night of wakefulness. It was as if her brain couldn't process quickly enough. Her thoughts kept flitting from one subject to another, so finally she left Keeper's Cottage and walked out to the patio and sat beneath the banyan tree that had all but wrapped itself around the lighthouse. The tree would have been there long before the lighthouse, and it was almost as if it were trying to protect this building, this "sanctuary" as Solana had called it.

I know how that feels. When someone puts arms around you and the world seems to be a safer place. And I'm glad Patrick has found peace for whatever his problems with the Church were. Does that mean he will stay here on the island? Perhaps it's too soon for him to think about any kind of relationship? But I can't deny that I'm drawn to him . . .but does he feel the same way? How will I know?

Oh, for goodness sake, Molly! Think about something else. . . like the autopsy report you haven't reviewed yet. Get this investigation over with and get on with your plans. Papa is home and you have help now.

She went back inside, sat at the desk in her bedroom and opened the autopsy report. She looked again at the note David had written across the top of the page. "Molly, I didn't get to complete the . . ."

What did you not complete?

The first observation she made was that he had written in pencil: "Probably Cause of Death is Fractured Cervical Vertebrae." She noted there were two fractured cervical vertebrae, C1 and C2. And she was aware injuries to those two vertebrae were often fatal. But why had he written in pencil? Perhaps he hadn't completed his review?

She began to dig further. Into the toxicology report itself. This analysis of arterial, venous, femoral, and cardiac blood, urine, gastric content, and various other tests are standard procedure in such a case.

There were findings she expected, such as elevated blood-alcohol concentration (BAC). Antonio's report of Ms. Hartwell having had too much to drink was confirmed. Among a long list of other detected chemicals, one grabbed Molly's attention: Tofranil. (Imipramine) Molly was aware this drug was given to patients who exhibited signs of depression or anxiety. But it was not commonplace. She sat back and thought for a moment.

Okay, so Gillian takes meds for depression or anxiety. Not something you see every day, but depression and anxiety often go undiagnosed. At least she was getting treatment for her problem.

She read farther down the page, taking her time to make sure she didn't miss something. The next drug listed was Chlorothiazide, used to treat hypertension.

So, in addition to depression, she had blood pressure problems. According to Antonio, she had imbibed heavily, which would not have been good for her blood pressure. Still, though, I doubt this amount of alcohol would have caused her death.

David, I don't know what it was you didn't complete, but so far I don't see anything here that would change your cause of death entry. She appears to have been diagnosed with depression and was being treated, but I don't think that fact changes anything.

Reading further on the list of medications she came to the next medication: Digoxin.

Oh, Ms. Hartwell had cardiac issues as well. So, what do I know now?

She let out a long sigh and looked toward the ceiling. Perhaps hoping to receive some divine guidance or information?

Keep reading, Molly. You haven't found any answers yet.

As she got close to the bottom of the page, a word there had her sitting up, leaning in to get a better look. Her eyes opened wider in an effort to make sure she'd seen what she thought she had. She wasn't one to swear very often, but if she had been, now would be a good time.

At the end of this list of medications was one that caused her eyebrows to shoot up of their own accord: Methylene Blue.

Alarm bells went off in Molly's brain and she hurried over to the bookcase where she kept her medical books and journals.

What do I know about methylene blue . . . and why is my brain insisting this is important?

It took only a moment for her to research the medication: *Methylene Blue: A potent, reversible Monoamine Oxidase Inhibitor used to treat a condition called methemoglobinemia. This condition occurs when the blood cannot deliver oxygen where it's needed in the body. To be given only under the supervision of a doctor. . . .and results indicate that Methylene Blue may be used to improve residual symptoms of depression in patients with bipolar disorder . . . increases mean arterial blood pressure . . . not to be used with certain medications such as digoxin . . . side effects may include changes in blood pressure, irregular heartbeat . . . etc. etc.*

Then, as if this information weren't concerning enough, the next sentence in the report had her holding her breath: *Enlarged heart; presence of large blood clots in coronary arteries.*

She had to sit very still and put one and one together . . . and come up with about fifteen! She was so in her element now. Deciphering medical issues.

Okay. Ms. Hartwell had (1) blood pressure issues which were being treated with Chlorothiazide; (2) depression and/or anxiety problems being treated with Tofranil, (3) cardiac issues as well as she was taking Digoxin, and (4) perhaps bipolar disorder being treated with Methylene Blue.

But Methylene Blue and Tofranil are contraindicated. Plus, she mixed an ungodly amount of alcohol with an antidepressant and . . .and . . .

She quickly returned to the middle of the page . . . wasn't there something here . . .something for . . . ah, yes . . . Ergotamine Tartrate . . . of course . . . treatment for migraine headaches . . .

So then . . . Ms. Hartwell mixed chlorothiazide with Tofranil which is contraindicated; mixed Ergotamine Tartrate with Digoxin and Tofranil, which are contraindicated . . . then mixed Methylene Blue and Digoxin which are contraindicated. And all were floating in a sea of alcohol. These combinations would have led to massive coronary artery blockage.

Oh glory. This poor lady had two cervical fractures, but that's not what killed her. She most probably died before she fractured her vertebrae.

She laid the report on her desk, stared at it for a moment, then closed her eyes.

David, you were writing in pencil because you hadn't completed your review of your findings. Were there more medications? Or what? Even if that is so, Gillian didn't die from fractured cervical vertebrae. Instead, she had a massive heart attack!

She sat back and whispered, "Oh what a wicked web our life-saving medications can weave."

Chapter 46

Deputy Harrison strode through the door at Sassy's Scones and Tea, removed his Stetson and smiled as he nodded his head.

"Mornin' Miss Sassy."

"Good morning, deputy. What can I get for you today? Your usual . . .three blueberry scones and a large cup of Scottish Tea?"

"Uh, no. Uh, yes, I mean yes. But I need six scones and two cups of tea today."

"Okay, then. Coming right up. Are you treating someone to some of my pastries this morning?" Sassy smiled at this gentle giant. She knew he had a heart of gold, but sometimes found his obvious "fascination" with her a bit much.

"Well, yeah, I suppose I am. I've got someone in our 'detention room,' and I'm responsible for feeding him."

"What? You mean you've arrested someone?" Sassy stopped and looked at the deputy. She'd never known him to put anyone in the detention room except a couple of drunks that couldn't find their way home.

"Did this person commit a crime? Or the usual? Had too much of a good time at Timmy's Nook?"

"Oh, no, Miss Sassy. This one is a real criminal. He's not just the usual type I pick up at Timmy's Nook. He's more . . . uh, no, I can't give out details about arrests."

"What? You've arrested someone who actually committed a crime?"

"Well, I . . . no. I'm not supposed to give out details about suspects who've been arrested. But, as soon as the officials from Fort Myers get here, it'll probably be all over the newspapers. I mean, it's not every day that we have a crime of this nature on Cayo Canna."

Sassy was sure this information had to be related to the recent death on the island. "I see. So, you can't divulge the name of the arrested person, but can I ask if Dr. Mac is aware of your arresting this criminal?"

"Oh, yes. In fact, she's the one who confronted him. And when the housekeeper at the lighthouse told me where Dr. Mac was, I hurried there and took him in hand. He's not going to hurt anyone else. You can bet on that."

"Uh huh . . . Dr. Mac confronted him, you say?"

"She did. She's really good at this investigation stuff. Her brain works out complicated facts and she figures out situations faster than most people. She's one smart little lady."

Sassy brought the scones and tea and opened the door for the deputy. She would keep this latest knowledge to herself until she talked to Dr. Mac. But knowing someone had been apprehended was reassuring. But, just yet, she didn't think she'd say anything to Debra.

Chapter 47

As soon as the sun peeked above the ocean, Molly grabbed the autopsy report along with her clues: the broken, gold chain and the evening bag belonging to Ms. Hartwell. Both items were in bags in order to avoid any new fingerprints being deposited on them. She ran up the spiral staircase with bare feet. Still in her pajamas.

Some things can't wait. Papa will be awake already. But I gotta tell him what I've discovered. Maybe now that he's "under the weather" he'll be available to help me with this blasted investigation.

At the top of the stairs she halted, then knocked lightly . . . just in case he was still sleeping.

A deep voice called out, "Solana? That you? Hope you've got my Cuban coffee ready," Papa was sitting in his chair taking in his favorite view, the Gulf.

"No, it's me, Papa."

"Molly Mac? Come on in. Up a bit early, aren't you?"

"Papa, I've spent the night going over the interviews I conducted, all the information I learned from various people on the island, and lastly, the autopsy from Dr. Strickland."

"I see. Then I would guess you've learned a great deal. I'd like to hear it, but first I need a good cup of coffee. That swill Bear has on the *Admiral's Lady* is abysmal. Cuban coffee is the best."

"Then, come down now. This is important, Papa. And time is of the essence. I think we gotta act on this new information. And soon."

Ensign led the trio down the spiral, skipping two steps at a time. Then Molly hurried down and watched as Papa took a bit longer, what with his leg still bandaged and not quite as flexible as usual.

When they got half way down, the aroma of Solana's coffee filled the air. "Ah, now that's what I call coffee," smiled Papa.

Solana looked especially colorful today, with a floor-length floral skirt and white blouse, and a beautiful hibiscus bloom tucked in her hair.

"Good morning, Captain . . . and Molly. What are you doing up so early? I know you're not sleeping much these days, so sleeping in might be a good idea."

"I've got too much to do to sleep, Solana. And you should sit here with Papa while I bring him up to date on this investigation."

"Then I'll bring the coffee and fruit."

Once they were settled beneath the banyan tree with their coffee and fruit, Molly lay the few clues she had found on the table: a scrap of paper torn from a larger piece, a rhinestone hair clip, the broken, gold chain and the black evening bag. Plus the autopsy report. Then she began to report her findings.

"Papa, David Strickland had written a note on the autopsy report saying he'd not completed something. Of course, he was coming down with whatever his illness is, so I assume that's the reason he didn't complete everything."

"Oh yeah. What is this about David being in the hospital?"

"According to Kathi, he and a few others have come down with a fever. And the fact that five of them have it, it could be contagious. He's in the hospital and Kathi will keep us advised. But I don't think he was feeling well enough to review all his findings.

"So, I went through the entire report, including toxicology, and found some interesting facts."

"Such as?" asked Papa as he sniffed his coffee and took a sip. He smiled, then gave her his undivided attention.

"Well, when I talked with Antonio the third time, he admitted walking Ms. Hartwell to her cottage as she was unsteady on her feet. According to him, as they were walking behind the shrubs, she turned to face him, grabbed him around the neck, gasped, and fell to her knees. He couldn't hold her up, so she fell backwards, hitting her head on a coquina stone on the path."

"Ah. I suppose he's stating it was an accident?"

"Well, yes, that's exactly what he said. Said he was afraid to report it as he knew he would be blamed for her death. So, he placed her body beneath the old dock and went back to the hotel."

"Every criminal blames his actions on an accident, Molly Mac. Remember that when you conduct any investigation. And sometimes it might be true. But not likely."

"So, seeing that David hadn't completed his review, I started at the beginning and went to the end."

"And? Find anything that brings any daylight to this situation?"

"Yes. I think I did. At the top of the report David had penciled in "Fractured Cervical Vertebrae" as likely cause of death."

"Penciled in?"

"Yes. I suppose that was because he didn't complete his review. Maybe there were more medications he needed to address. Whatever. I looked for anything that would give us information about this woman. David's note stated she had fractured vertebrae, C1 and C2, which can be fatal. When I reviewed the medications list, I learned she had several medical conditions that required treatment."

"So, two fractured vertebrae and several medical conditions. Such as?"

"Number one, she had high blood pressure and was being treated with Chlorothiazide; number two, she was also being treated with Digoxin, which tells me she had cardiac issues; number three, there was Ergotamine Tartrate on board, meaning she had migraine headaches; number four she was being treated with Tofranil which is used for depression and anxiety; and number five, she was being treated with Methylene Blue, likely for bipolar disorder which often brings depression."

Papa shifted in his chair and Solana poured him another cup of coffee. She sat then and listened as Molly continued her report.

"Many medical issues. Was she deathly ill?" asked Solana.

"No. None of these conditions would necessarily mean she was at death's door, and she was being treated. And by more than one physician I would guess. Not sure she was telling each physician about the others. But here's the problem: Chlorothiazide is contraindicated for use with Digoxin, Ergotamine Tartrate is contraindicated in patients with coronary artery disease, it's also contraindicated with Tofranil, Methylene Blue and digoxin are contraindicated, and . . . "

"Whoa, Molly Mac. Say it in English."

"Ms. Hartwell was mixing medications that can be lethal when combined. Plus, she had a tremendous amount of alcohol on board. And those facts alone could be important. But, another issue revealed itself as well.

"Ms. Hartwell had an enlarged heart and large blood clots in her coronary arteries. Papa, she had a massive myocardial infarction . . . a fatal heart attack."

249

No one said anything for a couple of minutes. Then Solana asked, "So, fractures and a heart attack. So how does that help us know who killed her?"

"Well, I've given this considerable thought. Antonio said: 'She turned toward me and grabbed me around the neck, breaking one of my chains. I thought she was trying to kiss me or something . . . then she gasped loudly and fell to her knees. I couldn't hold her and she fell backward, hitting her head on a coquina stone on the path. I shook her, hoping she'd come to. Then I checked her pulse several times. But I couldn't find one, and when I couldn't revive her, I realized she was dead. At that point I picked her up and placed her body beneath the dock because I knew I would be blamed for her death.'"

"Continue," said Papa as he poked at his pipe.

"Papa, I think Antonio was telling the truth. It was an accident. I think when Ms. Hartwell turned to him and gasped, she was having a heart attack. And when she fell and hit her head on the coquina stone, she fractured her cervical vertebrae."

Papa took a deep breath, "Well, my dear granddaughter. I'm not surprised you've solved this death. And you've done it all by yourself. And you thought you didn't know where to start. Looks like this case is closed."

Molly rubbed her neck, a sure sign there was more to come.

"But, Papa. There's just one problem."

"Okay. Come out with it. Can't be as difficult as the one you've just solved."

"Oh, actually I think it may be. You see, the last paragraph of the report shows the presence of an excessive amount of thallium in Ms. Hartwell's body."

"Thallium? Are you sure, Molly Mac?"

"Yes, Papa. I think someone either has been poisoning this woman, or she ingested thallium the evening she was killed, or something along those lines."

"Thallium poisoning is a very sly way of killing someone. I've known a couple of cases where that happened. But that was some time ago. Not anything I've heard about in the last few years."

He lifted the plastic bag with the broken gold chain. "Yep. Antonio wears these same chains. Seen them many times."

Then he picked up the black evening bag, still within the plastic bag. "And you confirmed this belonged to Ms. Hartwell?"

"Yes, Debra said she gave Gillian some headache medication . . . hmm . . . I think she said three capsules as she had complained of a terrific headache. And Gillian put the medication in that evening bag."

Papa turned the evening bag over within the plastic. "It's heavy. I think there's something inside."

"Oh, I haven't opened the bag."

"Well, I think we should," said Papa as he gingerly, through the plastic, opened the evening bag. The only thing inside was a small shiny item. Nothing else.

"Ah, a tube of lipstick. Funny, Margaret always had a small lipstick in her evening bag also," he said with a small smile as if this were a pleasant memory.

"Uh huh . . . along with that derringer you had her carrying," grinned Molly.

"Never know when you might need one, Molly Mac," Papa grinned back.

"The evening bag and the broken chain are important clues for the investigator. Along with the scrap of paper and the hairclip. Plus the photos you took. Those guys know more about this sort of crime than we possibly can. When do you expect him, anyway?"

"Could be later today . . . or not. Hopefully David is recovering and will come with the investigator. This is getting complicated. Thinking Antonio was the killer, then now, I don't think so.

"As I have said from the beginning, I'm not an investigator. Although I must admit that my brain has been challenged during these past few days. Something I haven't experienced in a while."

Papa smiled, "Sounds like the Molly Mac I know. The more challenging it is, the more you like it."

"So, Papa, I think we must visit the deputy and let him in on what the autopsy results indicate. But, should he release Antonio? It doesn't look as if he's guilty, but I don't know the proper protocol for a situation like this."

"Not sure I do either, but surely Deputy Harrison will have contacted the Lee County Sheriff's Office and they'll take over now. But you might check on David first. See how that situation is going. He's an experienced ME and since he didn't have a chance to complete his report, I know he would want to hear your rundown on the toxicology results."

Solana went to the kitchen and returned with a platter of warm *pastelitos*. Then the sound of high-powered engines had them staring across the water as a sleek watercraft flew by them so fast they hardly saw it before it was past them.

"Well, I do believe we may have a visitor shortly," Papa interjected. "That's the patrol boat from Lee County Sheriff's Office. Let's hope the investigator's on board."

They weren't surprised when, within fifteen minutes, Raphael's cab showed up at the lighthouse. Molly went to the driveway to greet the investigator, whom she was more than happy to greet.

But, to her surprise, the visitor was one she would welcome even more so than the investigator. David Strickland stood tall, smiled at Molly, and waved to Jack and Solana.

"David? You've recovered?"

"I do believe I have. There were five of us. Patients, that is. All ran extremely high temperatures, lost consciousness for a short period, had chills, then nothing. Lasted about three days. Then all symptoms were gone. The physicians are calling it 'fever of unknown origin,' which is what they always say when they can't figure out what's wrong with their patient."

Molly smiled, "Yes, and I know it happens, but I never like such episodes. Something has to be causing the problem. But I'm awfully glad you're doing well and truly glad you're here on the island. I'm ready to turn this whole investigative process over to you."

"So, give me a quick assessment of the situation."

"All right, then. Let's join Papa and Solana up on the patio. I have a few clues to give you and Papa may have some wisdom to pass on as well. He's an old hand at investigating such situations."

Papa and Solana greeted David, then they got down to business. Molly reiterated her findings at the crime scene, the shoe prints in the shrubbery, discovering the chain and the evening bag, then informed him of her interviews and what she'd learned from them. Then she lay the few clues on the table in front of David.

"Not much in the way of clues, just a number of photos I took, a scrap of paper, a rhinestone hairclip, a broken gold chain, and an evening bag.

"I interviewed a number of people and learned some information that helped me move forward. But some of it was just gossip about Ms. Hartwell perhaps bringing a tall man back to the cottage with her. I'm not at all sure that happened.

"So, after three meetings with Antonio Carlucci, manager at the Sandpiper, he admitted seeing Ms. Hartwell when she returned to the hotel."

"Three meetings?"

"Well, yes. After each of the first two interviews, I felt like he was keeping something from me, so I kept returning until he finally told me the whole story." Molly went through the entire scene as Antonio had explained it to her. David listened intently then smiled at Molly.

"That was a gutsy thing to do, Molly. Not everyone would have been so persistent. Especially if it looked like the person being interviewed could possibly be a suspect. Good job in ferreting out a criminal on your island. But maybe a bit on the dangerous side."

"Well, there's more to the story, David. After I read your report, I came to a different conclusion about Antonio. I believe he was telling the truth when he said it was an accident. I don't think he's responsible for Ms. Hartwell's death."

"Tell me more," David leaned forward. He was very interested in what Molly's thoughts and findings were. He was quite sure she was indeed a lady with many talents.

"Your autopsy revealed two cervical fractures and a heart attack. I believe Ms. Hartwell turned to face Antonio . . . as he stated . . . held him around the neck, then gasped loudly because she was having the heart attack at that very moment. She fell to her knees, then fell backward and hit her head, causing the fractured vertebrae."

"Okay. I'm with you. Molly, I'm embarrassed to tell you that I barely recall even performing the autopsy. That crazy fever came on so unexpectedly. One minute I felt fine, then the next I could barely hold my head up. The only portion of the procedure I can recall is that you were right in your earlier statement about cervical fractures. After that I hardly remember anything. Kathi says she found me, but I don't remember even seeing her.

"So, you say the report reveals Ms. Hartwell had a heart attack. Then that will be the cause of death. Cervical fractures would be secondary to the attack. I believe you're right, Molly. She would have collapsed following the heart attack, and certainly hitting her head on a coquina stone could have caused fractures. That's very good work, Molly."

Molly nodded. "There's more. She had blood pressure problems, cardiac issues, anxiety, migraine headaches, and bipolar disorder. She was taking medications for all her issues, but as you know, medications can be dangerous and sometimes fatal if they are taken together. When

253

I looked at them, I wondered if perhaps she was seeing several physicians and taking medications without sharing that information with each of them. A common problem in my world. But, if you, the ME, agree this was indeed an accident, what now? What happens to Antonio?"

"Before I leave, I'll call the Lee County Sheriff with these findings and my recommendations as ME on the case. He'll discuss the issue with a judge, most likely Judge Hal Clements, who works with me often. But I feel sure Antonio will be released immediately. I see no reason to hold him further. He has you to thank for helping him out of a most difficult predicament. And I must thank you as well. I had no business trying to perform an autopsy when I was not able to do so. Thank goodness you went through the report and discovered the true cause of death."

"But, David, there's one more issue we need to discuss."

"Oh? What's that?"

"The level of thallium was excessive. Do you commonly find that in your line of work?"

"Thallium? There have been cases on record where it's shown up as a criminal poison, but I've never run across it. It's used in rat poison and ant killer. And it has shown up in some Chinese herbal medications. Toxicity occurs by cumulative intake through inhalation, skin, respiratory, and gastrointestinal tracts.

"It's found in people who work in smelters, in the maintenance and cleaning of ducts and flues. It also can occur through contamination of cocaine, heroin, and herbal products. But I doubt this woman would be working in a smelting factory, and apparently there wasn't any cocaine or heroin."

"But, shouldn't we try to learn how she was exposed to it?" asked Molly.

David looked down at his feet. Lost in thought for a few moments. "Yes, we should. Even though the heart attack killed her, I fear someone may have been trying to poison her."

Captain Jack added, "I agree with you, David. Something about this whole affair doesn't wash. Molly has worked diligently on this case, but there are still some unknown facts."

Moments later the next visitor of the day arrived. Unannounced. Driving a golf cart with a bag of golfclubs on the rear, Patrick parked his wheels and walked toward the group on the patio.

Ensign hurried out to greet him and Jack was delighted to see him. "Patrick, good morning! Come have some of Solana's Cuban coffee and *pastelitos*. Molly greeted him with a smile that made his heart sing. Perhaps she was truly glad he returned.

"Patrick, come. There's room for one more," Solana chimed in as well.

Patrick grinned at Capt. Jack and then greeted David. "Dr. Strickland, I believe?"

"Yes, that's right, I'm David Strickland. And you're Father O'Brien as I recall."

"Just Patrick," he replied. With no further explanation offered.

David simply nodded, "I see. Are you here for a short visit?"

"Uh, not sure yet. Might be getting a place of my own on the island. Something about this place calls to me."

"Yes, it does have great appeal. Then I'll be seeing you around."

David stood then, turned to Molly. "If your phone is working, I'll call the Sheriff's Office and tell them our findings. There's no reason to hold Antonio as far as I'm concerned. He's gotta be tired of sitting in a cage. I feel sure Judge Clements will agree with my suggestion to release the man. Everything you say appears to be correct, Molly. He's not responsible for Ms. Hartwell's death."

Patrick looked to Molly, then to Jack. "That guy at the Sandpiper? He's not the culprit? The deputy arrested him and I assumed that was the end of the story."

"Well, not exactly. I'll fill you in later," said Molly as she led David into the lighthouse to make his call.

The call lasted only a few minutes and being that the ME was there on the case on the island, the Sheriff agreed to call Deputy Harrison and permit him to release his 'prisoner.'

The next call was to Raphael who showed up immediately. David took Molly's hand in his, "Again, thank you for everything. You have been a superb investigator, Dr. Mac. Something tells me we'll work together again. "

"Oh, let's hope not!" She laughed.

"I'll be in touch after I take these items to the investigator. They'll run them through several tests and we might have more information about the thallium. He may still come to the island if he has more questions. He won't close the case until he's satisfied it's been solved."

David hopped in the cab. Raphael waved to Molly as he headed his cab to the patrol boat. In a matter of minutes David was aboard the transport for the short ride to Fort Myers. He was determined to finalize this event, and the sooner the better.

Chapter 48

Sassy smiled when her next customers walked through her door—Adam Laramore and his little daughter, Wesley, Sassy's young friend. But as soon as they sat down at the table Sassy knew something was amiss. Wesley had a case of hiccups from having cried for such a long period of time. Sassy looked at Adam with a quizzical look on her face.

"Anything I can help with?" she inquired.

"No, Wes is upset because I've got to send her to live with her Aunt Susan in Fort Myers. I don't have much choice since Wiley can't take the kids over to Sanibel any longer. Charters start early, so that leaves me in a pickle."

Sassy nodded, "Yes, sometimes we have to make difficult decisions. And they aren't always to everyone's liking. Maybe a blueberry scone and a cup of milk would be good about now?" Adam nodded and gave a small smile. Sassy brought the goodies and put them in front of Wesley.

"Here you go, ladybug. Your favorites."

"Thanks, Sassy," Wesley murmured. But her little face looked so forlorn that Sassy leaned over the table and gave her a hug."

"And you, Adam? How about some of that strong Scottish tea and a couple of cinnamon scones."

The next customer was one of her regulars also. Raphael had dropped David Strickland, the medical examiner, off at the patrol boat mooring site and then scurried to Sassy's place. He did love those scones she made. Plus, he needed her help.

"Morning, Sassy. I know it's a bit late for breakfast, but I wonder if you got any of those blueberry scones left?"

Sassy smiled at Raphael, one of her favorite people on the island. He was always cheerful and had a great attitude even when things weren't necessarily going his way. Sassy thought him a definite asset to the island community.

He took a seat in the rear of the shop. Sassy brought his tea and scone, then cleaned up a couple of tables from earlier customers. Raphael sipped his tea, then brought out a large envelope and placed it on the table. Then he called Sassy over.

"Sassy, I wonder if you could help me out. I need a small favor."

"Probably," she smiled. "What do you need?"

Raphael lifted one of the flyers from his envelope and held it up for Sassy to see. "I was wondering if you would allow me to put up a couple of these flyers in your shop?"

Sassy read to herself: Raphael's School Bus & Water Taxi: Two daily trips to Sanibel and Captiva Departing Cayo Canna at 7:30 a.m. and 12:00 Noon. Return trips will depart Captiva at 2:30, make a stop at Sanibel, and depart for Cayo Canna at 3:30 p.m.

Sassy looked at him, "What's this? Raphael you're starting up a School Bus and Water Taxi Service to the other islands? What about your regular cab service? Will that still operate?"

"No problem. My cousin, Julio, from Miami, has moved in with me. He's young and eager to learn how the cab business works. I'll make the early morning School Bus run and he'll make the noon one. That way one of us will be here to answer calls on the island."

"That sounds great, Raphael." Sassy's mind was working overtime. This could be an answer to Adam's dilemma about sending Wesley to Fort Myers.

She took one of the flyers and ambled over to Adam's table. "You might want to look at this. Could be of interest."

Adam read the flyer and strolled across the room where Raphael was devouring a scone and asking for another cup of tea.

"Morning, Raphael."

"Adam, how's it going? Lots of snowbirds around. Should be good for your charter business."

"Yep. Staying busy. This flyer is pretty interesting. As it is, with Wiley Duncan no longer able to take Wesley and a few other children to Sanibel for school, I've got a problem. Are you serious about this service?"

Raphael nodded, "Yeah, I think it can work, Adam. Do you know how many children we have on Cayo Canna at this time?"

"No. Not really. But I know several families with children have moved here recently."

"Well, as of yesterday there were nine elementary age school children registered for school in Sanibel. And there's talk of opening a new school shortly. That's enough to warrant me starting this new endeavor."

"When did you think you might begin this school bus service?" Adam was afraid to get too excited. But he did hate having to move Wesley to Fort Myers. She was all he had at the moment.

"Right after the Christmas holidays. It's a good time of the year as the winter tourists will want to visit Sanibel and Captiva, and school will be starting back for the kids at the school in Sanibel. Several families have already agreed to use my service, so I think it might just work."

Adam held out his hand. "You can add my name to that list, Raphael. My girl here needs a ride to school in Sanibel. Your school bus service is a lifesaver for me."

Adam moved back to his table where Wesley was busy coloring the pictures on the placemats Sassy laid on her table. She had missed all the conversation going on around her.

Adam briefed Wesley on this arrangement. "Daddy? You mean I don't have to go to Aunt Susan's?"

"Seems that way. Raphael has a reputation for keeping his word, so I expect you'll be riding his water school bus after Christmas holidays are over."

"Oh Daddy! I love Aunt Susan but I want to be here with you."

Sassy took two of the flyers and placed one in her window and went next door and placed one in the window of The Writer's Block.

Would that all problems were so easily solved, thought Sassy.

She was waiting to hear something from Dr. Mac. Maybe today. And Debra was keeping herself busy re-shelving all her books. Anything to keep her mind off what happened to her friend.

Chapter 49

The Lee County Sheriff called Deputy Harrison and instructed him to release Antonio. Judge Clements agreed with the coroner and an investigator would now look at all clues and decide the next actions to take.

David called Molly with the news. As soon as the call came Molly thought she should go to the deputy's office and be the one to give an explanation to Antonio as to what was happening.

Papa Jack grabbed his pipe and made his thoughts known. "I think I'll go along, Molly Mac. Antonio is likely to be angry still. And I've known him a long time. But yes, I agree, you should be the one to give him a rundown on what has occurred since he was arrested."

Molly, Patrick, Captain Jack, and Ensign headed to the deputy's office. The four arrived just as Deputy Harrison was escorting Antonio out the door. The deputy quickly removed his hat and smiled at Molly, turning his hat in his hands constantly.

"Oh, Dr. Mac. The Sheriff called. Said for me to release Antonio. But he didn't offer any information other than that Dr. Strickland had approved him for release."

Molly came forward, "Yes, Ben. Antonio is free to go. He told the truth about Ms. Hartwell's death. She died of a heart attack. And even though she did have other injuries, Antonio was not responsible for them. It's complicated. But the autopsy has shown he did not kill Ms. Hartwell and should be released."

Antonio listened without comment. He opened his mouth to say something, but then didn't. What could he say? He knew the entire island would have heard that he "killed" that writer lady. And there was nothing he could do about that.

Captain Jack walked over to Antonio. "Antonio, your ordeal is over now. You've been cleared of any responsibility for Ms. Hartwell's death. It is unfortunate that any of this happened. But take it from one who's been around a long time, life has a way of dishing out unpleasant happenings to all of us. I know I've had my share."

Molly then came to stand with them. "Antonio, I hope you will forgive my hounding you for something you didn't do. I was doing what I was asked to do to keep the community safe. It was never my intention to bring such difficulty to you."

Antonio nodded, "I'm relieved you found out the truth, Dr. Mac. But my reputation is seriously damaged now. I'll need to leave Cayo Canna. My life here is over, even though I've been here for a number of years. The gossip grapevine will have had a field day with this incident."

Captain Jack cleared his throat, "Well, then. I think we should give them something else to gossip about. How about them gossiping about how Captain Jack McCormick and his granddaughter, Dr. Mac, are having a celebration to honor Antonio Carlucci, a valued member of this community, who has been cleared of any involvement with Ms. Hartwell's death. Such a celebration would be a good way to start the Christmas season . . . a season of giving as I recall."

Antonio stuttered . . . but, I . . . it would . . . do you think . . .Captain McCormick are you sure?"

Captain Jack put his hand on Antonio's shoulder, "Absolutely."

The last one to approach Antonio was Patrick, accompanied by Ensign who wagged his tail as he greeted Antonio, one of the folks who regularly gave him treats when he accompanied Molly or Jack to the Sandpiper.

Patrick slowly offered his hand. Antonio looked at it for a long moment, then held his out. Patrick sighed, "I hope there are no hard feelings. Molly appeared to be in trouble and I felt impelled to step in."

Antonio smiled for the first time. "No hard feelings. And if I ever need a security guard at the Sandpiper, I'll give you a call."

"Deal," said Patrick.

The deputy had been silent the entire time. But now he spoke up. "Thank goodness for you, Dr. Mac. You figured this whole mess out better than anyone could have. Maybe you should just work with the coroner and help with other crimes. They have a lot of crimes that are never solved."

"Oh, no. I'm a physician, deputy. But I need to tell you about a couple of developments."

She pulled him away a few steps from Antonio and the others. No need to let everyone know all the details of these latest findings.

"What we discovered was that Ms. Hartwell had a heart attack, fell backward onto a coquina stone and fractured her neck."

"Uh, huh. Right. She died of a heart attack and Antonio didn't hurt her. He never did seem like a killer to me."

"Yes, but the case is ongoing, still. Thallium was found on autopsy. Dr. Strickland will make some more tests and an investigator may still come over and have more questions. So, keep this to yourself and be aware that perhaps someone was trying to poison the writer."

"What? What's thallium?

"It's a chemical element whose use is limited as it's toxic. Poisonous. Used for controlling rodents and ants presently."

"What? That woman had swallowed it?"

"We're not sure how she got it. That's what Dr. Strickland will be checking out."

"But, Dr. Mac, that means we still may have a killer on the loose!"

"Oh, let's not get too far ahead of ourselves. Dr. Strickland will keep us informed of what he finds."

"Yes, Dr. Mac. I'll keep quiet. But I'm glad it wasn't Antonio. He's one of us."

Chapter 50

The next stop was Sassy's and The Writer's Block. The word about Antonio's innocence would spread quickly, and Molly wanted to be sure Debra was one of the first people to know what had transpired. Even though she was not sure she should tell about the thallium.

Papa led the way inside and Sassy's face lit up when she saw him . . . and Molly didn't miss that.

"Well, now, what a nice surprise. Two visits in as many days," said Sassy. Then she looked to Molly, then to Patrick. She remembered his face from his time on the island a few months ago, but couldn't put a name to it.

Molly introduced Patrick to Debra and he spoke to Sassy. "Good to see you again, Sassy. I've missed your fine scones and tea. You'll see me here often," he smiled his breath-taking smile and took a seat.

"Anything new in the investigation?" asked Sassy as she brought forth a platter of several kinds of scones and brought cups and tea for all.

"Well, yes. But I should inform Debra first I believe," Molly stated.

"Inform me of what?" asked Debra as she walked through from The Writer's Block.

"Oh, hi Debra. We've learned what caused your friend's death, and I wanted to let you know before the gossip grapevine gets too far."

Debra came closer, close enough for Molly to see her hair was thinning on the top of her head. One thing about medical training meant she was forever doing a mental "head to toe" assessment of everyone.

"Tell me, please. Was it her daughter's ex-boyfriend? The bartender at Timmy's Nook? The one from Tallahassee?"

"No. The autopsy report shows that Gillian had a heart attack which caused her death. She collapsed following the attack and hit her head on a stone, which fractured two of her cervical vertebrae. Antonio was trying to help her get back to her cottage, and he did not harm her in any way."

Debra frowned, "But . . . she told me the doctor who diagnosed her with heart failure had been wrong. She said it was just a misdiagnosis. It was just heart palpations and she now had medication and has been fine ever since. In fact, she was happier than I'd seen her in a while, which she attributed to taking antidepressants. Said they work wonders."

Molly's ears perked up with this new information. "We didn't find any medications in her cottage at the Sandpiper. Just a leather purse, several pairs of shoes, and a bit of clothing. But you're sure she was diagnosed with heart failure?"

"Yes, that's what she told me. And as for finding medications, Gillian often left her glasses, purse, and medications all over the place. She may have even forgotten to pack them, or left them somewhere. She wasn't the tidiest person."

"I see. Can you think of any other medications she may have been taking?"

"No, that's all she mentioned. Of course, that evening she drank an awful lot of alcohol. As did I. But I left her as she wanted to talk with the bartender at Timmy's Nook. He's a former boyfriend of her daughter. Then Raphael brought me home and that's the last time I saw her."

Molly kept pushing, "So, no other medications that you know about? Just the antidepressants and some medication for cardiac problems."

"That's right, and that evening she didn't complain about any heart palpations or pain. But did state she had an awful headache."

"Did she have chronic headaches?"

"I don't think so. She didn't mention it. Being a "headache" sufferer myself I always have some kind of pain medication in my purse, so I gave her the last three capsules I had as she seemed to need them more than I did at the time. Plus, I knew Jeri would bring me more if I needed."

"Did she take the medication immediately?"

"No, she put the capsules in her evening bag, which was empty except for a tube of lipstick. She'd never go without that."

Molly's brain was doing flip flops. New information that needed to be digested and considered with the other information running around in her head.

"This headache medication . . . do you have any with you now?"

"Of course. I keep some at home and some in my purse in case I develop a headache here at work. Which is a good thing since I feel one coming on at the moment.

"May I see it?"

Debra went to her shop and returned with her handbag . . . a crossbody bag by *Lilly*. She reached inside and brought out a plastic pharmaceutical vial filled with a number of brown-colored capsules. Molly took the vial and looked closely. The first ingredient listed was Chuan-Xiong-Cha-Tia-San followed by a long list of other ingredients, most of which were fillers and seemed innocuous. Greg Maxwell, PharmD, RPh, was listed at the bottom along with the date the medication was dispensed. So, then this was more information to be digested and considered in this constantly changing situation.

"May I take this vial and a couple of the capsules? I'd like to have Dr. Strickland check it out. It could be that some of her medications had adverse reactions when mixed together and played a part in her death." She didn't think it was a good idea to tell Debra about the autopsy report showing thallium in her friend's body. Better to let David do his checking before that.

"Yes, of course. But I have no way of knowing if she actually took the capsules I gave her. But she did say her headache was the worst ever. She was in a rather agitated state over having to talk with her daughter's ex, which probably brought on her headache."

"Thanks, Debra. When I learn anything more, I'll come by and tell you. And, if you like, I'd be happy to check you over. Might be something causing these headaches that's been overlooked."

"That would be so helpful. I'm forever calling Greg for advice and he always seems to have time to take my calls. However, I do get tired of having to go to Fort Myers for medical issues. So glad you're here. I don't think you'll lack for patients. Just let me know when you're open for business . . . I'll be your first patient."

Then Captain Jack joined in, "I believe we can now rest assured Antonio wasn't responsible, and Molly and I better get back to the lighthouse and inform Solana that she's got to organize a celebration for him. He's been the subject of some damaging gossip, so I think we should show the community he's one of our trusted citizens. A good way to start the Christmas season, I think. So, we'll let you know the date."

Sassy smiled, "Sometimes bad things happen to good people ... and Antonio could use a boost of confidence right now. I personally think a celebration is a grand idea, Jack. And Christmas is my favorite holiday." She'd not forgotten how helpful Jack had been in her own personal time of need.

Chapter 51

As soon as Molly, Papa Jack, and Patrick returned to the lighthouse, the three of them gathered on the patio to discuss what they'd learned from the discussion with Debra. Molly looked at these two men, both of whom were important to her, and both of whom she cared for whether or not she was ready to verbalize as much. With Patrick here again, it was as if time had stood still. As if he had never left. And she did admit, at least to herself, that this felt right. Patrick filled a void no one else could.

"Papa, Patrick, is it my imagination, or did you get the feeling that Debra and Gillian may have been friends, but there appeared to be a bit of animosity when Debra spoke of her?"

Papa chewed on his pipe, unlighted at the moment. "Yes, I got the same feeling. There might be more unknowns about that relationship that could have bearing on this case. What do you think, Patrick?"

Patrick sighed, "Yes, there was definitely some underlying, complicated current about these two women. Perhaps from events unrelated to this incident. Events that may have occurred long ago. Even when you've been friends for a long time, sometimes you learn information that is so incongruous with what you thought that you are forced to realize you really didn't know them at all. Debra appeared to be upset, certainly, but Gillian obviously had some traits and habits that didn't sit well with her."

"Papa, could you talk to the ferry pilot . . . what's his name . . . Skip? Ask him to take this medication over to Fort Myers on his return this afternoon? I know he's particular about what he'll take or allow on his ferry, but I want David to get this med as soon as possible. Chuan-Xiong-Cha-Tia-San is a Chinese medication. But I'm not all that familiar with what it's used for. I'll check my medical books, see what I can learn about it. And this may not amount to anything, but we've got to figure out where the thallium came from. She may have gotten it from something in any of her drinks that evening."

"I'll promise him one of Solana's dinners. He'll agree to just about anything in exchange for that," Papa smiled.

"Then I'll call David and ask that he or Kathi meet the ferry. We need to bring this case to a close. Speaking of dinner, why don't you stay and have dinner with us, Patrick?" Molly inquired.

"I believe it's shrimp scampi . . . Solana style, of course," offered Captain Jack.

Patrick sighed, "Well, I'm pretty busy, but I think I can manage to work a dinner into my schedule." He smiled at Molly and Papa. If he had wondered that returning to Cayo Canna was a good idea, then he now knew he'd made the right decision. Perhaps finding his place and purpose wouldn't be so difficult after all.

Chapter 52

David had gone over every inch of the autopsy report, knowing he'd been ill during the time he tried to complete it. But after checking his findings again, he was convinced he hadn't missed anything.

Kathi had hurried to meet the ferry and Skip handed her a small box with the vial and a couple of capsules of medication inside. She returned to the office and David immediately began to run his tests on the medication Molly had sent over to him.

The vial indicated it was Chuan-Xiong-Cha-Tia-San, followed by a long list of other ingredients and fillers. No names or pharmacies were included. He didn't often see Chinese medications in his bodies, but knew that many patients would take almost anything if they thought it would help their pain or soothe an illness.

Within a short time, Kathi heard him calling for her. "Kathi! Call the Sheriff's Office and have a transport ready for me. I've got to get to Cayo Canno immediately. Then call Dr. Mac and tell her I'm on the way!"

Kathi asked no questions. The Sheriff's Office assured her a fast transport would be waiting at the pier within fifteen minutes. Then she placed a call to Dr. Mac, hoping the phones were working on the island.

When the phone rang, Solana answered it. "Captain McCormick's residence."

"Oh, hello. This is Kathi from Dr. Strickland's lab. I need to speak with Dr. Mac, please."

Molly took the call, "Hello, this is Dr. Mac."

"Hi Dr. Mac, this is Kathi at Dr. Strickland's office. He asked me to let you know he's on his way to the island and must talk with you."

"What? David's coming this afternoon?"

"Yes, and he wants to make sure you'll be at the lighthouse. He's got information that's vital to your investigation."

Molly asked no more questions. "Tell him I'll be at the dock waiting for him."

Twenty minutes later David was aboard the fast transport, but his mind was elsewhere, desperately trying to put together new information with what he already knew regarding Ms. Hartwell's death.

The transport made the trip to Cayo Canna in record time. The Cuban Missile Crisis had brought about many changes in police work, and this transport was one he particularly liked.

Molly and Patrick met him at the dock. Molly found Patrick's presence calming and he had an ability to rapidly understand facts and most of all, an ability to relate to people, an issue she was still struggling with.

David leaped off the transport and strode up the long dock where Molly and Patrick were waiting. "Ah, Molly. Thanks for coming." Then he spoke to Patrick, "Patrick, you've been a great help sounds like. Not sure what would have happened if you hadn't come along when you did."

After learning Patrick had left the priesthood, David was beginning to get the picture. But he was never one to give up on getting something if he truly wanted it, so he'd not abandon his hopes of a closer relationship with Molly. Not just yet, anyway.

Patrick nodded, "Glad I was there, though she probably could have handled the situation without me intervening."

"What's so urgent that you had to come over here?" asked Molly.

"The medication you sent over on the ferry is the source of the thallium. The heart attack was what killed Ms. Hartwell, but if she had kept taking this, it would have killed her eventually. A slow death, but death just the same. We need to find out where this medication came from."

"What? But that wasn't Ms. Hartwell's medication. It was some headache medication that Debra gave her. And Debra has been taking this medication for some time."

She halted then, her brain sending out messages so quickly she found herself mired with conflicting information. "But . . . then . . . Debra . . . is in danger . . . and, oh yes, I remember seeing that her hair was very thin on top . . . and I know thallium causes one to lose their hair . . . oh good glory—we've still got a killer on the island!"

Patrick recalled the conversation with Debra as well. "Didn't she say the pharmacist . . . Greg somebody, gives it to her?" David looked toward Molly who was still frozen, reeling with flooding information. One thought tumbling on another.

"And Debra said Gillian had an awful headache so she gave her the medication . . .which Greg prescribes for her. From the label it appears to be just a common Chinese medication that's been used for centuries."

At that juncture, David interrupted, "Yeah, with a little thallium added for flavor I suppose. This is the first case of thallium poisoning I've ever seen. And I've seen a lot."

Patrick was putting all these pieces together. "So, the local pharmacist has been poisoning Debra? What do we know about this man?"

Molly took a deep breath. "I only know he has straying hands that make me cringe when he touches me. But, let's go see Papa. He'll know everything about this man. But surely the pharmacist wouldn't do such a thing. Perhaps the thallium was added to the medication that same evening. By someone at one of the bars?"

David piped up, "No. That's not possible. It's been added to the base properties, the Chuan-Xiong-Cha-Tia-San, and a number of fillers. No, this was done by someone who understands chemistry and medications."

When Molly explained the situation to Papa, he put his pipe down and stared at the three, Molly, Patrick, and David.

"That's quite a story. You're suggesting that Greg Maxwell 'doctored' this medication with thallium and has been prescribing it for Debra?"

"That's exactly what I think, Papa. I know Greg has been here a long time, but he's got a creepy side that you, as a male, may not understand. I can hardly stand to be near him."

"What? He's made advances or offended you, Molly? Why didn't you tell me?"

"No, Papa. He just has too many hands and I don't like him touching me. Just a female issue. No, he hasn't offended me. But there's something about him that bothers me."

"Hmm . . . I seem to recall Sassy saying something along those lines a couple of years ago. But she hasn't mentioned it again. Knowing Sassy, she nipped that behavior in the bud. She's half Scots, you know, and not inclined to beat about the bush about most anything."

273

"Even so, accusing him of putting thallium in Debra's medication is a serious accusation. But, as you and David seem to be in agreement, that's good enough for me. So, now we have to figure out the details."

"What do you suggest, Papa?"

"Oh, that's easy. I suggest we go directly to Greg with our suspicions and work from there. He's bound to know David will have checked out the body and found any toxic materials. That being the case, he may have already left the island, and we could be several plays behind in catching him."

"Papa, shouldn't we call the deputy? After all, we can't really make an arrest. Plus, if Greg is the killer, he may be armed and waiting on anyone who comes for him."

"I suppose that would be the proper procedure, but if he is the guilty party, I believe Patrick, David and I can take care of any difficult situations. I've brought in many "offenders" without an official officer on the scene. This wouldn't be too difficult. But, yes, call the deputy and ask him to meet us at the pharmacy. It's only mid-afternoon now, so it should still be open."

Deputy Harrison answered the phone on the first ring. "Deputy Harrison's office."

"Deputy . . . uh, Ben, this is Molly McCormick."

She could all but hear the smile in his voice. "Oh, Dr. Mac. Good afternoon. What can I do for you?"

"I need you to meet me at the Island Pharmacy. The medication that I sent to Dr. Strickland appears to be the source of the thallium found in Ms. Hartwell's body. We—Papa, Dr. Strickland and I—believe Greg Maxwell, the pharmacist, may have put the thallium in the medication he prescribes for Debra Morris, owner of The Writer's Block."

"He what? No, not Greg Maxwell. Hasn't he been the pharmacist here for a number of years?"

"Just the same, we need to confront him with this latest information, and it would help if you would be there as we discuss this with him."

"I . . . uh . . . yes. Of course. I'll be there in ten minutes, Dr. Mac. And don't go in before I get there. He might be armed and dangerous. You never know."

"As you wish. We'll wait until you arrive."

274

Chapter 53

Sassy was cleaning up the last of the table crumbs and empty coffee cups. The afternoon rush was almost over and she was ready for this day to end. There was so much she still didn't know about the death of Debra's friend. She hoped Dr. Mac and Captain Jack would come by again and keep her informed.

Debra, too, was ready to call it a day. "Oh, Sassy, do you think we'll ever learn what happened to Gillian?"

"Well, Dr. Mac appears to be very determined to get to the bottom of the case. And I can assure you that Captain McCormick will hound every clue until he gets all the answers. He's quite a fellow, Debra."

"Yes, and I think his granddaughter must be much like him. But, for the life of me I can't believe someone would deliberately kill Gillian. And I'm really glad Antonio has been cleared of any suspicion. He's always been such a kind fellow."

"Yes, he's kept the Sandpiper in tip-top shape and always offers to help at any social gatherings on the island. But, of course, with him being cleared, that just means the real criminal is at large."

As Sassy wiped down the last counter, the door burst open and Wesley, followed closely by Adam, came flying through, chatting so fast Sassy had trouble keeping up.

"Whoa, ladybug. Start again. I missed half of what you said."

Wesley rushed over to the counter and climbed up on a stool, "Sassy, Mom is coming home . . . maybe not for good, but for a visit. And I need to make her a cake . . . a really good one . . . can you help me with that?" Her little elfin face was bright with excitement and Sassy found herself smiling in response to such happiness.

"Colleen's coming for a visit?" Sassy lifted her eyebrows at Adam.

"A long weekend visit. Her physicians say she's greatly improved, but they don't want to rush her recovery, so they are suggesting she come home for a few days and see how it goes."

"That's grand, Adam."

Adam nodded. "Yeah, I just hope it goes well and doesn't set her back. She's come a long way."

"And let's pray she continues to get even better . . . and maybe your nightmares will disappear. No doubt they are connected with her being gone."

"That would be a blessing. And now with Wesley not having to go to Fort Myers for school, perhaps this family can get on its feet again."

Adam turned to speak to Debra, "Anything new on Ms. Hartwell's case?"

"No. We're waiting patiently. But I've contacted her daughter up in Tallahassee. She's coming down tomorrow, but I don't know when the medical examiner will release Gillian's body for burial. Speaking of nightmares, this event has turned into one."

Adam signed, "Yeah, seems we all have one kind of nightmare at some point in our life. Maybe mine and yours will be over soon."

Chapter 54

With Thanksgiving over and Christmas creeping up quickly, many island businesses were beginning to hang holiday decorations, and The Island Pharmacy was one of them. A couple of men were outside streaming colored lights across the front of the store, and a small Christmas tree could be seen in the front window.

"Looks like Greg and Jeri are getting into the spirit of the season," stated Captain Jack. He stood next to the golf cart and David, Patrick and Molly gathered close.

Deputy Harrison came screeching into the parking lot, and thankfully, without the siren blasting. "Dr. Mac, Captain, sir, Dr. Strickland, Father Patrick, he addressed everyone and removed his hat.

"We need to be careful here. He could be armed and dangerous. No telling what state of mind he's in if he could do such an evil thing. Killing Ms. Hartwell."

Captain Jack came closer, "Deputy, I think it might be a good idea if we take it slow here. I suggest we let Molly and David approach Greg and you, Patrick, and I should take a backseat. If they need our help, then we can step in."

"Yessir. I agree. Just keep things calm. No theatrics. Yessir."

Molly and David entered the pharmacy and within seconds, Greg wandered to the front and greeted them.

"Ah, Molly. And Dr. Strickland. What brings you to our establishment? Need some medications?"

David took over at that point. "Dr. Maxwell, I have a problem that I need your help with. It appears that you prescribe a medication for Debra Morris . . . something for her headaches."

Greg held out his hand as David offered the vial with two capsules inside.

"Yes, I do prescribe medication for Debra. She's suffered with migraines for a long time." He took the vial and looked at it, then opened it and took one of the capsules in his hand.

"What's this?"

"It's the medication you prescribe for Ms. Morris who passed it on to her friend, Ms. Hartwell. The woman who was found dead recently."

"No. What I give Debra is simply an ancient Chinese medication called Chuan-Xiong-Cha-Tia-San. It's been used for centuries and in Debra's case seems to be just the ticket."

Molly jumped in at that point, "Greg, Debra gave us this medication and said it's what you prescribe for her. How can you explain that?"

"Come, let me show you." He walked behind the counter and brought out a large container of white capsules with a small dark brown stripe around the center.

"This is the medication I give to Debra. I get it from a large pharmaceutical company in New Jersey. They have some unusual medications, such as the Chinese one I prescribe for Debra. I don't know what this is or where you obtained it, but it isn't what I give to Debra Morris."

David took over, "This medication is laced with thallium, Dr. Maxwell. If this isn't the medication you prescribed, how do you explain that it came in a plastic vial with your pharmacy emblem and your name as the prescribing pharmacist? That's a bit too much of a coincidence."

"Thallium? That capsule contains thallium? No . . . that isn't . . . "

Captain Jack walked over at that point. He read the look on Greg's face as one of anger and irritation and thought he'd better make his appearance.

"Greg, I think you're going to have to go with Deputy Harrison here. He'll have an agent from the Sheriff's Office in Fort Myers come over to ask some questions. Until then, you'll stay in the deputy's custody."

Greg stared at all of them. "Jack, you know me. You know I'd never do such a thing!"

"The Sheriff will made decisions regarding this, Greg. But now you've got to go with Deputy Harrison. Perhaps you might want to leave Jeri a note and let her know where you are."

"Jeri's out delivering pharmacy orders. She'll be back shortly. Can't this wait until then?"

Deputy Harrison stepped forward, "Let's not make this difficult, Dr. Maxwell. I don't want to use cuffs, but if you don't cooperate, then I'll be forced to do so."

"But, I never . . . this is ridiculous! I would never harm Debra. She's a very fine lady. This is not the medication I prescribed for her! Listen to me!"

Deputy Harrison was intuitive enough to realize Captain Jack McCormick was in charge of this proceeding, so he waited for a nod from the Captain before he touched Dr. Maxwell on the elbow. "Let's go now. I've already called the Sheriff. He'll be here shortly and will decide what the next steps are."

Greg looked first to Jack, then Molly, and finally to David and Patrick. As if hoping one of them would surely see he couldn't be the guilty party. But, when he saw the Captain nod to the deputy, he realized he would have to go with him.

David asked the deputy to hold on for a second. "Molly, Captain Jack, you two have been instrumental in helping discover evidence that could have easily been lost. We've still got work to do, but having a suspect in hand goes a long way to solving a crime. I'll ask Deputy Harrison to drop me at the transport. The Sheriff lets me use it because I help solve crimes, but he's got only two of these rapid boats and they are always needed. I am sure the Sheriff will call me, so I'll talk with you when I know the scoop on what he finds out. But, again, this isn't over. So don't be surprised if I call needing your assistance again. We work well together. He smiled at Molly and nodded to the Captain and Patrick.

Molly watched as the deputy placed Greg in the rear and David rode up front. The last thing she saw was the forlorn look on Greg's face. Was that because he'd been found out? Or was he just so astonished that he'd been accused of a crime, something that had never happened before?

Chapter 55

Solana was relieved when Captain Jack, Molly, and Patrick returned. She had *tapas* and drinks waiting on the patio. Sangria for Molly, Jameson for Patrick, and Glenfiddich for the Captain.

Captain Jack smiled, "Ah, *tapas,* my favorite. Solana you are a mind reader."

Patrick lifted his small glass of Jameson and smiled at her. Molly sipped at the sangria, her thoughts so scrambled she could barely keep them together. She stared at the ocean . . . just as she had seen Papa do when he was contemplating a complicated matter. Finally, she stood and began walking the patio from one end to the other in an attempt to order her thoughts.

Papa and Patrick looked to each other . . . neither wanting to be the one to interrupt her obviously serious contemplations. After another minute passed, she turned her attention to the two.

"I continue to say I'm not an investigator. And, that is true. But, at this moment, I do believe that we've missed something. Something vital."

Papa chewed on his pipe, took a sip of Glenfiddich, and then asked, "So, you have any idea what that may be?"

"Maybe. No. No. But, Papa, something about the look on Greg's face won't leave my mind. He was absolutely flabbergasted. And he . . . then what if . . . yes . . . it . . ."

"What, Molly Mac? Spit it out," called Papa.

But she didn't spit it out. Rather, she continued to stare at the two men, then over to Solana who had watched her the entire time. She'd learned that Molly, like the Captain, didn't like to make mistakes. But above all, would be fair to all and not wish to rush to conclusions without evidence.

"It's just...there's got to be...but if that's true, then...

Captain Jack and Patrick waited. No one knew what to expect, but Molly was walking faster, sipping her sangria, talking to herself, walking back the other direction, then she walked over to the old banyan tree and ran her hands slowly across it, then started mumbling.

"You know, banyans trees can live for a century . . . even longer. Hindu texts describe it as an upside-down-growing tree that has roots in heaven and branches that go down toward earth in order to deliver blessings. Its bark and roots are still used today to treat a variety of disorders, particularly in Ayurvedic medicine."

Patrick was the brave one to interrupt her dialogue, "You appear to know quite a bit about the banyan tree."

Molly looked at him, shook her head, "No, not really. But every day when I see this tree I'm reminded that, as opposed to this banyan tree, our lives are very short. Which means we should live each day to the fullest."

Patrick smiled, "I totally agree. Life is short. But sometimes it's not how long one lives that matters; it's how they live."

Molly looked at Patrick. *He may have left the priesthood behind, but inside he's still a very caring, compassionate man. One that I could care about. And I wouldn't want to lose him.*

That thought had her brain churning off in a new direction now. . . *one I could care about . . . what would one do when they truly care about another . . . and don't want to lose them . . . almost anything.* Then she stopped walking. Looked at Papa.

"Papa . . . oh no . . . we've done it again!"

Papa stood and came to Molly, taking her gently by the shoulders and searching her face for some clue as to her unusual behavior . . . walking about . . . talking about banyan trees . . . then this.

"What? Done what again, Molly Mac?"

"We've arrested the wrong person! I'm sure of it!"

"Why do you think that? Do you know something you've not told us?"

"No. But this is really quite simple. Greg was telling the truth. He does prescribe Chuan-Xiong-Cha-Tia-San for Debra. But prescribing it and delivering it are two separate issues."

"What does that mean?"

"Greg prescribes the medication . . . but he doesn't deliver it . . . Jeri does."

Papa put his pipe down, Patrick sat his Jameson on the table, and Solana put her hands together under her chin as if in prayer.

Molly continued as her story began to come together, "Jeri delivers the medication. I was actually in Sassy's shop when she brought it to Debra. I didn't see it, but I know it was this very medication.

"And recently I stopped by the pharmacy to pick up some antiseptic lotion. Greg was there alone, but shortly Jeri came in and all but shoved me out the door. I think she knows Greg has roaming hands and tries to keep women away from him . . . which may be why she brings Debra her medication."

Papa now began to walk as well. "Solana? Remember the Gasparilla Celebration . . . maybe last fall? Seems I recall a bit of a scene with Jeri and that spiritualist woman. Something about Jeri thinking she was giving Greg a bit too much attention?"

"Yes, Captain. I do remember that. Jeri and the spiritualist, Vedra, did have words. And, yes, Jeri does appear to be a bit on the possessive side where Greg is concerned."

Papa rubbed the back of his neck, "Perhaps Debra and Jeri have some history I don't know about?"

Molly shook her head. "No, Papa. But I'm quite sure Jeri has witnessed Greg's "too many hands" on more women than me, and she was determined to eliminate at least one of them that he pays special attention to, like Debra with her headaches. Debra told me she calls him often and he always has time to talk to her. And I'm sure that doesn't sit well with Jeri."

Solana began to clear the table and take away the empty *tapas* plates. She then turned to the Captain. "Women don't take kindly to other women getting too close to their man," offered Solana. "Especially women who know their man has a roving eye . . . or too many hands."

"But how will we ever prove Jeri put the thallium in the medication?" asked Papa.

Molly sighed, "Well, as David said. Only someone who has a knowledge of chemistry and medicine could concoct this medication laced with thallium. Using thallium is actually a very old scheme for killing someone. Agatha Christie wrote a book about it . . . called The Pale Horse. A novel that I read shortly after it was published last year."

"But again, how will we prove Jeri did it?"

"Maybe that's left to the Sheriff or his investigators . . . his real investigators."

Patrick joined in, "I think we might want to get to the deputy's office before Jeri does. No telling what she might resort to. When she learns Greg has been arrested, she will know the Sheriff will be coming to her with more questions. And, if she's desperate enough to contaminate medication, she might do anything."

Solana stayed behind, and Molly, Captain Jack and Patrick showed up at the deputy's office in a matter of minutes. But not before Jeri had gotten there. Her pharmacy vehicle was parked in the lot and the front door of the deputy's office was standing wide open . . . which was probably not a good sign. As soon as the trio got closer, they could hear Jeri's voice . . .screaming at the top of her lungs.

"Open that stupid cage and let him out! Now!"

The deputy's voice was the opposite: calm, clear, and low pitched. "Mrs. Maxwell, Jeri, you need to put that gun down now. It's loaded and very heavy and difficult for you to hold. It could go off without warning if you're not careful."

The voice was calm, but beginning to be just a bit shaky. The deputy was cursing himself for not removing his gun from the holster when he hung it on the wall. He'd not heard Jeri walk in as he had his back to the door. She'd grabbed his gun and now he had a real problem.

Then Greg's voice could be heard, pleading with his wife, "Jeri, put that gun down! You don't want to do this!"

Patrick and Jack exchanged a quick look. One that said both had been in situations such as this before. And both knew what must be done. Now.

Captain Jack turned to Molly. "Stay outside, Molly. We'll handle Jeri." Molly wanted to protest, but something inside told her to do as Papa said . . . at least this time.

Jack walked through the door and when Jeri turned to see who was coming in, Patrick rushed toward her, pushed her hand upward and the heavy .357 Magnum dropped with a thud to the floor . . . thankfully without going off.

Jeri screamed, "Captain! You can't do that . . . he must let Greg go . . . please . . . let him out of that cage! He's not a criminal!" She broke down with tears and Captain Jack escorted her to a small table in the corner.

"Sit, Jeri. This ordeal is over now. The Sheriff will be here any moment."

From the large detention cage Greg called out, "Captain, she's not herself at the moment. I think Dr. Mac should take a look at her. See what needs to be done!"

Jack went to the door and called for Molly. She hurried inside and one look at the situation was all she needed. The deputy was wiping sweat from his brow, so she attended him first.

"Ben, are you all right?"

"Yes ma'am. Uh, Dr. Mac. Just a bit shaken. It's not every day that your own gun . . . your own loaded gun . . . is pointed at you."

Molly smiled at him and helped him to his office chair. "Just sit here a few minutes."

Then she turned to Greg in the cage. "Greg . . . do you need anything?"

"No, Molly. Just see to Jeri. Something's wrong. She never behaves in such an outrageous manner. Help her, please."

When Molly turned to Jeri, she was surprised. The tears had stopped and Jeri presented her with a determined, calm expression. "Jeri, will you allow me to do a short assessment?"

Jeri shook her head from side to side. "I don't need to be assessed, Dr. Mac. I'm perfectly fine. The only thing you need to do to make me better is to remove Greg from that cage. He's not a criminal. He's a very fine man. One that I love."

Then she stood and held out her hands to the deputy. "I'm the criminal you're looking for. I always remove the medication Greg prescribes for Debra Morris. Then I refill the vial with the medication that has thallium. I've been doing this for some time, so Debra may expect to be experiencing some health issues soon. And for sure her hair will be falling out. Now, I have admitted my guilt. So, please remove Greg and put me in your cage."

Greg called out "No, Jeri. No. You're not a criminal. No!"

Deputy Harrison looked to Captain Jack, still not sure what he should do at this juncture. "Deputy, I think you can release Dr. Maxwell at this point. We'll all stay here until the sheriff arrives. No need for cuffs or cages. These people need help, now."

When the sheriff arrived, Molly explained the details as best she could. The sheriff thanked them all for their help and took Greg and Jeri to his fast transport which would take them to Fort Myers. He'd bring the ME, David, up to date and the case would finally be closed.

Molly stood next to Deputy Harrison, both glad this was coming to an end. "Deputy Harrison, you handled that situation quite well. Like an experienced deputy I would say."

He stood a bit taller then, squared his shoulders and nodded to Molly; "Thank you, Dr. Mac. Working with you has been a pleasure . .

. and a learning experience for me. Maybe we'll have the chance to do so again."

Now, with David stating the same "wish," Molly extended her hand to Ben and smiled. "I've learned that we never know what tomorrow brings, Ben."

Chapter 56

As agreed the night before, Captain Jack and Molly met Patrick at Sassy's shop. They needed to bring Debra Morris and Sassy up to date on the latest happenings. Ensign was in his accustomed place on the golf cart as this was one establishment where he was sure to get a treat.

Patrick pulled up just shortly before the others arrived. He was settled in the same bungalow he'd had before, but today he'd made a decision to buy a place on the island. He had no qualms about staying on Cayo Canna. This was where he belonged now. Thanks to his dear friend and mentor, Angus, he could entertain having a home here and another in Ireland.

Sassy's shop was now awash with colored fairy lights, a small tree in one corner, and Christmas carols playing softly in the background. And Sassy was ever so glad to see this motley crew come through the front door. She grabbed cups, a plate of scones, and brought a pot of tea to their table. Then she stepped next door and asked Debra to come over.

"Your place looks great, Sassy. Christmas is sneaking up on us. I better get Solana to work on the lighthouse. She loves this season," said Captain Jack.

Sassy chimed in, "And there's nothing like a cup of strong, Scottish tea and a couple of scones to start the day." She then turned to the door and grinned even more so when Wesley and Adam walked through.

"All my favorite people. This day is starting off to be a grand one."

Adam greeted everyone and Wesley hurried over to speak to Molly. "Dr. Mac, guess what I have in my pocket."

Wesley liked that Molly didn't appear to be like other doctors she'd met, mainly, those who had given her injections and put a cast on her arm when she crashed her bike last summer.

Molly bit her lower lip, then raised her eyebrows, "I have no idea. But I hope it isn't slithery or slimy."

"Not slithery or slimy . . . but this is something special . . . I've never found one before. Close your eyes and hold out your hand."

Molly slowly extended her hand and Wesley placed an item in it. Molly opened her eyes and smiled. There, in the palm of her hand was a shell unlike any she'd had ever seen on the beaches here.

"Oh, wow. What's it called?"

"It's a junonia shell. Well, actually, it's a Scaphella Junonia and it's really rare. I can't wait to show it to Mom. She's coming this weekend."

Molly smiled at Adam and he returned the smile, took a cup of tea, and left. He had a charter so Wesley was going to stay with Sassy part of the day, then she'd ride her bike down to the park with Mila and Ariane.

When Debra came in, Captain Jack stood and held a chair for her. "Good morning, Debra. Join us. We've got some information that you should know about. Won't take long."

A very tired looking Debra answered, "Any information will be good. I still don't know much of anything, except that my friend is gone, and I have no explanations for her daughter, who's coming here today."

"I see. Well, I think Molly can tell the details better than I," Captain Jack said. Then he picked up a cinnamon scone and took a bite, nodding to Sassy that her scones were as good as ever.

Molly took over, "Debra, I'm so sorry to tell you that Jeri has been exchanging the medication Greg prescribes for you and replacing it with some she has infused with thallium."

Debra stared at Molly then looked at Captain Jack. "Thallium? But, isn't that some kind of poison? Something we kill ants with? Surely this can't be true. Jeri would never do such a thing. I mean, she brings the medication to me in order to save me a trip to the pharmacy."

Molly continued, "I'm afraid that is what's been happening. And for some time. Jeri admitted she's been giving you contaminated medication for a long period. Which means you will be feeling its effects, and we need to check you out to see what can be done to counteract this thallium you've been ingesting."

Debra gasped, "Oh, heavens. So perhaps that's why I'm having difficulty walking sometimes? And lately I've had bouts of vomiting and diarrhea, for no apparent reason."

"Yes, those are all issues related to thallium. Plus, hair loss is a most common problem."

"Hair loss? Yes, I've been noticing my hair is getting thinner on top. But why would Jeri do this? She's always been so kind to me."

"That's a question none of us can answer. She obviously has some psychological issues and problems she needs help with. The sheriff from Lee County has taken her into custody and has asked Greg to accompany her to his office on the mainland. There are details that must be ironed out, but Jeri has confessed to putting the thallium in your medication, so we can all rest assured that there isn't a madman running about our island."

Debra began to cry. But her tears were those of relief. "So now we can all get on with our lives. I will miss Gillian. And I felt so guilty when we thought my medication killed her. But I don't feel responsible since we know she died of a heart attack. At least I can now tell Christina the truth about her mother. That girl has been a problem for Gillian since day one. I suppose I'll tell her to take her questions to the Lee County Sheriff who will know when the body can be taken for burial. Not a conversation I look forward to."

"If I can help you with these discussions with Christina, I'll be glad to," offered Molly.

"Thanks, Dr. Mac. But this is something I'll do alone. And Christina will go back to Tallahassee and continue with whatever her latest escapades are. I don't plan to keep up with her. And, thank you all for pursuing this until you discovered what really happened. It had to have been difficult."

She stood then, "Now, I've got a shop to run and I hope you will all become regular customers. You are all important to me. My friends. And Dr. Mac, I hope you will help me with my health issues."

Sassy walked to the bookstore with her and returned immediately.

"You are all the very best friends any of us could have. And let us hope we never have another such occurrence on our island paradise. Now, how about just one more cuppa and one more scone?" She laughed.

Chapter 57

When Molly, Captain Jack, and Patrick arrived back at the lighthouse, Solana was up on a ladder stringing fairy lights along the patio. She had six more boxes of Christmas decorations on the porch and ornaments spread out on the floor.

Captain Jack walked up the steps to the porch, then smiled, "Thanksgiving is just barely over. Don't you think it might be kind of early to be hanging Christmas decorations, Solana?"

Solana looked down from her ladder, "Christmas is a season, Captain. Not just one day in December," she responded. Then she started giving orders.

"Captain, if you would, please hang these snowflakes along the banister. And Molly, you need to place a wreath on the front door and one going into Keeper's Cottage. Patrick? You can string lights up the spiral staircase and put the star on top of the tree. It's a job for a tall person."

Patrick sighed, "Solana you know how I detest going up that blasted spiral staircase. My Irish feet are just too damn . . . uh . . . too darn big. I trip over them every time."

Molly and Captain Jack laughed as they recalled how Patrick always tried to get Jack to stay downstairs more often so he wouldn't have to maneuver those "blasted" spiral steps.

Captain Jack put his arm around Molly's shoulder. "Molly Mac, I do believe this Christmas will be the best ever."

"Papa Jack, you say that about every Christmas," Molly grinned at him. "And, you haven't told Solana about your plans for Antonio. Now might be a good time."

"Huh? Oh yes." He walked over where Solana was busy arranging a large group of poinsettias around the base of the banyan tree

"Poinsettias? Where did you find those?"

"I made a deal with Skip Lawrence. Told him if he'd bring them from the mainland, I'd cook a special dinner for him."

Captain Jack burst out with laughter, "What? Skip brought flowers over on his ferry? Well, then, looks like you two have worked out a deal. Speaking of deals, I have one I need to make. With you."

"I only make deals that work for me, Captain. Just tell me what it is you want and I'll decide if I wish to accommodate your plans."

"It's about a promise I made to Antonio. His reputation has been somewhat tarnished since he was arrested for a crime he didn't commit. He was ready to leave the island, but I promised him we'd have a Christmas celebration and he'd be the guest of honor. I figure that should let the islanders know he's still needed and wanted on our island."

Solana stood and looked at him, "Captain, I believe I can manage to accommodate you. A Christmas celebration in honor of Antonio. It will be my Christmas gift to you." She smiled and began placing even more poinsettias on the steps.

Patrick walked over and picked up one of the boxes of decorations. He looked at Solana, Captain Jack, and then to Molly. He placed the box back on the floor as Solana handed out cups of what she called *Crema de vie* (aka Cuban eggnog).

"Here, drink this. It'll give you all some energy and put us in the Christmas spirit."

Patrick lifted his glass, 'Since we're all gathered here on this island that has seen its share of difficulties and trials, I propose a toast."

And in that same deep, soothing voice that still made Molly's knees weak, he proclaimed:

"This is the day that the Lord hath made. Let us rejoice and be glad in it."

...just one more thing...

I hope you enjoyed reading this novel as much as I enjoyed writing it. So, if I could ask for "just one more thing," I'd like to hear from you and hope that you could take the time to post a review on Amazon. Your feedback and support will help me improve my future writing projects.

Use this link—**www.amazon.com/review/create-review?&asin=1943369225**—to take you directly to your Amazon review page.

Thanks so much for reading this book and I hope you will check out my other works available on Amazon.

About the Author

Florence Love Karsner, author of The Highland Healer and Molly McCormick Series, is a Registered Nurse and Clinical Research Professional who creates hand-built pottery and enjoys golf and gardening. She is a fifth generation Floridian of Scottish heritage who lives with her husband in North Central Florida.

Made in the USA
Columbia, SC
19 June 2024